starflower

TALES OF GOLDSTONE WOOD

starflower

TALES OF GOLDSTONE WOOD

✝✝

ANNE ELISABETH STENGL

BETHANY HOUSE PUBLISHERS

a division of Baker Publishing Group
Minneapolis, Minnesota

© 2012 by Anne Elisabeth Stengl

Published by Bethany House Publishers
11400 Hampshire Avenue South
Bloomington, Minnesota 55438
www.bethanyhouse.com

Bethany House Publishers is a division of
Baker Publishing Group, Grand Rapids, Michigan

Printed in the United States of America

Library of Congress Cataloging-in-Publication Data
Stengl, Anne Elisabeth.
    Starflower / Anne Elisabeth Stengl.
        p.   cm. — (Tales of goldstone wood)
    ISBN 978-0-7642-1026-6 (pbk.)
    I. Title.
PS3619.T47647675S83 2012
813'.6—dc23   2012028885

Book design by Paul Higdon
Cover photography by Mike Habermann Photography, LLC

12 13 14 15 16 17 18   7 6 5 4 3 2 1

For Esther,
my hand-reader friend.

A NOTE TO THE READER

STARFLOWER TAKES PLACE more than sixteen hundred years (as mortals count time) before *Heartless*. There are dramatic topographical differences between the Near World of Starflower's day and that of Una's, and some characters, though living, are not yet who they will become. Even the Prince of Farthestshore is known by another name. . . .

PROLOGUE

ONCE UPON A TIME, great Etalpalli, the City of Wings, was ruled by a Faerie queen. Her name has long since been forgotten. What is remembered are her youth, her beauty. Her hair was bright as the sun and no less vibrant than the feathered wings sprouting from her shoulders.

She was young when she came to the throne, and her heart was tender and full of love for her people. They flocked in the air, their wings a garden of many colors, and lived in the green-grown towers of Etalpalli. In those high places, they found it easy to hear the voices of the sun and the moon singing and would sing back in joyful echo.

Once upon a time, the City of Wings was a peaceful demesne full of life. Now it burned.

————

Hri Sora sat up, choking as though she'd swallowed her own tongue. Poisonous fumes filled her lungs. Surrounding her on all sides, towers of fire issued thunderheads of black smoke. She stared about, unblinking. Ashes and flying embers lashed the air, but these could not hurt her. Her thin face and form were those of a woman. But her yellow eyes betrayed her true nature.

The Dark Father stood with his back to her, a shadow, like smoke himself. At first, she thought he must be unaware of her presence. His head turned this way and that as he appraised the inferno surrounding him. The searing air shimmered red. Flames licked at his long black cloak, but it did not catch fire.

Hri Sora staggered to her feet, clutching her stomach. Her body was hollow and cold inside. She wondered if she should speak or back away, avoid the Dark Father's gaze. But he settled that question by addressing her first.

"That, my darling, was quite the tantrum."

She blinked at his broad back and said nothing. He did not seem to expect an answer but shook his head and continued, "Dear, oh dear. I wondered if I should say something to you when you started . . . remind you of those vows you made long ago. 'I shall never return to Etalpalli!'" His voice became a high, unflattering mimic of hers. "'Though I die, the City of Wings will live forever.' Such a fine sentiment. I'm sure you meant it at the time." He shrugged.

Hri Sora whirled about where she stood, dizzy with emptiness. Her eyes widened as she looked again at the towering flames, hundreds of fiery tongues tasting a blackened sky.

"No," she whispered.

"Oh yes," said her Father. He turned to her. The heat in the air rose so strong that the edges of his cloak floated up behind him in a dark swirl. He was more than seven feet tall, and his skin was white, stretched thin over a skull of black bone. He smiled, his fangs gleaming dully in the firelight. "I'm afraid it's true. You, my sweet, came blazing out of the Near World straight through Cozamaloti Gate and set fire to your own city. Do you not remember?"

Somewhere amid the roar of the flames came the deeper roar of a tower crumbling. Hri Sora gasped and clutched her head in her hands. "I did this?"

"Do you doubt it?" Her Father chuckled, rolling his eyes to the burning heavens. "You, who once boasted to me that your fire was greater than my own?"

"No," she whispered. Then, her voice a hoarse bark, she screamed. *"No!"*

She tried to walk, to run, but her feet betrayed her, and she collapsed on her hands and knees. The hot embers covering the streets should have burned her skin, but they did not, for she was a dragon, and this was her own fire. Rather than burn, they warmed her, bringing slow clarity to her addled mind.

Etalpalli. Her city . . .

Her Father laughed outright, the rumble of his voice itself like flames. Then he moved to stand beside her but made no offer to help her to her feet. Instead, he took another slow spin, as though he could not get his fill of the destruction.

"I will give you this, daughter. Not once have I seen any of my children burn so brilliantly before. You always were special, weren't you? My firstborn!"

She could not make herself rise but remained on all fours like a crawling beast. She, who had once flown to the highest vaults of heaven, into the presence of Lady Hymlumé herself! To what depths had she fallen? Closing her eyes, she strove to remember.

There had been the pure, hateful, cleansing light of the moon shining in her face. She had unhinged her jaw to swallow it whole—the light, the song, everything. Then came that horrible moment, the tearing across the center of her soul, deep into the core of her fire. The moment when her wings had been stripped away.

After that, the fall.

Her head throbbed, and Hri Sora forced herself to forget, at least for now. She was too weak in the wake of her last great flaming, the flaming in which, she guessed, she had destroyed Etalpalli. Her memory was full of ashes, and just then she wasn't sure she wanted it to clear. Spitting more ash as she spoke, she demanded, "When did I do this?"

"This?" said her Father, sweeping a hand to encompass the burning city. "About a hundred years ago, I should think."

"A hundred years?"

"Etalpalli is nothing but ruins now, all the greenery burned away, half the towers destroyed, the others hollow shells full of shadows. What you're seeing here isn't real. It's a dream. Rather, it's the death of a dream."

Hri Sora forced herself up onto her knees and stared around once more. The hot air caught at her hair, whipping it across her face. She licked her lips slowly and reached up to touch her cheeks, her nose, her mouth. "I'm still a woman," she said.

"Yes."

"You took—" She struggled with the memory, not wanting it to come. But it forced its way in at last. "You took my wings from me."

"That I did. And your dragon form."

"Am I no longer a dragon, then?"

The Dark Father sneered down at her. "Of course you are! Do you think any but a dragon could do something like this?"

Long ago, in the heat of her first flaming when she was newly reborn, Hri Sora had burned away the last of her tears, along with her former name. Her heart was gone, replaced with this raging furnace. But somehow, as she looked upon this destruction, dream though it was, she thought her heart must break should she still possess one. She wished for the relief of tears. For a moment, she saw Etalpalli as it once was, the high towers covered in green vines, the air filled with the wings of her people, their plumage bright and flashing.

"They were certainly glorious," said her Father, as though reading her mind. "All your former subjects. Such beautiful wings! I can see why you couldn't allow them to live."

They had still boasted wings when she no longer did.

"I killed them."

"They put up a fight," said her Father. "But you were in quite the rage when you returned. Though you walked the ground like a mortal woman, your fire blazed to the sky and burned their wings. They fell like shooting stars at your feet."

How she hoped that memory would not return, not yet! Hri Sora forced herself to stand, trembling. What a despicable thing was this woman's body. Much too weak to support the fire inside her. No wonder she had lost consciousness for a hundred years.

"Let me wake up," she said to her Father.

"Why?" he asked, chuckling again. "Don't you like this dream of yours? It is your finest victory!"

"Let me wake up. I have work to do."

He turned a cruel, devouring smile upon her. "What kind of work can a wingless dragon possibly pursue?"

Her mouth opened, but no words came. Her mind suddenly crowded with images, with hate. Her Father watched her face, reading more of her thoughts than she liked, so she turned away from him.

"What happened to you?" he asked.

"I don't know what you mean."

"When you fell from the heavens. I took your wings to punish your idle boasting, and you plummeted so hard and fast, I thought sure you'd die your third death then and there! Obviously, I was mistaken. You landed in the Near World and weren't heard from for ten mortal years at least. What happened to you during that time in the mortal realm?"

"I don't remember," she snarled.

"You burst back through to the Far World so suddenly, it took everyone by surprise. Even those cursed Knights of the Farthest Shore had thought you were gone for good! But no, back you came and, of all things, dragging two children behind you." He shook his head, a forked tongue flickering between his fangs. "Fancy—me, a grandfather! Ugly little brutes they are, too. Certainly not a brood of which to boast. I've found uses for them, however. There's always more room in my realm."

"They are mine." She bit the words out.

"Yes, yes, the little monsters are quite devoted to you," said he. "I've sent them out on several errands, but they always want to return to you, sniffing about and making sure no one comes too near." He shook his head at her. "But they can't reach you here. Not in your dreams."

"Let me wake up," she said again. "Let me wake up so that I may . . . so that I may find . . ."

"Find what?"

She chewed her lip with dagger teeth, drawing lines of dark blood. Flames burned the back of her throat. "None of your business," she said at last.

"All your business is my business," said her Father. "You have a look of revenge about you. Don't try to deny it; I know the signs. It's best not to think of it now, however. You are nothing without your wings. Oh, you can flame bright enough to destroy this whole city of yours. But that's just it, daughter. It was your city. Your demesne. Yours to keep or devour at will. Now it's gone, and you have nothing."

"I have my children."

"For what good they do you!"

Hri Sora turned to him then, planting her feet and throwing her head back. He towered over her, but she was still his firstborn, and she met him eye for eye. Her lank hair swelled behind her in a cloud, and her fists clenched at her sides. The fire in her eyes dominated every womanly vestige. She was a dragon, through and through.

"Give me back my wings!"

"And let you challenge my authority again?" He swept his gaze across the crumbling ruins, then back to her. "Not likely."

"Give them to me!"

"Why should I? You've done your worst, Hri Sora. You've earned yourself a place in history, both in the annals of Faerie folk and the legends of mortals. You have no need of wings or flame now."

But she did.

Somewhere in the world was a dark hut where a man lived—a man she had been unable to kill even when her flame was hottest. She remembered him now, though she wished more than anything to forget. She remembered those years of crawling about in the mortal dust when she had always been meant to fly!

"Amarok." She whispered the name like venom. "My dear one."

"What's that?" said her Father.

Hri Sora did not answer. She drew a long breath, sucking flames down into her lungs. "I must have my wings," she said. "I must. But I will not tell you why."

"In that case," said he, "I do not care to give them back."

"Everything has a price," she said. "Name it!"

In the jet-black depths of the Dragon's eyes, flames flickered. He looked upon Hri Sora's stance, took in the smoldering fire ready to burst from her breast. She was a beauty, he thought, or had been when he first turned her. A shame, really, that she'd puffed herself up so! Nevertheless, she had done more to strike terror of his name into the hearts of all peoples in all worlds than had any of his other children.

His firstborn . . . his prize. Even the Knights of the Farthest Shore had failed to quench her flame.

"There is a price," he said slowly.

"Tell me!"

He could make her do anything now. She would be willing to dive into the Final Water, to swim to the Farthest Shore and set fire to that unreachable realm if he asked her. Wretched fool! But he could get some sport from her yet.

"I want," he said, "the Flowing Gold of Rudiobus."

Her flaming eyes did not blink. She neither moved nor spoke for some time. At last she said, "It is hidden."

"Most definitely."

"Kept safe by Queen Bebo."

"Indeed."

"She who is oldest and strongest of all Faerie queens."

"The same."

Hri Sora shook her head slowly. "No one knows where it is. No one knows what it looks like. It is the chief treasure of King Iubdan Tynan, and no one else has even seen it!"

"A fine addition it will make to my Hoard. Don't you agree?"

The dragon woman blew a spurt of flame. "What you ask is impossible! Who can penetrate Rudiobus without a call? Who can take from Bebo and Iubdan what they wish kept secret?"

The specter smiled. "There is one other who knows the secret of Rudiobus. Or so rumor would have it."

"Who?"

"Lady Gleamdrené Gormlaith, Queen Bebo's own cousin, highly favored in the courts of Rudiobus. Of all Iubdan's merry subjects, it is said she alone knows the truth behind the legends of the Flowing Gold."

Hri Sora considered this. "It is well," she said. "But one must still penetrate the boundary protections that Bebo herself established. No one can enter Rudiobus uninvited. To even set foot in Gorm-Uisce Lake without leave would be death."

"So much for the power of the firstborn," said the specter with a mocking laugh.

She snarled at him, spewing drops of blood from her lips. If only she might tear him to pieces here in the nightmarish remains of her demesne! But he was without substance, no more than a shade. No fire of hers would ever harm him, she knew.

There was nothing left, then: No power without her wings; no city to call home. Only the hideous memory of former fires and that burning, driving lust for revenge. Such a pathetic creature she was, reduced to this form.

Unless . . .

Hri Sora smiled. This form was pitiable, but her mind was still good. And dragons command many powerful enchantments. An idea took root, and her smile grew.

Perhaps a soft and vulnerable woman was not so soft and vulnerable after all.

"Very well, Father," she spoke in a fearfully gentle voice. "I swear to you, I will do the impossible. I will get you this gold and make myself worthy in your eyes once more. Then"—flames flickered in her throat—"you will give me back my wings."

"Idle boasts," said he.

She roared. Her woman's face twisted almost beyond recognition, and fire fell from her bleeding lips. "Wake me up!"

The Dragon laughed at her. Then he put up one hand and snapped his fingers.

The dream vanished.

PART ONE

1

SHARP ROCKS TORE at the girl's bare feet as she ran. Her aching body cried out for relief, for rest, but she dared not stop.

Water lapped near her. Now, at high tide, the ground on which she ran was no more than a narrow stretch of pebbled beach with ocean extending forever on either side. Behind her were the mountains, but she would not look back. She could still hear the howls echoing and reechoing from peak to peak until she thought she might go mad. She fixed her gaze forward, struggling to see through the thick fog that rose up from the ocean and threatened to smother her. Yet the Path was firm beneath her bleeding feet.

The Wood watched her approach, its gaze curious and hungry.

She stumbled along the isthmus, crossing the bay from her own land to the greater Continent of the north. The Wood grew thick here. She had no choice but to pass into its welcoming arms if she wished to continue her flight.

The mist was so heavy she could not see two steps ahead. But she felt when the ground softened, the sharp rocks of the isthmus giving way to moss and crackling leaves. Her arms reached ahead as though to push the mist away; from her wrists dangled rough cords that chafed her skin.

She caught a glimpse of gold. No more than a glance, like the fleeting burst of sunshine through storm clouds, vanishing in an instant. Yet she turned to that sight, her eyes wide and desperate. For a moment, she stood as though blind. Then she saw it again, this time a form as well: slender legs, a shining coat, a powerful body disappearing into the shadows of the Wood.

Perhaps she dreamed it. It did not matter. Where else could she turn now that the world she knew was shattered?

A sob choked her, and she stumbled to her knees. How desperately she wished to lie down, to close her eyes, to will away the visions in her mind. But the howls were still too close in her memory, so she forced herself up and staggered on blindly, pursuing that distant golden form.

The Wood's dark arms encircled her as she plunged headlong into its domain. She felt no alteration as she stepped out of the mortal world into that place without Time, for her mind was spent.

But a voice without words spoke to her heart in a language she scarcely understood. She followed the voice, propelled by an urgency beyond fear and all human need. It sang to her as she fled:

See the truth, my child. See the truth and speak!

It was a night that would have gone down in history even without the events that followed.

Every night, the merry Faerie folk of Rudiobus Mountain found excuses to dance and sing and dance and sing some more, so that in itself was not unusual. But not every night marked the birthday of Queen Bebo . . . which was especially momentous considering the queen was so ancient that no one, not even her husband, would dare guess her age. The idea that she should have a birthday at all thrilled her subjects. They considered it so brilliant an occasion that they could bear to celebrate it only once every hundred years.

Bebo sat in splendor beside her raven-haired husband and watched with a smile while her subjects danced in her honor. She wore an ancient crown of goblin work (wrought in the ages before goblins forgot their craftsman skills), and a veil of delicate silver covered her hair.

The queen's cousin, Lady Gleamdrené Gormlaith, stood beside Bebo's throne, a jeweled goblet in her hand, ever ready to serve. She kept her eyes downcast, but a not-so-demure smile curved her lips. She was aware of how many doting swains turned their gazes her way, how many hearts beat in desperate hope that she might bestow favors upon them: a smile, a glance even. And oh! to think she might grace one of their number with a dance!

Lady Gleamdrené was the most desired woman in all Ruaine Hall. And she knew it well.

The young bucks pretended indifference. They shuffled their feet and elbowed their friends' ribs. They talked in loud voices of exploits in the great Wood beyond Rudiobus, hoping their voices would carry above the pipers' playing and strike Lady Gleamdrené's ears. A few even vowed to themselves that, before the night's end, they should ask to take a turn about the dance floor with Queen Bebo's fair cousin.

But Gleamdren, slyly peeking out from beneath her lashes, missed one particular face in the crowd. Her smile slowly melted into a frown and her covert glances became more and more pronounced. "Lumé love me," she whispered. "Where *is* he?"

Yet she could not find the one she sought. He stood in the shadows just outside the reach of torchlight and lanterns. One of the side passages leading from Fionnghuala Gate into King Iubdan's central hall provided darkness enough that a man might prowl there beyond the gaze of searching eyes.

The people of Rudiobus wore green. From the queen's apple-green gown to the rich forest tones in her husband's robes to the olive jerkin worn by the lowliest imp, the kingdom of merrymakers were a verdant garden of emerald and spring leaf, moss and teal. This man wore scarlet.

The Merry People of Rudiobus were rarely seen without smiles, and so it was with this man. A grin tugged at the corners of his mouth, waiting to burst across his pale, angular face. But his golden eyes were serious.

He watched the shadows of the dancers winging across the walls of the mountain hall. He smelled the richness of the fresh-hung pine and holly boughs festooning the rocks and littering the floor. He heard the sounds of ageless voices raised in song. He saw how every man in the room turned eventually to gaze with longing upon Lady Gleamdrené Gormlaith. But she would have none of them.

She looked for him. He knew it with a confidence common only in his kind. He lived ever assured of the ultimate desirability of himself. Who would not crave his presence, nor vie for his esteem? He himself admired no man more, for was there ever such a handsome, a quick-witted devil as he?

"We are alike, you and I, my lady Gleamdren," he whispered to himself as he watched that fair maid scan the crowds, her face sinking into deeper frowns when she failed to see his. "The Flower of Rudiobus. That's what they call you. Any man here would give his right hand for your pleasure!"

The smile, which had been tugging at his mouth for some time, finally won out. He grinned, and his eyes shone even beyond the torchlight. "You, my sweet, should be my wife."

"A fine sight, eh, poet?"

The scarlet man did not startle at the gruff voice that suddenly spoke behind him. He turned, his eyes narrowed, and icily replied, "The queen's birthday is always a fine display, which is nothing new. It holds little interest for me."

"Little interest, you say?" The speaker took a step nearer to the poet, entering the light of the nearest torch. He wore a moss-green doublet that would disguise him from hunting eyes should he venture beyond Rudiobus Mountain, and he carried a lance. His appearance was stocky, broad-shouldered, and powerful, opposite of the scarlet man's in every way save for his shock of yellow hair. In that aspect, the two might have been brothers. Perhaps they were. But they, like all the men and women of Rudiobus, were so ancient in their immortality that none could remember their heritage. "You're blind, my friend, if you can find no lovely face to light an interest in you."

"Fine sentiments, Captain Glomar of the Guard," the scarlet man said. "I was unaware that *your* kind entertained feelings of the higher order."

Glomar ignored this last with masterful stoicism. Setting his lance momentarily aside, he crossed his arms and leaned against the wall, his face cast into shadows by the torch. "If none other can touch your heart, there's one I think who might." His eyes were bright as he gazed across the hall. "Aye, she's the image of what every lass ought to be; that's what I think."

"I'm going to pretend I haven't the least notion what you're talking about," the scarlet man said. "And I'd advise you to take advantage of my pretense and sneak away now."

Glomar's sandy eyebrows shot up. "Don't tell me you've not noticed for yourself!"

"Noticed what?"

"That lass! What else?"

"*Which* lass, Glomar? There are a hundred and more ladies careening across the floor as we speak."

"Ah, but only one so far as I can see," answered Glomar, settling back comfortably to continue his long-distance admiration. His voice, though rough as dirt and rock, was almost wistful. "I dare you to find a maid alive who can rival Queen Bebo's cousin."

The scarlet man was not surprised. Why should he be? Who beside fair Gleamdren could have caught even stony Glomar's eye? Nevertheless, momentary jealousy surged in the scarlet man's breast. Had he been a cat, the fur on his back and tail would have stood on end. As it was, his lips drew back in something like a snarl, and he turned on the starry-eyed captain a look that might have pinned the poor man to the wall. But before Glomar saw, the snarl melted into a smile.

"You should ask her to dance, good captain."

Glomar's face paled noticeably even in the shadows, and his eyes went hollow and round. "Ach, no! That I could never! Nay, I would not dream to so much as step in her slim little shadow, much less ask to hold her hand in mine! I'm not much of a dancer in any case."

"Wise, then. Wise, indeed," nodded the poet. He too leaned against the wall, his arms crossed. Though in breadth he could never equal Glomar, he stood a half head taller at least. The better to look down upon the captain. "You'd never have a hope with her."

Glomar sighed. "Don't I know it." Then he glared up at his companion. "Nor can any man in Rudiobus hope to be fair Gleamdren's match!"

The scarlet man shrugged. "I could dance with her. If I wished."

Glomar snorted.

"I could," the scarlet man said, smooth as butter. "Anytime I choose."

"Ask her, then. I'm always game for a joke."

"I'm not so much in the mood."

"Not in the mood? To dance with that vision?" Glomar barked a laugh that caught the attention of several of the nearest dancers, who turned startled faces toward the darkened passage. "You amuse me, friend. Are you a bard or jester? Not in the mood, my eye. Ha! You're more a coward than all the rest of your kind together, aren't you?"

The scarlet man opened his mouth to give a reply, but fortunately, King Iubdan chose that moment to cry out in a voice that instantly silenced the music and the laughter of the revelers.

"Where is my Chief Poet?" he bellowed. His tones were round and rich as plum pudding, and his eyes, though black, were the merriest in the room. "Where is Bard Eanrin? Send him up to me at once! Make way, you dancers, and find my poet!"

The scarlet man stepped away from the wall, smoothing down his yellow hair, then jamming a jaunty red cap in place. "Anytime I choose," he hissed in parting before springing from the shadows, leaving Glomar behind in the gloom.

The crowd made way for the scarlet man as he crossed the dance floor, his golden face beaming with smiles. He approached the thrones of his monarchs and swept a bow made all the more dramatic by the flourish of his gold-trimmed cape.

"Ah! There you are, Eanrin," said the king.

"Greetings, most noble Iubdan Tynan, Dark Man of the Merry People, Lord of Rudiobus, who sits enthroned above all in fair Ruaine Hall!" cried the poet, his hand raised in salute. "And most illustrious queen," he continued, turning a gaze of adoration upon Iubdan's wife. "Fair Bebo, who walks among the stars and sings with the Spheres to the cheer and gladness of the Far World. My best wishes upon the anniversary of your birth!"

"Many thanks, Eanrin," said the queen with a graceful nod.

But Iubdan shook his head and bellowed, "No, no, no! What do I keep you around for, bard, if not for barding? I won't accept wishes to my queen spoken thus. You must ballad, Eanrin! You must versify!"

Poet Eanrin gave another bow, less hearty than the first; when he stood again, his face was full of woe, and many a lady in Ruaine put her hand to her heart at the sight of such tender feeling. "I fear, my king," said he, "that a song is not within me this night. You see before you a man broken. And though I would fain—"

"I didn't ask you to feign," said his sovereign, his dark eyes snapping. "I require that you perform your duty, Chief Poet, and perform it in proper spirit. It is Bebo's birthday, and she must have a song."

"Pray, my Dark Man," said Bebo with a kindly smile, "do not tax the poet. If he has no song in him—"

"When have we known our good Eanrin *not* to have a song?" Iubdan cried, then quickly added in a gentler tone, "Pardon my interruption, sweet one. But my Chief Poet will earn his keep! I put it to you, Eanrin. Can you dredge up a song?"

The poet raised melancholy eyes to his king's face and replied, "I can, my king."

"Then sing for us, will you? Sing in honor of your queen!"

Eanrin placed a hand to his heart and turned to Bebo. But his gaze strayed, if but for the space of a heartbeat, to her cousin standing just behind the queen's throne. And Lady Gleamdren lowered her gaze to the goblet in her hand and blushed most prettily.

"Queen of my heart," Eanrin said, a tremor in his voice, "to you I dedicate this ode, composed spontaneously here at your feet."

Bebo gave a gracious nod. Gleamdren raised an eyebrow, and the corners of her mouth twitched in expectation, but she schooled her face into a frown a moment later. A lady must take care how much she reveals.

The poet, unaccompanied, lifted his arms and sang. His voice was so sweet and so golden that he needed no instrument to fill it out, and his song carried to all corners of Ruaine Hall, into every cranny of that vast cavern, even to places where the torchlight could not penetrate.

"Hers the voice, the look. Obey
And sing a humble, longing lay!
Within the Hall of Red and Green
Behold my sweet, my love, my queen.
With merry song and manic pleasures,
Light of foot in lyric measures,
First pursue and then retreat.
Bright upon their fiery feet,
Within the circling dancers' meeting
In time to ancient drums a-beating
Solemn strains, her homage must declare.
Where falls her glance, the Graces honor pay.
I would behold the luster of her hair
And seek the arms of Lady Gleamdrené!"

A gasp rushed through the hall. The last echoes of the song died away, leaving the merrymakers wide-eyed and openmouthed, and Captain Glomar looking much more like a badger than he had a moment before. Queen Bebo hid either a smile or a frown behind her hand, while her cousin's face was a conflict of blushes and scowls.

Only Iubdan laughed.

He threw back his head and howled so loudly that even Poet Eanrin had the sense to look abashed. When he was quite done, Iubdan cried, "So that's how it is, bard? And here I thought you were singing as fine an ode to my queen as ever I have heard!"

"Forgive me, Your Majesty," said the poet with a bow. "Did I misspeak?"

"Indeed you did. Where we should have heard the name *Bebo* sweetly sung, we heard instead that of her cousin. Don't tell me this was a mistake?"

"If mistake it was," said Eanrin, turning to fix his gaze upon Lady Gleamdren, "it was a mistake of the tongue, not of the heart! Can I help it if the words that burst from my lips are the truth I feel most keenly?"

Iubdan guffawed again, and this time much of the court joined with him. Even Bebo no longer tried to disguise her laughter. But more than a hundred pairs of fists clenched, more than a hundred jaws set on edge as the young men of Rudiobus turned angry eyes upon the poet. Not least among these was Glomar, who took up his lance and squeezed it nearly to the point of breaking.

Gleamdren, however, refused to look at the poet, who stood, hand upon heart, gazing up at her.

"I thank you, good poet," said Queen Bebo at length, stilling the laughter with a wave of her hand, "for bringing such jollity to our hall. I look forward to another song when next my birthday is celebrated."

Then she bade the musicians take up their playing again, and the dancers returned to the floor. Iubdan rose and offered his hand to his queen, and they joined the others, whirling away in time to the music. Their removal to the floor left Gleamdren momentarily alone behind the thrones. She fixed her gaze upon the dancing monarchs, refusing to look even when Eanrin climbed the stairs and bowed in a fine impression of humility. Her face was fetchingly flushed.

"Fair lady," the poet began, "please allow me to—"

"Not another word!" Gleamdren said, holding up a hand. "Your impertinence does you no credit, Bard Eanrin. Though really, I should be surprised by nothing you say or do. But good Lumé! Must you embarrass me so in front of all the court?"

"I never meant to embarrass you, sweet maid," the poet protested, his hands outstretched in supplication. "I intended nothing other than to sing the praises of our queen! But my heart must always dictate my tongue, and my heart said—"

"I care little for your heart and its fool notions," said Gleamdren with a pretty toss of her head that indicated quite the opposite. She was flattered, and Eanrin knew this. "You're a dragon-kissed fool, Eanrin, that's what you are. And tonight you've proven it to everyone."

Here she tempered her words with a smile. It was a subtle dance, this art she practiced, and she was a skilled dancer. She must discourage her beaux just enough to keep them interested, not enough to drive them away.

The poet smiled in return. "Oh, come now, Gleamdren!" he said. "I know you can't mean that. You were watching every darting shadow for a sign of me. Admit it!"

She turned up her nose. "I admit nothing." But she gave him a sidelong glance that spoke volumes.

He leapt at the bait. "Not one man in this room is your equal." He took a step nearer and reached for her hand. "Not one man, save me."

She avoided his touch with an "Oh!" and gave him an arch frown.

He ground his teeth in a smile and spoke softly. "Enough of this nonsense, fair Gleamdrené Gormlaith. You know you are bored to tears by all these fools vying for your attention. What have they to offer you compared to me? I am the Chief Poet of Iubdan."

"You're a silly cat, Eanrin."

He slipped a hand about her waist. She pursed her lips, struggling to frown when her whole face longed to smile. She dropped her gaze to her goblet once more but did not resist—at least, not too much—when he drew her to him.

"I will go down in history," he whispered. "The greatest bard of all time. The prince of poetry!"

She rolled her eyes and gave a little shrug. "For what *that* is worth!"

"Every song could be yours." He bent his head to whisper in her ear. Her white-blond hair tickled his nose and smelled of pine needles. It was an exciting scent. "I shall dedicate my work to you. Every song I write. Every lyric stanza . . . yours! What say you to this?"

"Is what you sang just now an example of things to come?" she asked, turning her face suddenly up to him. Her nose bumped his, and he drew back, startled. Then he leaned in to kiss her.

"No! No!" she cried with a laugh and backed out of his grasp, tossing her head. "Such bosh and nonsense! What girl wants all that romanticized drivel dedicated to her? Throughout history! People will get silly notions about me. They'll start to say I'm some sort of famous beauty. Insignificant me!"

She was fishing for compliments, but Eanrin was no longer feeling generous. "Come now, dearest of my heart," he growled. "Give us a kiss, won't you?"

"Oh, Eanrin," said she, still laughing. "A kiss you will never have from me!" Her glance said otherwise.

"A dance, then?" said the poet, emboldened by that look. "This reel is your favorite, I know. Give me your hand, Gleamdren, and we'll show these beggars what dancing is!"

Gleamdren blinked at him, long and slow. Then she turned, swept down the steps, and grabbed the arm of the nearest unengaged gentleman, declaring in a voice of honey, "I'll not dance with you, Eanrin, for I have already promised this dance to—" She turned to discover the identity of her new partner. "Who are you?"

"Captain Glomar of the Guard!" gasped he, his face full of the beautiful terror of a dream come true.

"Yes, you then," said Gleamdren.

Glomar stared down at the little white hands clutching his arm. A flush swept over his face, as red as Eanrin's cape. "Why . . . why, my lady! I'm not much good at dancin'."

"But you have promised to dance with me, haven't you?" said she, gazing up at him in such a way that he would not have contradicted her for the world. Without another word, Glomar swept her into his arms, dragged her across the floor, flung her in a twirl, caught her at the last second, and hurled her again. Gleamdren was out of breath and gasping within moments. But her face fixed into a smile that was intended less for Glomar's pleasure than for Eanrin's misery.

And every man in Ruaine Hall saw the Chief Poet's disgrace.

Eanrin stood, his mouth agape, his heart beating strangely in his breast. This must be what jealousy felt like. Best to remember it; a poet must be keen on his emotions, able to dredge them up at a moment's notice. Gleamdren cast him one last dogged smile, and her eyes flew wide as her arm was nearly wrenched from the shoulder.

The poet could bear no more. He turned on heel and stalked from the hall.

2

THE PATH AT HER FEET was narrow indeed.

The mortal stumbled through the Wood. Once or twice, she still thought she glimpsed the golden form running ahead of her. Strange guide though it was, it was the only guide she had, and she forced her bruised body to follow. But her mind was so tired, full of clashing images and sounds.

Her father's face, pale for loss of blood.

Moonlight on stones like teeth.

"Run!"

The girl gasped, her mouth twisted in a silent scream.

The trees drew back from her as she continued her flight. They dared not interfere while she walked that Path, no matter how they might wish to. She took no notice of them. How long had she fled now? Had it been one night, or days and weeks of this nightmare? And always the howls pounded her memory.

Suddenly, the howls vanished. A new voice spoke from the gloom.

Come to me, pretty maid.

The girl stopped, swaying where she stood, on the verge of collapsing. Slowly, as though she dared not hope to find what she sought, she turned her head to the left. Between the trees a river sparkled like a ribbon of pure light and sweetness.

Her thirst was overwhelming. Even the snarls faded from her mind, replaced by the River's inviting babbling. *Come to me, pretty maid,* it said, though she heard only the sound of water.

Her feet left bloodstains on the moss and rocks as she hastened down to the River's edge. A glint of gold shimmered in the tail of her eye, shining even in the Wood's oppressive shadows. She ignored it. Falling to her knees on the bank of the water, she plunged in both hands. The water stung her wrists where the harsh cords had bitten into her skin.

Drink deeply. Drink.

The water flowed about her arms, fresh and alive. She cupped her hands and lifted the cooling liquid to her lips. She drank.

She drew a long, shuddering breath, then fell upon the bank, one arm extended into the water, the other upon the shore. Her black hair covered her face, and the River ran its fingers through the ends of it, pulling, pulling.

Sleep deeply. Sleep, said the River.

From the shadows of the trees, a fine, narrow face watched with solemn dark eyes. The shape was that of a hound with a coat of white-gold luster. But the eyes shone with an angelic light, or a light of a higher order still. Unhurried, he approached the girl and looked down upon her sorry state. He saw the Path she had walked and would later walk again. He saw how the twisting and winding of this Path would baffle her.

The shining one bent his head and placed a kiss upon the girl's forehead. Then he turned and loped into the forest, vanishing as though he had never been. The girl slept where she had fallen, her thirst unsatisfied.

Eanrin sat on the banks of Gorm-Uisce Lake, which lay at the base of Rudiobus Mountain and reflected both the mountain and the stars above. On such a night, with all the Merry Folk dancing in the Hall of Red and Green, the lake was a lonely spot. The voice of Fionnghuala Lynn, the waterfall gate into Rudiobus, was distant enough to be no more than a murmur. The only living soul within calling distance was the guardian of Fionnghuala, who would recognize a poet's need for solitude and leave him in peace.

Eanrin stared across the still waters to the far shore, where a dark forest stood. *"Woe is me, for I am undone,"* he whispered. He quite liked the phrase and thought he'd round it out with a lyric stanza or two. *"Woe is me, for I am undone . . ."*

Unfortunately, he had no more. What rhymed with undone? Homespun. No. Bludgeon?

"Poetry be dashed!" he snarled and clenched his hands into fists. "What in the name of Lumé, Hymlumé, and the entire starry host is *wrong* with Lady Gleamdren?"

Neither the lake nor the stars seemed inclined to answer.

Eanrin frowned. Obviously, the first fault lay with Gleamdren's womanhood, he decided. Had he not already written a score of popular verses on the fickleness of women, on their temperamental, unpredictable natures? That much, at least, was no surprise. But he knew without a doubt that Gleamdren wanted him. She must! They were so alike, she and he. She, with her beauty and her pretty ways, bidding every lad to join her entourage even as she simultaneously repulsed romantic advances. If hers was not a heart akin to that of a true poet—desperate for notice, still more desperate for solitude—than whose could be?

"Why then does she resist me?"

Eanrin sighed, casting his gaze to the heavens, which offered no sympathy. So he took a comb from his pocket and leaned out over the lake. It was quiet enough beneath him to make a fine mirror, and he began smoothing his hair. With his mind so unsettled, a good grooming was the only recourse. He slicked his golden locks into place and slicked them again, the rhythmic motions soothing until he found himself better able to think.

"Patience, Eanrin," he told himself, tilting his face above the lake to get a better perspective on his features. "Patience is all you need. A turn or two about the dance floor should be enough to settle this business. Once Glomar has shown the lady his paces, she will be sick to death of him and longing for my return."

The poet's smile broadened at this thought. By pure comparison, how could he fail to shine the brighter in his lady's esteem? And he had time. His merry life had extended more centuries than he could remember and would continue, so far as he could imagine, for many centuries still. He need not hurry.

"Though I wait a thousand years and more," he whispered to the stars, "I will yet win the hand of Lady Gleamdrené Gormlaith. This I vow upon the crown of the moon, upon the scepter of the—"

A chilling howl trembled on the edge of the night.

Eanrin startled and fumbled to catch his comb before it was lost forever beneath Gorm-Uisce's glassy surface. He stood and backed away from the lake, his eyes fixed upon the dark line of forest across the water. The sound must have drifted from the worlds beyond, from the Wood Between or even the Near World of mortals. Such a cry, so lost and so horrible, had never been uttered in Rudiobus.

The guardian of Fionnghuala emerged from behind the waterfall and trotted along the lake's edge to stand beside Eanrin. She was a golden mare with a scarlet tail, a beautiful and solemn animal. Her name was Órfhlaith, and she spoke to Eanrin in the language of horses.

"Did you hear that?"

Eanrin nodded. "The Black Dogs," he said, and trembled. "I know them when I hear them. That was the cry of the Black Dogs. Are they come to Rudiobus?"

"Not they. Their prey." Her nostrils flaring, the mare tossed her head to indicate the far shore of the lake. The white light of Hymlumé above, which had been bright only minutes before, had vanished behind a cloud, and the poet could discern nothing on the far shore. "Some poor soul they pursue has fallen on the edge of Rudiobus."

"But not entered," said Eanrin quickly, as though to assure himself. "No one can enter Rudiobus uninvited. Not even Death or his minions."

Órfhlaith stamped a hoof, splattering Eanrin's shoes with silver droplets. "You're right, king's poet," she said. "Quickly, on my back!"

"Why?"

"The Black Dogs are terrible. They always run down their quarry in the end. But they may not enter Rudiobus, and perhaps we can offer their luckless victim shelter."

"It's not our business!" Eanrin protested.

"No," agreed Órfhlaith. "But we can make it so. On my back, at once."

Eanrin nearly argued. But his eyes lit suddenly with an insatiable curiosity. Who might the Black Dogs pursue that would think to turn to Rudiobus and the Merry Folk for aid? The poet licked his lips. He had never glimpsed the Black Dogs. Word of them had first come to Rudiobus in the last century, and he thought them a dreadful tale, but one he was unlikely to encounter. According to rumor, they chased only those upon whom they were set, pursing their quarry without flagging until they ran it down. But no one would set the Black Dogs upon Iubdan's Chief Poet. It would be a safe enough venture to take a peek beyond Rudiobus.

"I suppose I should investigate anyway," he said. "My duty to the king and such."

With that, he scrambled up on the golden mare's back and held on to her mane as she leapt out onto the warm waters of Gorm-Uisce. She did not swim, for she was herself so light, so airy, that she could not sink. Her hooves left spreading ripples where they glanced on the water's surface. The water was dark without the moon to shine upon it, and darker still the nearer they came to the far shore, where the trees swallowed all light.

The forest beyond the lake marked the edge of Rudiobus. Although many boasted of it, few of the Merry People actually walked the shadows of the forest beyond the lake. To pass amid those trees was to pass into the Between, the thin realm of existence that separated immortal Faerie from the mortal world. The undying folk of Iubdan Tynan avoid proximity with mortality. But Eanrin was more daring than most of his kin. Always eager for some inspiration for new songs with which to delight his king and queen, he had explored deeply into the treacherous Wood. He had learned which Paths he might safely follow, and which he would do well to avoid.

So it was with little care or concern that, when Órfhlaith drew close to the far shore, Eanrin leapt from her back to dry land, avoiding wetting his feet as much as possible. A strange thing happened the moment he stood upon that shore. While neither he grew nor the mare shrank, suddenly he towered above her, and she was so small that she might have fit into his hand. For he no longer stood in Rudiobus, and height and girth could keep no rigid hold on him. But these alterations on the fabric of reality were as commonplace as breathing to Iubdan's bard, and he took no notice.

"I'll just have a look," he told the mare. He took two strides into the shadows of the Wood and left behind the realm of his birth.

The trees themselves did not change in the Between. The lake had vanished; Eanrin could no longer smell it behind him, nor the scents he always associated with Rudiobus—pine sap and rock and the heady scent of laughter, which only a nose as keen as his might discern. Stepping from the darkness of night into the gloom of tree-shadowed midday gave the poet momentary pause.

The Wood was lit in half-light. Perhaps above the woven branches a sun shone brightly. No one could say for certain. Eanrin took a deep breath, glad to be once more in the Between and the thrill of danger it offered. Fire lit his spirit, and he took three steps.

Then he drew up short as a foul stench assaulted his nostrils.

It was a wonder he had not noticed it the moment he stepped from Rudiobus. It was the smell of a dying body. It was the smell of mortality.

The poet made a face, his lips drawn back from his teeth. The Black Dogs must have been set on the trail of some poor mortal who had wandered foolishly from the Near World into the Wood. He cast about for the source.

She lay fainted beneath an old caorann tree. Did she know how close she had come to Rudiobus? But of course not, how could she, ignorant, dying beast that she was? Her hair covered her face in a tangled snarl, and some of the caorann berries had fallen in it, like drops of red blood.

From where he stood, Eanrin could not tell if she breathed.

The poet stood a while regarding her, struggling to keep from gagging. If there was one thing he hated, it was obligation. He knew, now that he had seen this creature lying in such a helpless state, he should feel obliged to help her. The Black Dogs could not be far off. If they came upon the mortal lying thus, they would rend her to pieces and carry her spirit down into the Netherworld.

"But really," Eanrin muttered to himself, "is that any of my business?"

Órfhlaith would expect a report, as would Iubdan and Bebo, who, even in the midst of celebration, must have heard the voices of the Black Dogs baying. They would even now be standing by Fionnghuala Lynn, awaiting news. He had best investigate, at least discover if the woman lived.

He approached her, placing his feet gently so as to make no sound. She did not stir. Even as he drew near, he did not think she breathed, she lay so still. No features were visible beneath her hair. Ragged, colorless garments covered her body, and what little he could see of her skin was just as colorless. She was slight, gaunt even. He put out a tentative finger and touched her shoulder.

He hissed, drawing back quickly. A blister swiftly developed on his fingertip.

Something was wrong. His nostrils flared as he drew another long whiff of her scent. She absolutely reeked of humanity. But why would her skin burn? He stepped back, and his heart raced. Did she suffer some dreadful fever? It was not unlikely here in the Wood. Humans reacted strangely to many of the plants or beings dwelling here. She may have caught a burning curse or some disease, neither of which would affect Eanrin. He had no reason to fear, he told himself again and again.

Yet he could not still his beating heart. What if she wore a glamour?

He raised his gaze to the caorann tree under which the woman lay. These trees were known to protect against witchcraft and enchantments. It was said their berries would reveal the truth of all but the deepest spells. If this woman was a witch wearing a glamour to disguise her true nature, lying beneath the caorann tree would be a mistake. The berries fallen in her hair would swiftly dissolve her spell.

Only one creature, so far as Eanrin knew, could cast an enchantment strong enough to deceive the caorann. Everything in him told him to flee. But his curiosity was so intense that he stood unmoving.

After all, he had never seen a dragon.

There were many known to stalk the worlds of Faerie. The most infamous, of course, was the Flame at Night, scourge of the mortal realm, who had once been a Faerie queen herself. But there were possibly hundreds of other minor dragons, or so the rumors had it.

His eyes as round as moons, he approached the woman again. Once more he put out a finger but did not touch her right away, trying to feel the heat emanating from her body. The air was cold all around her. Had he imagined the burning? But no, his blistered finger was no lie. Frowning, he touched her again, lightning fast.

Nothing.

Licking his lips, Eanrin rested his finger on her shoulder for a longer moment before drawing back. Still neither heat nor sign of life. He grabbed her shoulder fully, and she did not burn him, nor did she move.

Not a dragon, then, he decided. He must have been mistaken. Perhaps she did indeed suffer from a curse that made her sometimes burn to the touch? Stranger things had happened in the Far World.

Eanrin felt beneath the tangled masses of hair to find the stranger's neck. There was no pulse, none at all. He took hold of her shoulders and rolled her over into his arms. Her face lolled to one side, half covered in her long hair, which was as colorless as the rest of her. He put an ear to her mouth and nose but could discern no breath.

"Are you dead, then?" he asked and received no answer. He had rarely been so near to death. It did not frighten so much as fascinate and simultaneously appall him. "You appear remarkably dead-ish, at least. Perhaps I should just leave you here to the Dogs."

He realized, suddenly, that he had heard not a single note of the Black Dogs' baying since he stepped into the Wood. Odd . . . Should they not be even now bearing down upon their prey? He sniffed the air but could catch no scent other than the dominating smell of mortality. Shivering, he looked down at the woman again and brushed the hair back from her face.

She was strangely beautiful. Too beautiful, he thought, to be mortal, despite her lack of color. Rather like a sketch before the pigment had been added, every shadow and contour perfectly defined but unfinished. There was a hardness to her lines, however, a certain set to her jaw and about her lower lip as well, which should have detracted from her beauty.

Somehow it didn't matter. She was beautiful enough to make his heart lurch.

But was she even alive?

He could picture Fionnghuala Lynn's falls alight with torches as the Merry People awaited his return. Iubdan would be anxious for news, and Bebo hardly less so. Eanrin needed to make a decision—either bear the woman back across the lake or leave her here.

"How can I bring a corpse into Rudiobus?" he whispered. "If corpse you are, that is." He shook his head, setting his jaw. "No, I cannot do it. Death cannot come to Rudiob-AYIEE!"

The stranger's hands had come up and clasped about his neck. He leapt to his feet, screaming as though bitten by a snake. If he'd been a cat, the fur on his tail would have stood on end. As it was, he lost his cap in a brief struggle to loosen her hold and danced several paces away.

"Dragon's *teeth*!" he bellowed. "Dragon's teeth and wings and tail! You nigh unto scared my whiskers off, woman!"

The mortal lay in a heap, supporting herself on her elbows, breathing now in rasping gasps that sounded as though they would tear her lungs to shreds. With an effort, she raised her face. Her eyes pierced Eanrin.

"Help me!" she gasped. Then, with a moan, she collapsed once more.

"Dragon's teeth," the poet swore again, his voice venomous. He approached on tentative feet, sniffing just in case some trace of a spell had escaped him before. The caorann tree waved its branches gently, as though trying to reassure him. But he knew better than to trust any of the trees in the Wood. They were deceitful devils when they got the chance, even the caorann on occasion.

Kneeling but hesitant to touch her again, he said, "Gentle lady, I thought you were dead."

She was still but for the faintest rise and fall of her chest as she drew breath. Setting his jaw, Eanrin reached out and took her in his arms. She was so thin that he expected no difficulty in lifting her. To his surprise, she was far heavier than her size would indicate, and he struggled to stand upright. Yet she moaned piteously in her semiconscious state, her arms draped across his neck.

She smelled sweet to him suddenly. He put his nose into her hair and drew a long breath. All the prettiest scents of the world danced alluringly through his senses.

"I should put you down," he whispered, but his arms would not obey. "I should leave you here. You'll do me harm if I bear you in. I know you'll do me harm!"

But his heart would not believe his head, and his arms clutched her close.

He heard the Black Dogs' voices.

The darkness of their baying rolled across the Wood, dragging shadows with it, dousing lights. Eanrin turned, his face pale as a ghost's, expecting to see their great bodies bearing down upon him, teeth flashing, eyes blazing.

Instead, he saw something far more dreadful.

He was a hound, but he was not black. Where he stood, the shadows of the trees drew back, and light fell in a bright aura upon his white-gold coat. Tall and slender, with a long, noble face, he stood on delicate feet and gazed at the poet from out of the Wood's depths. He made no sound but took a single step forward.

Eanrin screamed.

In that instant, his decision was made, though he did not make it for himself. His feet moved in a surge of terror and, still clutching the woman tight, he sprang back across the borders into Rudiobus.

3

EANRIN STOOD ONCE MORE upon the banks of Gorm-Uisce. The Wood was behind him, but he felt the protections of Rudiobus all around, the boundaries set in place ages ago by Queen Bebo. Nevertheless, he stood scarcely breathing, his limbs all atremble. Then he squeezed his eyes tight shut and bowed his head. He would not think of it. He would not remember it! That vision was unbearable, unthinkable, and he would not allow himself to dwell upon it. Better to have seen the Black Dogs!

With a shudder that shook his whole body so that he nearly dropped his burden, he at last opened his eyes again. He found the woman gazing up at him, her face solemn and unreadable.

Eanrin's mouth was dry, and his voice croaked when he spoke. "You're safe now. I will take you to my king. Death may not come to Rudiobus, and neither will his Dogs."

Wordlessly, she buried her face once more in his chest. Eanrin carried her, staggering to the water's edge. Órfhlaith waited there, still tiny as a mayfly.

"Is she the victim?" the mare asked.

Eanrin nodded.

"Iubdan would wish to offer refuge. Put her on my back."

Eanrin, for once in his life, obeyed without a word. The magic (if magic it must be called) worked again. When he stepped forward to put the woman on Órfhlaith's back, their sizes altered without ever seeming to change. The woman did not shrink; Órfhlaith did not grow. Yet each fit the other perfectly.

Eanrin sprang up behind the woman and put his arms around her to keep her in place. The mare cantered smoothly back across the lake. Eanrin said nothing. His heart beat too fast, and his head still whirled with terror. Several times in his absentmindedness, he almost lost hold of the stranger and allowed her to slip into the water.

He knew what he had seen. He only wished to the Spheres Above that he had not! Perhaps he could forget. Perhaps he would not be forced to remember. . . .

At last Órfhlaith passed through Fionnghuala Lynn to where Iubdan, Bebo, Gleamdren, Glomar, and all the court of Rudiobus, having heard the awful voices of the Black Dogs, had gathered to discover the source of all the excitement. Queen Bebo's delicate veil covered her hair and glinted in the torchlight, and she lightly held Iubdan's arm.

"What have you there, poet?" demanded the king as soon as Eanrin and the mare appeared.

"A mortal," said Eanrin, his voice subdued. He looked at the woman held before him and thought, *What a fool I was to have thought otherwise. She is so obviously what she is. How could I have suspected a glamour?*

When Eanrin seemed unwilling to tell his tale, Órfhlaith explained what she knew. As she spoke of the Black Dogs, a hush settled on the crowd, broken a moment later by a rush of excited babble, like birds chattering their morning chorus. Black Dogs! How tremendous! The stuff of one of Eanrin's exotic tales! Meanwhile, Gleamdren stepped forward and put her hands up to help the woman off the mare's back.

"Careful, darling," said Eanrin hastily. "She might have died while crossing, and you shouldn't be touching death."

The stranger moaned before the words had quite left the poet's mouth.

Gleamdren gave Eanrin a withering glance and assisted the stranger to the ground, supporting her with gentle hands. The people of Rudiobus looked upon her and gasped.

"What a pretty creature!" said Queen Bebo, pressing a hand to her heart.

"And mortal?" exclaimed the king. "A princess of the Near World, perhaps. And pursued by the Black Dogs! Such a dreadful fate."

"Especially for one so fair," agreed his queen. All those gathered murmured their agreement. "Can she speak, Gleamdren? Can she tell us her story?"

Eanrin hopped off Órfhlaith but hung back. Ordinarily, he would have stepped forward and demanded his fair share of the attention. After all, the mortal was his find. But his limbs felt weak, and his stomach roiled with the too-near terror he had just experienced. It was all he could do to stay on his feet. When Bebo turned to him and repeated her question, he murmured only, "Not much. She said *help me*, or some such nonsense. That is all."

Gleamdren gave him a quick glance. She had never known Eanrin so restrained. Her lips thinned. Then she turned and whispered tenderly to the stranger, "There, there. Can you talk, then?"

The stranger's eyes, which had been half closed, suddenly opened wide. Colorless yet beautiful, they rolled as she struggled to take in all the assembled people, the laughing faces wearing unnatural expressions of concern. "Wh-where am I?" she cried in a voice rough with mortality. Then she moaned and buried her face in Gleamdren's shoulder as though it was all too much to bear. "The Dogs . . ."

"Hymlumé's light!" exclaimed Iubdan, his own dark eyes snapping with something between sympathy and anger. "How could those brutes chase this little mite? We must learn what goads them!"

"No," said Bebo softly. "Not tonight, my Dark Man. Can you not see how close she is to fainting? The poor thing is spent. Let us allow her a sound night's rest before we ply her with questions."

"Aye, that is wise," agreed her husband. "Lady Gleamdren, can you find accommodations for our guest?"

Gleamdren nodded. "I shall put her in my own bed. She'll rest easy enough there and hear nothing of those monsters while she dreams."

Eanrin gasped. All in a rush, his own fears vanished, and he stared at his lady, at the stranger, and back again. "Gleamdren, my sweet," he said, stepping forward and putting a protective hand on her shoulder. "We don't know anything about this creature. We don't know what she might have done to provoke someone to set the Black Dogs on her. They don't chase without reason, you know."

But though the words spilled quickly from his tongue, no one paid him heed. Gleamdren shrugged off his hand and, with nothing more than a withering look, ignored him. She walked away with the king on one side and the queen on the other as she assisted the woman back through the caverns of Rudiobus. Glomar trailed behind, and all the rest of the court, sparing not so much as a glance for the crimson poet.

He found himself at last standing alone beside Fionnghuala Lynn with the king's mare. He turned to Órfhlaith. "I tell you what, my friend, something about this puts my hair on end."

She whuffled and shook her ears. "Do not mistrust Master Iubdan or his lady. Would they allow evil into Rudiobus?"

Eanrin did not hear. He watched the torchlight vanishing up the caverns, his heart sinking. The last thing in the world he wanted was to become tangled in some mortal's affairs. But he had brought the creature into Rudiobus of his own free will. Whatever happened next, he could no longer extricate himself.

With a curse, he left Órfhlaith and the waterfall, sprinting after the crowd.

The colorless woman opened her eyes to the warm glow surrounding her. The room was full of gold. Gilding on the bedposts and walls, golden threads in the bed curtains, a gold frame surrounding a mirror of pure water—she closed her eyes again and turned away from that. The last thing she wanted to see was her own reflection.

When she raised her lids again, there was more gold. The gold of candlelight shining on the white-gold braid draped over the shoulder of a Rudioban maiden.

Flowing Gold.

"So. You're awake." Lady Gleamdren sat on a chair near the bedside, her eyes narrow, her arms crossed over her chest. "It's about time."

The colorless woman opened her mouth, but her throat was raw and she found it difficult to speak. Then she gasped, a tearing sound in her chest, and cried out, "The Dogs!" She sat up in the bed, her long hair falling about her shoulders like a shawl and partially covering her face. But one bright eye gazed out from between the limp strands. "The Black Dogs! Are they near?"

"Nice show, that," said Gleamdren, twisting her lips. "I'd almost think you were truly frightened."

The stranger blinked. As an afterthought she took another deep, shuddering breath. "How long have I slept?"

"Don't give me that. You haven't slept at all."

The woman swallowed. The counterpane was heavy, and she pushed it back. Even it was quilted with golden thread on gold-spun cloths. "Who are you?" she asked the maid.

"Lady Gleamdrené Gormlaith. As if you didn't know."

A smile touched the woman's mouth, tugging at its corners. "I did not know. But I am pleased to make your acquaintance."

"Less pleased am I!" Gleamdren hopped up from her chair and strode to the bedside. "You're wearing my nightdress. Did you know that?"

The woman looked down at the soft green gown embroidered at the neck with dark leaves and, sure enough, more gold. She said nothing but picked at the rich collar.

"And do you want to know why you're wearing my nightdress?" Gleamdren persisted. "Because every glamour-dazzled fool in Rudiobus has gone and fallen in love with you. Every one of them! Do you think I've a single suitor left this night to think of *me*?" As she spoke, her hands touched her own face as though to assure herself that she was still as pretty as she'd always been. Her mouth formed a hard line as she brandished her fists the stranger's way, and the woman drew back a little from her.

"My only choice," Gleamdren continued, "was to offer you my bed and my gown. Display my sweet-natured heart, you know. At least then, when the novelty of *you* has worn off and you're long gone from Rudiobus, my suitors will still remember the kindness of Gleamdren."

The smile on the woman's face grew, and in her eyes, fires danced. "I am sure rumor of Lady Gleamdrené Gormlaith already flies across the worlds. Rumor of her beauty and of her favor in the court of Iubdan."

Gleamdren looked mollified. "Well, it's all Eanrin's verses, you know," she said modestly. "They do have a way of getting about, his being Iubdan's Chief Poet. Not that I give him the time of day, mind you. I'm not such a fool as that. You give a lad an inkling of favor, and suddenly he forgets all that undying passion of his! Best to string them along—but you distract me."

"Indeed, such was not my intent." The counterpane fell back as the woman slid her legs around and over the edge of the bed. "Did you have something more to say to me, Lady Gleamdrené?"

"I want you to kidnap me."

"What did you say?"

"I want you to kidnap me." Gleamdren set her jaw. "I'm not a fool, you know. I did not fall for your little glamour."

The woman said nothing. She stared into the maid's eyes, momentarily uncertain.

"I'm not the sort to fall in love," Gleamdren continued in a most practical voice. "So it's not in my nature to fall for glamours either. Not even a spell is going to make me love someone so unconditionally! No, when I saw you, I felt neither love nor pity for you, no more than that silly Eanrin did, I'm sure. But unlike Eanrin, I stop and think about things now and then. So when you were brought inside and even Bebo was taken in by your 'great beauty'—though, I must say, I don't see what's so great about it. Even with enchantments, you're far too scrawny to be beautiful—I thought to myself, 'Who could possibly deceive even my queenly cousin?' Not another Faerie, surely. Bebo is older than all of them. No enchantment of the Far World would get past her eye.

"Then I thought, well, what about a witch? Not a mortal witch, of course; those poor hags and silly sorceresses couldn't begin to deceive even Eanrin, much less my cousin! Perhaps a Faerie witch, then. But even Vartera, the Witch Queen of Arpiar, couldn't get past Queen Bebo's protections. And she tried! Lumé love you, how she tried, so desperate to find the Flowing Gold was she! Everyone wants the Flowing Gold. And every gold-hungry witch and monster of the Far World has tried to take it at least once. But you . . ."

Gleamdren's stream of prattle died away as she smiled knowingly upon the colorless woman. "You did what even Queen Vartera could not—you deceived Bebo. You wheedled your way into Rudiobus, extracted promises of safe haven from the king and queen. You are more than a mere goblin witch, aren't you?"

"What, then," the woman whispered, "am I?"

"A dragon."

The candles all about the room flared, then sank on their wicks. The warm glow vanished, exchanged for a dull redness. Gleamdren and the stranger gazed at each other. And slowly the glamour unraveled.

Hri Sora sat on the edge of Lady Gleamdren's bed, clad in her soft green nightgown. Her skin was stretched too thin over her frame, and in places it broke, revealing cruel scales beneath. These were black with a red-hot iridescence that was painfully beautiful to behold.

"I thought as much," said Gleamdren with a satisfied smirk. "You smelled burnt like a dragon, not dead like mortals do. So tell me, dragon, are you looking for the Flowing Gold too?"

"I am," said Hri Sora. Her voice rasped between her sharp teeth.

"Of course you are. I know where it is; did you know that?"

"I did. And you will tell me."

Gleamdren laughed outright. Her laugh was artificial, as though she'd forgotten long ago what a real laugh was supposed to sound like. She wiped one eye with her thumb and turned a smile upon the dragon. "Oh, honestly! Do you really think that's how it's going to work? I'm not about to just tell you a secret like that, older than the foundations of the world! You're going to have to kidnap me."

Hri Sora hissed and fire gleamed in her mouth. "Tell me what I want to know, and there will be no need for kidnapping."

"What? And spoil all the fun? I think not! No, no, it's much better that you steal me away to . . . wherever you live. I do hope there's a good high tower there. It's proper if you lock me in a high tower. That's how these things are done."

The dragon rose from the bed. Fire burned through her skin, and the green nightgown caught and smoldered at the neck and sleeves. "Tell me what I want to know." The heat of her words melted the gilding on the bedposts, on the walls, on the mirror's frame.

"No. Sorry. Kidnapping it must be."

"Are you not afraid?"

"Why should I be afraid? I have *scores* of suitors, and they'll all come to rescue me. Can you imagine how romantic that will be? Much more so than epic poetry. I've never been kidnapped before, but I've always rather liked the sound of it! So yes, why don't you just spread your wings like a good dragon and carry me off?"

Hri Sora gnashed her teeth. Fire fell from her lips, setting the counterpane ablaze. Even Gleamdren had the sense to take a step back, blinking rapidly. But Hri Sora reached out and took hold of the front of her dress, dragging her so close that Gleamdren thought her nose might melt away. For the first time that evening, a flutter that might be akin to fear stirred in Gleamdren's breast.

"I'll carry you off, little maid," snarled the dragon. "I'll lock you away fast and far. And believe me, you will tell me what I wish to know, or you will die."

"Don't . . . don't make a fool of yourself," Gleamdren gasped, still trying to keep her voice light. "The people of Rudiobus don't *die*."

"Perhaps not." Fire surrounded the dragon's tongue as she spoke. "But you can be killed."

Gleamdren opened her mouth to speak but found she had no words. That thrill of fear she'd known for the first time only moments ago returned suddenly, paralyzing her. She went limp in the dragon's grasp, made no struggle as she was caught up in two powerful arms and borne to the window. It may have been some spell. It may have been the overwhelming poison of the dragon's breath no longer disguised by an attractive enchantment. Either way, Gleamdren found herself unable to move, unable to speak, unable to so much as cry out for help.

The dragon flung wide the casement, and the fire of her hair and her eyes lit up that dark street within the mountain, angry red light bursting through every window and startling all sleepers into instant, panicked wakefulness. Then she roared in a powerful voice that carried not only throughout all Rudiobus Mountain, but also across the lake, into the Wood and the worlds beyond. The language was one never before spoken in the land of the Merry People, and it would never be heard in those halls again.

"*Yaotl! Eztli!*"

War and blood. Fire and terror. The words cracked rocks and broke hearts even as they sped through the passages and pierced the boundaries of worlds to fall upon the ears of those to whom they called.

Then the baying began.

The voices of the Black Dogs filled the ears of every man and woman living in the mountain. Called at last from within, those awful hunters burst through boundaries heretofore unbreakable, sped across the water, and hurled themselves like a hurricane wind through the gates of Fionnghuala Lynn. No one dared stand in their path as they hurtled forward, dragging a vicious dark Midnight in their wake.

Gleamdren saw them within a moment of the dragon's call. She glimpsed huge bodies; she glimpsed flaming eyes all tangled in a snarl of sounds and shadows and raging winds. Her hair whirled about; even the fires of the dragon's hair were threatened with extinction. But the dragon's claws clutched Gleamdren by the shoulder, and she was dragged through her window and mounted on the back of a black body she could not see with all that assailed her senses.

Then they were gone: Dogs, dragon, maiden. Vanished from Rudiobus so quickly that no one saw their passing, not even Iubdan's mare standing dumbstruck at the gate. But the baying of the Black Dogs echoed through the byways of Rudiobus for hours afterward. And when the echoes at last died away, the heavy darkness of Midnight lingered for hours more.

All this while, the girl in the Wood slept on the River's edge, and it pulled at her hair with its wet and wanton fingers. Her sleep was deep indeed and troubled as only enchanted sleeps may be. In her dreams she lived again and again that dark moment when the moon vanished behind a cloud. When a looming shadow appeared between two jutting stones.

She heard the wolf howling in a voice so like those of the Black Dogs that it may almost have been the same.

4

Eanrin scowled at the blister on his finger. There it was, right in front of him. Swollen and ugly, painful even to look at.

Yet he had carried a dragon into Rudiobus.

"Dragon's teeth," he hissed, quietly so as not to be heard. He stood hidden in a gallery above Iubdan and Bebo's council chamber and did not want his voice to echo.

They rarely used this chamber for anything resembling a real council; their council members were unused to being summoned at all, especially at this hour. Everyone sat ill at ease, some in their nightshirts, some in uncomfortable robes of office that looked as though they had not been worn for centuries (most of them hadn't). Iubdan sat with his face very red behind his ebony beard.

"How can this have happened?" he demanded.

Eanrin strained his ears, waiting for someone to remind someone else that it had been the poet's fault. As much as he hated to admit it, it probably was. He should have seen through the disguise! Even the caorann tree had been deceived, but that should have made him still more cautious. Only dragons, it was said, could fool the caorann. And only a dragon—he knew this now with rueful certainty—could burn a man at the slightest touch.

What a fool he'd been. The longer he dithered over her, the longer her glamour had worked itself into his brain. Had he acted upon his first instincts and left her there, none of this would have happened. She could have scraped and scrabbled on the edge of Rudiobus for a hundred years and never found an opening.

"But it wasn't my fault," he muttered, unwilling even now to admit a mistake. "I might have put her down, if it wasn't for that . . . that . . ."

He could not bring himself to speak the word. A dragon in Rudiobus was bad enough. *Only one monster at a time,* he told himself. *You needn't worry about that other. Not yet.*

With a shudder, he returned his attention to the scene in the chamber below.

"How can this have happened?" Iubdan demanded for perhaps the tenth time. The councilmen cast one another accusing glances, as though any one of their neighbors must be at fault and why not confess now and let everyone else go back to sleep? By the king's black beard, it was going on noon already, and all of them should be properly tucked away in bed!

Glomar stood like a lump to the king's right, arms crossed and his brow more badger-like than ever, offering not one useful word. "We've got to fetch her back!" was all he said, as though no one else was capable of coming to this conclusion. Eanrin, from his hiding place (poets are never officially invited to secret council meetings), sneered at the man and his fellows.

"We've got to fetch her back!" Glomar stated again after another interminable silence crept by. "Immediately! I'll set out now and track them down."

"Track the Black Dogs?" one of the councilmen said.

"I'll do it!" Glomar roared.

Eanrin watched as the councilmen exchanged glances. Even those dunces, less blinded by love than the captain, knew how foolish such a venture would be.

"You'll end up on the road to Death's realm," said Iubdan, thumping his fist on the arm of his chair. "That's where you'll go, and that's no help to anyone. No one is setting out that way unless we've a good plan for how to venture both in and out. Ugh! I little like the notion of stepping into the Netherworld again! Poor cousin! Taken by such fiends . . . she must be well on her way to that dark place herself. Where else would the Black Dogs carry her?"

"Etalpalli."

All eyes in the chamber, including the covert pair in the gallery, turned to Queen Bebo. She sat apart from the table of councilmen, on a humble chair of twisted roots growing up from the mountain floor. Her green sleeves, delicately picked out in spider webs of exquisite work, draped over the arms, and her silver veil still covered her hair, though she had long since removed the goblin crown. She sat apart and scarcely raised her eyes from her hands as the menfolk talked and argued and forgot her presence. But when she spoke, they all remembered and turned to her as schoolchildren might turn to a benevolent teacher for advice. For Queen Bebo was older than they, older than the mountain. And she heard the voices of the sun and the moon.

"What's that you say, my dear?" asked her husband the king, raising his great bush of an eyebrow. "You spoke a name, I think, but one with which I am unfamiliar."

"Etalpalli," she repeated in her gossamer voice. "The City of Wings."

Something in the way she spoke sent a burning dart through Eanrin's heart. For a moment, his breath steamed the air before his face. He shook himself and hunched his shoulders, leaning out of hiding to better see her face. The councilmen gave one another uncomfortable looks.

Iubdan, however, leaned back in his seat, his face thoughtful. "Ah yes," he said. "I remember. Once upon a time, we journeyed beyond the Cozamaloti Gate into the City of Wings, did we not?"

"For the coronation of the new queen, yes," said Bebo. "Two thousand years ago, if you count the hours as mortals do."

Iubdan rubbed his mustache. Rarely did the Merry People see their king's face so solemn. "A bright little girl she was," he said, musing with remembrance. "Newly crowned and so pretty on her great throne, with those wings of hers still overlarge for her wee frame."

To Eanrin's horror, the king bent his head and hid his face in his hand. The poet stared, wondering if his own eyes deceived him. Did Iubdan weep?

"Her name is forgotten," said Queen Bebo, her soft white lashes closing over her softer blue eyes. A single look at her face, and Eanrin knew that one person at least remembered the young Queen of Etalpalli's name. But he also knew that Bebo would not speak it. Instead, she swallowed, and the sight of his queen forcing back tears was enough to make the poet want to hurl himself from the gallery and burst into some manic song. Anything to make her laugh! The Merry Folk were not intended for tears, especially not their queen.

There was a catch in Bebo's voice when she raised her eyes and again addressed the assembly. "Her name was forgotten long ages ago. When she gave up her heart and succumbed to the voice of him we call Death-in-Life. When his kiss sealed her, her name was lost. And she became the firstborn of all dragons."

The councilmen drew their robes and nightshirts close; several wiped sweat from their brows.

"She abandoned her people in the passion of her first burning," Bebo continued quietly. "But she did not forget them long. A hundred years ago, she returned to her own demesne and burned it beyond recall. The City of Wings is no more. Its empty ruins rise to an emptier sky."

The men in the hall hung on her words, holding their breath as though afraid she would say more, afraid she would tell them some horrible detail of the story at which she hinted. But the queen was lost in her own thoughts, her face tight and closed as though she listened to something no one else could hear. Iubdan, his face still covered in his hand, did not look up.

At length Glomar crossed his arms and cleared his throat loudly. "What can dragons have to do with any of this? It's the Black Dogs we're after."

Eanrin nearly burst from hiding then and there to rain insults upon the captain. But he was spared by King Iubdan, who put up a silencing hand and turned a near-violent face upon his guard. "My lady knows of what she speaks, badger-man. Do not take so disrespectful a tone in her presence. Of course there's a dragon involved in all this mess! Who but a dragon could spin a spell so powerful as to trick all Rudiobus?"

"And of all Death's offspring, only one has the power to deceive me," said his queen.

"The Flame at Night!"

Which of the councilmen whispered the name remained unknown. But everyone heard it, and all traces of amusement vanished from their ruddy faces. This was not a name to be spoken lightly, and each man desperately hoped Queen Bebo would contradict the assertion, would assure them that no, such a dire suggestion was unwarranted.

She did not. She said only, "Hri Sora, the Flame at Night, firstborn of her kind. She alone, the onetime Queen of Etalpalli, could blind my eyes to her true self."

"But she is dead!" said one of the councilmen. "Did we not all see her fall flaming from the sky? Sir Etanun of the Farthest Shore slew her twice with the sword Halisa. Then she fell from the vaults of Hymlumé's Garden and lost her third life. We saw the fire of her fall ourselves!"

"It seems she did not die after all," said King Iubdan in a voice as dark as his eyes. "The Flame at Night still lives her final life."

"But why the Black Dogs?" someone else asked. "Why would she call them into Rudiobus? If she is indeed the Flame at Night, why did she not transform and fly from here herself?"

"That," said Queen Bebo, "I do not know. Nor do I know why the Black Dogs obey her. But of all Death-in-Life's children, she is the only one with the strength to command them. So it must be she who has taken my dear cousin, not into the Netherworld . . . no! No, she would not venture into the realm of her Dark Father. Not yet. She must have ridden the Dogs into the realm that once belonged to her. Into Etalpalli."

"But why?" Glomar's voice boomed in the hall, and he clenched both fists in his fury. "Why would such a monster steal away Lady Gleamdren? I don't understand!"

Bebo turned her mild eyes upon the captain. Though her voice was gentle, it carried more force than his bluster ever could. "Gleamdren knows the secret of Rudiobus. She knows the whereabouts of the Flowing Gold."

A silence like a trance held the room captive as the truth of this statement soaked in. At last Iubdan said quietly, "Aye, that must be it. Even Hri Sora would not dare attempt to wrest the secret from you or me, my girl. But your cousin is not so strong. How could she hope to withstand the firstborn's fire?"

For the first time since the commencement of the meeting, Captain Glomar turned a baleful glare up to the gallery shadows where Eanrin stood. He shook a fist, crying, "And *you* carried the monster right through our gates!"

"And just what do you imply?" Eanrin appeared at the railing, leaning so far out one would have thought he'd lose his balance. Then, with a cat-like yowl, he leapt right over the rail and landed in a crouch just in front of Glomar. He paused a moment, his knees up and elbows out, catching his breath, for the fall was greater than he'd anticipated, before he rose and grabbed Glomar by the front of his jerkin, pulling him nose to nose. "Dare you imply that it is *my* fault my lady has been placed in such dire peril? Dare you insinuate that *my* actions have led to this terrible state?"

"That I do!" Glomar snarled.

Eanrin narrowed his eyes and set his jaw. Then he smiled and released his hold, leaving Glomar to stagger backward a few steps. The poet gave a dismissive toss of his head and addressed himself to his sovereigns. "He may be right, my good king, my fair queen. But I put it to you and all this wise council that the fault came only from a heart too easily moved to compassion at the sight of one apparently helpless! Can you lay guilt upon intentions so pure if so misled?"

Glomar snorted but Queen Bebo said only, "We were all deceived. We all welcomed her to our bosoms."

"As does us credit!" Eanrin cried, still smiling. "We are a darling lot, aren't we? But darlingness aside, we've got ourselves in an awful fix. Not only does the sweetest maid that ever walked the meadows of Faerie lie even now in the clutches of Evil's own daughter, but also, how long shall the protections we have enjoyed in our own dear realm last? For should the Flame at Night, by her fell arts, wrench from Gleamdren's lips the secret—though she will find the courage of my queen's cousin nigh unto impenetrable, I grant you!—what should stop her from storming

Rudiobus once again? Or even—and I shudder at the thought—holding fair Gleamdren for ransom?"

"Enough babble!" cried Glomar, turning to Queen Bebo. "Talking will get us nowhere, my queen, and Lady Gleamdren is even now in danger! I shall set out at once for Etalpalli to see if what this idiot says is true."

"And I," declared Eanrin, "shall go with you."

"Never! I'd not have you for a companion though my life depended upon it."

"You have no choice in the matter, my blundering badger. I shall go whether you wish it or no, and you may do as you like with your life."

"I know your games, cat. You'll do nothing but put yourself in my way!"

"If that is so, I'd suggest you get out of mine."

"Why, I'll—"

"Stop."

Queen Bebo's face was quiet when poet and guard turned to her. They dared not speak, though both thought her silence lasted too long. She appeared to be listening, but there was nothing to hear in that chamber of rock deep within the mountain. A muscle in her jaw twitched and her eyes first closed, then opened slowly.

"You shall indeed go," she said. "Badger and cat. Soldier and poet. One who loves too much; one who loves not at all." She stopped again, once more listening to voices no one else could hear. Eanrin and Glomar shuffled their feet and looked about, but a glance from Iubdan quieted them again, and they stood like statues.

Suddenly Bebo smiled. It was strange, considering the dire events. But she smiled, her face lighting up with unexpected joy that radiated down upon the two would-be heroes.

"Go to Lady Gleamdren's aid, both of you!" she cried. "Seek out Etalpalli, storm its gates, and demand the prisoner freed. But—" Here she laughed outright and shook her head as though disbelieving what she herself was about to say. "But I tell you this, my little darlings: Only one who truly loves will at last break through the Flame at Night's defenses and bring my cousin safely home. True love! Only true love . . ."

The poet raised his eyebrows; the guard lowered his. "My feelings for

Lady Gleamdren are well known throughout Rudiobus," said Eanrin. "Did I not sing just last night of my undying passion?"

"Undying rot!" snarled Glomar. "The truest love is that least spoken."

Eanrin shrugged. "Time will tell, my friend. And time enough have I!"

But Bebo said no more. She smiled at her husband, who watched her with keen eyes and suspected much, though he could make no final guesses.

In the Wood Between, the girl by the River dreamed.

The sun is hot upon her back as she follows the winding path. Spring has met a swift end, giving way to a brutal summer. But though her body is drenched in sweat, she shivers with a cold that freezes her from the inside out.

Up the path into the mountains flows a long, fluid line. Warriors head the procession, solemn torchbearers armed with stone daggers. Next come three men in robes of deerskin dyed brilliant scarlet, their faces smeared with black streaks like streaming tears. Behind them walk the elders of the united tribes, the Red Feet, the people of Black Rock, the North Walkers, and more. The Eldest follows these, and his is the face of a man who died long ago.

Behind the Eldest march twelve maidens to represent each tribe. They are hooded in black, and their feet are bare and bleeding, marked with intricate cuts. They weep silent tears.

In the midst of these maidens walks one in white. Her black hair is her only hood, hanging over her face, shielding her even from the eye of the sun, who watches her progress. Her feet are bare but uncut. In her hands she carries a wooden bowl filled with blood and struggles to spill not a drop even as they climb the uneven pathway up the mountain. Starflowers adorn her head, a circlet of red blossoms.

Following the maidens march the people of the Land, members of every tribe and village. The girl feels their eyes upon her as they climb higher and higher into reaches where the air is thin—people she does not know who look to her for salvation. When she dares cast a glance behind her, she sees that they all wear the same face. In that one face is sorrow and pity but no mercy, for they have no hope. They are a beaten people. But they are determined to survive.

The girl turns her eyes upward again, up that long, winding path. For the first time since this endless journey began, her eyes fill with tears.

The girl by the River moaned and stirred. And the River fed her enchanted sleep and suffered her to go on dreaming.

5

GLOMAR CALLED on every ounce of honor in his brawny being to wait on the far shore of Gorm-Uisce while Órfhlaith carried the poet over. The last thing he wanted was to make this journey in the company of Bard Eanrin, and only the strongest of all the vows he had made to King Iubdan kept the captain rooted to the spot as the mare trotted across the lake with her scarlet burden.

But honor is honor, however inconvenient. After all, had not Queen Bebo declared that the two must venture out together and fetch her cousin? That was as good as an order, and Glomar always followed orders. He could not, in good conscience, sally forth alone. Especially not with all the people of the court gathered at Fionnghuala Gate, cheering for all they were worth.

So the captain stood on the shore just outside the shadows of the great Wood, hefting his hatchet from one hand to the other and watching how the sunlight gleamed upon the blade. The thoughts he indulged were perhaps unworthy of his captain's rank, but he did wait.

Eanrin slid from the mare's back and stepped onto the shore before him. Both of them, to the common eye, appeared as tall as an ordinary man, though Órfhlaith, standing still on the lake, was as tiny and delicate as a child's toy.

"What-ho, good Glomar!" Eanrin beamed. "Shall we off?"

"I'd like to off you!" Glomar growled, or rather, thought about growling five minutes later. He was not one for witty comebacks on a moment's notice. At the time he bowed to Órfhlaith and ignored the poet, turned, and stamped into the Wood. Eanrin did not follow him. The Chief Poet of Iubdan never *followed* anyone. He happened to go the same direction, and happened as well to be a few paces behind.

Within those few paces, they stepped from the boundaries of Rudiobus into the Halflight Realm. The forest extended for an eternity around them. Lingering in its darker shadows were still some traces of the Midnight of the Black Dogs, but for the most part it had lifted.

Eanrin stood a moment and sniffed. Glomar gave him a sidelong glance and wondered if his eyes deceived him. Did the poet look . . . anxious? But that was ridiculous. Indeed, Glomar would have liked to dismiss his rival as spineless and despicable; however, he knew too much about Eanrin's exploits beyond Rudiobus to believe it.

Granted, most of those exploits had been recounted by Eanrin himself. Nevertheless, Glomar could not recall ever seeing the poet out of his depth. He knew Eanrin had traveled many times through the Wood, more than Glomar had himself. Why, then, did the poet's face look so drawn? Why did he sniff the air with such care? The smell of the Black Dogs was pungent enough, leaving an unmistakable trail. Glomar drew a long breath himself, trying to catch whatever scent it was his rival sought. He smelled nothing but the Dogs . . . and fear.

He shrugged and shouldered his hatchet. "Hurry up, cat," he growled and started off in the direction the Black Dogs had run, bearing their mistress and captive on their backs. The caorann tree standing nearby waved its branches tremblingly at the two Rudiobans. Well, it should be sorry, Glomar thought. Some protection it had been! What was the use of having caorann trees that couldn't see through a glamour, dragon's or otherwise? He stumped past it without a nod and started into the foliage.

He had made scarcely ten paces, however, before Eanrin grabbed his arm. "Just where do you think you're going, my fine, meatheaded friend?"

"Don't be touching me, poet!" Glomar snarled, shaking off Eanrin's hand. "Nor even speaking to me!"

"That will make our little adventure rather tiresome, now, won't it?" The poet grinned.

"This ain't *our* little adventure."

"Oh no?"

"I'm not the fool you take me for, cat. I know your game."

Eanrin rolled his eyes, but the smile remained fixed in place. "Tell me, then, since you know it so well: What is my game?"

"You're a two-faced monster; that's what you are," said Glomar. "Aye, you'll make yourself out to be the hero with all your fine words and fine ways. But you'll stoop to backstabbing if it serves your purpose."

"How enigmatic is our good captain," said the poet mildly. His eyes half closed, and he looked as smug as the cat who got the cream. "Do, pray, continue. Enlighten me to my own treachery."

"You need no enlightenment! You'll wait until the opportune moment, I have no doubt." The captain's lips pulled back so tightly from his teeth that they cracked. He licked them angrily. "You're wanting to prove your mettle to the queen's cousin, and you'll do everything you can to make me look the fool."

"Is that what you fear? That in this venture of rescuing my lady, you might come out the shabbier of the two of us?" Here the poet laughed outright, tossing back his head so that his cap fell off and he was obliged to catch it. But he went on laughing, and Glomar's face went red as a beet.

"Do you deny it?" the captain demanded.

"Certainly not," replied Eanrin. "I have every intention of demonstrating to my lady—"

"She ain't *your* lady!"

"—my superiority in every respect. If you insist upon aiding me, who am I to stop you? Contrast often makes a jewel shine all the brighter. Our little sojourn in Etalpalli, should we survive it, will be the stage upon which I perform my true devotion to the goddess of my heart. And with you as my supporting cast, how can my performance help but shine?"

The guard lunged, but Eanrin expected this and danced out of his reach. "My good Glomar!" he cried, scampering behind a twisted elm tree, keeping the trunk between himself and Glomar's hatchet. "In all seriousness, you haven't a hope of success without me. Did I not just watch you plunge into the Wood without a thought?"

"I'm following the trail of the Black Dogs, which is clear enough."

"A trail and a Path are two different things!" The poet jerked his hand off a branch just in time to keep from losing a finger to the guard's swinging weapon. "It is dangerous to walk the Wood without a Path, as you should know by now. The Wood will twist you up and drag you places you never expected. And Etalpalli is no easy realm to find."

"What makes you think I don't know the way?"

"Do you?"

Here Glomar paused in his assault and gave Eanrin a sly smile. "You don't remember."

For the space of a heartbeat, Eanrin could not breathe. Then he said brightly, "It would seem that I don't. Tell me, what is it I'm not remembering?"

"I've been to Etalpalli." Triumph, albeit premature, flooded the captain's face. "I've been there myself, passed through the Cozamaloti Gate. When Iubdan traveled there for the last queen's coronation, I went with him as his guard. And where were you, poet? Gallivanting off in the Wood somewhere and unable to join your king's entourage?"

Eanrin shrugged. "It matters not. I know where Etalpalli lies. Better than you, it would seem, what with your rushing off on the Black Dogs' trail! There are sure Paths and there are foolish Paths, and to pursue the Black Dogs is invariably foolish. But everyone knows that to find Etalpalli, one has only to follow the River."

"True," said Glomar. "Follow the River, why don't you, Eanrin. But it is I, not you, who knows the key to Cozamaloti's unlocking."

"Oh, is that so?" Eanrin continued grinning, but he had not, in fact, considered this point. He had assumed that the gate's locks were broken when the city itself was burned. He wasn't going to let that on to Glomar, however. "How nice for you!"

"Aye. Nice for me, indeed," Glomar said, playing with his hatchet's balance. "For I know you'll never unlock it! Cozamaloti can only be opened if you enter for the sake of another. If you try to open it for selfish reasons, the gate remains locked. And you, my friend, will die." The guard licked his lips, his eyes for a moment cruel. "A great, watery death."

Eanrin blinked. He turned this information about to observe it from a few angles. "But of course," he said at last, still smiling, still pretending he had the advantage. After all, advantage lay in the perception of power, not the fact. "I shall pass through Cozamaloti for the sake of my beloved."

Glomar growled, but it was more of a laugh than a threat. "You never loved anyone but yourself, cat."

"What good is there in protesting?" Eanrin's voice became silky. "Can one expect a dirt-bound lug-about to understand the higher, more tender feelings of the soul? No indeed, dear captain, with your earthy snuffling about in fair Gleamdren's shadow. I am certain you believe your feelings true and noble, but in reality—"

The captain roared at this and took hold of his hatchet in both fists. "Do you think me a fool?" he bellowed.

"In point of fact, yes."

The captain swung, missing the poet's head by inches. "I'll hew you limb from limb. Honor be dashed!"

The poet eluded the blow on feet as light as thistledown. He'd incensed his rival, and the advantage was his once more. "My dear, blustery captain, you must learn to bear with my upstaging you, or you'll never see my lady—"

"She ain't *your* lady!"

"—again." The poet put out a hand. "Shall we shake and say peace, at least until Gleamdren is returned to my arms?"

Captain Glomar hacked at the hand. The poet darted back with the air of a slandered saint, drawing his cape close about him. "Very well," he said with a sniff. "If that's the way you feel about it, allow me to make another proposition. It's hardly a fair one to you, but—"

"I'll hear none of your propositions!" The hatchet sank into the trunk of the elm tree. A shudder ran from the roots to the topmost branches and back again. The hatchet stuck.

"You'll hear this one," said Eanrin. "I propose we part ways, here and now. And to make things interesting, I propose a race."

The captain, tugging at his hatchet, paused. A tremor passed through the ground, like the rippling of roots beneath the soil, but neither he nor Eanrin noticed. Glomar's face sank into a deep scowl, yet there was interest in his eyes. "A race, you say?"

"Aye. Rather than drag me down with your sour company and lumbering blundering, I suggest that you race me instead. To Etalpalli and back. He who rescues my lady Gleamdren first and carries her triumphant back to the Hall of Red and Green will be declared victorious. And," he added slowly, "the loser must agree to forgo his suit to the winner forevermore."

Here, Glomar smiled so knowingly that Eanrin, for all his confidence, felt a twinge of concern. He masked his discomfort, however, and answered smile for smile, even as Glomar said, "You may not like that so much as you think, poet. This meathead may possess more knowing than you realize."

The poet gulped, but he spoke lightly. "That risk I am willing to take."

With a final heave, the captain pulled his hatchet free. "Well—"

That was when the tree snarled.

There is only burning. Forever and ever, it seems.

But this fire, like all fires, must run out of fuel and dwindle until nothing remains but smoldering embers. When that happens, she begins to remember.

At first there is little enough for her mind to grasp. She sees a girl whom she recognizes but whose name she does not know. A lovely creature with wings of many vivid colors spreading from her shoulders. Upon her head she wears a simple crown, and her hair and her eyes are as vibrant as those wings. Such a fair creature is she!

Why, then, does Etanun not love her?

Hri Sora's eyes flew open.

She stood, she discovered, at the summit of a high tower on a wide, flat roof. The stones beneath her feet were blackened. All embellishments that might once have made this tower beautiful were obliterated, all greenery long since killed.

She knew this place. Turning about, her dry eyes studying every cranny and crevice, Hri Sora recognized Omeztli, the Moon Tower. It was the queen's tower, had been hers ever since her brother died. Before she herself died.

It was not the sight Hri Sora had seen in her dream. No colossal bonfires engulfed the green towers—the flames were gone, leaving behind blackened, flaking stone through which the red rock beneath showed like raw wounds. Many of the towers had crumbled into the streets, carcasses fallen in war. She searched for Itonatiu, the Sun Tower, which should stand opposite Omeztli. The home of her brother, the home of kings.

Where it had once stood was a great, gaping hole.

"Lights Above be eaten!" she cried, but the words caught and strangled in her throat. Fire rushed to her mouth, ready to drag her into madness and oblivion. When she had been a whole dragon, that rush of flame inside had led to her bursting into true dragon form, wings pounding the air, great, sinuous body tearing and destroying as the furnace erupted from her belly.

But now she had only a woman's body, wingless and weak. A body that could not support such a fire. To let it build, to let it take over, meant to give herself up to the blaze, to sink into burning dreams and lose all memory.

No, Hri Sora could not allow herself to succumb to those fires again. Not yet. Slowly, she forced the fire down into her belly. As she did so, more memories returned.

"I did this," she said. Once upon a time, leafy vines had cloaked those stark walls, causing the entire city to look alive, lush, and growing. "I burned it all."

She stood like a statue, watching smoke rise from the pit where Itonatiu had stood so proud and golden.

Then she smiled.

She knew who she was again. The memory of her death and rebirth as a dragon returned to her, and her teeth gleamed with a smile.

"The queen is dead," she said and laughed. "Long live the queen!"

She strode to the edge of the tower and looked out from that dizzying height. For a moment, her fire vanished in a dreadful coldness—something akin to fear. How dreadful it was that she, a dragon, should fear to fall! She who had once flown upon wings of iridescent blackness, rising even to the highest vaults of the heavens!

Hri Sora put a hand to her head. The fire inside was so great sometimes. How often did it drive all thought away? "Cruel, cruel fate!" she growled, and fire gleamed in her mouth. "But . . . but have I . . ."

Oh! How her head pounded with mounting heat and pressure! She would have to flame it out, burn the air until it melted away. But when she flamed, she could not think. And she must think! She must devise some way to regain her wings.

Another memory stirred. "The . . . the Flowing Gold," she whispered.

"I was wondering when you were going to bring that up."

The voice came from somewhere near. Though the throbbing in her temples did not diminish, Hri Sora raised her head slowly. It swung on the end of her long neck like the weight of a pendulum, back, forth, searching for the speaker. The voice was familiar somehow, but she could not place it, nor even see from whence it came.

"Down here."

A little iron cage sat on the stone floor near the center of the flat tower roof. Her heritage, nearly forgotten, flared in her memory for a moment. Cages! Those with wings could not abide them. The impulse to fling it from the tower nearly overcame her. But she strode over to it, the remnants of a green nightgown wafting about her limbs, and knelt to peer inside.

A tiny woman with white-gold hair gazed up at her from furious blue eyes.

The Flame at Night startled back, her lips curled into a dreadful snarl. "What are you doing here?"

The tiny captive folded her arms and shook her head, disbelieving. "Well, I like that! Here you go through the bother of kidnapping me, laying siege to unsiegeable Rudiobus, dragging me off in the middle of the night after I'd given you my own bed for your comfort . . . and you have the gall to ask what I'm *doing* here."

Hri Sora hissed again. When she said no more, the tiny woman kicked the bars of her iron cage, rattling them with such force that the dragon drew back. "You kidnapped me!" the tiny woman cried. "You kidnapped me and shoved me into this cage, forcing me to take this insignificant size! And now you'll attempt to wrest the secret of Rudiobus from my unwilling lips!"

"What . . . what secret?" The fire in her temples was mounting. Thinking was agony, as was remembering. Perhaps she should flame it out and destroy this creature, destroy this foul cage, and sink into forgetfulness.

"What secret?" The tiny woman flung up her hands, then planted them on her hips, shaking her head. "See here, you stole me away from my home because you desire the fabled Flowing Gold. I am one of only three who know its whereabouts, therefore—"

"Why should I desire gold?"

Gleamdren blinked. "How should I know?"

Hri Sora pressed her hands to her forehead. Her breath came in short pants. "I desire . . . many things. But not gold."

Lady Gleamdren tilted her head to one side. "If you don't want the gold, why bother kidnapping me? Pure sport? Well, you'll have plenty of that, I can assure you. I expect no fewer than two dozen brave suitors have set forth from Rudiobus by now. Stalwart heroes bent on my rescue, fired with the passion of their adoration for . . . well, for me." She simpered prettily. "I have quite the assortment of beaux, you see. They'll all be in a state now that I've been torn from the bosom of my homeland. How do you like the notion of two dozen or more heroes bringing war to your demesne?"

For a long time, the Flame at Night stood silent, warring against her own inner furnace. When at last she spoke, her voice was so hot that the air about her mouth shimmered.

"In my day," she said, "I have swallowed more than a hundred heroes in a single breath. Armies of every nation, every world, have set upon me with arrows, with engines, with weapons beyond your imagination. These I have devoured."

She stood, her arms wrapped about her belly, where the depths of her flame flared into greater, more awful life. Her voice rose even as she forgot to whom she spoke. "The warriors of Etalpalli, winged and helmed, spears in hand, flocked to me in angry legions, ready to tear me apart, to mount my head upon my own city gates! I, who ruled them. I, who ate them. Ate them and burned their city, for they were mine to devour, and it was mine to burn!"

Her eyes squeezed tight, and when they again flared open, sparks flew. Flames ringed her eyelids. Lady Gleamdren screamed at the sight and covered her face, though the iron cage kept away the shower of fire that fell about her.

"You see, little creature with your laughing face," Hri Sora said, "I do not care for whatever sport you may bring upon my realm. Even without my wings, I am the most glorious of my Father's children! But what—"

She broke off, bending double with the pain in her gut. For a moment she was lost, perhaps never to return from this agony. She struggled against it. In a barely audible whisper she gasped, "What shall I do? I must have my wings!"

Then she was gone. The flames swallowed her once more. With a roar that tore the sky and brought rocks tumbling from the higher towers of her realm, she spewed fire from her belly. All memory was gone, all plots and plans. Lady Gleamdren, who lay prostrate on the floor of her cage, watched between her fingers as the dragon spat and writhed in the agonies of her burning.

"Lord Lumé love us!" Gleamdren whispered, though she could not hear her own voice above the dragon's din. "She's quite mad."

When at last the Flame at Night fell spent upon the tower roof, her body smoking and ash spewing from her tongue, Gleamdren heard these words gasped from a tortured throat:

"Amarok. My love."

Then she was still. She did not sleep, for dragons never know rest. But she lay quiet for a time, and Gleamdren sat in silence in the middle of the cage, keeping well away from the iron bars. She realized, with a sinking heart, that she was likely to be here for a long, long time.

She wondered if she'd got ash on her face.

6

THE SNARL OF A TREE is unlike anything else in the worlds. It is deeper than a lion's roar, more piercing than an elephant's bugle. It slices through the senses, striking fear into every beating heart.

This tree snarled and three roots burst from the soil like enormous witch's hands, gnarled fingers grasping. One root went for Eanrin, another for Glomar, and the third for the hatchet in Glomar's hand.

None found what they sought, however, for a tree, no matter how angry, is never agile. The moment its snarl interrupted their argument, both poet and captain vanished. Anyone observing would have seen instead a bright orange tomcat with a plume of a tail streaking one direction and a lumbering badger, all silver and black, bowling his way through the undergrowth opposite. The roots, which were snatching at man-shaped objects, found only empty air. But the tree continued roaring, its roots blindly reaching after them, and the two animals continued running until far beyond that hateful sound.

At last the cat made himself halt. He stood a moment, his hair on end, his eyes saucer-round, then turned and began to groom his tail. This done, he sat with his front paws together and his ears pricked, pretending to any who might be watching (one never knew in the Wood) that his heart wasn't racing double-time. When at last he could make himself breathe normally, he raised a white paw and gave it a lick.

"Well, that does it for Glomar, then," he said to himself. "Gave him a good shock, didn't it? And he's run off in the wrong direction! Probably still trying to follow the Black Dogs' scent, poor fool. He'll get twisted up in moments, and I've got the advantage on him for miles. So much for rivalry."

Somehow, this wasn't as comforting as it might have been. The cat slicked back his whiskers thoughtfully. To all appearances, he might have been dozing at a hearthside on a summer's noon, not just escaped being pulverized by a tree given to righteous anger. Usually, if the cat pretended enough indifference to circumstances and people around him, he began to believe it, which made life simpler.

But he could not convince himself that he liked being in the Wood alone.

Until today, he had never been uneasy exploring the byways of the Between. Many an adventure he had met in his time, and on more than one occasion he had come close to losing more than a tuft of fur. Spooks and monsters aplenty could be found in the Wood, and the cat was happy to root them out. Danger added flavor to a life otherwise far too long, and he was never afraid. At least never before.

But then, never before had he seen the Hound.

The cat shivered, wishing he had not allowed that thought to slip through. The vision he'd glimpsed the night before pressed upon his memory. The slender but powerful body; the great head held high as though crowned.

With a meowl, he shook himself hard and dropped the semblance of a cat, assuming his man's shape once more. It was not a drastic shift. It was as though the cat turned his head and, in turning, revealed a new but natural view of himself. Man to cat, cat to man: It was all the same for him.

He drew a long breath and slowly let it out. "Don't think about it,

Eanrin," he told himself. "It was a trick of the light, that's all. You heard the Black Dogs, and the dragon's spell was working on your mind. You invented the rest of it. Curse that lively imagination of yours!"

The sound of his own voice calmed him. He even managed to laugh. The notion of *that* one taking an interest in the Chief Bard of Iubdan? Incredible! Unbelievable, so why bother believing it?

"You have worries enough," he told himself, getting to his feet and brushing leaves and dirt from his cloak. "No time to consider this foolishness. You have a demesne to infiltrate!" This thought was enough to drive all other concerns from his mind, at least momentarily.

Cozamaloti. His lips thinned as he considered the name and what he knew of that gate. Faerie gates can take many forms and substances, depending on the need of the demesne. He could not guess what this one might look like, and it troubled him that Glomar knew. All Eanrin knew for certain was that it was the only way into Etalpalli.

Cozamaloti had been locked, Eanrin recalled, by the last King of Etalpalli. Presumably the last queen had left those locks in place even after she abandoned her realm and became the Flame at Night. Locks or no, Cozamaloti had been unable to withstand her return. Though turned dragon, she had retained her rule, and her demesne would not dare to prevent her reentrance.

Anyone else trying to pass, however, would find their way much more difficult.

"Only true love," Queen Bebo had said, would save Lady Gleamdren. Eanrin believed there was nothing to worry about. Never was a love so true as his! Gleamdren was meant to be his wife, so naturally he was in love with her. He needn't worry about Glomar's silly threats and omens. Need he?

"Don't think on it!" Eanrin commanded himself. "Watery death, indeed. What does an old badger know about such things? He's been listening to rumors, or he's confusing it with some other story he's heard. No matter. He's long gone off in the wrong direction, trailing those fool Dogs. Everyone knows that the only way to Etalpalli is by the River, so it's off to the River I go!"

With a determination found only in a cat that has absolutely set its mind on something, Eanrin proceeded through the forest, following his nose toward water. After a quick search for a safe Path, he found one fit for the folk of Rudiobus, a Path probably built by one of the Merry People long ages ago, or at least by someone friendly with King Iubdan. This Path, he sensed, would lead him safely enough.

The trees melted away as he walked, and he covered leagues in a stride. Such is the magic (as some might call it) of Faerie Paths. A journey that would have taken a mortal man hours, if not days, constituted little time at all for the bard. Only when the music of running water caught his attention did he step from the Path back into the shadows of the forest. The trees became solid once more, not the vaporous phantoms they had been.

The River ran just ahead. Though the Wood itself was gloomy, the River was bright and cheerful. Not friendly, necessarily. Its cheer was of the mischievous kind. Eanrin was not taken in by the smiles its watery surface wore.

He nodded as he approached its bank, and the River laughed back. It was in a jolly mood, Eanrin could tell, though somewhat distracted. All the better. If it was distracted, it would have little time to pester him. He need only follow its course, and so long as he did not allow himself to be drawn aside, he knew he would come at last to Etalpalli.

He took a step. Then he froze.

Not twenty paces down the River stood the Hound.

He was the size of a pony, perhaps a horse. His coat was like white silk but with hints of gold where the reflection of the River gleamed upon it in shivering patterns. His head, viewed in profile, was long and narrow with an arched muzzle. The shoulders were powerful, the feet huge with claws that could tear into the hardest turf in pursuit. He was a creature made for coursing, for running down his prey and rendering it immobile.

He directed his gaze across the water, on into the far Wood, or perhaps looking into a world the poet could not see. He did not look at Eanrin, not yet. The poet's knees began to tremble. Any moment, the creature could turn and see him.

Eanrin could not wait for that moment.

He spun about so fast, he almost unbalanced into the River. Then he was a cat, running as swiftly as his four legs could carry him, streaking along the riverbank, leaping damp, moss-covered rocks, stumps, and debris washed from unimaginable places. There was no time to be afraid. When he was safe, he would have the luxury of fear, but now there was only running, running, running as fast as he could.

Was he pursued? He dared not look back. But he must! Were those graceful limbs, in deliberate, unhurried chase, set upon his tail? That majestic head bent to the scent, eyes fixed upon his quarry? He must know! He dared not look. But he must know!

The cat leapt for a tree near the water's edge. He expected to feel teeth tearing into his back even as he scrambled for higher cover. He reached the lowest branches safely, however, and there turned and, from this vantage, looked back the way he had fled.

The Wood was empty behind him. Only the River flowed past, chuckling to itself as it went.

Was that a flash of gold among yonder trees?

The cat did not wait for a second look. A hiding place in a tree's boughs would not stop that Hound, not for a moment.

He dropped to the ground and continued his flight, speeding over the terrain until his paws bled. *Stick to the River!* he told himself. Otherwise, in his madness, he might set foot on a Path he did not wish to take. No point in running himself into a trap just to flee that Hound. But he must get away! *Stick to the River and don't look back!*

If the Hound caught him, he would lose everything. If the Hound caught him, he would swallow him whole. Not just his physical body . . . no, no. Much worse than that.

When the Hound caught his quarry, he swallowed it down to the essence of the soul. There would be nothing left of Eanrin, nothing at all.

The River rocks could tear the cat's feet to ribbons, and still he would not slow. He would run the rest of his long, long life, run until eternity ran out.

Or so he thought.

He took a turn in the River, scrambling to round the bend, and encountered a body lying on the bank. He should have kept going. Years later, he would often wonder what would have happened if he had followed his natural instincts, leapt over that fallen form, and sped upon his way unheeding.

Instead, he came to a scrambling halt, just before his weary paws trod upon the person's arm. And he swore violently.

"Dragon's spittle and flame! What kind of fool do you take me for?"

Lying on the River's edge, collapsed with her arms and the ends of her hair trailing in the water, was a young mortal girl.

Someone was kissing her face.

The knowledge came to Hri Sora before she was truly conscious. She felt the kisses on her cheek, on her forehead, and they were tender. Her body shuddered in revulsion before her mind was even awake, a natural reaction against affection.

Who was kissing her?

The question was the first coherent thought that returned to her fire-blackened mind. She could not remember her own name or where she was, but that question forced itself upon her angrily, demanding an answer. Was it—

She sat up with a snarl. *"Amarok!"*

He was not there.

Her eyelids were heavy, but she forced them open. She wasn't inside the dark hut on the hill. Rather, she lay upon an empty street. The stones were hot beneath her, pleasantly so. Her dragon spirit relished the heat and the pain, though her woman's body suffered from it.

Shaking herself and wiping the memory of the kisses off her cheeks, she cast about to get her bearings. Ah yes! Her city. Her demesne. It was dead now, just as she was, but like her, it was reborn in this monstrous form. Burned beyond all recognition, it reflected its mistress to perfection.

Hri Sora smiled. How she had loved her city, once upon a time. How she hated it now! But it was hers more than ever. Hate was a fearful binding.

She got to her feet. It took time to recognize where she stood, on Ehikatl Road. This road had led straight through the city once, from the Omeztli Tower to Itonatiu. But it wasn't a road intended for walking. Hri

Sora swore as she took her first step. The Sky People had never walked these ways; even the fledglings had flown.

Yet here she was now, picking her way along like a guest of the city, or an enemy. But she was no enemy. The city belonged to her! The inhabitants, they had been the enemy when they dared to fly when she could not.

She must get her wings back.

A shadow caught her eye. She turned and caught a glimpse of a small form darting into hiding behind one of the towers. The riddle was answered; she now knew the source of the kisses.

"Away with you!" she cried, flinging up her arms, tearing at the air with her talon fingers. "Out of my sight, monsters!"

She received no answer, and this was good. The creatures had fled, then. They were useful beasts, but they looked too much like their father.

She continued up the road, uncertain why. Trapped in a woman's body, exhausted from a fire that was too powerful for this form, she struggled once more to regain her memory. She could not yet recall Gleamdren or the Flowing Gold, so she wandered without aim, feeling the death of her city beneath her bare feet. What a malevolent force Etalpalli had become! She felt the hunger in its stones. Helping her destroy its inhabitants had whetted its taste for death. But no living creatures remained aside from Hri Sora. And of course her children. They, however, could not be eaten, for they were of her own flesh, heirs to Etalpalli.

She'd have to provide more food for her city in time.

The road turned unexpectedly. Why? In olden times, it had run straight from Moon Tower to Sun Tower. Hissing, Hri Sora took hold of the city with her mind, trying to wrench it back. But then she saw where the turn had brought her.

The tombs.

Hri Sora cried out at the sight. The tombs of the Kings and Queens of Etalpalli! Tall and grand and horrible were they, especially now with all their green growth stripped away. The dragon woman turned wildly, her gaze flying about her to see the names inscribed above the door of each tomb. Faerie kings and queens were not meant to die! Yet here the beautiful immortals lay, their remains secreted away in darkness. Here lay her mother, her father. And . . . oh!

Hri Sora fell to her knees, hands pressed to her cheeks. Before her, looming to the tortured red sky, was the tomb of Ttlanextu. Her brother.

She could not cry. She had been a dragon far too long, dying twice in fire. The tears she might have shed were long since burned away. So she sat, hollow and empty, before that awful edifice. Once, long ago, a little Faerie queen, her head bowed with the weight of her new crown, had carved that name above the solemn doorway. That Queen of Etalpalli had cried; this one did not.

Shaking her head, Hri Sora forced herself to stand and turn away. A new and more terrible sight met her eyes.

Across from the tomb of Ttlanextu was that of his sister.

"They built me a tomb," Hri Sora whispered. "They built me a tomb when I left them and took the fire of my Father. They thought I was dead!"

Wonderingly, she stepped closer, gazing up at the great tower without windows that was, she knew, empty inside. As empty as she herself was without her fire. But the fire was mounting once more. She felt her furnace rising, painful and inevitable.

Then her eyes flew wide, and her furious roar shattered the silence of that dead city.

"They carved her name!" she screamed. "They carved her name above the door! Her name, which must be forgotten!"

The fire overcame her then. It burst from her mouth, her nose, her eyes, overwhelming everything. Her children, who had lurked nearby, fled. The towers of Etalpalli trembled.

And high at the top of Omeztli Tower, Lady Gleamdren looked up from her twiddling thumbs and gazed out across the city. She saw the explosion in the street, the flames shooting to the heavens.

With a heavy sigh, Gleamdren rolled her eyes. "That dragon-witch will never keep her mind straight long enough to begin questioning me," she muttered, twiddling her thumbs some more. "Lumé love me, what a bore this imprisonment business is! I thought for sure she'd try some torture. And I wouldn't give in, because I am the heroine of this tale, and it wouldn't do for me to breathe a word of what I know."

Another heavy sigh puffed between her lips. "No torture. Not a single question about the Flowing Gold! There's something wrong with that

Flame at Night. I do hope the lads are on their way. I'll *die* of boredom if they don't get here soon!"

To entertain herself, she began singing—a song written by Eanrin, of course, as were most of the songs sung in Rudiobus. She liked it because her name was in it many times over. All the best songs, she believed, were about her.

> *It gleams and glows like river shine*
> *And swiftly golden flows.*
> *In lustrous locks or silky vine,*
> *Which none but Gleamdren knows.*
> *With silver comb and silken twine,*
> *Fair Gleamdrené does bind*
> *The Flowing Gold, so soft and fine,*
> *The Dark Man's favorite find.*
> *The Flowing Gold of Rudiobus,*
> *The Flowing Gold of Rudiobus.*

Anyone who might have caught sight of that iron cage on the tower roof would have heard the chirping of a bright yellow canary as she sang her little heart out. But not even the sun dared peer into that dreadful demesne, so Gleamdren sang for herself alone.

7

E ANRIN PEERED around the trunk of a sheltering tree, down to the River's edge, where the mortal lay. After his first shock, he had leapt into the deeper forest, intending to continue his flight in a new direction. But curiosity had a way of getting the better of him, and he could not keep himself from looking back.

The River's voice was clearer here. *Pretty maid, be mine!* it said. And because it was a river and, therefore, rather repetitive, it said it again and again. *Pretty maid, be mine, mine, mine!*

The girl, lying helpless before that lecherous entity, did not stir. Her attitude suggested that she had fainted while bending over for a drink. Her face was pillowed on one extended arm while the other trailed almost completely in the water. Of all things—here Eanrin the dandy did not try to suppress a derisive snort—she was clad in what looked like animal skins. It was enough to make the poet's tail bristle.

She was mortal, Eanrin knew even before he worked up the courage to draw near and smell the death on her body. After all, only mortal women were foolish enough to listen to the River's seductions and drink its water. And always princesses. Mortal princesses, wandering into places they had no business going, listening to voices that any simpleton among the Faerie folk would know to ignore.

"Serves her right," said Eanrin. "And I won't be dragged into her business."

The River continued whispering, either unaware of or bound to ignore Eanrin's presence. Otherwise, no one else spoke. No one argued with the poet or urged him into action. He looked around, expecting to catch a glint of gold or to hear the scrape of large paws upon stone. But there was nothing. As far as he could conclude, he was alone with the River and the maid, the Hound vanished into the oblivion of an overactive imagination.

Defensive nonetheless, Eanrin folded his arms. "I won't!"

The River pulled its fingers through the long hair. *Pretty maid. Pretty maid . . .*

The River held something else in its eager grasp, Eanrin realized with a frown, something tangled with the girl's locks. At first he thought it must be riverweeds. On second glance, however, he realized that they were ropes, roughly woven cords tied about the mortal's wrists. Traces of blood washed down the current, lapped up by the eager River.

Eanrin licked his lips. "It's not my business," he said. How had he allowed himself to be turned aside? Everyone knew the danger of letting an outside source determine one's Path in the Between. Yet here he was, far from his goal, almost afraid to move for fear of bringing the Hound down upon him again.

The girl's sides heaved with labored breathing. At least he knew she was no dragon like the woman he'd found in the Wood only the night before. That one had not breathed, not with her fire sunk so low beneath her glamour. This maid struggled for every breath.

Cursing himself for a fool, Eanrin took a few steps nearer, crouched, and leaned out to catch a better look at the girl without touching her. As he balanced himself, his hands sank into the wet mud on the River's edge, and he shuddered. He hated dampness!

The girl's hair veiled her face so that he could not discern her features.

He sniffed. *Faugh!* How she reeked of mortality! This could be no glamour, no disguise. The scent of a swiftly dying body—perhaps still living, but for so brief a span of years!—filled Eanrin's nostrils and left him gagging. He pulled away, his lips curled back in a hiss, more cat than man for the moment.

"I've had enough of damsels in distress to last me a lifetime," he said, standing and drawing his red cloak about him. "What kind of fool do you take me for? Ha!" He backed several paces up the bank. "I'll not become involved in a stranger's affairs again. She should have stayed in her own world, where she belongs. And, light of Lumé, what was she thinking, drinking from a Faerie river? Everyone knows what happens when mortals drink from our waters. Serve her right if she sleeps a thousand years and wakes up with a beard a mile long. If mortal maids grow beards. I forget. Either way, it's not my business!"

Eanrin turned to pursue his Path down the River's winding way toward Etalpalli. But he made a fatal mistake: He cast a last glance at the girl's bound hands.

"Poor little thing."

Wait! Was that *his* voice speaking? He shook his head violently and forced himself to stride three steps downriver, his sandals squelching in the mud. "You fool! Don't think that way! Remember what happened last night? You should have thrown the creature back to the Dogs. It was the Hound's doing. He frightened you, bullied you. But you're not blind! You saw the results of your charity, and they are not results you need repeated. Get on your way and rescue your lady!"

Despite this verbal barrage, he had already stopped in his tracks again. Against all sound judgment, he looked back at the girl, at her frail form, her dark skin and hair, her torn and bleeding feet. And especially those harsh ropes, dragging in the water.

"Glomar will find his way to Etalpalli before you at this rate," Eanrin muttered. "Sure, he's a blunderer, but even a blunderer can be quick when necessity pushes. You'd be foolish indeed to underestimate your opponent."

And yet he turned on heel and lost those three steps he'd gained. The River growled at him, *She's mine!*

Eanrin ignored it. He didn't much care for rivers anyway; they were so often wet. He gazed instead upon the girl.

"You're an odd princess, dressed so," he mused. "What a primitive nation you must hail from. I wonder what realm of mortal history you have fled?" He frowned, considering the problem she posed and disliking the answers he saw. "It'll take a kiss to set you right."

The River snarled, threatening murder. Eanrin, unbothered, knelt beside the maid's still body. For some reason, he found her smell less repugnant now. Perhaps this sort of thing happened when one took a turn for the heroic. He must be a hero indeed to turn aside when he knew the risks.

Eanrin whispered, "Surely a quick kiss couldn't harm anything?"

He didn't believe himself.

The girl did not stir when he lifted her into his arms; her sleep was profound indeed. The similarity of the situation to the scene just outside Rudiobus the night before gave him a shudder. The girl's head lolled over his arm exactly as the dragon's had. He was obliged to part the hair to uncover her face, just as he'd done with the Flame at Night. And just as then, her face was uncommonly beautiful for a mortal girl's.

However, this girl's beauty was different. For one thing, her skin was a rich dark brown, and her hair glossy black. For another, she was imperfect. Her teeth, visible between gently parted lips, were a little crooked. Mud stained her skin, making it darker still, and her brow, even in sleep, was puckered with anxiety or fear. Her dreams must be wicked indeed.

Eanrin grimaced at the sight and almost put her down again. After all, a princess with dreams like those probably had a tale of woe to match. She would certainly wake with expectations of a handsome hero to aid her. As far as Eanrin was concerned, a dash of heroism was one thing, but commitment to a cause? Never. Rushing off to the rescue of Lady Gleamdren was different, for he had determined that she must be his wife and the sole inspiration of his life's work. Besides, he loved her.

This creature meant nothing to him.

But blood oozed from the abrasions on her wrists. And her body, mortal and vulnerable, lay in his arms. Eanrin rolled his eyes heavenward though to seek some holy aid. Then he braced himself and wiped of the mud off her lips with the edge of his cloak. She frowned in her sleep and stirred but did not wake.

"Nothing for it," he muttered. Closing his eyes and trying not to smell her any more than he must, he leaned in and kissed her.

"Do not forget!" cries a voice as old as the hills, as young as the wind. "Do not forget the horror loosed upon your grandsires when they failed to heed my warning! They called your servant a liar and refused to satisfy the Beast's demands. Who among you remembers the screams? Who among you remembers the slaughter? I remember!"

The world is dark, heavy with decay even as the sun beats down in incredible heat. Sweat beads the brows of every man, woman, and child in the crowd listening to the man who speaks. He is the tallest of them, clad in gray wolfskins. His beautiful face is made hideous by the rage in his voice.

"I remember mothers wailing, children lying in pools of blood, warriors choking on their own gore. I remember your elder slain, mauled beyond recognition! You remember, do you not, Panther Master?"

The tall one turns and locks his gaze with that of a mortal man who stands apart from the crowd. This man is stern and strong, yet he trembles under the vicious gaze of the speaker.

"You were there," the tall one says. "You were a small child, and you saw the death of your grandfather. You remember."

The stern man cringes away, a young wolf submitting in terror to the alpha.

"Give the Beast what he asks!"

Eanrin drew back with a gasp, his mouth open. Slowly, his ability to breathe returned. He narrowed his eyes at the young woman in his arms. It took all his willpower not to drop her and run.

The images ringing in his mind were clearer than the reality surrounding him. The voice of that tall stranger was stronger and more vivid than that of the River. In that instant when the scene flashed with painful clarity across Eanrin's mind, it was as though he'd lived it himself.

The River laughed, a lascivious sound. It put up a watery hand and snatched at the girl's face. Eanrin glared ferociously and pulled her back, clutching her to his chest. If there was one thing he hated, it was being laughed at. His face tightened, and his ears would have flattened to his skull had he been a cat.

Then suddenly he laughed back. Perhaps it was forced, perhaps not even the River was fooled. Still he laughed, smoothing back his hair with his free hand.

"What a joke!" he cried. "Took me by surprise, that did. Never kissed a mortal girl before. An unpleasant experience, to be sure!"

He gave the River a final sneer, then looked down at the girl, still fast in her enchanted sleep. Her brow was more deeply drawn into a line, but otherwise she did not stir.

"Well, I like that," Eanrin said, raising an eyebrow. "So it must be one of *those* kisses, eh? A prince, or nothing. Well, am I not the prince of poetry? Come, come, don't be fussy. It's not as though many princes walk these woods. You'd better let me wake you, or you'll remain here a good hundred years at least, unless the River gets you first. Let us try again!"

He inclined his head and gave her another kiss. This one was longer, deeper.

With rhythmic beats, the girl drives a stake into the ground. She is young and lovely, with large dark eyes. But her face is set, her mouth a grim line.

A child tugs at her garments. When she looks down, she sees the little one make silent gestures with small hands. But she shakes her head and continues to pound the stake. When it is securely placed, she turns and claps her hands.

A young dog, shaggy and gray, rises from its resting place in the shade and comes to the girl. Its tail is low and still, its eyes full of dumb worry. It whines as the girl ties a cord around its neck. Then she secures the end of the cord to the stake, pets the dog once, motions for it to sit, and walks away. The dog's whimpers rise with every step the girl takes. The child begins to cry silent, pulsing tears. She runs after the girl and grabs her hand, pulling.

The girl kneels and takes the little one in her arms, holding her close. Her own tears run into the child's black hair. Then she stands and gestures firmly. The little one, still crying, obeys. She goes to sit beside the dog, which puts its head in her lap.

The girl watches them, her eyes full of things she does not speak. Then she turns from them and marches up the hill, disappearing over the crest. The morning is cold and gray as it settles about the abandoned child and dog.

The image faded. The poet withdrew, more slowly this time. He did not bother to hear the River, which was by now roaring with merriment at his failure to wake the mortal. Eanrin's face, for once, was thoughtful. He tilted his head to one side and licked his lips as though to taste and understand better those things that had flashed so vividly through his mind.

"Well, little princess," he said at length, "you've had an odd life so far, haven't you?" Gently, he brushed more hair back from her forehead. The line on her brow relaxed a little, and she turned her face toward his palm, like a kitten nosing after a caress. She did not moan, but a sigh escaped her lips.

Was the sympathy he felt due to some enchantment? Eanrin shook himself and leaned in to sniff with greater care. He smelled no sorcery, but he'd smelled no sorcery the night before either, and where had that gotten him? He wished he had a caorann tree on hand with which to test the girl. Not that the caorann had proved any help against the Flame at Night!

But the Flame at Night had worn no such bindings on her wrists.

The poet growled, "My dear girl, you have no idea the Time you are wasting. And if you waste an immortal's Time, that is waste indeed! But you won't meet a prince here. The Faerie princes will not look at you, and all the mortal princes who are foolish enough to lose themselves in the Wood are almost invariably picked up by Lord Bright as Fire or the serpent, ChuMana." He grimaced. "It's not my business. And I am *certainly* not paying a visit to Bright as Fire's demesne!"

He made as though to lay the girl back down upon the bank but instead looked once more at her face. She was so young. Like a child in this place, unable to cope with the greatness of many worlds. And he knew the River. It would swallow her up if given half the chance. Or age her far before her time so that she would wake at last wrinkled and white-haired, her beauty and youth spent. It wasn't as though mortal life afforded her much time to enjoy beauty and youth as it was!

"Dragon's teeth and ears and snout," the poet swore. "I should *know* better than this."

With a groan, he got to his feet, lifting the girl in his arms. She was not tall, and her mortality made her light. He slung her over his shoulder, and her long hair trailed down his back.

"I'll not visit the Tiger," said the poet as he set off through the forest. "But ChuMana . . . well, the serpent owes me a favor. Never thought I'd collect that debt for the benefit of a mortal creature!"

He left the River behind, its waters churning with frustration and fury. He did not see the Hound watching from the deepest shadows across the water.

8

I N THE SWAMP OF CHUMANA countless columns rose from the
murky waters. Straight and elegant, built of white marble, they were
taller than most trees. One might imagine they had grown up from the
ground itself, sprouted from randomly scattered seeds, for there was no
rhyme or reason to their placement. They supported nothing. No roof,
no arches, no platforms high above. The sky was heavy with iron-gray
clouds, always threatening rain, though rarely offering it. Perhaps the
columns supported the sky. They certainly reached high enough, save
for those few that had crumbled and lay half submerged in swamp water.
The weight of the sky must have been too much for these.

All about the marble block bases of each column—carved with elegant
depictions of young women in scanty clothing and young men in laurel
wreaths—brown water slurped and scrag-grass grew in unsightly clumps.

And the very air vibrated to the voices of a thousand and more frogs.

ChuMana draped herself along one of the fallen columns. She might
have been sunning but for the lack of sun. Her face was neither relaxed

nor severe, neither satisfied nor discontent. It was a complete blank. She listened without interest to the songs of the frogs, all mournful and hectic with a smattering of sullen *"Graaaups!"* thrown in for emphasis.

ChuMana was mistress of this demesne, and she understood every word of the songs being croaked around her. Frogs have limited interests (there were a few toads scattered about too, whose interests were more limited still). They tended to harp on the same theme:

"Kiss me. *Graaaup!* Kiss me. *Graaaup!*"

It was a bit monotonous. Yet ChuMana's mental state remained tranquil. As life was, so it should remain. Consistency was the chief end of all aims—a steady, forever sameness.

Thunder rumbled overhead, threatening yet unlikely to follow through with its threat. ChuMana did not smile, nor did she frown. She merely slid a little farther along her column, stretching herself out to a glorious extent. The nearest frogs shuddered and ceased singing when this movement caught their blinking, bulbous eyes. But they quickly forgot what they'd seen and resumed their song: "Kiss me. *Graaup!*"

No one, ChuMana thought, had a collection to rival hers.

The thought had scarcely passed the innermost recesses of her mind— so deep inside that it was more a warm vagueness than actual thought— when the shudder came.

It was a shudder like an earthquake through the air. Someone pushed at the threads of enchantment that every Faerie queen spins on the borders of her demesne. Whoever pushed, pushed hard. ChuMana slowly raised her head and focused her lidless eyes on the direction from which this assault came. Her movements were as gentle as marsh weeds waving underwater.

Another push. Another shudder.

Then she heard it, on the edge of her lands. Someone called in a voice that burst like sunlight into the gloom. "Oi! ChuMana, m'dear! Are you about, then?"

"Viper's bite!"

Her equilibrium shattered. The sameness broke into shivering pieces. Muscles beneath ChuMana's skin quivered as, in a single, fluid movement, she slipped from her column and submerged herself in the swamp murk. She swam with uncommon grace, gliding her great bulk between scrag-grass, hillock, and column bases while innumerable frogs fled before her, still singing after kisses. She followed the shuddering that shook her enchantments with every inward step the intruder took.

She knew who it was.

She herself had given him entrance to her world long ago. Memories flooded back, unwanted visions that had no place in this heavy, languorous place of dampness and forlorn song.

How his singing had charmed her! She should have let him taste her poison, but instead, she had fallen for his song, the little devil! And when he left her demesne, oh, how she had sighed for his return! Monster. Bewitcher. What a fool she had been to leave the safety of her swamp and pursue him into the wild Wood.

The water was black before her eyes, but she followed her nose and that sixth sense of magic that led her unquestioningly forward. The Mistress of the Swamp hissed out curses as she swam. Then she smelled that familiar scent. A scent associated with bindings, with slavery.

The poet. Her savior.

Eanrin stood up to his knees in mud, cursing the heavy sky above him. Whenever he tried to step on what appeared to be a patch of solid ground, it turned out to be no more than an illusion, and he sank once more, oozing mud slurping at his sandals and soaking the edge of his cloak, all this while burdened with the weight of the mortal girl slung over his shoulder. Her long hair trailed down his back, the endmost tendrils collecting swamp refuse behind him.

"Sweet ChuMana!" Eanrin called, unaware of the serpent's proximity. "Do be nice and come greet your old friend!" He swore again, lifting one foot and shaking it, then obliged to put it back in the water before he could lift and shake the other. What a muck he was becoming!

"ChuMana, Lumé smite you, do come out. I have no wish to venture any farther into your demesne; no more than you wish to have me! But you owe me, and you know it. Don't think you can thwart the laws of Faerie. I've come to demand my dues, and I won't leave until I've seen—*mrrrreeeowl*!"

ChuMana rose from the reeds like the sinuous growth of a black, limbless tree, startling the poet so that he almost dropped his burden.

Her head emerged first, her eyes bright and unblinking. Mud fell from her scales, blobbing into the pool about her, and still her great neck stretched higher and higher. Her scarlet underbelly flashed redder even than the poet's grimy cloak.

At last she reached her full size, towering over Eanrin. Her tongue flickered once. Then a tall, slender woman in a black robe stood before the poet. The front panel of her robe was embroidered in rich red threads, and her eyes were like two rubies. She was strange and horrible to look upon, for she was so tall and thin. But strangest of all, she had no arms.

"Poet of Rudiobus," she hissed. She slowly lowered her chin to her chest, her long neck bending gracefully. Her gaze never shifted from Eanrin's face. "Many years have I wondered when you would return to claim your rights."

"Yes, well." Eanrin gave a shrug and the sweetest of smiles. He dared not bow for fear of dropping the girl. "I hadn't intended to make it so soon. But I was thinking to myself today, 'See here, it's been some time now since you laid eyes on that sweet ChuMana, hasn't it?' And then I asked myself, 'Why not stop in for a chat and inquire after—'"

"Still that wandering tongue of yours, charmer!" ChuMana's long body swayed gently, as though moved by some soft breeze. "I fell for your pretty words once, and once is enough!"

Eanrin met her red gaze with his own steady stare. "Charmer, eh? You misrepresent me to all those present." He swept the hand that did not hold the mortal girl to indicate the hundreds of frogs peeping out from the weeds and rushes. "Why should you say such harsh things, m'dear? Can you possibly have forgotten that little run-in with the Roc?"

The memory crashed back upon the serpent's conscious mind, images she had long tried to forget: a form like a mountain hovering in the air; wings like thunderclouds; talons like lightning.

"You tricked me!" Her whole body swayed now, rocked by some internal force. A grotesque vision, for without arms for balance, she should have toppled into the pool. Yet her lithe body undulated with perfect, unnatural grace. "You sang your pretty songs and entranced me!"

"I'm a bard. We bards were born to sing. As I recall, you asked me my business, and I told you."

"You led me from the safety of my realm!"

"You followed without my invitation."

"You lured me into the Karayan Plains, where the great Roc hunts and where there is no cover for one such as I!" A shudder ran up her body, and she flickered between snake and woman form. When the shudder passed, she stood as a woman again, though her flickering tongue was forked. "You knew what would be my fate."

"Oh, I wouldn't say that," said the poet with a disinterested shrug. "The Rocs are odd ones, and you never know what they might want to bring home to their nestlings. And it was your own fool fault, you must admit, for crossing into Arpiar. Vartera was sure to be upset."

"Vartera?" The serpent hissed and showed long fangs between her womanly lips. "It was never Vartera's doing! It was yours. Yours, poet!"

"It was my doing that you're still alive," said he. "I saved you from the bird, and at great risk to my own limbs, I might add. And . . . well, a fellow hates to bring it up, but you know the law as well as I." His eyes glinted. Despite the misery of that damp land and the burden of the mortal girl slung across his shoulder, he was enjoying himself. It was not often that he found himself holding the upper hand to a Faerie queen. And such a queen as ChuMana, no less!

He watched how she coiled and churned, losing her womanly semblance to that of a snake flashing her red underbelly as though to ward off some danger. Eanrin leapt back for fear of getting lashed by the sharp scales at her tail's end. He staggered and almost dropped the mortal girl but managed to brace himself at the last.

Everything in ChuMana wanted to devour the poet. Her jaw swung open and shut in its urge to unhinge and swallow him whole. But the laws of Faerie were unbreakable, and she owed him a favor. Whether by trickery or fair dealing, he had saved her life, and she was at his beck and call until such a time as she might repay him.

Finally she regained her woman's form, her head bowed so that she need not look at her enemy. Her long tongue flickered again. "I am in your debt," she said.

"Yes, you are," said Eanrin, grinning. He could feel the dampness of the land seeping into his bones. "And as it happens, I need a tiny little favor from you."

"Name your price," said the snake. "I can refuse you nothing."

"Well, all I really need for the moment is one small part of your collection."

ChuMana gazed at her intruder, the rubies of her eyes flickering with thought. Then, like water falling, she slipped from her upright stance down into the slime of her realm. Once more a serpent, she circled the poet, sometimes sliding over tufts of dirt, otherwise half under water. Her bulk was thicker than Eanrin's waist, and her length greater than a fallen pine. Eanrin swallowed, his heart racing in his throat. He wasn't used to being afraid. He should not fear ChuMana now, bound as she was by the laws of the worlds as every Faerie queen or king must be. Yet this inarguable fact failed to ease his mind.

At last ChuMana said, "What do you need of my collection?"

"Just to borrow one, that is all," said Eanrin. "This girl here"—he lifted his shoulder to indicate the mortal—"has had a bit of trouble, as it were, with the River. Fallen asleep, you see? She needs a prince to wake her."

The serpent's head rose from the water. "And you wish to borrow one of mine?"

"Any will do. It's only for the kiss, you understand," said Eanrin. Though he trembled under that cold gaze, he met it eye for eye and never ceased to smile. "You cannot possibly refuse such a small request. Not after our history, ChuMana! Not after—"

"Cease your talk!" ChuMana stood once more as a woman, her eyes flashing, her tongue flickering like lightning in and out between her teeth. "I will loan you one prince. But I will not give him up!"

"Oh, quite so," said Eanrin. "The *last* thing I need on my hands is a mortal prince as well as this princess! Let them rescue themselves, I always say. Makes for better epics. But just this once . . . you know how it is. Every rule needs to be bent now and then to test its mettle."

"Very well," said the Mistress of the Swamp. Then she knelt in the water, her eyes scanning the murk. Suddenly the frogs stopped singing. Dead silence hovered as heavy as the black-clouded sky.

Though her form remained that of a woman, from somewhere several yards away, the end of a serpent's tail moved. It darted out. There was a splash, then a loud, *"Graaaaaup!"*

The tail emerged, holding, wrapped in its coils, an enormous bullfrog. It boasted the most mournful face ever seen on one of its kind, its great back legs kicking, its eyes rolling skyward with heavy resignation.

Eanrin nodded, satisfied. As gently as he could, he slid the mortal girl from his shoulder, kneeling so he could support her across his knee. He hated putting her in that swamp water, but she was already so dirty it could hardly matter. He took the offered bullfrog from ChuMana. Turning it until its bulging eyes were level with his, he addressed it sternly:

"Now, you know your part. Kiss the girl like you mean it, and we'll all be better off, understand?"

"Graup," it said without enthusiasm. With a nod, Eanrin twitched the frog and its dangling limbs about and pressed its mouth to the mortal girl's lips.

The River was angry.

As far as Glomar could tell, however, it wasn't angry with him. His Path had been long and winding indeed, trailing the Black Dogs. Perhaps Eanrin was right and he should have stuck to the simpler way. One would think the Dogs would take the swiftest route back to their lair, but instead they had led Glomar over hill and dale, doing everything in their power, he suspected, to lose him. Well, they got more than they bargained for! Glomar of Rudiobus was no mean footman. He was Iubdan's captain, a soldier of the field. He knew a thing or two about tracking.

Nevertheless, he frowned grimly as the Path he followed finally led him to the River. If Eanrin took this simpler road, he might indeed have already entered Etalpalli far in advance. Glomar knelt and put his badger's nose to work, snuffling the turf for any sign of the poet. There was none to be found.

Yet the River was angry. Furious, even. Glomar found it growling like a wild animal with unsuppressed ferocity, tearing at its own banks.

But the force of its personality focused elsewhere, farther upriver. What could have caused it so much ire?

Glomar swallowed hard and adjusted his grip on his hatchet. Not that it would do him a great deal of good should the River decide to vent its anger on him. Still, he felt better for handling it. He picked his way from the higher banks down to the water's edge, following the course it cut through the rocks and roots. The River, like all the Wood, was a treacherous sort; one could never be overcautious when dealing with it. Glomar, his face set in stern lines of concentration, made slow but steady progress.

That fool poet thought he couldn't get into Etalpalli. Hmph!

The water rushed faster and faster, churning white foam and dangerous currents only inches away from Glomar's Path. He must be nearing the gate, he thought. He had passed that way once before, and he knew what to expect. There the River's waters fell in great, rushing torrent. There the mists of its wild careening billowed far below. There, with his heart in his throat and his courage grasped firmly in both hands, a man could stand on the brink and gaze upon the gate of the City of Wings.

Only a soul who wished to pass for the sake of another might enter. Glomar licked his lips and thought of Lady Gleamdren. Sweet Lady Gleamdren, who would be Eanrin's fair quarry should Glomar fail. The captain gnashed his teeth. He could never let that happen! Gleamdren was too fine a gem to belong to that brute of a cat.

Within another few paces, Glomar beheld Cozamaloti Falls.

9

A T FIRST HER MIND crawled slowly out of the deep recesses of fading dreams, back into the waking world. Enchantments often cause pain as they break and fall away, especially spiteful enchantments like the River's. They pulled at her, struggling to keep hold even as her body forced her to wake. A smashing whorl of colors and impressions filled her mind, allowing no coherent thought to take form. She was hot; she knew that much. A damp, soaking, dirty sort of hot, sweating from every pore.

Strange, for the last she remembered, she had been shivering.

Every limb was paralyzed and heavy, but her mind was returning to her. She wanted to wake. She did not want those dreams to pull her back down. So she fought the last fading shreds of the enchantment, mentally hurling herself against their hold. The more she struggled, the more she felt the damp and awful heat. But it was better than dreaming.

She strained again, and this time thought perhaps her body moved as well. At last she regained enough consciousness to open her eyes.

And found she was kissing a bullfrog.

Immediately, use of every limb surged back into her body. Her eyes flew wide; her arms flew wild. One hand struck the frog away, the other struck something or someone else. She heard a croak and a curse, and the next thing she knew, she was submerged in water. It closed over her head, stinging her eyes and filling her mouth. Thrashing madly, she pushed herself up again, coughing out a stream and pushing her hair out of her eyes.

For a frozen moment, she stared up into the face of a pale man with fiery gold hair and yellow eyes.

"Quite the clip in the jaw you just gave me, my girl! Come, now, let's make up and be friends, shall we?"

In her haste to turn about and simultaneously scramble to her feet, she slipped and went under again, this time face first. Her hands and elbows sank into mud, and swamp weeds wrapped about her arms and tangled with the ropes still attached to her wrists. But her flight instinct was strong, and though exhaustion threatened to betray her, she shoved forward even before she brought her head to the surface again.

She heard a shout and a splash and felt someone's hands grabbing at her shoulders. With an animal snarl she twisted away, writhing in the muck and kicking. She heard an *"Oooof!"* and a body landed partially on top of her. She pushed out from underneath, managed to gain her feet, and stood a dripping moment, poised to flee but without bearings.

Her gaze met that of the serpent.

ChuMana's long neck rose from the dark water, her flat head looking down. A forked tongue flickered from a mouth that could have swallowed a small pig whole.

A bead of water fell from the girl's nose.

Then she dropped like a stone, not asleep but in a dead faint.

Hri Sora awakened on the brink of a chasm.

She stared down into blackness, and her head whirled with that sickening sensation that was still so new to her: the fear of falling. All in an instant, she relived that plunge from the heavens . . . that moment when her wings were stripped from her and the mortal world dragged her down.

Then she wrenched herself back from the chasm and sat gasping, her feet inches from its edge.

Slowly, the flames in her head cooled and she was able to open her eyes and survey the world. She remembered her name, and she knew where she was this time. She felt Etalpalli pulsing with the pain of its wounds beneath her. And she remembered the Flowing Gold and her bargain with the Dark Father. What she could not remember was why she was here, on the rim of this drop.

On trembling limbs, she got to her feet and slowly spun about. The memories returned but without pain. She could not, at least at this moment, feel pain. She recalled the tomb of her brother. Poor Ttlanextu.

Heat filled her mouth at that thought. "He was weak," she said aloud, her words burning the air. "He was weak, or he would never have succumbed to Cren Cru. *I* didn't! It took more than that parasite to bring me down."

It took only my fire.

The trembling of Hri Sora's limbs ceased in frozen horror. Then she turned to the pit, the black and gaping hole in the ground where Itonatiu Tower had once risen to the sun. She strode to the edge and, though the emptiness falling away below made her sick inside, she opened her mouth and spat fire into the darkness. The flame fell in a ball down and down, deeper and deeper. At last it was nothing put a pinprick of light. Then it was gone.

A moment of stillness. Then screams.

They were so far away that Hri Sora almost missed them. If Etalpalli itself was not so deathly silent, she never would have heard them. But they rose from the darkness and pierced her ears. She hissed and stepped back quickly.

The Dark Father spoke again in her head: *Are you ready to come home to me?*

"No!" she snarled. "I will have vengeance first."

Vengeance upon whom?

"None of your business. Give me my wings."

Give me the Flowing Gold of Rudiobus.

Hri Sora gnashed her teeth. She remembered now the iron cage up in Omeztli, where her Faerie captive waited. Curses upon this raging fire that kept consuming her mind! Curses upon this frail body that could not support such flame! But she must not let herself grow angry. She must not allow the fire to take her again. How much time had she wasted already? Not that there was any need for haste. Gleamdren was immortal. Etalpalli was unassailable.

And Amarok was going nowhere.

This thought made her smile. No, Amarok never dared leave his self-styled demesne. Not with his children on the loose.

What is that smile for, daughter? Why do you keep secrets from me?

Warmth filled Hri Sora now, a pleasant warmth of anticipation. "Don't you wish you knew?" she crowed to the empty air. "Don't you wish you could read my mind?"

I don't have to read your mind. I can predict your every thought!

"But this you don't know," she laughed. "And you won't. It's my business, not yours."

Well, child, my business is your wings. Which you will never have if you fail to give me what I ask.

"All in good time, Father, all in—"

Etalpalli shuddered.

Hri Sora broke off with a gasp and fell to her hands and knees, feeling the ground with her fingers, tearing the rocks with her talons. Her demesne had been linked to her spirit the moment she was crowned queen. Though she'd burned the city, this link was unbroken. She felt every shudder, every change.

She felt now the intruder nosing along the edge of her borders. Beyond her world, out in the Between, but so close.

"You want it, don't you, my Etalpalli?" she whispered, stroking the trembling stones like a pet. "You are hungry for more deaths. Were not all my people enough to satisfy this newly awakened appetite?"

What a crude animal your demesne has become. I'll leave you to your games, daughter. But don't forget our bargain.

The Dark Father's voice receded into the pit. Hri Sora hardly cared.

Rising, she sped her gaze to the far reaches of her land and on into the Wood Between. There he was, one of the Merry Folk, testing the strength of her gate. He'd never get through on his own, selfish little beast that he was. Ttlanextu had been weak, but he was no fool when he set those boundaries in place!

Yet just as the king could make the rules, so the queen could break them. Hri Sora raised a hand and, with a twist of her wrist, opened the Cozamaloti Gate.

"Light of Lumé be doused forever, look what you've gone and done!"

It was unclear if Eanrin spoke to the serpent, the girl, or even the bull-frog as he scrambled up from the muddy water, rubbing his middle where he'd been viciously kicked a moment before. He was soaked through, his hair plastered to his head, his cloak clinging to his body. But he darted forward to lift the fainted girl from the murk and thump her back to be certain she hadn't swallowed more water. She lay limp as the dead against him, and he muttered a stream of curses.

A shadow fell across them both, and Eanrin looked up into the face of the bullfrog. Only it was no bullfrog now. It was a prince.

"Dragon's teeth," Eanrin snarled.

The prince was tall, dark, and perhaps what mortals considered handsome. His clothing, though slimy as a frog's hide, was of fine weave, all blue and silver. In that hasty first glance, Eanrin decided he was probably not from the same Time as the girl in her skins. Time being unpredictable, it was possible for princes and princesses of different eras to meet when once they entered the Wood Between. Eanrin (though he paid little attention to mortal history) estimated a good thousand mortal years between girl and prince.

The prince swept a bow both to the poet and the fainted maid, saying, "Fair creature of untold beauty! How long have I awaited the deliverance brought by your sweet kiss?"

"Enough blathering," snapped Eanrin, adjusting his hold on the girl, trying to brace her so he could stand. "She's unconscious and cannot hear you. Just as well if you plan to speak in clichés." He gave the girl a shake. "Come, this is ridiculous. One doesn't faint upon waking from an enchanted sleep! Rise and meet your rescuer; there's a good girl."

Though her skin was dark, it wore a chalky pallor. Eanrin feared she had died from her fright, but when he put an ear to her mouth, he found she still breathed.

"Spitfire!" the poet swore in relief. With more sloshing and wallowing, he managed to get himself upright, the girl in his arms. Her neck was limp, and her mass of hair trailed over his arm. "Here," he said to the prince. "Take her. I've had quite enough of this heroics nonsense. And have I mentioned that it's none of my business?"

The prince blinked at him. "She isn't mine."

"She is now. She kissed you out of your froggishness, didn't she? Take her and deliver her kingdom like a man, then marry her, why don't you?"

The poet staggered a step forward, intending to drop the girl in the prince's arms. But the prince stepped back. "M-marry?" he said. "Oh, now, Sacred Lights!"

Eanrin offered the prince the coldest possible of stares. "Don't tell me you have any complaints?"

Thunder rumbled in the heavy sky above. Prince and poet startled and hunched their shoulders, as though afraid the heavens would drop on them. "Oh, I'm certainly not complaining," said the prince. "Much obliged for the rescue, of course. But—"

"But what?"

"Well, *marriage* . . . I am expected to marry well."

"To a princess, I would imagine?" Eanrin shrugged the girl in his arms. "This one is as much a princess as you'll ever find. She drank from an enchanted River. Who but a princess does that? True, she's not much to look on right now"—She wasn't. The wet skins she wore stank of swamp and clung to her limbs. Her hair stuck to her face and neck and sagged in a heavy, tangled lump down to the swamp water. Mud covered every visible inch of skin yet failed to disguise the sickly color of her cheeks—"but she'll clean up well enough. And she rescued you, by Lumé, from a fate amphibian! Just the girl to bring home to mum and dad."

The prince rubbed the back of his neck. A drop of rain landed on his nose. More drops began to fall, dimpling the pools around them. The poet began to growl.

"The thing is," said the prince, "I need to find myself a bride with a certain amount of dowry. Never mind why. But this girl . . . I mean, look at her. Princess or not, one must wonder if she'd recognize the value of a gold coin if it hit her in the eye!"

Eanrin felt the dampness of ChuMana's realm seeping into his bones. Even his smile had been soaked from his face. "You won't take the creature because she has no riches?"

"It's a sad business, I know," said the prince with a sigh. "But what is a man to do? So, I'll just be moving along, then. When she comes to herself, give her my thanks. It has been a pleasure, and her kiss was nothing to frown upon, take my expert word for it. Farewell, princess! Farewell, stranger! I must take my leave—" He turned.

And found himself eye to eye with ChuMana.

The serpent looked mostly like a woman just then, but she smiled like a snake. "And where do you think you are going?"

"Oh, dragon's—"

Her bite was swift, sinking with deadly accuracy into his shoulder. The prince had just enough time to give a startled yell. The next moment, a bullfrog sat once more in the water. It gave a mournful *"GRAAAAP!"* and hopped away with a splash, disappearing among the reeds. Its bellowing voice joined those of its countless brothers while the rain continued to fall.

"I like him better that way," Eanrin said, looking down his nose at the frogs. "Some men are more natural for a little slime."

ChuMana, hissing still, turned to the poet. "So, Eanrin of Rudiobus," said she, "my debt is now paid."

"Aye, that it is," agreed Eanrin with something that was probably meant to be a smile but was much too soggy by now to count. "Always a great feeling, isn't it, paying off one's—"

"Away from my demesne!"

Eanrin needed no convincing. The laws of Faerie satisfied, nothing but quick feet would save him now. Without a thought, he slung the mortal girl over his shoulder and fled the swamp, avoiding the serpent's parting kiss by no more than a hair's breadth.

Thunder growled. Rain, free at last, beat down. ChuMana, the equilibrium of her realm restored, slithered into the darker reaches of her swamp, frogs scattering before her.

10

First to return were sounds, though from such a great distance, she could not be certain she even heard them. At least they were gentle sounds: the rustling of leaves, the sighing of wind. More faintly still, she thought she heard soft breathing, but that was most likely her imagination.

Next came a sensation of light that slowly pushed the darkness back into a hazy tunnel. Sparks burst on the edges like exploding fireflies. But soon things began to take more solid shape and color. She saw leaves, brilliant green on dark branches against a vibrant blue sky. She lay in a forest, she realized, though she couldn't remember how she had come there.

Oh, beasts and devils! Was that *her* head hurting so badly?

With a groan, she struggled to repossess her own limbs. How had she— No! She wouldn't think about that, not with her head throbbing so. But what was this place—no, no! No thinking!

Grinding her teeth and drawing deep breaths, she sat up. Almost immediately she curled forward, her elbows digging into the dirt, her palms pressing into her eyes, and wished to die. People should not be obliged to live with heads in such a state. But after another lungful or two, she felt better and was able to look about again.

She sat in a small clearing of pure green grass. Sunlight broke through the otherwise intensely heavy foliage to fall just here, making the green brighter still (and not helping her head). Beyond this circle of light lay the Wood, as black and ominous as any wood has ever dared be. The trees whispered to each other, gossiping with the wind. Otherwise, she was alone.

"So, you are awake at last."

Not quite alone.

The girl peered into the shadows of the trees just beyond the clearing. A form sat in the darkness, but she could discern no details. The voice was a man's. Not a warrior's voice, she thought. It wasn't deep but smooth with a golden timbre. Coming from the shadows, however, it was ominous. Her heart began to race, and she stood and took a step back. This wasn't her world. She felt the strangeness in the ground beneath her feet, in the air she breathed. And this stranger, whether man or monster, could not be her friend, not in this place.

The form slinked from shadow to shadow with barely a flicker she could follow. But her eyes were quick and her ears quicker still. She turned as it moved, making certain she faced it.

"You have been wasting my Time, mortal woman," the stranger said. "With every breath you take, my rival draws nearer to stealing from me what I desire most. Do you see your crime, creature of dust?"

She stepped back slowly, setting her feet so gently that they scarcely made a sound. How odd was the speech of the stranger! She thought, somehow, that she should not be able to understand, should not know his language. But the words he spoke shifted in her mind even as he spoke them, and she understood as clearly as though he spoke the tongue of her people. His voice was not unfriendly, but the meaning contained a possible threat. Her eyes darting even as her head remained still, she cast about for a stout stick. But in this otherworldly forest all the trees grew straight and never dropped a dead branch.

The figure in the darkness moved again, sidling around as though to get closer to her. "It's my own fault," he said, "for allowing myself to become involved. I am more than ready to take responsibility for my foolishness!"

She stepped sideways, one foot crossing delicately behind the other as she moved. The grass was soft beneath her feet, but she did not like it. It was deceptively comforting. How could one trust a forest such as this?

"But for my pains, I think I deserve an explanation or two," the stranger continued, slipping behind a tree so that she lost sight of him altogether. Her knees bent and her hands spread to lend her balance should she need to run suddenly.

"Tell me, girl, what *were* you thinking, drinking from the River?"

The voice was directly behind her. She whirled about. How could he have moved so fast? Her eyes searched the dark deeps, struggling to see through the glare of light around her. She spun in place, her gaze darting. Where was he? Where was—

"Speak up, if you please."

She looked down. An orange cat sat at her feet, tail lashing. He grinned a feline grin at her. "What's wrong?" he asked. "Cat got your tongue?"

She ran.

Sparks exploded in her peripheral vision as her body screamed for her to stop. She did not care. She'd had enough of this place. Enough of animals who spoke with the tongues of men and men who were worse than animals. She sped through the trees, pushing branches from her face. Why did they reach like snatching hands to stop her? Her head pounded, her stomach roiled, her damaged feet pleaded for ease.

How long had she been running now? Ever since the moon vanished behind the clouds on that night so far past, which also seemed but a few hours ago. She could never have passed through the mountains in so short a time. She should have died from exhaustion! Perhaps she had. Perhaps this was the world after death. This hell where she must keep running, running, and never know a moment's peace.

She fled the clearing, fled the nightmare, fled that cat. But in her mind, it was the wolf she heard howling at her heels.

The trees shifted from her way so that she ran in a straight line. But their shadows became longer and darker, like thick curtains falling. The only light she saw came from the flowers on the vines twining everywhere in this wood, gleaming little stars. She thought she heard them speaking to her in voices not human, pleading with her to go back, to turn around.

But there was no going back now. They would kill her if she returned. They would bind her to the stone and leave her to be devoured. No, she had fled, and she must never return!

Oh, Fairbird! Her mind cried out in desperate silence. *How could I have left you?*

There had been no choice then; there was no choice now. She must run, she must lose herself in this forest so deeply that she would never be found.

The Wood put out its grasping arms, ready to swallow her whole. Its shadows fed into her fear, and without knowing what she did, her feet fell upon a dark Path that made promises she understood without knowing she heard them. Promises of safety, of hiding, of dark holes where no one could pursue.

How cold the air had become! Her breath frosted, her fingertips were blue, and her lungs begged for relief. The harsh cords on her wrists cut more sharply, the dangling ends lashing at her bare legs. But she could not stop.

A pit opened before her.

Her arms swung wide, grasping at empty air, for the trees had pulled back to give her no handhold. A gaping hole from which rose a fetid stink ate away the ground at her feet. She scrambled on the edge, struggling in vain to throw herself back. She saw the face of the devil in the dark, saw its hands reaching for her throat.

"This one isn't for you, Guta!"

The golden voice of the stranger rang in her ears, as horrible to her as the face of the devil. But she felt strong hands grasp beneath her arms and haul her away from the pit. She staggered and fell, scraping her legs against hard soil, but two arms wrapped about her and held tight. She closed her eyes, bracing herself . . .

. . . and opened them in a flood of warm sunshine.

The pit was gone. She lay on a soft patch of earth once more in a bright part of the Wood. Did this mean she was safe? Moaning, she closed her eyes and shook her head, desperate to clear her thoughts. Then she looked at the man kneeling beside her.

"I must say, you mortals are a flighty lot."

His features were human enough, but there was something feline about the rest of him. Not his appearance but the essence of him. He clucked and shook his head at her disapprovingly. His voice was that of the cat.

"I really should have left you in the first place," he said. "Or the second place! But after all that nonsense—giving up my favor from ChuMana, Lumé love me—I feel I'm owed an explanation. Curiosity always was my chief fault, and now look where it's gotten me! Ah, well. What's a man to do?"

She should be afraid. But just then she was too spent to be frightened anymore. She took a deep, shuddering breath and let it out slowly. Otherwise, she could not move.

"That part of the Wood is dangerous, you know," the cat-man continued. "It'll draw you into darker places with folks you don't want to meet. Guta is a foul-tempered demon, to say the least. A beater. He would beat you to death upon sight, believe me! He's done it to many stronger than you. It's a good thing I caught up when I did. I don't know if I'd have been able to pull you back out once you'd fallen into Guta's pit!"

Though her limbs did not want to move, she made herself sit up. Every muscle screamed ill-use, but she could not lie there forever. She held her head between her hands until the dizziness cleared, then blinked at the cat-man.

One moment she saw him in one form, the next moment in the other. This creature was simultaneously all cat and all man, and despite the shining youth of his face, he was ancient.

She knew one other like this one, may the spirits of the mountains protect her! Though they wouldn't, actually. They had never protected her or any of her people. When the man who was an animal entered the Land untold years ago, had the mountains moved to intervene? No. They remained stone and slept as they had since the dawn of time. And he who was as ancient as they came among her people and worked his will unchecked. Man and animal. Monster and master.

Yet that one had never smiled.

"There, now," said the cat-man, seeing how her face slowly relaxed. "There, you'll be all right, my girl. Can you stand?" He helped her to her feet. She staggered a little, but he caught her and patted her shoulder gently while she clung to his scarlet doublet. "Light of Hymlumé," he swore softly. "Since when did I transform into the caring sort? Dangerous business, I tell you. Perhaps you are a sorceress?"

She looked up and saw that he still smiled, though he asked the question sincerely. She shook her head and stepped back, releasing her grip on his shirt. They stood in the same clearing where she had first awakened, she thought. Or one exactly like it, with a patch of bright green grass bathed in sunlight.

"I'm glad to see you on your feet," said the cat-man. "First an enchanted sleep, then a fainting spell, now this little mess . . . It's been one thing after another, hasn't it?"

An enchanted sleep? The girl frowned and put a hand to her head. She did not remember that. She remembered nightmares unending but couldn't be certain which were dreams and which reality. Her only clear memory was of a bullfrog and a kiss . . . but that, she desperately hoped, was another dream!

"No harm done in the end," the cat-man was saying. "I tried to kiss you awake myself, but that didn't do much good. Not that your kiss wasn't sweet enough, I'll grant you—"

Her eyes flew wide and her jaw dropped. Raising both hands, she formed silent words in the air. "You *kissed* me?"

He did not know the language of hands. Men never formed the Women's Words. He went on talking. "As everyone knows, only princes' kisses work on enchanted sleeps, and dear ChuMana did owe me a favor."

It would make no difference, but she signed even so: "You had no right to kiss me."

"I was strolling the Karayan Plains one day, minding my own business. Then suddenly, what did I see but the great shadow of a Roc blotting out the sky! I looked up and saw that old serpent caught in the Roc's talons, twisting and thrashing and screaming for all she was worth. What a sight that was! I knew a favor from ChuMana could prove useful someday, so I picked up a rock, and— My name is Eanrin, by the way. Chief Poet of Iubdan Rudiobus, Bard of the Golden Staff, etcetera. You've possibly heard of me?"

She shook her head.

"What? No?" The cat-man's smile faltered and his eyebrows went up. "Isn't that just the oddest! Are you sure?"

She nodded.

"Well, what a primitive lot your people must be, never to have heard the celebrated verses of Bard Eanrin! But then, you probably sing nothing but war chants and suchlike. I, however, write all my poetry out of the inspiration of my deepest heart." He tilted his head and gazed meaningfully into the leaf-twined sky as though from thence fell that deep inspiration of his. "It is my way of expressing the longing I feel for my great love, and so on and so on. Her name is Gleamdren. Lady Gleamdrené Gormlaith, fairest maiden to walk the merry halls of Rudiobus Mountain. I intend to spend my life regaling her ears with verses to her honor and splendor."

The girl blinked at him. Then she raised her hands and signed, "Poor lady."

"I shall make her name famous across all the worlds . . . almost as famous as my own." The soulful eyes blinked, then turned to the girl with a frown. "Are you *certain* you've never heard of me? Eanrin? Bard of Rudiobus? Golden voice and all that?"

"No," she signed.

"Why do you keep flailing your hands about like that? Some native dance of your people, perhaps? Such unusual cultures you mortals have. But come, have done with it. Tell me your name, girl."

She chewed her lips, narrowing her eyes at him. Then she signed, "I cannot speak." This involved a slicing motion across the neck.

"No need to make violent gestures," said the poet-cat, who looked more like a cat when affronted. "Just give us your name, if you please. Then we'll say, 'Splendid meeting you!' and go our separate ways."

She shook her head and signed again, "I cannot speak."

"I must say, I do think you're a bit rude."

Exasperated, she tapped at her throat and grunted. It wasn't much of a sound, no louder than the groans she had made in sleep. It was a painful noise both to hear and to make.

The poet frowned. Her black eyes stared at him so earnestly that Eanrin wished to look away. But being a cat, he did not like to break gaze first. At last he said slowly, "Are you . . . you mean you're a mute?"

The girl opened her mouth wide. He saw the muscles in her throat move. He even saw her tongue and lips trying to shape a word. But not a sound emerged save a whisper of a moan, and even that caused her obvious pain.

The poet put both hands up and backed away, frowning severely, which was a terrible sight on his merry face. "You're cursed."

She nodded.

"Great hopping goblins!" Eanrin turned away, pulling the scarlet cap from his head and twisting it in his fists. "Great *ugly* hopping goblins! What am I doing? This is just brilliant, Eanrin, brilliant. You've gone and rescued a princess from one curse only to find out she's under another! That's what you get from reaching out the hand of friendship to a stranger. Listen to yourself next time and don't get involved."

He prowled the little clearing like a caged animal while the girl watched him, irritated. After all, she had not asked him for help, and she certainly wasn't asking now. She folded her arms and waited.

The cat-man whirled on her, his eyes flashing. "What I *don't* have time for is you!" he declared. "So you'd best get up and go on your way. Do you hear me? Break your own curses."

Her jaw set. Her shoulders went back. Her hands dropped in fists to her sides, and she turned from the poet and marched from the clearing into the waiting Wood.

"Stop!"

The poet leapt forward, spreading his arms as he blocked her way. "Where do you think you're going? Carry on that way, and before you know it, you'll land right in the middle of Arpiar. Terrible demesne, that! All barren hillsides and deep mines, goblins crawling everywhere. And didn't I just tell you about Rocs hunting on the Karayan Plains?"

She drew back from him, wrapping her arms about her middle so that the bindings on her wrists slapped against her legs. She turned on heel and started in the opposite direction. But she had made no more than a few paces when the poet shouted again.

"You mortal creatures are as helpless as blind kittens!" He placed a restraining hand on her arm. "You go on that way, and you'll tumble right into the realm of Lord Bright as Fire, the Tiger. He doesn't like company. And you're so puny, it won't take him more than a mouthful to put an end to you!"

She shook off his hand. With a still more resolute stride, she picked another direction and started at a run. But the cat-man easily outpaced and blocked her, a warning hand upraised. She scowled, planting her hands on her hips. The poet sighed as though he bore the curse himself.

"The Wood is dangerous without a Path," he said. "Especially for you, mortal as you are." His merry face became drawn with long-suffering. "I've never much cared for your kind. You live and die so swiftly, it's like becoming attached to a mosquito. But now I've gotten you this far, I can't leave you out here to get yourself killed or enchanted all over again. What's the point of waking you if you're just going to go back to sleep?"

The girl shook her head slowly, her eyes narrowed, her mouth closed tight. Oblivious, the poet heaved a frustrated sigh. "I shall have to take you with me."

"No," she signed.

"Eventually," he continued, ignoring her, "I must discover where you belong and return you there. But I haven't the time to waste on such nonsense at present. For once in my life, Time is of the essence! My beloved, the fair and glorious Gleamdren—you know, my poetic muse?—has been captured by a most foul evil. The dreadful Hri Sora, curse of the Near World! Exciting prospect, yes? The stuff of epics."

"I'm not going with you," she signed.

"See here, girl, I don't know what you're saying, but consider this: What other choice do you have? Do you want to end up battered by Guta or devoured by the Tiger?"

The girl gazed up at his strange, beautiful features. He was different from every being she knew save for . . . save for that one terrible face with eyes devoid of either kindness or mercy. And yet, while this man was definitely a cat and selfish to the bone, she thought perhaps, deep inside his gaze, she glimpsed a spark of compassion.

Besides, as he said, what choice did she have?

"Very well," she signed. "I will go with you. For now."

"Is that a yes?" guessed the cat, his eyes following the movement of her hands.

With something close to a smile, the mortal girl nodded.

"Excellent!" said Eanrin.

11

COZAMALOTI FALLS roared with the voices of a thousand lions, its white mist shot with rainbows. Only the brave man who dared dive from the bridge at the brink of the falls for the sake of another would enter the City of Wings. Many had journeyed to this brink and gazed into those mists, only to turn their backs upon greatness. These had never seen the city of the Sky People or the tall green towers of Etalpalli, where Lady Gleamdren now languished in a dragon's keeping.

Now was the hour for the brave to come forward and make that leap of faith! But no story ever told about the mighty Cozamaloti Falls had prepared Glomar for this challenge.

The captain stood on the rope bridge strung above Cozamaloti's edge and looked down the falls. Though the waters were indeed shot with rainbows as promised, they hardly roared with the voices of a thousand lions. A thousand kittens, perhaps.

A two-foot trickle gurgled over a lump of rock into a pleasant stream below.

Glomar frowned. He rather hoped there was some trick here, that this was an illusion disguising the true power of Cozamaloti from his eyes. After all, it took nary an ounce of courage for a man to make this leap! The most he had to fear was slipping on a wet stone and giving his rump a good soaking.

He looked up and down the River. How strangely calm it was! Glomar knew from previous excursions into the Wood that this part of the River should be rushing with rapids and building to a final climax. Instead, it had dwindled to little more than a sweetly bubbling streamlet. What, by all the Lights Above, could be distracting it so thoroughly upriver?

Ah well! No use in musing on unfathomable matters. Glomar turned back to the falls (more like the dribble) and studied it. Perhaps that hazy mist where the rainbow arched was actually a deceptive death plunge? Not likely. But if he really made himself believe as much, he might work up enough terror to make the jump a courageous one.

He climbed over the rope guard on the bridge and held on to it, hanging over the side. It swayed out and back again in gentle rhythm. Dragon's teeth, it was like being a babe rocked in mother's arms! This was no way to storm Etalpalli's gates.

Shrugging, Glomar waited for the bridge to swing back out over the little drop. Then he let go.

Eanrin led the way through the Wood. Or at least he hoped he did.

Sometimes he thought he caught a gleam of gold, a flash of white, up ahead. But it vanished every time he looked twice. He trembled at the possibilities crowding his mind and forced himself to dismiss them. His life was what it was. Nothing was going to change.

Just because he hadn't left this mortal girl to rot on the River's edge did not mean he cared for her or her paltry story.

He picked his footsteps carefully, following a Path he believed he chose for himself. The mortal girl walked a few paces behind. He glanced back at her with a smile, admiring how quietly she proceeded, making surprisingly little noise for a human. Her bare feet were cut and sore, he noticed, yet she moved with grace, save when those awful cords dangling from her arms caught in the underbrush.

Something needed to be done about those.

Eanrin stopped and reached out to snatch the girl's right arm. She jerked away, her eyes flashing curses as she backed up several paces. Eanrin laughed and shook his head. "You startle like a fawn, my girl! Come, don't be so skittish. Don't you think if I had intended to harm you, I would have done so long ere now? Use your brain and don't be a fool. I want to examine those bindings of yours."

The girl's eyes searched his face. Truly she had been at his mercy for some time already, she told herself. Then again, he had made her kiss a bullfrog. Ugh!

But his face was not like that other.

Licking her lips and drawing a deep breath, the girl held out her hands. He lifted them to his face, sniffing. How like a cat he was in that moment, though his features remained those of a man.

He caught a certain scent and dropped her hands. For the first time since she'd met him, she saw fear in his golden face. It vanished so swiftly that she wondered if she'd imagined it; but she did not imagine the step back he took or the swift intake of breath.

Eanrin blinked once, then smoothed both eyebrows with the back of his hand. "Well, little one," he said with a smile, "you have collected quite the variety of acquaintances, haven't you? But I don't want to know more. It's not my business what friends you make, or enemies, for that matter. I'll get these cords off you in any case."

He drew a knife from his belt. Once more the girl gasped, but this time she forced herself not to flinch. *He is a friend!* she told herself. *He won't hurt you.*

She looked away as he pressed the cold blade against her skin, slipping it under the painfully tight cords. He was gentle and did not cut her. In her mind, however, she saw another knife. A stone one, the blade jagged and stained.

The cords fell away, first from one wrist, then the other. As they dropped, the girl knelt, curling up in a ball. She thought she would be sick and struggled to force her stomach back down where it belonged.

"Oh, Lumé's crown!" said the poet-cat, looking down at her. The next moment, an orange cat rubbed across the girl's knees, purring noisily and flicking his tail in her ear. She sat up and, after a brief hesitation, ran a tentative hand along the cat's head, back, and up the plumy tail. The fur was matted with mud in places, but his ears were softer than the soft skins she wore, and his body was warm and rumbling with life.

Frostbite, she thought, and a tear dropped down her face.

"Crown and scepter!" the cat meowled. It was strange indeed to hear the man's voice from the animal's mouth, though not as strange as it might have been. The two forms were both such natural extensions of Eanrin's nature that they hardly seemed disparate; it was only her perspective that altered. "If a purr like that can't cheer you, I don't know what will."

The cat sat and started grooming, his ears quirked at an offended angle. The girl wiped away her tear and gave the top of Eanrin's head a scratch. He paused, pink tongue sticking out, and she smiled.

"I'm going to have to give you a name." The cat vanished and the man sat cross-legged before her. Surprised, she pulled her hand back quickly from his head. He, with an air of disinterest, pulled a comb from the depths of his cloak and continued grooming. The comb's teeth caught on mud tangles in his thatch of hair, and he tugged at these vigorously, all the while keeping up a steady stream of talk. "I cannot keep calling you 'girl,' or even 'princess.' You are a princess, though, aren't you?"

The girl, rubbing her wrists, looked up with some surprise at this odd question and shook her head.

"Nonsense," said the poet-cat, pausing a moment in midtug. "Didn't you disenchant the bullfrog? Everyone knows it takes a princess's kiss for that kind of magic."

The girl shuddered and suppressed a gag.

Eanrin grabbed a clump of his hair and began tearing at it with sharp little digs from his comb. "You must be a princess without being aware of it. Or perhaps they don't call it 'princess' where you're from. The emperor's heir, maybe? No, no, you look more like a chieftain's daughter. Some rugged tribe lost in the wilds of the mortal world . . . That's a bit romantic, actually."

She shook her head again, smiling at the thought of this odd poet imagining romance in her life. She looked down at her clothing, the soft white skins now mud gray and torn. No princess was she. Nothing but a woman's child.

"I must pick a name for you," the cat continued. "Something royal enough to suit. Don't expect me to play any guessing games! You'll just have to take the name I choose. How about *Clodagh*? It means 'muddy,' and you're certainly that! What, no? All right, all right. *Pádraigín,* then. It means you're of noble descent, which I'm telling you, you are. Princess Pádraigín." He made a face. "I'd certainly not be writing any ballads to you."

The girl, still rubbing her wrists, shook her head vehemently. A shining brightness in the shadows nearby caught her eye. Looking, she saw a familiar vine climbing a tree. Amid dark, blunt leaves, its flowers glowed bloodred in sunlight. In darkness they turned from red to gleaming white, like tiny stars. This vine grew in her homeland in wild abundance, and the sight of it here made her smile, like seeing a friendly face among strangers.

"*Úna* might be nice," the poet was saying. "It's always been one of my favorites. . . . Oi! Where are you going?"

Eanrin turned where he sat to watch the girl step over to the vine and gently lift one of the branches without plucking it. Then she turned to the poet and pointed at one of the star-shaped blossoms.

Eanrin, watching her, blinked his wide gold eyes. He spoke coldly. "Well, you needn't like *Úna*. I've plenty of other choices for you. What about *Mallaidh*?"

She shook her head. Once more she pointed at the flower.

"*Dollag?* That's getting a bit pretentious, but—"

She glared at him and signed, "Don't be thick!" though she knew he wouldn't understand. Yet again she pointed at the flower and raised her eyebrows at the poet.

He tilted his head to one side, opened his mouth, thought better of it, and closed it again. Swallowing, he said, "Are you trying to tell me something?"

She mentally cursed back at the curse that had taken her voice. Grinding her teeth, she jabbed more forcefully at the blossom.

"Pretty that, yes," said the poet. "The little starflowers."

She nodded and smiled. Her teeth, though crooked, were white against her dark face. It was a pretty effect, Eanrin noticed, and he blushed.

No, wait . . . *blushed*?

He shook himself. Eanrin of Rudiobus, Iubdan's Chief Poet, did not blush; he *caused* blushes. Among all the ladies of Rudiobus. On the scaly face of ChuMana. Any woman he met would fall for his voice, the charm of his swift-flying words, and dissolve into the reddest flushes!

This was all wrong. This girl must be an enchantress of some kind. What a mess he'd gotten himself into! He wished he'd left the girl to the River, and this forlorn wish made him sulky.

He crossed his arms over his chest. "How about *Éibhleann*? It means radiant beauty. Not that you can ever boast beauty like that, mortal creature that you are!" he quickly added.

Her eyes narrowed to slits. Setting her jaw, she stepped over to the poet and took hold of him by the scruff of the neck. The moment she did so, she held an enormous growling tomcat, which she carried to the vine. She stuck his nose up to the flower.

The cat twisted out of her hands and landed on sandaled feet, once more a man. He shook himself and gave her such a look as would have curdled milk. "Yes! Fine, lovely flowers those! I agree! We call them *imralderi*, the starflowers."

She nodded again, pointing.

The poet scowled at her. "Is that your name?"

Nod.

"You're sure of that?"

Nod, nod.

Suddenly his face was all smiles again. "Ah! What a fine and pretty name it is! And so unusual for a mortal girl. I would not have thought anyone in the Near World knew the Faerie tongue." He snatched up one of her hands and, raising her fingers to his lips, saluted her ceremoniously. "I am ever so pleased to make your acquaintance, Princess Imraldera of the mortal realm."

She drew back her hand. "I am no princess," she signed, "and that is not my name!" Once more she indicated the little flower.

"Indeed," said the poet, still smiling. "You are named for the flower, yes?"

"Yes!" she signed.

"The little starflower?"

She nodded and smiled as though to a simple child. "Yes, yes!"

"Princess Imraldera, then. Lovely name! Not one I've heard more than a handful of times, and never among my own people. Well, Imraldera, it's nice to be on such friendly terms, isn't it?"

She flung up both hands, then rubbed them down her face. But the poet's mind was settled on the matter. He had named her Imraldera, and Imraldera she must be.

"Well, now that's decided," said the poet, adjusting his cap and cloak, "we really must be off. Glomar has such a start on me, I wouldn't be surprised if he's already found the gates to Etalpalli! This whole 'helping the helpless' business really is for the dogs. You can't begin to understand how drastically you've slowed me down, Imraldera, and every moment is precious! If Glomar rescues the fair Gleamdren before I've so much as set eyes upon the Cozamaloti Falls, well, it's all up for me! I will have to abandon my pursuit of the true love of my heart, and with it abandon all dreams of poetic greatness! You see what a tragedy that would be, don't you?"

And he started off through the Wood, following a brightly lit Path, singing as he went:

> *"Oh, woe is me, I am undone,*
> *In sweet affliction lying!*
> *For my labor's scarce begun,*
> *And leaves me sorely sighing*
> *After that maiden I adore,*
> *Who something, something, something more . . . "*

He called back over his shoulder, "Thus does the poet's work progress! Do, please, withhold all judgment until further notice."

Newly christened Imraldera stared after him. Then with a sigh, she picked up her feet and made them follow her noisy guide. For now, she would let her path wander with the poet's. But soon, she would have to part ways with him. She would have to plunge alone once more into the threatening Wood.

Etalpalli shuddered.

The towers had stood vacant for a hundred years. The streets were crumbled, melted from that old fire. Like a sad and lonely graveyard, the city had stood undisturbed in the ruins of its once fair demesne.

So when a stranger fell through its gates and landed hard upon the stones, the city trembled to its core. And somewhere, deep within that tangle of streets, two Dogs started baying.

Hri Sora, returned to the summit of Omeztli Tower, gazed with far-seeing eyes across the many spires to the edge of her city and saw the intruder. The fall had been, apparently, much greater than he had expected. She smiled. Her little deceptions could still govern the borders of her realm, ruined though it may be. The man had landed on the stone and fallen, his face twisted in pain. She watched him reach down to one ankle, which was already showing signs of swelling. Yes, that fall had taken him by surprise. Cozamaloti was not to be underestimated!

"What are you staring at?" The petulant voice of her prisoner rang through the otherwise silent air. "I don't recall ever seeing you so alert. You look almost conscious!"

"We have a visitor," Hri Sora responded without looking around.

"A likely story," said Gleamdren with a sniff. "Who would come calling on . . . wait a moment. My suitors! They've arrived!"

"Suitors? No." Hri Sora smiled as she watched the poor captain struggling to get to his feet. "Only one."

"What?" Gleamdren pressed herself up against the bars of her cage, her sulky eyes wide with disbelief. "You're teasing me. I demand you let me see!"

"You can make no demands here," said Hri Sora, turning suddenly. "You are bound by my pleasure, Gleamdrené Gormlaith." Nevertheless, she lifted the cage by its handle, not caring how it swayed. Gleamdren, unbalanced, fell to her hands and knees. "But it is my pleasure," Hri Sora continued, "that you should see." And the dragon carried her prisoner to the edge of the roof and held out her arm.

Gleamdren gasped. She hung suspended over a drop of unbearable length. As the cage swung, she caught glimpses of the red stone so terribly far below. Without the cage, she would not fear. Heights never bothered her little head, and she would gladly cast herself from the highest peaks of Rudiobus Mountain. Such was her nature, flighty as she was. But not in a cage, without freedom of movement. Not with those iron bars surrounding her, pulling her down . . .

But the dragon did not let go. "Look," said Hri Sora.

Gleamdren looked and gasped again as her gaze sped across the miles, seeing over the distance with such unnatural clarity that she felt dizzy. "What are you doing to my eyes?" she demanded.

"Giving you my sight. Behold your suitor, queen's cousin!"

And Gleamdren saw Captain Glomar writhing on the stone street at the city's edge. She frowned, her fear forgotten. "Where are the others?"

"What others?"

"My suitors. Where are the rest of them?"

"There are no others."

"You're wrong. There should be a dozen at least. More, even!"

"Only one." Hri Sora's smile was cruel and cold. "And that one not for long." She raised her other hand, gleaming with long black talons. She snapped her fingers.

Gleamdren saw the movement of darkness deep in the city. The flow of a black shadow that was deeper than shadow, moving like a living animal through the streets. And even at that distance, she heard the baying.

"I have put the Black Dogs on his trail," said Hri Sora. "They'll drive him into my city. He will never find you, Lady Gleamdren. Unless, of course, you tell me what I wish to know."

Gleamdren watched that blackness flowing like spilled ink, drawing ever nearer to where Glomar lay still, clutching his swollen ankle.

"Tell me the secret of the Flowing Gold," hissed the dragon. "Tell me, and I may even now let him go."

The voices of the Dogs were the death tolls on a booming bell.

"Tell me," said Hri Sora. "Tell me what I need!"

Gleamdren's face was pale and cold, as though a piece of her had died as she watched the scene being played out below her. At last she pulled herself to her feet and walked unsteadily across the swaying cage floor to the other side, where she could face the dragon. Though the iron made her dizzy, her small white hands grasped the bars, and she raised her gaze to meet the dragon's as she said:

"I cannot believe there's only one. I have scores of beaux! Are you sure there aren't more knocking at your gates?"

Hri Sora nearly flung the cage over the roof's edge then and there.

12

THEY TRAMPED THROUGH THE FOREST for what seemed both forever and an instant, though the light never changed. All was still, yet Imraldera sensed that life moved through the blurry shadows just beyond the Path she trod behind the poet. Life, and death as well.

How long had it been since she'd last eaten? Since she'd last sipped water that was not ensorcelled? Her steps shortened and she stumbled.

Eanrin whirled about, his eyebrows drawn into an irritable line. "You mortals are such a poorly put together lot, it's a wonder you survive as long as you do! You look as though you're ready to fall into little pieces, and who will be left to pick you up?"

She glared at him but could not suppress a relieved sigh when he continued, "Sit down and rest. This is as safe a place as any. Can't have you fainting on me again, especially once we come to Cozamaloti Gate."

This name meant nothing to Imraldera. But it didn't matter. Though she hated to demonstrate any weakness in front of the Faerie cat, at the word "rest," her knees gave out beneath her, and she sank gratefully into a cushion of soft moss, resting her head on her crooked arm. She was too tired even to sleep.

Eanrin prowled about the periphery of the grove of silver aspens, his long nose sniffing and twitching so that she almost thought him in cat form. "This was a Haven once," he declared at last.

She watched him, offering no response.

"A Haven of the Farthest Shore," he went on, for he never required encouragement to talk. "Built by the Brothers Ashiun, two knights who came to these worlds from across the Final Water. Run down beyond recognition now, isn't it?" he added, tapping one of the tree trunks and shaking his head dismissively. "That's what happens with knights. Everything begins new and shining, the worlds all praising their virtue! It ends like this Haven. Abandoned. Empty."

But Imraldera, her eyes slowly traveling about though she was too tired even to lift her head, saw how gently the trees swayed in some almost imperceptible breeze. There was nothing here to disparage, she thought. Vines climbed the trees, spreading their curtains of many-colored flowers among the branches, including gleaming starflowers. It was wild, but it was beautiful in its very wildness.

Imraldera's breath caught in her throat. In a single instant (very like when she had first seen that the cat was also a man), she saw that the grove was also a chamber. A beautiful round room with walls of dark wood and diamond-shaped windows through which golden light poured upon a floor of green marble. She lay not on a bed of moss but on a pile of silken cushions, their colors faded. Yes, the windows were broken, the marble was chipped, and in many places the ceiling had fallen in, crumbling walls with it. But it was, nevertheless, the richest, the most beautiful room Imraldera had ever seen. More lovely than her wildest dreams could have conjured.

She blinked again, and the vision was gone, replaced by the aspen grove. But the image of what she had seen remained in her head. *This is what holy places should be,* she thought as her eyes slowly closed. *Holiness should be beautiful. Not bloodied.*

A sob caught in her throat. Still lying on her side, she covered her face with her arms, hiding herself. And she fell into fitful dreams.

"Will you let me take your name with me?"

Sun Eagle's eyes are dark as the night, but with a bright golden quality shining in their depths. When he looks at her, she believes he sees her . . . not the lowly woman's child, or the mute servant who must always keep her head down and obey. She thinks he sees who she is, the person hiding inside. The person who longs for a voice.

"It would give me great pride to carry your name. The name of Panther Master's daughter."

Shyly, she holds out her hand. A blue clay bead painted with a white starflower rests in her palm. She offers it to Sun Eagle, who smiles in return.

But his smile melts. His face elongates. And then it is not Sun Eagle who stands before her, but the High Priest.

"You belong to the Beast!"

She runs in the dark. The tunnel closes in, and she cannot breathe the air here. She will suffocate, yet still she must run and run, though the rocks cut her feet and her eyes cannot discern two steps down her path.

Behind her, just at her ear, someone is breathing. . . .

"Wake up, princess. Wake up, I say!"

Imraldera's eyes flew open, and she gasped. She lay in the grove of aspens. Everything around her—the smells, the sounds, the feel of moss beneath her hands—was comforting and safe. Even the sight of that cat-man, his eyes expressing something between concern and irritation, was a relief.

I am far from the Land, she told herself as her racing heart slowly calmed. *I need never return.*

Eanrin, who was on his hands and knees beside her, drew back, his eyes narrowed. "It's time to move on," he said. "Cozamaloti is near, and I can't afford to waste any more time on you."

Despite these harsh words, he offered a hand and helped her to her feet, holding her arm until she had steadied herself. Her muscles ached and her head whirled, for she was still hungry. The cat-man watched her closely.

"Your dreams stink," he said at last, then turned and led her from the Haven, back into the Wood.

A little swing hung from the roof of the iron birdcage. Just a single bar suspended between two delicate threads, but Gleamdren's weight was featherlight, and she balanced on it with ease, swinging back and forth. She held on to a thread with one hand. With the other, she played with a strand of her long flaxen braid, which was coming undone. *"I would behold the luster of her hair,"* she sang under her breath, *"And seek the arms of Lady Gleamdrené."*

Her hair wasn't so lustrous now, was it? After hours and days, weeks, perhaps, without a comb! One by one, she had lost her hairpins, and now only three remained to hold any semblance of style in place. "Not that it matters," she whispered. She huffed a sigh.

In the distance, she heard the howls of the Black Dogs. They were on the move, she guessed. Perhaps Captain Glomar was giving them a bit of a chase, despite that swollen ankle of his. Well, Lumé light his path . . . but it wouldn't do Gleamdren a lot of good if only Glomar showed his sorry face! What kind of reputation could she hope to boast if she returned to Rudiobus with only one of her gallants in tow?

The Dragonwitch, as Gleamdren was beginning to think of her captor, perched on the edge of the flat roof, bundled up like a gargoyle in the tatters of Gleamdren's own nightdress and her lank, colorless hair. She might be watching the city below, feasting upon the sight of the Black Dogs hunting down their helpless prey. More likely, she was asleep. Or at least that version of sleep dragons know: an outwardly frozen stupor while their insides burned.

High towers notwithstanding, Gleamdren decided that captivity was as boring a lot as she'd ever known.

"So I've been thinking," Gleamdren spoke out loud, with little real hope that Hri Sora was listening. "It does seem a bit odd for you to want the Flowing Gold, doesn't it? Queen Vartera wanted it to flatter her vanity—she is a stuck-up pig, for all she's a goblin! Nidawi the Everblooming made a snatch for it once, just for a lark. Even the Mherking tried to find it as a gift to woo Linaherea, the mortal girl he fancied.

"But you? You do nothing for a lark, and I can't imagine you vain. It doesn't make sense, you being so glum and unattractive. My best guess is that you want it as a gift for someone, like the Mherking. Ugly as you are, you probably have some trouble getting a fellow to notice you. Am I not right?" Gleamdren simpered on her swing, patting at her limp hair. "I'm something of an expert in these things! So yes, I think that must be what this is all about. But it's not that knight you were in love with long ago, is it? I remember the story from the *Ballad of the Brothers Ashiun*. He died, didn't he? Or his brother did. I can never keep it straight."

The swing creaked as it swung, the only sound besides Gleamdren's prattle and the distant howls of the Dogs. The Dragonwitch herself might have been a stone gargoyle for all she moved or responded.

"But you don't want the gift for the knight." Gleamdren licked her lips. She was playing with fire, she knew. "You mentioned someone else a while back, when you were having one of your . . . fits. You want the gold for this Amarok, don't you?"

The explosion was beyond what Gleamdren expected. The blast of it knocked her from her swing. She had the good sense to curl up in a ball and tremble as waves of heat and smoke rolled over the little birdcage. When at last she dared look up, she was surrounded in such a thick cloud of black, she could have sworn the Black Dogs themselves had descended upon her.

Instead, two burning eyes cut through the smoke. Hri Sora gazed in at her captive.

"There is only one gift I will ever give Amarok," she said.

When the smoke finally cleared, Gleamdren was alone atop the roof under the blistering sun of Etalpalli.

Give her back! Give her back to me!

Eanrin heard the voice of the River long before he saw it. This stretch of the Wood was otherwise silent, as though the trees themselves were afraid of attracting the River's notice. The poet-cat shivered at the voice.

They were drawing near to Cozamaloti. He had never seen the gate before, did not know what it might look like. But he had passed in and out of many realms of Faerie in his day, sniffed out dozens upon dozens of hidden gates. He knew the signs and smells. And he knew that Cozamaloti was near, possibly on the edge of the River itself.

But they could not hope to pass through the gate without the River's compliance.

"Iubdan's beard," he swore, pausing in midstep, his nose high, his tail low (for he was in cat form at the moment). He'd hoped the River would have forgotten Imraldera by now. A vain hope; rivers have long memories.

He looked back at the girl. Her head was down, and she moved slowly, though always just keeping pace with him. Despite the few hours' rest he'd allowed her at the Haven, her eyes were glassy with fatigue. She didn't seem to understand the River's voice. That should make things easier.

The trees tended to point as the two made their way along the Path, especially the aspens, which are terrible gossips as it is. The girl was a sight, Eanrin had to admit. So dirty, her hair a mess of twigs and leaves, the rough-skin dress she wore torn at the hem. At least her face was lovely.

The cat swore again. What was he doing? Never in all the centuries of his life had he considered altering course to help a mortal creature! Much less allowing one to shadow his footsteps like this. Even now, if he stopped and truly thought about it, everyone would be much better off if he left her here. After all, dragging her along to the River was no end of dangerous for her, but he couldn't, for Gleamdren's sake, turn aside from his own quest. No, it would be much better to slip away now, to vanish into the shadows and let her learn to fend for herself.

It was all the fault of the Hound. They said, when once you saw him, your life was forever changed.

"Dragon's teeth and tail!" the cat whispered through his fangs. "Changed, like the Brothers Ashiun, no doubt. And look what happened to them. Dead. Or disgraced. And they, so noble! I'll be dragon-kissed before I follow in their footsteps."

Imraldera stumbled.

Eanrin, before his reason could catch up with his reflexes, took on his man form and caught her. Her hands gripped his sleeves as though they were her final lifeline, and her face pressed into the front of his doublet. An almost inaudible moan escaped her lips, cutting him to the quick.

"Steady, Imraldera," he murmured, gently setting her back upright. "Steady."

The girl shook herself and stepped back from him. She signed something he did not understand but which he guessed from her face to mean, "I'm fine on my own!" A bold-faced lie, but at least the creature had spirit.

"We're nearly to the falls," Eanrin told her. He rubbed a hand uncomfortably down the back of his neck. Why did he still feel the warmth of her hands gripping his arms? A strange sensation, not altogether unpleasant, but utterly terrifying. "When we get to the River, be sure to stay close beside me. Not too close, mind! Don't get in my way. But . . . well, do not touch the water. Understand?"

She nodded. Her gaze met his, eye for eye. She seemed to be daring him to try something. What, he could not guess. To coddle her? To treat her like a helpless kitten? Well, was it his fault if that's just what she was?

"Keep up," he said in almost a growl.

The voice of the River was unmistakable now. *Give her back to me!* it roared, and Eanrin guessed they must be near indeed to the falls. Weeping willows grew thickly here, at the water's edge. He parted a curtain of trailing leaves, gazed out, and nearly turned back then and there.

He had not realized that Cozamaloti Gate, the only entrance to Etalpalli, was on the very brink of a waterfall.

Imraldera, curious to see why the poet, even in his man's shape, bristled from head to toe, pressed up behind him and, standing on tiptoe, peered over his shoulder. She gasped at the sight that met her eyes. She had seen waterfalls in the Land before, places where the rivers met and rushed white over steep drops, and she had thought them beautiful. But nothing in the Land compared to this. A vision of absolute power. The beauty of it, the awfulness made her tremble. For a moment, she was thankful—she would change nothing from her previous life and risk losing the chance to gaze upon something as marvelous as Cozamaloti.

"Well," said Eanrin through dry lips, "that's certainly more than I expected. Is that a bridge?"

Suspended across the brink of the falls, attached by ropes to tree trunks on either side of the River, was a rope bridge of a sort. Its fibers were frayed, and many of the planks along the walk were rotted and broken. It swung above that mist-shrouded chasm, stirred by even the slightest breeze.

And just beyond the brink, just where the water took its final gasp before making that plunge, was the invisible Faerie gate.

Eanrin drew a long breath. That was an awful lot of water. He did not care for water.

"Mighty deeds await," he told himself. "Fair Gleamdren must be rescued . . . and besides, no one ever called a cat a coward!"

Imraldera gave the poet a look. When he started his descent to the bridge, she caught his sleeve. "What are you doing?" she signed when he looked back.

"Come along, sweet princess. We must reclaim my true love, which means taking the dive." Eanrin continued down, calling over his shoulder as he went, "My one comfort is that Glomar could not possibly have gone before me! I cannot imagine the faithful badger working up the nerve to jump off the bridge, for all his noble intentions. We've got the advantage, Imraldera, my girl, I feel it in my whiskers!"

Imraldera's jaw dropped. *Jump off the . . . No!*

She latched onto the branches of a weeping willow, bracing herself as though afraid that, by sheer force of will, Eanrin would draw her after himself. There was no chance she was going anywhere near that bridge.

Eanrin stepped onto the rotting boards and fraying ropes, the River roaring beneath him, its words drowned out by its own noise. Taking cat form for better balance, the poet slinked out to the middle and, his ears flat, crept to the edge.

"Oh, Great Lights preserve us!" he gasped and drew back his pink nose, pressing his orange body flat.

The River laughed at him.

Yet Eanrin was no coward. He was simply bracing for the proper spring. Any moment now, his muscles would flex, his paws would gracefully clear the ropes, his body arching elegantly as he soared over that death drop and landed on his feet (as a cat must) in the demesne of Hri Sora. He could see it all in his mind, a leap worthy of epics!

He was simply preparing himself. That was all.

He realized suddenly that Imraldera was not beside him. His whiskers quivering (along with the rest of his body), he looked back up to the bank. There she stood, staring after him with those wide eyes. Coward indeed! At least he'd had the nerve to venture this far! That little mortal, living forever in fear of her own imminent death, hadn't made a single step down. Serve her right if he left her there, leapt into Etalpalli, and continued his quest alone. And that's just what he would do.

As soon as he was ready.

Maybe a quick groom was in order? After all, one doesn't want to step into a foreign demesne looking shabby, especially not when on a mission of rescue.

The River moved.

Of course the River was in constant motion, flowing and churning and rushing to this moment of cascade. But this was a movement unnatural to rivers. It swarmed up the side of the bank, a long, sinuous, grasping arm.

Mine! it roared in a voice mortal ears would not understand. *Mine!*

Eanrin gasped. The next moment he was a man clutching the bridge's rope to balance himself as he shouted, "Run! Imraldera, *run!*"

She could not hear him. She could see him shouting and waving his arm, his cloak flapping like a warning flag. But she could not hear him.

And she did not see the River's arm until it wrapped around her legs.

Eanrin saw her mouth open in a silent scream. Then she was gone, dragged down the bank in a moment, vanishing into the churning white water. He stared, gasping as though it had been he who was dragged beneath the deathly waters, his mind unable to accept what his eyes saw.

For an instant, her dark, matted head surfaced. She vanished again, only to reappear moments later. Her desperate arms reached out, grabbing at a boulder. The River tried to smash her against it, but instead she was able to wrap herself around it, holding on. The River was cruel. It pressed her, harried her, battered at her. She could not hold on long.

The falls waited.

In a flash, Eanrin saw the only escape appear before his mind's eye. Only one instant to decide.

Then he was hauling himself over the side of the bridge farthest from the falls. The River pulled, and Imraldera lost her grasp, disappearing once more into the foam.

"I hate water," Eanrin growled. Then he jumped.

His fall seemed to take forever. But it ended suddenly as he plunged through roiling whiteness into black depths. The pull of the falls was incredible, and he thought he would never break the surface.

Yet Imraldera's head popped above the water just as his did. Her eyes locked with his in a moment of terror.

MINE! the River roared.

Eanrin reached out and grabbed tight hold of Imraldera's shoulder. Then they were on the brink. Eanrin had just enough air in his lungs to scream, *"Etalpalli!"*

Cozamaloti hauled them down.

13

A VOICE RUSHES *in her ears. The voice of the River.*
Pretty maid, be mine! Mine!

How silly. Rivers do not speak the tongues of men. But then, many incredible things have happened around her. No world exists beyond the Land. Yet when she left the mountain circle, had she not fled into this very forest? Animals cannot speak with intelligent words. Yet had she not conversed with the cat? Or perhaps it is one long nightmare.

Pretty maid, be mine!

The words tumble through her mind with the power of the waterfall. Then they transform, and it is no longer the River she hears snarling on the edge of her consciousness.

"You were always meant to be mine."

"No," she pleads, but no one hears her, for she has no voice. "No, please . . ."

"Wet! Wet! Wet! *Wet!*"

Imraldera opened her eyes and found that she lay on bone-dry stone, her soaking hair heavy around her. So she wasn't dead. Every muscle in her body remained tensed for impact, but otherwise she could discern no hurts. Except she could not breathe.

When her lungs heaved, she rolled over and coughed up a fountain of river water. It darkened the red stone underneath her to deep brown. She kept on coughing and retching until she thought she must heave up all her insides. But at last she stopped and lay immobile, her face pressed into the dark patch of stone.

There was no waterfall, no River. Sucking in a great lungful of air, she pushed herself up onto her elbows and pulled back her dripping hair. Sniffling and sputtering still, she looked around for the poet. Being a cat, he had landed on all fours, of course, and was shaking his feline body with such violence she thought his legs might drop off. He paused to give his paw a lick, then shook again, dappling the stones with droplets. He looked like a large, orange, waterlogged rat, all his fluff plastered to him.

"Ugh. *Reeeeowl.*" He swore in cat and Faerie tongue and set to grooming his bedraggled tail. "My coat is ruined. My life is over."

Imraldera, her breath beginning to come in more normal draughts, sat up slowly, drawing her knees beneath her. Her eyes could not have grown larger as she struggled to take in what she saw.

They were no longer in the Wood Between.

The towers of Etalpalli were blistered by heat on the outside.

Inside, they were full of palpable shadows.

Hri Sora sat in the darkness inside Omeztli, hiding from her own prisoner, that wretched Faerie maid who knew Amarok's name. Oh, how could she have let that slip? Trust the little gnat to pester and harp on it! Bite, bite, bite—she could worry even a dragon to death! Hri Sora would devour the creature if she dared.

But she could not risk Queen Bebo's wrath. Nor this one chance to find the Flowing Gold.

She clutched herself into a ball, rocking slowly back and forth. The shadows did not frighten her. They were shielding, so different from her fire. In here, no one could see her shame. No one could see her without her wings.

Outside, the children were brawling.

Wait. That could not be true. It was only the sound of the Black Dogs chasing that intruder. She was in Etalpalli. She was in her own city, not back in that dark, dank little hut in the mortal world. She was queen here. Queen over nothing but the ghosts of her people, yet queen even so.

But she heard them just outside, scuffling. Their voices raised in battle against each other.

Hri Sora rocked herself, her mind slipping in and out of the present as the fire inside flickered, rose, diminished, and flickered again. Her dragon mind was precarious without the appropriate body in which to house it. Time itself could not hold her. She was simultaneously in Etalpalli and in . . .

. . . her prison.

Outside, the children snarl like the little beasts they are, flailing in the dirt, bashing each other's faces. They will come to her when they are through, full of cuts and bruises, expecting her sympathy.

The fire roils in her gut. How long has she suppressed it, here in this world full of mortal stench? How long has she believed herself one of these decaying creatures of dirt? For years now, the fire of her dragonhood has stirred so faintly that she hasn't noticed it. But now it grows. And with it grows her memory.

"I . . . I am no woman," she gasps. Smoke escapes her mouth.

If only those children would stop their squabbling!

She sits in a hut high in the mountains. It is dark. She should light a fire. Her man will be home soon, expecting a meal. But her fire circle lies empty, the ashes cold. A fresh kill is piled against the outside wall, undressed, swarmed over with flies. She can smell it, the stink of mortality. Her throat constricts and she gags.

"I hate this world," she murmurs.

Someone outside, one of her young, yelps in pain as its sibling catches it with a hard hit. Monsters! She hopes they'll eat each other up and never bother her again.

A groan escapes her lips, cut off abruptly by a sharp hiss. Her eyes bulge, and in the darkness of that mountain hut, they gleam like two bright coals. The pain, the fire in her gut—it threatens to explode.

The children fall silent. Drawing a deep breath, she smells the reason. Their father has returned, reeking from the hunt. She hears his heavy breathing as he approaches the hut, hears the soft scramble of her young as they hasten out of his way.

Then he is at the door.

"Woman!"

His voice is a growl.

She sees him silhouetted against the dusk. His shoulders are broad, his hands enormous as they grasp the doorway on either side as though to bar her passage. But she makes no move to escape her prison. She sits on the hut floor, in the dirt, in the dark, her teeth clenched.

"Woman, how can you let our brood tear into each other so?"

Her gaze rises to meet his.

The shadow of his form draws back in surprise. "What— No, swallow it back!"

The woman gasps as though breathing for the first time in years. Then she speaks:

"Swallow what back, Amarok? My words? Or my fire?"

Her jaw drops, and flames pour from her throat.

Fire lit up the walls of her tower, and Hri Sora was once more back in Etalpalli. Her flames hurled themselves against the stone and died ineffectually as they struck and found no hold. With difficulty she swallowed them. The last embers fell and sizzled upon the floor, leaving her standing once more in darkness but in possession of her true mind.

Or so she hoped. It was so difficult these days to tell past from present, waking from dreaming.

Etalpalli trembled.

Someone else had entered her city. Someone she had not herself opened the gate to. Which meant someone had actually dived over the edge of Cozamaloti Falls in its true form.

She snarled and felt her way to the wall, searching with hands and feet until she found the narrow stairway. The Sky People had never used stairs when they lived in Etalpalli. Why would they? But they had built crude stairwells out of courtesy to foreign guests who were not blessed with wings. Hri Sora had always sneered at these. Now she found herself painfully grateful. Otherwise she, the city's queen, would have been unable to access her own tower.

Lady Gleamdren's voice was a canary's twitter coming from the birdcage in the middle of the rooftop. Hri Sora ignored her, striding to the edge of the roof and looking out. She saw the dark patch in her otherwise flame-bright city where the Black Dogs still pursued that luckless captain. This did not interest her. They would catch him eventually. They always did.

But who had dared cross her boundaries without her knowledge? Only one of great courage. Someone powerful.

She saw them, there at the edge of her city. She frowned.

"What are you looking at, Dragonwitch?" Gleamdren cried, her chirpy voice setting Hri Sora's teeth on edge. "Have they caught poor Glomar?"

"We have more visitors," the dragon replied.

"*Really?*" Gleamdren could not have been more delighted. "I *knew* they would come at last! How many? Oh, I do wish I had a mirror and some sort of comb. I'll be such a wreck by the time they get here! I can't wait to see their dear faces when they realize what peril I am in. Such a battle it will be! I do hope Eanrin has come along so he can put it all down in verse."

"It is the poet," said Hri Sora. Her eyes were mere slits as they pierced the distance. "I recognize him, for he came to me in the Wood and nearly saw through my glamour. By some miracle, that selfish rat has now entered my world. But who . . . who is that with him?"

"Might be Sir Danu. He pretends indifference, but I know he's quite mad about me. A girl always knows. Or it could be young Rogan, such a favorite—"

"It is a woman."

"A *what?*"

Hri Sora hissed, and smoke twirled in the air as it rose from her nostrils. She studied the maid crouched on the stone beside the poet.

She took in her clothing, her skin, her hair. And when the girl raised her face and seemed to look across the long miles, straight at Hri Sora, the dragon gasped.

The girl was from the Hidden Land.

"Silent woman!" Hri Sora snarled. Fire dripped from her tongue.

All was red stone around them. At first, Imraldera could have sworn she and the poet had landed inside a deep red canyon. But when she blinked the water out of her eyes, she saw that the rocks formed towering buildings, windows and doors and spires and balconies, all stretching to the seared sky as though they would touch the heavens. The stone blocks of which they were made fit so seamlessly together that each structure might have been chiseled from a single huge boulder. Carvings of feathers and wings in patterns more complex than she could discern wrapped around each tower and formed the banisters of stairways and balconies.

Imraldera had never seen anything like this place. Her mouth moved in a soundless prayer to some unknown god. Then, with a moan, she covered her face with her hands. The air was so hot that her wet skin and hair steamed. Her clothes shrank and shriveled as they dried, smelling almost as bad as the sodden cat.

"Well," said Eanrin, "I must say I'm relieved." He didn't look relieved. He looked a sight. Even when he took his man form, his appearance did not improve. His bright red cap had lost all shape, and his cloak and clothes looked uncomfortably damp in that sultry air. He fumbled with the buckles and let the cloak drop to the stone cobbles, all the while looking about him. His nose twitched as he sniffed. "I was uncertain what to expect at that gate. This place was once known as the City of Wings, and the Sky People lived here. They had wings sprouting from their shoulders, if you can believe it. Wings! Great, shimmering feathers. Or so I'm told. I never saw them. And naturally, being winged, they flew everywhere. I half wondered if Cozamaloti Gate would open into empty sky . . . which would have been the worse luck for us today. We'd have had a hard landing!"

Imraldera wiped her face, now wet with perspiration. The city, as far as she could see, was dry. Nothing had grown here for decades.

The poet-cat added his outer doublet to the discarded cape, leaving only a thin white shirt and breeches beneath. "All my beauty stripped," he sighed with a forlorn shake of his head. "What has my life become? But all and more for the sake of my beloved! She owes me a new hat."

He shook his hair one last time. It was nearly dry already and standing out like straw all around his face, which made him seem quite wild. But he smiled and strode over to Imraldera, offering his hand. "Up, up, my girl. Hymlumé spare me, but you smell a fright! We must away ere darkness falls. These streets will be perilous at night."

Imraldera accepted his hand but frowned at his words. The sky was red, not with sunset but with burning heat, as though it had been wounded by fire and never recovered. It was hard to imagine night falling in a place such as this.

She turned to the cat-man. "You jumped to save me," she signed.

"Stop all the hand waving. It looks perfectly ridiculous, and you know I don't understand."

Imraldera bit her lip uncertainly. In all the terror that was her life, she must cling to those few good things: to memories of a little girl wrapping skinny arms around her neck; a house on a hill; and a gray lurcher standing in the yard, eyes fixed on the road, waiting for her mistress. The good things were so rare, so precious.

Now added to their number was a cat-man who looked and spoke like a buffoon, but who had risked his life for her, perhaps more than once.

More for herself than for him, she signed: "Though I am a stranger, you have been a true friend. I am grateful. I will help you find your beloved. I swear on the—I swear on my hand. Before I try to find my own way in this awful world of yours, I will help you, Bard Eanrin. I will rescue your lady Gleamdren."

He watched her hands fly, his quick eyes moving to follow them. Then he laughed and caught them between his own palms. "Enough, I say! You look like a clown when you flail about so. We must get moving." Keeping hold of one of Imraldera's hands as though she were but a child, the poet strode down the narrow street as confidently as if he owned the place. Such is the way with cats.

Imraldera cast a backward glance over her shoulder at the pile of scarlet clothing steaming on the stones. But they turned a corner, and she saw them no more. Despite the heat, a cold sensation inched up her spine. She felt as though, when they turned that corner, the street they'd walked but a moment before had vanished entirely. Not merely from view but from existence.

There were no doors on the lower levels that Imraldera could see. There were, however, tall windows at least three times Eanrin's height. These were set high but within reach if Imraldera were to jump. Although the sky was bright and the red stone glared almost blindingly, deep shadows lurked within the towers.

Imraldera looked at the street they followed, winding among the red buildings. Every turn it took seemed to her much like the turn before. She wondered if they were going in circles. But when she took time to study the carvings adorning the towers, she saw that each one was unique, as though carved by a different hand. No two buildings they passed boasted the same arrangement of feathers or clouds. They were as individual as faces, and beautiful too. So they couldn't be going in circles.

The buildings cast no shadows.

Imraldera realized this truth rather suddenly. Already it felt as though they had wandered the streets of the empty city for hours. How could one sense the passage of time in a world that cast no shadows? Everything was wrong. When she looked ahead, she could not make heads or tails of the street. Did it extend forever, or only a few paces? Was that a turn coming up, or did it continue straight? Everything was distorted. Straight lines waved before her eyes. And everywhere was blistering red stone.

Her stomach clenched, and she gagged, doubling over. But she was empty inside, and nothing could relieve the churning in her gut. She could only stand, bent over and panting.

Eanrin dropped his hold on her hand and stood aside, his arms folded. "Poor creature," he muttered. Then he firmly shook that thought away. After all, she deserved what she got, fool mortal, for venturing into worlds where she didn't belong! Served her right if she found the ways of Faerie beyond bearing.

And yet, there he went, stepping to her side once more and gently putting a hand on her shoulder. He should be taken by the scruff and shaken until his teeth rattled!

"It's all right," he heard his own voice saying, no matter how he struggled against it. "This place would be difficult for anyone. There's hardly a soul in Faerie who could walk these streets and not feel a hint of what you're experiencing right now. Perhaps my good Queen Bebo, but few others. It's a nasty city. The Flame at Night has wounded it to its heart. Even the ground is unstable."

Imraldera shuddered when she breathed. She was, Eanrin realized, probably hungry and parched as well. He recalled hearing somewhere that mortals could not go for as long without food or drink as the folk of Faerie might. Her face was drenched and gleaming with sweat and her eyes were dull.

"Look, we're getting nowhere like this," he said, wrapping an arm across her shoulders and helping her to stand once more. She swayed and leaned heavily against him. "Come," he said, supporting her as she walked, "let's get you inside one of these towers. Then I'll climb to the top, yes? And get a good scout out of the city."

She rallied at these words and shook her head. But he clucked dismissively. "Never fear, princess! I know what I'm doing. Am I not the Chief Poet of Iubdan Rudiobus, renowned throughout Faerie for my heroic verse? One cannot write that much heroic verse without learning a thing or two about heroics. This is a good plan, I tell you."

While he talked, he led her to the nearest of the towers. Like all the others, its windows opened into nothing but blackness beyond, and there were no doors. Eanrin leaned Imraldera against the red wall. The stone was hot but not unbearably so. Then he scrambled up onto the windowsill and peered into the shadows. He saw nothing, smelled nothing. "Seems fine enough," he lied through a charming smile.

Imraldera glared up at him.

"All right, all right, let me just . . ." Holding on to the windowsill, he leaned into the shadows.

They were thick, almost tangible. As though all the shadows of the outer city had taken refuge inside, allowing no light to enter. Eanrin took a deep breath. His sunny disposition disliked all that darkness, yet he transformed into a cat and hopped down inside.

For a split second, he felt as though he would fall forever. But he landed on all fours on a solid floor below the window. His cat's eyes, skilled at seeing in the dark, took a moment to adjust. Then he saw that the room was empty. And it was, he realized the next moment, vast.

Not in circumference. In floor space it was no greater than his own modest bedchamber back in Rudiobus. But in height, he could not begin to guess its dimensions. The shadows concealed details, but he got an impression of . . . perches. Of landings and chambers without passages between, without stairs. This was a world intended for those with wings.

He sniffed and prowled the ground floor, finding nothing of interest. It should be safe enough for the mortal girl to hide here while he scaled the outer wall and took stock of their surroundings. With this conclusion in mind, the cat stood up into his man's form again. It took several attempted leaps and a certain amount of ungraceful scrambling before he gained enough purchase on the windowsill to pull himself up out of the shadows. He recovered himself on the sill, smoothing back his hair, and smiled down at the girl.

Only she was gone.

14

WHEN THE BLACK DOGS HUNT, they never stop until their quarry is found, or so rumor would have it. Glomar saw no reason to doubt that rumor as he hobbled down the twisting streets of the firstborn's city.

They were always just behind him, just one bend away. If he dared a glance back, he saw the looming Midnight that always followed in their wake and knew it as the shadow of his own doom.

But Glomar was a man of Rudiobus, and fear was unknown to him. So he staunchly limped on, groping the hot stone walls for support, swinging his bad leg and stretching his good one for all it was worth. Lights Above, what a jump that had been! He'd been right after all in thinking the little two-foot trickle was a deception. Trust your instincts . . . how often had he pounded that maxim into the heads of trainee guardsmen? Your instincts are a better guide than your reason nine times out of ten!

He took badger form. While not swift, this shape at least gave four legs to hobble on rather than two. Panting, he rounded yet another bend in that shadowless world. Perhaps he'd not escape the Dogs . . . not in the end. But he would find Lady Gleamdren and deliver her before they got him! He was Iubdan's man, and failure was not part of his vocabulary.

He took the turn and met a Dog nose to nose.

The Midnight swarmed in to surround him.

※

The Dragonwitch smiled. The Black Dogs had done as she asked. She reached out to them across the distance, calling into the dark recesses of their minds.

"Find the poet," she said. "And the maid."

"Maid? Hmph!"

Gleamdren pressed her face against the iron bars of her cage, little caring how dizzy they made her. Her stomach churned with something much more potent than dizziness.

"How *dare* he bring a maiden on a rescue?" she muttered. "Eanrin. Of all people! What happened to those romantic verses of his?"

She was so angry, she thought she might split in two!

So the dragon watched the story play out in the streets, and her captive watched the dragon. And they were watched only by an empty, burning sky.

※

The moment he disappeared through the window, Imraldera knew the poet was not coming back. Whether he had vanished from the world entirely, she could not guess. This world was unlike her own. The rules of nature were different, if rules existed at all.

Imraldera stared up at the windowsill, where a cat had sat just the moment before. Not for the first time in her life, she wished for the ability to scream. Not, she rationalized, that it would do much good. But it might *feel* good.

As it was, she could only stand there and stare as the silence pressed in upon her, both inside and out. How, by the stone teeth, had she come to this?

Almost without her realizing it, her fingers made signs of grief, of passing. Perhaps they were useless. After all, she could not know if the poet-cat was alive or dead. She only knew he would not come back. So she made the signs traditional to her people, her hands moving fluidly through the hot air.

"May he walk safely through the void beyond the mountains," she said. Then she added a sign she had been taught, not by the High Priest or the underpriests, but by her mother long ago, when she was a little girl. "And may the Songs sing him to life."

Tears blurred her eyes. How many times had she made these signs in her lifetime? For her mother. For Sun Eagle. For her father . . .

Had Fairbird remembered to add that last line for her?

Shaking herself, Imraldera dashed tears from her eyes. She was the daughter of Panther Master. She must not weep. She had vowed to the poet-cat that she would find his ladylove before she gave thought to her own troubles, and find her she would, or die as she was meant to die.

Turning away from the window and back to the streets, she forced her mind to review what Eanrin had told her of Etalpalli . . . a dragon . . . Gleamdren . . . It all tangled up in her mind. Her head was light with hunger, and her eyes blurred, though whether from heat or fear she could not have said. Part of her wanted to curl up in a ball and let the heat melt her away into nothing. Instead, she found herself walking. What was the good of waiting under a window? She would fulfill no vows that way. She must find a way to solve the puzzle of these tortuous streets.

Her thirst was great and she stumbled as she went. When was the last time she'd eaten? The wafers fed her by the priest . . . but no! She would not think of that. That was another time, another world entirely.

The street bent.

It was a sudden, jerking movement that threw her off balance. Imraldera landed on her hands and knees, stunned. For a moment her head whirled, and she thought she would be sick. Then her stomach settled, just as the street did.

She raised her face and found that she was surrounded by thick, black Midnight.

It was the darkness of a night without a moon, that hour when children awake in their beds, terrified because the sunset is long gone and sunrise far away. There is no escape from such darkness. All one can do is wait and hope.

Imraldera found she'd had enough of waiting.

Grinding her teeth, she scrambled back to her feet. Her knees were scraped and one palm bled. She did not care. She'd already sat once in moonless darkness on the top of that mountain. No more! She would keep moving until she dropped.

The only sound was the slap of her bare feet on cobbles still hot to the touch. The street now stretched before her without turn or bend, and it was too dark for her to make out either its beginning or its end. It was as though the city itself had decided upon her path and shaped it for her.

A sob rattled across the silent stones.

The sound startled her, and she backed up against one of the tower walls; having rock at her back was somehow comforting. She strained her ears. Sure enough, a second sob followed the first, and this one gave her some idea of the direction. It was a pitiful sound made by a small voice. She should be afraid, she knew. This darkness was dreadful, this world more dreadful still. She should be cowering, running for her life.

But the sound wasn't one she could fear.

Picking her way quietly down the street, walking on her toes so as to make no noise, she followed the sobs. At length her searching eyes made out a form sitting in one of the high windowsills. *Eanrin?* Her heart leapt with the hope. Then she realized that the sobs came from this creature, and the voice was not the poet's.

It was a child.

The instant Imraldera recognized this, the Midnight vanished. It was as sudden as snuffing out a candle, only the opposite. One moment, she stood in darkness. The next, blistering red sky leered down at her. The abrupt shift hurt her eyes, and she shielded them with both hands.

When at last she dared look again, she saw the child still perched in the window. One thin leg dangled down the wall; the other rested up on the sill. The little urchin was so thin and underfed as to have lost almost all traces of childhood. Boy or girl, Imraldera could not guess. It covered its face with bony hands and sobbed its heart out.

Imraldera wished yet again that she had a voice. She could only stand and watch. Even if she could speak, what could she do to ease such painful sorrow? This little one's heart was broken. And there was nothing worse, she knew, than a brokenhearted child.

Suddenly, as though it felt her gaze, its hands dropped away. A pinched, wolfish face turned to her, and Imraldera saw how its eyes gleamed yellow. They were animal eyes.

She recognized them.

Her heart stopped beating where she stood. She might as well be dead. That animal gaze held her in place. Then the child bared its teeth and snarled. With an agile leap, it landed on all fours in the street, crouched and emaciated. The sob was replaced by a low growl.

Imraldera swallowed and discovered her heart once more—it raced double-time. But when the child advanced, still moving on its hands and feet in a grotesque crouch, Imraldera advanced as well. She did not break its gaze. It snarled again, half lunging. She showed her teeth and took another step forward, still not shifting her eyes.

With a wolfish yell, the child barreled at her legs. Imraldera leapt to one side, caught it by the back of the neck, and pushed it firmly to the ground, holding it there. The child roared and howled and flailed its limbs, but though it struck Imraldera several times, she did not let go. She braced herself, pressing into the little one's back as well as its neck. As it struggled, she clucked to it gently, sounds she had once made to her baby sister. The only sounds she could make, as natural and mild as wind-murmuring branches in a tree.

She could not guess how long it took; at last, however, the child ceased struggling. Sweat dripped down Imraldera's forehead. But she did not move. The little urchin lay perfectly still for some time. Then softly, it moaned. The sound was not human. Imraldera hadn't expected it to be.

Carefully, she loosened her grip and sat back. The child scrambled up, sitting cross-legged with its hands planted on the ground before it.

It shook its head, and even this close, Imraldera could not guess its sex. It turned those snapping yellow eyes upon her, head tilted to one side.

Very slowly, Imraldera put out her hand, palm up. The child leaned forward and sniffed. Half expecting to be bitten, Imraldera leaned in and gently ran her hand along the top of the little one's head, down around behind its ear. The child blinked. It pushed into her hand, still whining, still panting.

Then, much to Imraldera's surprise, it crawled forward, climbed into her lap, and immediately fell asleep. Imraldera scarcely dared to breathe. She wrapped her arms around the scrawny limbs, feeling every bone in the creature's body. Tears formed in her eyes and escaped in swift drops down her cheeks.

Poor thing, she thought, rocking gently to and fro, as a mother rocks her newborn. *Poor, loveless little thing.*

"I must be mistaken."

Hri Sora stood transfixed upon her roof, watching the scene being played out on the streets of Etalpalli. She could not believe her eyes. The fire in her breast flared in her fury at such a picture of tenderness enacted in this place of death. She gnashed her teeth and tore at her own hair, leaving lines of blood streaming through the lank strands.

"I must be mistaken!" she raged. "How can a woman of the Land be . . . be compassionate to one of them? The little monsters! The little fiends! They have *his* eyes, yet she stretches out her hand to them?"

The fire boiled like sickness inside. She doubled over and vomited flame and ashes that fell from the rooftop down to the street below, burning the stones black.

15

"IT SERVES ME RIGHT. I should never have become involved."

Eanrin sat on the windowsill, looking up and down the street. Iubdan's beard! He had turned his back for two minutes! Why were mortals incapable of staying put?

This was unfair, though he hated to admit it. Though the streets of Etalpalli had a tendency to look alike, he knew that this street was not the one he had left only a few moments before. Things had shifted when his back was turned. That, or the room he had just explored was some sort of portal, rather like the Faerie Paths themselves, only smaller and undirected. He should have guessed. He should have known when he sniffed those heavy shadows that they would cut him off from his companion.

What if something happened to her? A lonely mortal without guide or direction in this place of empty ghosts . . .

"Not your business!" he snapped at himself, leaping down into the street. "You should have left her by the River to begin with. How many times have I told you? Thank the Lights Above you lost the girl at last! Good riddance, I say!"

He started up the street, paused after two steps, turned, and started back down. Crouching and becoming a cat, he sniffed and strained his ears, searching. But the street was absolutely empty, without a trace of Imraldera. The girl had never been here.

"Dragon's teeth," the cat hissed. He sat and wrapped his tail tightly about his front paws, ears turned back and looking so much like horns that he could have been a fluffy orange devil. He closed his eyes the better to listen, the better to smell, the better to sense with that strange sixth sense of cats that would alert him to any other nearby soul.

But there was nothing.

"This is the way it will always be," he growled, still with his eyes closed. "This is what you must expect when the Hound hunts. You'll be driven to Paths you never chose, driven to duties you never wanted. And then, it will all fall apart about your ears! Give in once, and you're doomed. Allow yourself to care, and—"

Here he snarled, and his eyes opened wide. "I got attached. Me. *Attached!* Lumé, Eanrin, you should know better! Look what happened to others who've walked the Paths of the Lumil Eliasul. Look at Etanun: All those holy places burned! Look at Akilun: Killed at his brother's hand! Renowned hero to despised villain within a generation. And where are you left at the end?"

He listened. He strained all his cat senses as though waiting for an answer to this question. But none came. With a sigh, he got to his feet. "He drives us until he's through, then he abandons us. Such is his way. Well, he's driven you, Eanrin, into this burned demesne, though it's unlikely you'll see him here. And thank the Lights for that!"

It flashed across his mind that it had been his own idea to come to Etalpalli; also, that he would never have passed through the gate had he not first met the mortal girl on the River. How could he ever have worked up the nerve to jump had he not been compelled for her sake? Cozama-loti would have remained as barred to him as were the doors of heaven.

He owed the girl much.

Silence surrounded him. With a shake and a flick of his tail, he turned back into a man, picked a direction, and started down the street. "If Imraldera wants to wander off and get herself killed," he muttered, "so be it. It's not my business. I'm a good fellow, and I will rescue my lady Gleamdren just as I intended. No more involving myself in strangers' business. She can live her life, and I will live mine. Never again to—"

He turned a corner and stepped from daylight into darkness in a single stride. He drew a sharp breath, his nostrils flaring. He knew what this darkness was. It was not like the palpable shadows hiding within the towers. This was Midnight.

His cat's eyes blinked once and drew in what light they could. But he still heard before he saw the Black Dog. A low growl rattled the core of Eanrin's bones.

If there was one thing he hated more than water, it was dogs.

He turned and ran. Enormous teeth snapped shut in the place his head had been an instant before. Baying, like a hundred voices all in one, filled his ears, and he fled down the streets of Etalpalli, racing with the daylight.

Midnight and the Dog followed two steps behind.

The child snored in Imraldera's arms. How it could sleep in this heat, she could not begin to understand. Her arms, chest, and neck were sticky with sweat where the little one's body pressed up against her. But she did not try to put it down. For one thing, she could not guess at the consequences.

For another, the creature was so affection starved, how could she bear to withhold what little she could offer? She felt the child eating it up, draining kindness from her in its need. And still she rocked it back and forth, clucking and pressing her cheek to the little one's dirty black hair. The child stirred, and its moans were inarticulate but full of meaning. It nuzzled its head under her chin, pressing its cheek to her breast.

Oh, Fairbird . . .

Sweat and tears mingled on her cheeks, and her grip unconsciously tightened about the bony little body.

The child woke. Every muscle tensed, it stared up at her with its wolfish eyes. For half a moment, Imraldera was afraid. She saw the gleam of teeth and felt the strength in those scrawny limbs.

But the child merely leapt from her arms, spinning about on the red stones and shaking as though released from a cage. And when it turned to her again, it wore a great smile upon its face. The teeth gleamed. They were sharp. Yet the smile was real.

Prancing like a puppy, the little one darted up to her, grabbed her hand, dropped it, ran away again, only to spin about and return at a mad dash. It made little grunting sounds like laughter but still no articulate words.

Imraldera got unsteadily to her feet, swaying a little. Her dark skin was used to incredible summer heat, but this was unlike any she had known before. If she did not find water soon, she feared she would faint . . . and never wake again.

She had no sooner found her balance than the child rushed at her and flung its arms around her middle, clinging to her in a desperate hug. She almost fell but braced herself and hugged the little one back. It laughed. A strange sound coming from that animal face—harsh, almost a growl. But it was a laugh, and the child flashed her another smile. It bounded away from her, kicking up its heels and laughing and swinging its arms.

Imraldera steadied herself and gazed after the child. What could she do? The creature was obviously as ignorant as she herself was mute. Not stupid, exactly—she could see the sharp intelligence in those animal eyes. And there was language in the grunts and growls and even the body movements, a language Imraldera could almost interpret. But the child had no power of speech.

Imraldera raised her hands. Creatures of this new world could not possibly know the silent language of women. But desperation drove her to sign:

"I need water."

The child tilted its head to one side, still smiling. Then haltingly, it signed back, "There is a well. Follow me."

Imraldera stared. She must be dreaming, she thought. Hallucinating in her thirst and fatigue. Of all the impossible things she had seen and done, this was by far the most impossible.

"You speak the Women's Words?" she signed, her mouth gaping.

"Follow me," repeated the child. "Follow me to water."

It wasn't right! Only the women of the Land knew the language of hands. Not even the men would bother themselves to learn those signs. As old as speech and as secret as the hidden face of the moon, it was their one strength, the one thing the men could not take from them in a world where women were nothing but slaves.

How could this creature know? This otherworldly being that may or may not be female?

The child darted off down the street in a gangly, loping stride. Imraldera had no choice but to follow. Her bare feet were so burned and callused by now, they scarcely felt the hot stones beneath them. She thought she would lose the child, who dashed on ahead so wildly. But the street did not shift as it had before. It remained straight as far as the eye could see. When Imraldera thought she saw a tower or a pile of rubble blocking the street, by the time she reached it, it had moved. And still the street pointed straight ahead. She saw the child running up ahead and heard its barking laughter.

At last the street blended into what looked like it had once been a market square. Above Imraldera's head, many platforms like bird perches stuck out from the high towers, yet these cast no shadows on the stones. She scanned the rest of the square, following the erratic movements of the child. In the center was an enormous well with an arch and pulley built over it. A large, iron-fastened bucket lay on its side beside the surrounding stone wall.

And tied by his feet in that place where the bucket should be, suspended above the black mouth of the well, was a man.

For one heart-stopping moment, Imraldera thought she'd found Eanrin. The hair color was the same, and the aura of immortality. But the clothing was wrong; whereas Eanrin's was bright, mud stained, and flashy, this stranger was dressed quietly in shades of the forest. The rope twisted, the body turned, and she saw the face and form. It wasn't the poet she'd found.

It was another Faerie, one who was also simultaneously man and animal. A badger, she guessed, though he did not wear his animal form at the moment. His face was ghastly, and she wondered if he was dead.

But no . . . the immortal quality still shone from him, vivid and full of life. He hung upside down like a hunting trophy, but he was alive.

The rope creaked. The stranger's eyes opened. He saw Imraldera. He saw the child. His mouth opened in a great O, and he bellowed wordlessly for all he was worth.

Imraldera startled, clapping her hands to her ears. But the child laughed, ran up to the poor man, and poked him cruelly in the stomach. The man bellowed even louder and made a snatch at the creature but missed. His body swung sickeningly above the well, and the rope strained.

Imraldera waved her hands. "Stop! Stop!" she signed, but the child did not see her. It circled around the captive, slapping him on the backside and shrieking with delight at the roars the poor fellow made. Imraldera could not endure it.

Her thirst momentarily forgotten, she ran across the square. The child, absorbed in its brutal sport, did not see her until she had taken it by the arm. Then it whirled upon her, teeth bared, yellow eyes flashing. She glared back and signed, "No!"

It pulled out of her grasp and snapped at her, not seriously, merely as a warning.

"No!" she signed again, scowling still more severely. "Go back!"

The child growled. But it could not break her gaze. Lowering its head, it backed away, its bony body trembling with either fear or fury. Yet it obeyed.

She turned to the captive.

"Madam," said he, craning his neck to still see her even as the rope twisted him around, "you are a witch or a sorceress. No one can control those beasts!"

Imraldera shook her head impatiently. Princess, witch . . . these Faerie folk had such ideas about her! Her hands fumbled with the heavy ropes, but the knots were too strong and too thick. The fibers tore at her fingers. She bit her lip impatiently.

"Lass, look there. My hatchet," said the twisting man, pointing to a weapon lying on the ground near the tipped-over bucket. Gratefully, Imraldera knelt to pick it up. What a fine piece! She hefted it in both hands, amazed at its make and balance. And what stone was this forming the head? Not any she knew, so bright and so sharp! There wasn't a man in her father's village who wouldn't give his firstborn child for the sake of owning a weapon like that.

"Great dragon tails," the stranger muttered as once more he spun around and caught sight of the girl with his hatchet in hand. "Oh, great dragon tails and spikes, I hope you know how to use that—"

She swung. The blade hacked deep into the rope where it wound up from the wooden arch. The whole arch shuddered, and the man swayed uneasily. She swung again, and this time the rope broke. The stranger had just time enough to catch himself on the lip of the well to avoid making a terrible (and rather damp) plunge. Imraldera dropped the hatchet, which rang upon the stones, and flung herself at the stranger, grabbing his shirt with both hands. Together, with much swearing on his part, they hauled him up and out. He collapsed, and she fell to her knees, panting, beside him.

She remembered suddenly how thirsty she was.

But they had only the space of three breaths. Then the stranger sat upright and yelled, "Ware! The Dog!"

Imraldera, blinking and breathing hard, turned.

The child stood only a few yards back. Its head lowered, and a rumbling growl filled its throat. Those sharp teeth gleamed in a dreadful, mirthless smile. Imraldera's dry throat constricted. Her hand reached unwittingly for the fallen hatchet.

The child's eyes darted. It saw the movement. Its growl became a gnashing snarl, and it crouched down on all fours. And suddenly it became what Imraldera had known it must be all along: a great, hideous Dog.

Midnight fell upon the square.

The only thing she could see at first were those burning eyes. Wolf's eyes, she thought, but with flames deep inside. The Dog took a step forward. Enormous paws nearly the size of her head, with claws that could tear the hardest turf, scraped at the stones, shooting sparks.

For an instant, Imraldera's fingers tightened about the hatchet shaft. The Dog spat saliva, twisting its head as it showed its teeth. Unable to breathe, Imraldera sucked in her lips as though to suppress all the screams that longed to burst from her mute throat.

She let go of the hatchet and stood, empty-handed.

"What are you doing, woman?" the man hissed, pushing himself up on his elbows.

Imraldera ignored him. She advanced upon the Dog just as she had advanced upon the child. It made as though to lunge, but when she did not retreat, it backed away. Its head and tail were low, its shoulder blades like knives moving up and down as it tried to circle her. She would not let it pass or go anywhere near the fallen man.

"Quiet," she signed.

It barked, its whole body shaking and lunging and cringing at once.

"Down," she signed.

Its flaming gaze followed her hands. The dark of Midnight emanated from its black body, surrounding them in a heavy cloak. But Imraldera did not shrink.

"I am not afraid of you," she signed. It was a lie, but her face betrayed no falsehood. "I have faced the Beast on the mountain and passed unharmed. I have walked the Pathway of Death and lived to tell the tale. I have looked into the eyes of the River and the serpent, and I have not perished. I am your better. I am your mistress."

The Dog threw back its head and howled.

Imraldera put out her hand, palm up. The Dog made as though to tear it off. She flinched but otherwise did not move, her gaze never shifting. She clucked gently, just as she had before. *Poor, lost creature,* her eyes spoke for her. The Dog understood. She knew dogs; she knew their language, their manners. She took another forward step.

"What are you doing?" the stranger cried.

Startled, Imraldera turned. He was on his feet, reaching for his hatchet. A snarl shredded the darkness, and a heavy black form leapt past Imraldera. She had no time to think, only to react. Her hand darted out, and she grabbed the Dog behind the neck, pushing it to the ground just as she had the child. It was huge, and she felt powerful muscle within that skeletal frame. This was no ordinary dog or wolf, but a Faerie beast of absolute brute force.

Inside, however, was still a child.

Imraldera flung herself on the body, throwing it off balance before those powerful jaws could close on the stranger. Though its strength was far greater than her own, it trembled at her touch, shying away from her, submitting without an order. It shook free, and she stood between the stranger and the monster, her eyes blazing, uncertain which she was angrier at. "Bad!" she signed.

The Dog whined pitifully. Then, to her great surprise, it crouched down, pressing to the ground. Rolling onto its back, it exposed its belly, whining still and lolling its red tongue out from its jaws. Pleading eyes gazed up at her.

With a last furious glare at the stranger, Imraldera stepped forward and knelt beside the Dog.

"Good," she signed and stroked its head. "Good Dog."

The stranger stood beside the well and stared. "By my king's beard!" he muttered.

Imraldera, still stroking the Dog's head, looked up at him, shook her head, and made a silencing motion with one hand. She continued petting the Dog, which rolled upright and laid its ugly head in her lap. The tail flapped once, twice, three times on the stone. It did not look as though it had often wagged before. Imraldera continued stroking, pouring every feeling of love she could into her touch . . . though she was so spent, she had little enough to offer.

At last she rose and staggered back to the well. The Dog, its shoulders rising higher than her waist, followed at her heels, ignoring the man, its eyes fixed only on her. Exhausted, she leaned against the well wall.

The stranger uncertainly bowed. It was an awkward movement, as unlike Eanrin's flashy manner as it could be. "Glomar, Captain of King Iubdan Tynan's guard, servant of Rudiobus," he said. "I am in your debt, m'lady witch."

"I am no witch," she signed, though of course he did not understand. She pointed to the bucket lying near his feet.

Glomar obediently picked it up and handed it to her. Moving slowly from fatigue, Imraldera attached the handle to the cut rope and began lowering it the long way down, praying that water waited at the well's bottom. She heard the splash, and it was better than the clink of gold in her ears. But she was too weak just then to crank the bucket up herself.

Glomar, frowning, stepped forward and assisted her. "Not sure you want to drink, m'lady," he said. "Not all wells in the Far World are safe. You might fall into an enchanted sleep."

She gave him a cold look. At that moment, she would have gladly slept for a thousand years. If only that flea-ridden poet of a cat had never woken her to begin with! As soon as the bucket emerged from the well, she plunged both hands in and drank deeply. The water was stale and flat, but she did not care. Neither did she fall enchanted.

"May I know to whom I owe my life?" the captain asked in his gruff, earthy accent. He did not sound the bright immortal he was, though his skin remained luminous even in the heavy Midnight shadows.

Imraldera shrugged. She had no desire to go through that routine again. The Dog, sensing her distress, pressed up against her side and growled at Glomar. She put a hand on its head.

"AYYYYYEEEEEEERRRRRRREEEEEEEOWWWWL!"

The three of them—maid, captain, and Dog—startled and turned to look across the square. A bright orange tomcat flew across the stones, tail low, eyes wide, fur bristling.

At his heels charged the other Black Dog.

16

IMRALDERA HAD JUST TIME to draw breath before she found herself clutching an armload of trembling fur. Paws wrapped about her neck, claws digging into her shoulder, and she gasped with pain and surprise.

The other Black Dog bore down upon her, fire falling from yellow eyes, black coat like the shadow of Death. Unconsciously she clung to the cat, frozen in place. She saw the great red mouth open, gazed into teeth-lined doom.

The next moment, the monster crashed to the ground under the assault of its sibling. The two Black Dogs snarled and tore at each other, flames and sparks burning the stone around them, their horrible voices echoing through the city so violently it seemed the towers must crumble.

Somewhere just beyond the din, a voice shouted, *"Run!"*

Imraldera felt her arm taken in a powerful grasp; then she was running, dragged behind the captain, still clutching the cat. In a vague, distant way, she heard the captain swearing with each step he took. He moved with a limp, but he ran anyway, his face grim and gasping.

It did not matter which street they took. All were buried in Midnight. The only thing that mattered was putting distance between themselves and the battle being waged in the square. In that rush of terror, all Imraldera's weariness vanished. Her whole existence was taken up with flight.

Flight through a dark tunnel.

The Pathway of Death.

No escape . . .

The cat leapt from her arms. She staggered, nearly unbalanced, but suddenly Eanrin was beside her, his steadying hand on her arm. On they ran. And the howls of the Black Dogs pursued them.

Her legs gave out before her will. Imraldera would have sprawled headlong had not the poet still gripped her arm. As it was, he caught her and just prevented her from hitting her head. She could not move. She lay gasping, conscious but inert.

Glomar, who had continued many more paces before realizing he wasn't followed, stopped. His face was drawn with pain, his ankle swollen double. He barked, "What's wrong with the witch?"

"She's not a witch; she's a princess," Eanrin replied. "I think she's broken."

"Broken? What do you mean?"

"She's a mortal! I don't know how these creatures work. Her body just seems to have . . . stopped."

Glomar hastened back to them as fast as he could move. The noise of the Black Dogs was all too near. "She is not mortal," he said, kneeling down.

"She is."

"Can't be! She tamed one of the Dogs."

Eanrin ignored this last and gave the girl a once-over. "We've got to hide. She's not good for a step more."

"Quick!" said Glomar, getting to his feet. He limped to the nearest tower with a window low enough to access.

Was the baying of the Black Dogs closer? Had they forgotten their quarrel and taken up the chase? Imraldera's heart raced so hard that for a moment she did not realize what Glomar intended to do.

She saw him in the window, beckoning to Eanrin. "Pass me the lass," the captain said. "We'll hide in here until this Midnight lifts."

Her gaze flew to Eanrin's face, but she saw only an instant's hesitation. Then he shrugged, stood up, and picked her right off the ground, carrying her more easily than she'd carried the orange tomcat. Glomar reached down to her, and only then did Imraldera realize.

She shook her head and struggled, nearly causing Eanrin to drop her. He let her slip enough that her feet landed on the stone once more. But she would have fallen had he not kept his arms about her. "I say, steady!" he cried. "No use in fussing. You can't go on, so we've got to hide, and this is the only place. We'll go in together, I promise. We won't be separated."

You can't promise that, she thought. But he was right. What else could they do? At least now she knew he hadn't died when they were parted before. That was some comfort.

Eanrin passed her to Glomar, then climbed up, and they held her between them, crouching on the sill. There was no doubting it now; the Black Dogs were certainly getting closer.

"We've got to jump together," Eanrin said, "else we might lose each other in the dark."

"And wouldn't that be a tragedy," Glomar growled.

"Lumé's crown, Glomar, there's a time for—"

Imraldera took hold of their hands and jumped into the shadows.

The fall was not great; she was prepared for one much greater. But the landing jarred her, and she lost her hold on Eanrin's hand. That was it, then. He was gone. She would never find him now.

"Gah! My ankle!" Glomar roared in one of her ears. Then in the other, a golden voice yowled, "Dragon's teeth and tail, my girl! You could give a fellow warning."

She had never thought she'd be so glad to hear the cat. Her hand darted out and caught his, clutching as though she would never let go. So the shadows hadn't separated them. The streets moved, not the space inside the towers. At least, as far as she could guess. Who could fathom the rules of this awful place?

The three of them sat in the dusty dark base of the empty tower, feeling rather than seeing the vastness above them. Imraldera waited several breaths as her heart relearned to beat. Slowly, two separate thoughts formed in her mind. First, the noise of the Black Dogs' pursuit was gone, replaced with silence.

Second, there was light shining through the window above them. The Midnight was gone.

"Now, I call that a stroke of luck," said Eanrin, rising. The gloom was so intense, Imraldera could scarcely make out his form, much less his face. But his voice was as bright and relaxed as ever, giving no indication that he'd just been pursued by beasts of the Netherworld. "Not a sound of them! Shall I pop up for a peek?"

"Be my guest," said Glomar.

But Imraldera, seeing the poet outlined against the window as he made to jump out, scrambled up and caught him by the foot. She feared that if he climbed out, the streets would shift again, and they would still be separated. He looked down at her, smiled, and seemed to recognize her concern. Rather than climbing all the way onto the sill, he merely held himself up and peered out.

"Sure enough," he said, "the street has changed. For once the unsettled foundations of Etalpalli do us a favor! As far as I can discern, the Black Dogs are miles from here."

He lowered himself down into the dark and sat with his back against the wall. It pleased him rather frighteningly when Imraldera settled in beside him, so near he could feel her warmth without touching her. How familiar that mortal smell of hers had become in so short a time. How nice to know she wasn't dead.

Glomar's rumbling voice carried through the dark. "You two seem to know each other. Will you introduce me, Eanrin?"

Eanrin, who disliked sharing, said shortly, "Glomar, Imraldera. Imraldera, Glomar," and crossed his arms.

"Imraldera? A strange name for a mortal lass," said Glomar. "I didn't know mortal folk knew the Faerie speech. Is she—"

"She's none of your business, that's what she is."

"I am beholden to her for saving my life," the captain replied. Imraldera thought she heard his teeth grinding in the dark. "I was at the mercy of the Black Dogs, certain I was bound for the Netherworld. But she saved me. This little mortal maid with a Faerie name—where did you find her, Eanrin?"

"Like I said, none of your business."

"Then whose business is she?"

"Mine."

"Is that her notion or yours?"

The poet's eyes flashed in the dimness. Then he shook his head and, without a word, began searching his pockets for his golden comb. Realizing he'd left it in his discarded outer shirt, he cursed and started running his fingers through his mud-crusted hair instead.

"Well, Glomar," he said as he groomed, "it has been awfully nice running into you, as it were. So you made it through Cozamaloti in one piece? Wouldn't have thought it possible. Cats, of course, always land on their feet, so the fall was nothing to me. But badgers aren't known for their grace, now, are they? No wonder you bungled your leg, eh? Any luck in locating my lady Gleamdren? Didn't think so. You know what they say: No points for starting first if you finish last."

"I'm not finished yet," growled Glomar. Judging from his voice, Imraldera thought, he really must be a badger. She could think of no other sort who would speak with that growl. But he sounded honest, which she liked.

She wondered what kind of woman Lady Gleamdren was to boast two such dissimilar suitors.

Eanrin got to his feet and put out a hand to Imraldera. Surprised, she took it and allowed him to assist her up. The interval out of the blistering heat had revived her somewhat, and she found she retained some residual strength in her limbs. But how hungry she was! She wondered if her fate was to starve in this barren world.

The poet bowed to Glomar. "We must be on our way. We hasten to my lady's rescue, and since your company would prove more hindrance than help"—he indicated Glomar's ankle—"we must here make our farewells. Farewell!" He turned and hopped up into the windowsill, his lithe body blocking the light and making the inner tower still gloomier. "Come, Imraldera," he said, bending to reach her, hauling her up beside him before she quite had a chance to think.

"Wait!" Glomar struggled upright. Imraldera, grabbing the window frame to keep from tumbling out into the street, turned around to face him. His bow was much less graceful than Eanrin's, but his gruff voice was respectful when he addressed her.

"My lady," he said, "you need not cast your lot with that dragon-bitten mog. You've done me a good turn, and I am grateful. I must continue my search for sweet Gleamdren—she's this fine lass, you see, the finest, exceptin' your fine self—but if you would accompany me, it would be my honor, and I'll see to it you leave Etalpalli safe and sound—"

"I think not!" Eanrin, once more a cat, arched his back and flattened his ears, snarling down at the captain. His tail lashed. "She's with me, Glomar."

"Why don't you let the lady speak for herself?"

"Because she can't, that's why. She's a cursed mute, and she's mine!"

"Yours? And what would Lady Gleamdren say about that, I wonder?"

"That's not your business either."

"But this poor lass is yours?"

"Absolutely! I rescued her!"

"Is that so? It wasn't *her* I saw leapin' into anyone's arms just now!"

"I'll claw your eyes out, badger!"

"I'd like to see you try, cat!"

Imraldera, ready to burst with her desire to scream, scooped up the hissing tomcat and hurled him at Glomar's head. Howls, snarls, and bloodcurdling curses filled the darkness, but she didn't care. She leapt down into the street.

Eanrin tore at Glomar's nose; Glomar snapped at Eanrin's ears. Then both stopped midbrawl, realizing what had just happened.

"Dragon's teeth!" Eanrin swore.

"She'll be lost to us!" Glomar growled. He pushed the poet, who was once more a man, off of him, and they scrambled for precedence at the window. Pushing, pulling, they scrabbled up onto the sill and looked out. Both breathed in relief.

Imraldera sat in the middle of the street, collapsed on her knees, her shoulders and head bowed. But she was there. They climbed hastily out of the tower and crept on quiet, repentant feet behind her. Neither spoke but stood, waiting for her to acknowledge them in some way. She would not turn. They saw a shudder pass through her body, but otherwise she sat still.

"Is she . . . crying?" Glomar whispered to the cat-man.

Eanrin shrugged.

"Speak to her. Say somethin' to . . . to make it right," urged the captain.

"Why me?"

"You're the poet. You're the one with the words. Besides, she's your responsibility, remember?"

Eanrin gave the captain a dirty look. But he took his cat form and, purring shamelessly, sidled up to the mortal maid. He bumped her elbow with his nose, adorable as a kitten, and rubbed his body around until his paws were in her lap. "Imraldera?"

Her face was pale, her eyes closed.

The cat wormed his way still more fully into her lap and trilled, "Don't be cross. That's just how Glomar and I are with each other. The whole rivalry business is all in good sport. We're on a race, you understand. Whoever rescues Gleamdren first gets to continue wooing her while the other backs off. You see how it is?"

She opened her eyes slowly. He blinked up at her, as sweet and charming as he knew how to be. She licked her cracking lips. Then, raising her hands, she signed:

"I do not know your true name."

He watched the finger movements like he might eye a buzzing fly. Sitting up on his haunches, he caught one of her hands between velveted paws and gave her fingertips a firm lick. "You know I don't understand. Just nod yes or no. Are we friends?"

She sighed and tried to swallow, but her mouth was dry. Shooing the cat from her lap with no concern for his ruffled dignity, she leaned forward and started drawing in the dirt of the street. He watched her hands tracing lines and patterns.

The tip of his tail twitched impatiently. "Are you trying to tell me something?"

She nodded. Her jaw was set, and she shifted where she sat to broaden her drawing, giving as much detail as she could with her finger and dirt.

"Is this . . . is this the story of how you came to be by the River?" the cat hazarded, dancing backward out of the way of her arm.

She nodded again. At last she sat back and pointed. Her eyes pleaded with him to understand, to try. Under that gaze, Eanrin had no option but to sit and stare at the scribbles in the dust, stare with all the intensity a cat can muster. His pupils dilated until the golden irises were like rings of eclipsed sunfire. Imraldera watched him, chewing her bottom lip and waiting.

At last the cat lashed his tail and raised his whiskered face to her. "I'm sorry, my girl. It looks to me like the Greater Stick Bug pursues the Lesser Stick Bug over the back of a giant alligator. Can't make a thing of it otherwise."

Imraldera tossed up her hands and shook her head, desperate to force back the tears that would insist on springing to her eyes. The cat, ever sympathetic, purred again and rubbed his cheek along her bowed shoulder. His whiskers tickled her skin, and she pushed him away. So he became a man again and, suddenly embarrassed, backed away from her.

"See here," he said, crossing his arms over his stained white shirt, "I promised you that as soon as this little adventure was through, I'd help you find your way home."

"What if I don't want to go home?" she signed.

"Please stop waving your hands! Help me, and I'll help you. That's a nice way to work, isn't it? But we've got to find Lady Gleamdren and, as you know, neither Glomar nor I"—Eanrin cast a glance back at the captain, who waited several paces away, avoiding as much female emotion as possible—"has any notion how to navigate this dragon-blasted city. But we've got to find some way."

Imraldera scarcely listened as the poet rattled on. She gazed at her drawing, at the scenes she had tried and failed to depict.

If only the Beast had devoured her.

See the truth, Starflower.

She squeezed her eyes shut, shaking her head, willing it to clear. But when at last she opened them again, she saw something in the dirt, just beyond the marks of her drawing. Interested, she got up and, still ignoring Eanrin, stepped over for a closer look.

It was a Dog's enormous footprint.

"What are you looking at?" Eanrin demanded as both he and Glomar stepped up beside her.

She pointed. Glomar swore. "So they have passed this way! We'd best get away quick-like, or they'll double back and find us."

Eanrin agreed and both turned in the direction opposite the footprint. But they'd not gone two paces before looking back to find Imraldera, still intent upon the street, following another print, then another.

"What are you doing?" Eanrin demanded, beckoning her. "Come back, princess!"

She looked his way and shook her head. Then she started off at a trot, following the trail of the Black Dogs. Eanrin and Glomar gave each other bewildered glances. With shouts of "Beard and crown!" they hurried after the girl, along the ever-shifting streets.

But where the Black Dogs ran, the road remained straight.

Fascinated, Hri Sora watched the events playing out in her city like a grand lady in a theater box watches a haphazard play. It was a mess, a disaster, a tangle of impossibilities, yet she could not look away.

"The girl is no fool," she observed.

"I beg to differ!" Gleamdren's voice twittered and chirped as she blustered about her little cage. "If she's keeping company with that fool Eanrin, she can be nothing but a fool herself!"

The Dragonwitch ignored her noisy captive. She saw the Black Dogs loping through the streets, dragging their darkness behind them. She saw how the maid picked up their trail and led the others through twisted Etalpalli as straight and true as a flying arrow. "She caught the Path of the Black Dogs." Hri Sora hissed, impressed and frightened all at once. "The Faerie folk could not think to catch onto my children's trail, but she caught and pursues it. A real woman of the Land!"

Yet this knowledge contradicted her earlier observations. The gentleness with which the girl had managed one of Hri Sora's own dark brood conflicted with the story. "None who have met Amarok could bear to show kindness to one of my beasts," she whispered.

She must test the girl. She must know for certain.

So she stretched out her hands and cast a glamour over Etalpalli. Not a glamour of beauty. No, this was a vision breathed into being by Death's own daughter, as much a truth as her hate, as much a lie as her love.

17

THE SKY BOILED RED ABOVE ETALPALLI, its heat oppressing Imraldera as she led the poet and the captain straight through the writhing streets. She heard a rumble like thunder, but how could there be thunder in this cloudless atmosphere? Perhaps the sky itself growled with a voice greater than those of the Black Dogs, threatening these intruders, warning them away.

A flash of blue drew her eye. Before her mind caught up with her leaping heart to shout its silent warning, she turned. She looked.

Oh, gods and devils! Not here!

Before her spread, not the towering red structures of Etalpalli, but a sweeping vista of a thousand colors, of light and shadow and depth. Green valleys and dark forests; great rivers cutting the land in gorges; scattered villages, and smoke from a thousand hearths curling to a deep sky. Not a tortured sky scalded as though by brands. A healthy, thriving, blue sky with a warm sun. A sun that shone down upon the Land she had known and loved all her life, never realizing she loved it until it was taken from her.

Only one place in all the worlds afforded this view.

Not the dead mountain!

If she gazed south, would she see the home fires of her village? Would she see the light of her own hearth shining from the top of the hill? Would Fairbird sit in the doorway, waiting?

No!

She grabbed her head in her hands, forcing her eyes away from that view. *The prints. Look at the footprints!*

She saw them. They swam before her dizzy vision, but they were there, solid in the red dirt of the street. For she did not stand on the mountain, and the Land did not spread below her, awaiting her return. She had left that life behind when her people abandoned her on the mountaintop. This world, this dead, twisted world, was all the reality left, and she would not lose her mind to visions and dreams! That would be the final defeat in a life born defeated.

Her feet were heavy weights, but she lifted one, then the other, following the rubble-strewn street of red. Dead, just like the mountain, yet not the mountain. She must not look right or left. She must follow the trail.

The footprints, she saw, were no longer those of a Dog. They had become the prints of a small child.

Glomar and Eanrin, a few paces behind, exchanged looks. The girl was staggering drunkenly, bent over as though climbing a steep incline while the street remained level.

"What ails her, do you think?" Glomar whispered.

"Mortality?" Eanrin suggested.

"Hadn't we ought to . . . I don't know . . . help her? Give her an arm, or something? She looks about to topple." The captain, favoring his twisted ankle, made a face. "I'd volunteer but, you know, with my game leg and all—"

"Of course, leave it to Eanrin," sighed the poet. "Seems to be the popular theme these days. Let *Eanrin* take care of mortal maids. He's bound to like the task! Let *Eanrin* mind the weak and infirm. He's got the stomach for it!"

"You said she was yours, didn't you?" Glomar snarled.

"Oh, well, she is. I'm merely pointing out—"

Imraldera screamed.

It was a sound she should not have been able to make. Even hearing it was pain, the pain of fire and ice. In that tormented moment, the curse holding her trembled, then renewed its grasp with agonizing strength that Eanrin and Glomar, both attuned to the workings of Faerie, felt almost as keenly as the girl did. Both gasped and recoiled from her, even as silence once more slapped upon her so heavily that she fell facedown in the street, her arms around her head, her body crumpled.

"Imraldera!" Eanrin, shaking himself free of the curse's aftereffects, sprang forward, putting his arms around her and trying to draw her to him. "What is it? What's wrong?" He struggled to make his voice soothing, but his body quaked with fear of her and the curse she bore. She fought him weakly at first, then fell against him, quivering with noiseless sobs.

"Is it the city?" Eanrin suggested, stroking her hair and rocking her gently. "It is a wicked place. It gets to you, I know. I feel it too."

Her shudders eased, but her face, when she finally gazed up at him, was stricken. He did not see that they sat in the Place of the Teeth.

It is only an illusion, she told herself. If she put her hands to the ground, she felt, not the smooth sacrificial stone, but the edges of broken cobbles, the dust and ash of the city's destruction. And she smelled the burning stench of Etalpalli. Her vision alone was manipulated, making her see what was not there.

She gagged and might have been sick had her stomach not been empty.

Eanrin could smell the enchantment. Etalpalli reeked of dragon smoke and dragon death, but this was a dragon's enchantment, similar to the glamour placed over his eyes on the shores of Gorm-Uisce. Only this time it was directed at Imraldera, so he could not see it; and unlike that time by the shore, he could sniff it out.

He took Imraldera's face in his hands. "Princess, my dear," he said, "I know you're seeing something. I don't know what it is, but obviously it is none too pleasant for you. You know it is false, don't you?"

She nodded, staring desperately into his eyes. It could not be real . . . but oh, at the same time, how real it was!

Eanrin glanced about quickly, then focused on Imraldera, holding her gaze. "This is a place of power. Perhaps the center of Etalpalli. It's good you've brought us here!" That was a lie. As far as he could tell, the center of the labyrinth held no more answers than its edges. But the poor girl needed some encouragement. "You did well, Imraldera. Much better than I could have expected from a mortal maid! Now just keep looking at me, and the enchantment will wear off. You will see we are on the same dirty old street in the same dirty old city."

A tear trailed down her cheek. She must look at him. She must not see the stones like teeth rising beyond his shoulders. Her dark skin took on a ghastly hue.

"Dragon's teeth!" Eanrin drew her to his chest, laying her ear against his heart. "Close your eyes," he said. "Rest and close your eyes." He felt each breath she took trembling through her body. Pressing his cheek against her tangled, dirty hair, he shut his own eyes and sang.

It was a song so old, he'd forgotten when he first heard it. Perhaps he had composed it himself, back in the days of his forgotten youth, when first he had learned that life was not all joy—the first great step one must take if one is to grow, but a step he seldom paused to remember. Why should he, whose life extended forever before his feet, pause to consider pain?

But when he was young, he had known.

> "'*Lilla lay, lilla lay,*' *softly she sighs,*
> *The fair willow maiden with silver-gray eyes.*
> *But over her sighing, the white birch maid laughs:*
> '*Lilla lay, lilla lay, sorrows won't last!*'
>
> "*So listen, sweet child. Oh, lilla lay, ly!*
> *To the voice of the birch tree who laughs to the sky.*
> *For today may be gray, and the rain may be falling,*
> *But lilla lay, lilly, a new day is dawning.*"

He rocked the girl and felt her body relax as the mellow tones of his lullaby worked their own enchantment. She slept, and it was, he smelled, a sleep without dreams.

Glomar stood over them, his weight shifted off his bad leg. "That was . . . very pretty, Eanrin," he said, his voice gruff. He sniffed and wiped his nose. "It was like something . . . I don't know. Something I heard a thousand years ago, perhaps. When I was young. I didn't know you could sing like that."

"Shhhh," said the poet with a sharp glare. "Don't wake her. Let the glamour wear away."

But he dashed a stray tear from his face before the badger might see. No wonder he had forgotten this song! And as soon as he could get rid of this maid, he would make every effort to forget her as well. He was a fool to allow himself to care.

The longer he cared, the longer he risked that which he feared most.

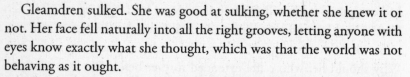

Gleamdren sulked. She was good at sulking, whether she knew it or not. Her face fell naturally into all the right grooves, letting anyone with eyes know exactly what she thought, which was that the world was not behaving as it ought.

What was this fascination with mortal women? First, Rudiobus falling for the glamourized dragon (which, granted, only *looked* mortal) and now this! The Eanrin she knew wouldn't be caught dead speaking to a mortal girl. He certainly wouldn't drag one along on a noble quest! Was he going to start writing poetry in her honor too? Insufferable man.

And now even the Dragonwitch was enthralled by the little insect. *Her* dragon. *Her* captor, who was supposed to be torturing her, striving to wring secrets from her unwilling mouth! Instead, Hri Sora spared not a glance for the iron birdcage and its inhabitant. Her attention was fixed upon whatever events were unfolding in the streets of Etalpalli.

Perhaps, Gleamdren thought, she should bring up the subject of Amarok again. That would get a reaction from the Flame at Night! Setting her jaw, Gleamdren scrambled to her feet and approached the bars of her cage. "Oi!" she began.

Howls split the air, drowning her voice.

The Black Dogs raced each other up the stair spiraling up the outside of their mistress's tower. Midnight followed swiftly on their heels, giving Gleamdren's eyes their first relief from the glaring red of Etalpalli's sky since she'd come to this place. Not that it felt like relief. Used as she was to the bright ways of the Merry People, it was oppressive. She stepped back from the cage bars to avoid attracting attention from the two monstrous Dogs barrelling across the rooftop and bellowing like an entire pack of wolves.

The Dragonwitch silenced them with a look.

Cringing like whipped puppies, the Dogs crawled on their bellies to her feet. Their heads were bigger than hers, their jaws capable of breaking her in half without a thought. But they were in terror of her, the shabby queen of this city, standing above them in a tattered green nightdress, her hair wild about her face.

"My children," Hri Sora said.

They whined; they groveled. One dared the barest wag of a tail. This one she struck across the face. Not with any force that could have hurt the creature, but with a cruelty that wounded its spirit. It rolled onto its back, exposing its belly, the picture of subservience. Gleamdren felt sick at the sight but could not tear her gaze away.

"I was right," said the Dragonwitch. Her eyes barely saw the beasts abasing themselves before her. They gleamed with a light that was full of memory and hatred. "I was right. How such a girl came to my demesne, I do not know. Perhaps, for once, the fates work in my favor? She is come, and it is a sign. I know it is a sign!"

She knelt and took one of the Dogs by the scruff of its neck, lifting its jowly head so she could snarl in its face. "Bring her to me. Alive."

The Black Dogs rose and fled the tower, tails tucked, ears flattened. They would obey. They were too full of fear and love to consider otherwise.

The Midnight lingered long after they had gone. Gleamdren, her sulk momentarily forgotten, huddled down on the far side of her cage, warily watching the Dragonwitch pace along the roof's edge.

Imraldera sat with an orange cat pressed up against one side of her and a badger on the other. Both were fast asleep. How odd these Faerie creatures were. They flaunted their immortality with such casual ease! In the midst of this evil city, enchantments surrounding them and the Black Dogs on the loose somewhere close by, these two slept as peacefully as a pair of kits.

Imraldera, however, could not. When the last echoes of Eanrin's lullaby faded from her mind, she had awakened to find her two companions snoring soundly. Careful not to wake them, she idly stroked the ears of one furry bundle, then the other. How long it felt since she had sat thus in her father's house, her gray lurcher sleeping with its head on her lap, her baby sister leaning against her shoulder. Those were beautiful days, she realized. Days she had always known must come to an end.

But what a strange, terrible end!

When she looked about, she still saw the Place of the Teeth, the central stone slab, the five jutting stones like fangs rising from each corner and the center. But she knew, now that her heart had calmed its mad racing, that what she saw could not be the truth. The winds were always harsh in the Place of the Teeth. Here, there was no wind. The illusion affected only her vision.

It was fading. Slowly, the stones, the mountain, the vista of green below her melted away, and she saw the burned streets and towers, red and shadowless once more. How had she come to this? She could make no sense of it, find no underlying reason. She had fled, and her flight had brought her here, to a world she could scarcely begin to comprehend, to companions who wore their fur coats as naturally as their cloaks and doublets. Imraldera did not want any of it to be real. If only reality consisted of nothing more than a dimming hearth, a small child, and a faithful dog! How sweet life might be then.

The Midnight descended.

She saw it creeping softly across the red stones like a bloodstain spreading as it soaked into the ground. It crawled up and over her own limbs, shrouding her and her sleeping companions. And ahead of her, Imraldera saw the flaming eyes of the Black Dogs and heard their deep breathing.

Eanrin and Glomar slept on.

The creatures approached, their heads low. Imraldera looked from one to the other. They were as like as twins can be, their grotesque faces more monster than Dog. But she saw the difference in their gazes.

She turned to the monster on the left and signed, "Good Dog."

Its tail came up and its ears pricked. Softly, it whined. But its sibling snarled and snapped at its ear. Both lowered their heads and growled deep in their throats. Then they turned and marched at a sedate pace back up the street. One paused and looked around, its eyes beckoning.

Imraldera understood. She could not pretend otherwise. She rose quietly, careful not to disturb either the poet or the captain. Somehow she knew they would have slept on even had she kicked them. The Midnight carried with it an enchantment of stealth. The Black Dogs wanted her and no other.

She wondered if the Dogs led her away to devour her as she should have been devoured long ago. She almost hoped so. The Midnight was so heavy as she followed her guides that she could scarcely make out the street. But at last the Dogs came to a tower identical to the other towers, except perhaps more blackened than some.

They trotted up the outside staircase, which spiraled high into the gloom. Imraldera followed without question. Round and round, higher and higher. Her heart beat fiercely from fear and exhaustion. She must follow; no more flight.

The stairway ended. Imraldera found herself standing on a flat, circular rooftop. She turned about, observing the whole city from here, both the dark patches where Midnight lingered, and on to the outer stretches, where the red burning sky arched over all. The city went on for miles and miles on all sides, but from this vantage, her vision extended just as far. She saw all the way to the city's edge, where the crumbled towers trailed off into . . . nothing.

What an isolated world this was, Imraldera thought vaguely. More isolated even than her homeland. Her bare feet moved silently across the flat roof, feeling the way in the dark. She stubbed her toe on something and heard a tiny voice shout, "I say! Watch where you're going, blundering mortal oaf."

Imraldera knelt and peered between the iron bars of a birdcage. It was difficult to discern the inhabitant, but she heard the rustle of wings and thought she glimpsed a furious, sputtering songbird.

Lady Gleamdren, she thought.

"Stop staring at me!" the songbird chirped and was suddenly not a bird but a tiny woman shaking her fists at Imraldera's nose. "Stop staring! Go back where you came from and tell Eanrin that if he wants to rescue me, he'd jolly well better do it *without* the aid of a sniveling mortal wench! What have you to say for yourself? Speak up, witch, or I'll—"

"Pay no attention to my prisoner."

Imraldera sat upright and turned at the deep voice speaking from the shadows. She had never before heard such a voice. It was ancient and dark, bound in a body it was not meant to inhabit. A figure stepped into view, slight, rag clothed, and flanked by the Black Dogs. Those monsters made the figure seem smaller, though she stood a full head taller than Imraldera.

She was a woman.

Imraldera stared, not believing her eyes or her ears. Leaping to her feet, she bowed after the fashion of her people and made the sign for "chieftain," for what other word could describe this person before her. A woman! A woman who spoke in a voice both like and unlike a man's! There never was such a marvel, such a horror. Imraldera, dizzy with both fear and hunger, feared that she might faint. And what a dreadful fate would that be, to display such weakness before a woman of such power!

The Dragonwitch smiled. "Perhaps I should speak to you in your own language," she said. Then she raised her hands and formed the words known only to the silent women.

"You are from the Land Behind the Mountains."

Imraldera gasped.

18

S HE HAS PROBABLY BETRAYED US. You know how mortals are."
Eanrin and Glomar sat in the street in their animal forms, staring at the fresh footprints of the enormous Dogs heavily pressed into the dirt along with the lighter prints of Imraldera. They had slept so long and so deeply that by the time they woke, the Midnight had already lifted on the street, and Imraldera's scent was fading.

The poet-cat fixed a glare upon the badger, his ears twisted back irritably. "Idiot," he growled. "If she'd betrayed us, we'd be dragged off to the Netherworld by now. She's been kidnapped."

Glomar stood, taking his man's form as he stretched. He tested his weight on his ankle. The men of Rudiobus heal quickly. Sure enough, he found his ankle almost as good as new. "I wouldn't be so sure," he said to the cat, who was eyeing him with a blend of disinterest and dislike. "I saw how she was with the Dog yesterday. Wee little girl like her, and she forced one of those brutes to the ground! I could break her arm between two fingers! Either of the Black Dogs could swallow her whole without a thought. But she bullied it and made it obey her. That's witch work."

"I told you: She's no witch. She's a princess."

Glomar shrugged and looked up and down the street. He wondered if he could find his way through this maze back to the square with the well and locate his hatchet. He felt bereft without it, like a man who went out one day and forgot one of his arms. But there was no telling where the well might be. Shrugging, he picked a direction and started walking.

"Where do you think you're going?" the cat meowled. He remained where he was, sitting very upright, but his tail lashed, sweeping dust up in a cloud.

"I'm going to fetch Gleamdren," Glomar replied without looking back. "Just as I said I would."

"You don't know where she is!"

"Neither do you, so I don't see much use in keeping your company."

"What about Imraldera?"

Here Glomar stopped and slowly turned about. He was a badger down to his bones, his mind full of tunnels and rock, the good clean smells of fresh-turned dirt. In badger form, his nose was long, capable of sniffing out all manner of things through many layers of sediment. It took time for his mind to catch up with notions that his nose had sniffed out in a moment.

"You like her," he said with a snort that may have been a laugh.

"What?" The cat's ears pricked and his whiskers twitched. "What did you say?"

"I said, you like her. The mortal."

"I never!"

"You really do."

"Impossible!"

"You, who've never liked anyone but yourself all your life."

And the captain snuffled again, his rugged face lit up with laughter. Eanrin stood with his mouth open, whiskers bristling, which was funnier still. Glomar had never known the Chief Poet of Iubdan Rudiobus to be at a loss for words. Miracles still happened in Faerie after all.

The cat hissed at the captain. "Now you've done it, Captain Glomar, meatheaded bungler. *Badger!*" His ears went back like horns. "Now you have incited the wrath of Bard Eanrin, Prince of Poetry!"

"And what will you do, poet? Versify me to death?"

"You think I can't?" A light of fire blazed in the cat's eyes. "I'll find my lady Gleamdren," he said. "I'll find her so fast, it'll make you ill! And when I've carried her home to the Mountain and all Rudiobus is singing my praises, where will you lay your shamed head to rest? And when songs of my valor fill your ears, where will you go to find peace?"

Glomar raised his bushy eyebrows. Then he shrugged. "Do your worst, cat," he said, turned on heel, and continued down the street, snickering to himself as he went. The cat hurled insults at his back, but these had no effect. Within a few paces, the street made a sudden, gut-wrenching twist, and Glomar knew without a backward glance that he was now separated from the cat by distances he couldn't begin to guess.

The separation caused him little anxiety. Lumé's crown, he was happy to be rid of the orange devil! The shift, however, left him uneasy. It reminded him that, since he no longer followed in the Black Dogs' Path behind the slight mortal lass, the city could do with him what it liked. It was no longer grounded as it had been before its queen destroyed it. It was as changeful and untrustworthy as the Wood Between, and angry besides. Its spirit had been killed, leaving behind a hollow shell of wrath, more than willing to swallow up intruders. A reflection of its furnace-hearted mistress, no doubt.

So Glomar proceeded with more care, his lumbering pace slower than before. Dragon's teeth, being pursued by the Black Dogs had been easier than this! Every street, every tower, looked just like the one before.

The captain stopped suddenly. What a fool he was, using his eyes! Every badger knew to trust his nose first and foremost. He sank down into badger form, closed his beady eyes, and sniffled and snuffled long and hard. He caught an unpleasant scent that drew his interest. At this point, any change must be preferable to the continuing sameness. Perhaps it would be a clue to lead him to his lady.

He trundled off in pursuit of that scent, glad to have a goal. But when he found the source, he swore in badger tongue.

The towers had given way to a street lined with tombs. These were nearly as tall as the towers, but their purpose was unmistakable. There were no windows, for one thing, no doorways opening to the sky. They were carved all over with wings, wrapping around as though enfolding each tomb in a fond embrace. Glomar knew they must be the final resting places of the city's former kings and queens.

A dreadful thought: The Sky People, like all Faerie, were not meant to die.

The death of a Faerie king or queen was a horror even to one of Glomar's stoic nature. He took on his man's form when he beheld the tombs—so many of them for one kingdom!—and fell to his knees. Each one signified three deaths for those entombed.

Glomar's hard face melted into that of a young boy struggling to hold back tears. He had seen the work of Death before upon occasion. In the war with Arpiar, he had put an end to the immortal lives of many goblins and had seen comrades fall, their spirits carried (he was told) across the Final Water. But never a Faerie king or queen. Iubdan and Bebo had ruled Rudiobus since the Mountain was no more than a small Faerie hill. Etalpalli must be a land of fearful history to have lost four of its kings and queens to Death's appetite.

On trembling legs, he advanced, drawn to this horrific street as though against his will. And he saw that the names of the monarchs were carved in Faerie tongue over the doorways: Citlalu the Star King; Queen Mahuizoa the Glorious; Tlanextu of the Coming Dawn. All names of power. All names of those who succumbed to unnatural death three times.

The name on the last tomb had been obliterated, the stone melted until the letters were indecipherable. A recent destruction, by the smell of it, Glomar decided. Its doorway on ground level was open; the doors of the other tombs had been blocked up. Their walls rose sheer and unbroken to the sky.

Glomar thought, *This is* her *tomb. They built it for her when she changed and lost her heart. For she died that day, and they mourned her. Poor Sky People.*

"Glomar! Captain Glomar!"

The voice came from the darkness. It startled Glomar so badly that he fell back into badger form, teeth bared. But he knew that voice, and when his ponderous mind caught up with his beating heart, he recognized it.

"M'lady Gleamdrené?"

Out of the shadows within the tomb's doorway, a face appeared. There she stood, lovely in her green dressing gown, her flaxen hair wild about her face. She smiled at him. At *him*, Glomar, the oaf to whom she'd never cast a glance save to irritate Eanrin! How beautiful she was, and how frail and sweet she looked here among the awful sepulchers of Etalpalli.

Glomar lurched forward, his baggy hide quivering with delight. "M'lady!"

She laughed and reached her hands to him. "You have come for me at last! I knew you would, faithful Glomar. Hurry now! I'm caught by a spell, but you can break it. Only you, Glomar! Only you, my dearest!"

He realized after the fact that he should have known better. It was so clearly a trap, he should have laughed. Gleamdren would never call anyone her *dearest*, after all. Not a soul could claim that honor from the maiden who simultaneously held all her suitors in highest regard and lowest contempt. But that voice and those tender words fulfilled the deepest wishes of his simple badger heart, and he lacked courage to face the truth of the matter while making the split-second decision to run to her arms.

To run into the gaping doorway of the tomb.

The shadows pulled him in, and he was blind. Glomar heard the rumble of the door closing behind him and knew he'd been had.

Curse all females and their pretty talk!

Eanrin took a stroll.

Being a cat, he disliked appearing out of his depth. So as he sauntered down Etalpalli's malevolent streets, he did so with the air of a dandy on his way to call on some maiden aunt, anticipating an evening of dreadful boredom, yet keenly aware of his own charm. His tail was up with the faintest curl at the tip, his whiskers were smooth, his eyes half closed.

No one would have guessed how madly his heart raced.

He couldn't tell which distressed him more, his outward circumstances or his inward fury. Possibly the fury, which would be much more manageable if he could figure out exactly what he was furious about.

"Glomar and his heartless accusations, clearly," he told himself. "The boor, hurling such slanderous notions my way! I am a Faerie, a Rudioban, an immortal bard. And I do *not* like the mortal girl."

But he did. Which was the worst part.

At least for the moment he could enjoy the gift of solitude. He needed it desperately if he was going to clear his head and reevaluate his situation. Here he was, deep in Etalpalli. Why was he even here? He remembered the rush of the River, the feel of Imraldera's hair in his hand, the fall . . . He had leapt into the water to save her, but why had they even ventured near the River?

"Gleamdren," he said. "Of course, Gleamdren! You are here for your own purpose. Forget the other wench. You are well rid of her, and you never wanted anything to do with her in the first place. It was all the—"

He stopped. The face of the Hound appeared before his mind's eye. With a shudder, he shook it away.

What a shambles his life had become since he'd glimpsed the Hound! He'd rather have been run to the ground by the Black Dogs, torn to shreds in their ravenous jaws, and dragged to the Netherworld. In Death's realm, though but a ghostly vapor, he would remain Eanrin.

But once the Hound caught him, what of himself would be left?

"He drove you to the mortal girl," he muttered, walking on. "He drove you against your will. And now see what has become of you! She ran you completely off course, and now she's . . . gone."

His heart hurt in his chest. The thought of Imraldera dragged off by those monsters to some unknown fate sickened him. He reeled, shaking his head, and suddenly took on his man's form again. Leaning against the wall of the nearest tower, ignoring how the stones burned through his thin shirt, Eanrin took his head between his hands.

"You should never have done it!" he snarled. "You should never have helped her. Curse that Hound! Curse that girl! Curse them all and let them rot in their curses, or they'll destroy everything you are."

No time passed in Etalpalli. No shadows or drifting clouds. It might have been a thousand years, for all Eanrin knew or cared, before he stood and shook himself out. He was hollow inside.

Once more in cat form, he continued on his wandering way. The streets he walked were more ruinous than those he had traveled earlier. More than half of the towers were toppled into rubble; most of the cobble road was burned and blackened. A thousand evil smells assaulted his pink nose, and his pupils dilated until his eyes were large black disks on his face. "At least it's a change," he told himself without conviction. "At least it's not the same street again and again."

He wondered how many hundreds of immortal lives had ended in this very spot in a flood of torrential fire.

Ahead of him lay a pit.

In this place so blasted by fire, the ruins gave way to flattened, melted rock that vanished into blackness at the center, blackness more absolute than the shadows hiding within the towers. Eanrin felt the pull like the currents of a river dragging him to this place. He realized suddenly that all Etalpalli was nothing but a whirlpool of hatred, and the center of that whirlpool was here, down that pit.

He must resist it, he knew. He must back away and flee up the street, fight with everything in him against that inexorable draw. Instead, he found himself creeping low to the ground, placing each paw carefully, but drawing ever nearer to the edge. He smelled rather than saw indications that a tower had stood here once, perhaps the greatest tower in the city. But it was long gone, swallowed up in that hole.

It gave Eanrin the wild urge to jump.

He knew that was wrong, evil even. Yet something about that chasm, that plunge into nothingness, beckoned to him, filling his body with unholy need—a need for the pitch, the fall, and the swallowing that must follow.

Shaking himself and backing up a step or two, he cast about for some anchor, anything at all to hold him back! He knew in his rational mind that this wild, consuming craving was suicidal. Yet all the deathly smells of Etalpalli rolled in upon him, urging him to give in. His ears pricked, then went flat to his head, for he thought he heard thousands of voices calling, rising from the darkness. Did the dead Sky People call his name? Did they cry out for him to join them?

It was the foul city! He knew, but the pull was so great he did not want to fight it. Etalpalli would swallow him, and he would willingly leap down its gaping throat.

A new voice, like a caress, crooned to him.

Choose my darkness, Eanrin.

Eanrin had never before in his life been so afraid. Until that moment, he realized, he had not known what fear was.

Choose me.

There must be some escape! There was always an escape for the heroes of epics. Hissing, flashing his sharp fangs, Eanrin drew himself together. The fur on his spine and tail bristled, but there was no one to combat. Only the pit.

Choose me, before I choose you.

As though a noose had closed around his neck and dragged him, Eanrin found himself pulled to the lip of the void. He strained and twisted, but deep inside he knew he could not resist, wasn't even certain he wanted to. The choice was so easy! The fall, so inevitable.

Then suddenly his front paws were out over the edge. He scrambled and snarled and felt that terrible rush through his body that precedes a plunge. He had only an instant to cry out, inarticulate in his terror.

Then his voice was lost as he fell into the arms of darkness.

Hri Sora's eyes were two yellow candles, flickering but intent. The only other light on the roof of that Midnight-shrouded tower came from the smoldering eyes of her children. The Dogs crouched on either side of her, tense and trembling, as though expecting a blow at any moment. Their gazes followed their mother's hands when she moved them in deft signs or folded them quietly before her. There was fear in their ugly faces, fear mixed with unfathomable love.

But Hri Sora spared them not a glance. Her attention fixed upon the maiden from the Land.

She was unmistakable. Hri Sora could have laughed at herself for ever doubting. This girl with the mark of slavery all over her face could only come from the Land Behind the Mountains. She was enslaved to her own beliefs, to the laws of her people.

She belonged to the Beast.

The silent language of women was hateful to Hri Sora. But her fingers did not hesitate as they formed the familiar signs. How long now since she'd been taught this language of slavery? How long since she too had been rendered mute under the curse? She shuddered, wishing not to remember, struggling to keep at bay the fire that always raged to life with these memories. No, she could not succumb to it yet, no matter how tempting those surging flames might be.

One thing only she desired more than the return of her wings. One thing . . . and this girl might prove the key.

Though her hands shook, she formed the necessary words. "Tell me who you are."

"Starflower," the girl replied. "Daughter of Eldest Panther Master."

"I do not know this Eldest." Hri Sora blinked slowly. "There were many elders in the Land when last I was there."

"There is but one Eldest now," the girl signed. "All elders bow to Panther Master." Then her face contorted, the skin of her forehead puckering while her mouth fixed in a firm line. Her chin quivered, and she bit down on her lip. Then she hung her head, and her hands signed a correction. "They *bowed* to Panther Master."

"Look at me," Hri Sora snarled. The girl raised her swimming eyes and watched the dragon form more words with her hands. "In my day, the elders bowed only to the Beast."

The girl nodded but offered no other reply.

"Does the Beast still rule the Land?"

The girl nodded again. A shudder passed through her small frame, and Hri Sora wondered if the little mortal would faint then and there. Such a puny creature!

The dragon licked her dry lips. She hated the girl. She hated everything she represented: dirt, degradation, and despair. She wanted to swallow her up and then let herself descend back into the fire of her hatred. But no! She must focus.

"Tell me, child," said Hri Sora, her hands moving harshly. "Tell me how you came to escape the Beast. Tell me how you fled from behind the Circle of Faces."

The mortal girl closed her eyes, and a tear slipped down one cheek.

One of the Dogs, seeing her distress, whined softly. Hri Sora turned to it with a snarl and cuffed its muzzle. It backed away, its tail tucked, and dared not whine again.

When the dragon turned back to the girl, she found those large black eyes fixed upon her in anger.

"What?" Hri Sora said. "Do you disapprove of how I treat my own slaves?"

The girl ground her teeth, her jaw working. Her hands remained still, but she spoke from her eyes with clarity.

Hri Sora realized suddenly that, for all her mortality, there was strength in this girl. Strength much deeper than what could be outwardly seen. Strength stemming from some source the Dragonwitch could not fathom. But women of the Land were never strong! They were beaten, downtrodden, worthless rags, just as she had once been. Where, then, had this girl come by such power? It took power indeed to feel compassion for one of the Black Dogs. Such power the Flame at Night, in her most potent wrath, had never known. Hri Sora growled, but a shiver ran down her spine.

The mortal's eyes did not leave the Dragonwitch's face. At last she signed with her clay-formed hands, "They are *his* children, aren't they."

Hri Sora hissed, and fire fell from her lips when she answered aloud rather than with her hands. "His monsters. Yes."

The girl signed, "And yours?"

The fire would swallow her whole. Hri Sora felt a mounting desire to blast this girl into oblivion!

"Tell me," she repeated, her claw-tipped fingers ripping at the darkness, "how you came to escape the Circle of Faces. You have his mark in your eyes. You have gazed upon his true face. Yet you lived. Mortal that you are, you lived." Her lips curled back, and fire licked at the corners of her mouth. "Tell me!"

Imraldera stared at the devil before her, this creature out of her peoples' darkest stories. Though she saw no wings, no scales, no long sinewy tail, she knew what this woman must be. A dragon, like the one that fell from the sky and smote Bald Mountain, killing everything within miles of its dreadful summit. Though her form was not right, the fire brimming inside her was unmistakable.

Yet somehow, Imraldera could not fear her. She could not decide what she felt instead. Was it hatred? Or merely pity?

"It is a long story," she signed.

"Time does not matter here in the Far World," the dragon said. "Tell me your story. Tell me from the beginning, as you remember it. Tell me everything."

So with halting fingers, Imraldera began to weave the tale in the darkness. Her brown hand danced, but it was a solemn dance. A dance of mourning. And as she worked her tale, she felt as though she relived it.

She relived the days of death.

PART TWO

1

STARFLOWER

I REMEMBER THE NIGHT my mother died. I remember it because, until that night, I had never heard her voice. But that night she screamed. Not even the curse of the Beast could stifle those screams.

I do not like to recall my mother that way. It is difficult to prevent those final moments from overshadowing everything else. Her hands were gentle. They were not the hands I saw clawing at the animal hides upon her bed. They were not the hands I saw tearing at the shadows, begging for help in broken signs. No, let me remember them as they were before! Brown as doeskin, rough as lizard hide, hands that contained so many stories.

Her fingers . . . how they could dance out a tale! How they would fly for me when I was little and just learning to form words of my own. She told me stories of heroes, of elders back in the days before the Land was united under one Eldest. She told me how the mountains that surround the Land were once giants, tall and grand and glorious. But they sinned a dreadful sin; because of this, they are bound forever in stone. Only if they allow their hearts to become soft once more, to beg forgiveness and listen to the Songs of the Spheres, will they ever be free.

My mother taught me the names of things. I remember that best of all. Her fingers, elegant and strong, would help mine to form the name of the sun, the moon, the name of each mountain and lake and tree. They are silent names, known only to the women. Men do not speak our language of hands. They do not know the hidden names of things.

"Before a creature may truly live," my mother told me, "it must be known by name. Every living thing, be it man or woman, animal or angel, sleeps inside, waiting for that day when it will wake and sing. But until it is called by its true name, it will remain asleep.

"A true name is a powerful thing. Dangerous. Many go through life asleep inside, because no one has ever called their true name. And so, they think themselves safe."

"Safe?" I asked. "How can this be? If they must be called by their true name to come alive, why wouldn't they want that name to be known?"

"Because to know a true name is to have great power. The one who knows becomes so strong . . . and also, so weak. Just as you too, when your name is known, are both stronger and weaker than you would otherwise be."

"If one person knows many true names, is that person then very powerful?"

"Yes," my mother signed. "But also very fragile."

I shook my head, confused by this. How can one be both strong and frail at once? It is a great mystery. Perhaps the greatest mystery of all.

"Well, I know my name," I told my mother in my ignorance. "I am Starflower."

"That is the name your father gave you, yes," my mother replied.

"Is it my true name?"

She smiled. I know the reading of faces as well as I know the reading of hands. And in her face, young as I was, I read her answer: "I know your true name, my child. I know, though no one else does. And I will keep it safe."

My father is Eldest of the Land. All the elders of all the villages, the Crescent Tribes, the men of Black Rock, the tall North Walkers, all of them pay tribute to Eldest Panther Master. They bickered among themselves, however, and only their loyalty to their Eldest kept them from violent warring.

But my father had not produced a son. Only me. Only a worthless woman-child.

Without a son, my father risked losing the loyalty of the elders. Their squabbles became more bitter every year, and their trust in their Eldest, a sonless chieftain, faded. After all, who can trust a man who can father no heir?

The men of our village pleaded with Father many times to set aside my mother and take another wife, one who would give him sons. But Father refused. I would say it was because he loved my mother, but how can a man love a woman? We, who have no voices. We, who are born slaves. It is too much for me to understand.

But I know Mother loved the Panther Master. She loved him for his strength, but she loved him more for the kindness he showed her by not putting her aside when, in the ten years since she had given birth to me, she still gave him no heir.

Then, after all hope had been lost, she came to be with child again. Stone giants above! I had never seen her so joyful! How beautiful her hands became during those months. And I saw her sign these words:

> *"Let me praise the One Who Names Them.*
> *He named this child from the Beginning.*
> *Since before the worlds were made, he knew*
> *The name of the child I bear."*

Her hands moved in song, though she could not sing aloud. I thought it strange and beautiful. And I wondered who it was who gave the names to living things, even the unborn.

Father, his warriors, and many elders journeyed to Bald Mountain to make sacrifices to the Beast. The High Priest, Wolf Tongue, journeyed with them to be certain these prayers were heard. If Wolf Tongue prayed on behalf of the Panther Master, then surely a son must follow!

While the men were gone on their long pilgrimage, my mother grew heavy with child. One day, I remember, she drew me aside, and her hands were full of secrets.

"Starflower," she signed, "you will have a sister come next full moon."

"A sister?" I replied, horrified. "No, Mother. No, Wolf Tongue has gone with Father to the mountain. He will pray to the Beast, and surely the Beast will give you a son!"

But Mother shook her head. "Child, the Beast cannot give life. He can only crush it. He has no power that his worshipers do not confer on him, and even they, no matter how fervent, cannot grant him the power of life-giving."

"How can you say this?" I asked. "This is blasphemy!"

I was afraid for her. If Father were to learn these secret thoughts dwelling in Mother's heart, he would be forced to kill her. But perhaps he would never discover it. After all, men do not know the language of women. It would be a sin for them to learn it or to acknowledge that they understood it. Maybe she would be safe?

Mother must have seen these thoughts racing across my face, for she smiled. "Not blasphemy but truth. You will learn it yourself one day."

I could not stop the tears that sprang to my eyes. If this was the truth, if Mother did indeed have a daughter and not a son, then she would still die. The elders would put her to death, along with the child. No woman who birthed two daughters and no sons could continue being the Eldest's wife.

Mother's face was peaceful; there was no fear in her eyes. This frightened me more. But she put her arms around me, holding me, breathing comfort into my hair. When at last she put me from her, she signed, "You must be brave, Starflower. And you must learn to search out the names of things as I have taught you. When you know them, you must store them in your heart. And one day . . ." She smiled and drew a deep breath before continuing, her hands shaking. "One day, you will speak those names aloud, and in speaking, you will be stronger than death or life-in-death!"

She placed my hands over her rounded stomach. I felt the baby moving there. "Promise me," my mother signed, "that you will watch over your sister."

She read the promise in my eyes.

Father and the elders returned before the next full moon. Wolf Tongue was not with them. But he had declared that the Beast, though unseen, had nonetheless heard their prayers. The Panther Master must have a son! The elders were confident.

I don't believe I had ever heard a woman's voice before that night. Perhaps I had and smothered the memory because it was too strange for me. But that night, my mother screamed and screamed, and nothing the midwife did could stop her.

Father prowled the opposite side of the dim, smoke-filled house, his body dark against the light of the fire. He saw me at last, crouched in a corner. I could not take my eyes off my mother. I hardly recognized her, so contorted was she in awful pain.

Father came over to me and hauled me to my feet. I do not think he intended to hurt me. He was too frightened himself to realize what he did. His face was gray and his teeth flashed in the firelight.

"Get out of here, girl," he said. "Get out!"

I fled the house.

The hillside was black that night, for the moon, though full, hid behind thick clouds. The Eldest's house was set high above the rest of the village, greater than all other buildings save the Long Hall. Light poured from the windows of the Hall below me, and I knew that the elders waited there for word of the Eldest's new son. I could hear their brutal songs.

I sat in the darkness halfway down the hill, afraid to venture any nearer to the village, afraid to look back up at the house. Mother's screams were dulled by distance, but each one hacked my ears, hewing at my sanity like a great hatchet.

Oh, Mother!

The moon broke suddenly through the darkness above me. Light poured onto the hillside around, like water rushing in spring rains. It startled me so much that I forgot, if only for a moment, the cruel sounds filling the night. A moment later, I could not have heard those screams or those raucous songs had I strained my ears for them!

Music filled the world.

It flowed from the moon above in a language I had never heard, but which I understood. A language like water, like light. For an instant, I understood everything! Only for an instant, but it was so clear while it lasted. I understood that the Beast was not the giver of life. No, not even the giver of death! I understood that I had always been made to sing, to raise my voice to join with those of the moon and the sun and that greater, more beautiful voice that had taught them the songs! Such a moment it was . . . a moment beyond life, beyond death.

But when I opened my mouth to sing in reply, instead of my own voice, I heard that final scream.

The moon vanished behind the clouds. The song was gone, as though it had never been. I turned to gaze up at my father's house and knew, as I looked at the light shining dully through the low doorway, that my mother was dead.

But the baby . . .

The next moment, my feet were flying back up the hill. There was no time for thought. I burst through the curtain hung over the entrance. The hearth fire cast horrible shadows upon the walls, like the giants of old etched in darkness. Mother lay so still upon her pallet. The midwife beside her wrapped something in soft skins. The bundle mewled unhappily.

The Panther Master stood across the room, his arms folded and his face like a stone. He saw me in the doorway. "I told you to go," he said.

I heard him but could not make myself understand his words. The midwife, still carrying the crying child, stepped over to the fire and stirred an evil-smelling brew that bubbled in a pot. Noxious fumes rose with the smoke.

Poison!

I flung myself across the room and snatched the baby from the midwife. A foolish gesture, I knew, for where could I go? The midwife, crouching by the hearth, lunged after me, staggering under her own heavy bulk so that I easily eluded her grasp. I backed away from her until I hit the far wall. Both the midwife and my father approached.

"Give back the child, Starflower," said my father, putting out both hands. I held the infant closer. "You know the law," my father said. "Hand over the babe and let Doefoot feed her the brew."

I bared my teeth at him like a mongrel. When he took a step closer, I ducked under his arms and fled to the doorway.

I ran into Wolf Tongue's arms.

The High Priest was taller than any man in the Land, so tall that he could scarcely fit inside my father's house. His strong hands, which could have broken my neck without a thought, pinched deeply into my shoulders. I was a rabbit caught in a hawk's talons. But I clutched the baby close to my chest.

"Wolf Tongue!" the Panther Master gasped as he ducked his head to exit the house. "You have come already."

"The Beast sent me," said the priest. At the sound of his voice, my body trembled so hard, I feared I would drop the baby. I had never before stood so close to Wolf Tongue, never heard his voice so near. I had always seen him at a distance, offering the harvest sacrifices or giving his dark blessing to the warriors before they marched off to bloodshed. Even from a distance, he had seemed too terrible and enormous to be flesh and blood.

But now I stood near enough to hear his deep-throated breathing, to smell the mustiness of his wolfskin robes. This nightmare was real. I felt his eyes upon me, though I ducked my head and hunched over, trying to hide the wailing baby.

"Have you an heir?" Wolf Tongue asked.

My father stood for a silent heartbeat. Then he shook his head. "I have a second daughter."

Just as Mother said. The Beast had not heard the Panther Master's prayers.

One of Wolf Tongue's hands let go of my shoulder. I heard the scrape of a knife being drawn.

My body reacted without thought. I brought my heel down sharply on the priest's bare foot, then drove an elbow into his stomach. He grunted, astonished if not hurt, and I took that moment to wrench myself free. I stood then in the empty place between my father and Wolf Tongue, a cornered deer with hounds and hunters all around. My senses whirled with the need to flee, and the baby screamed. But my limbs were frozen.

Wolf Tongue clutched a flint knife in his hand. He did not look at me. His eyes bore into my father instead.

"You know the law, Panther Master."

The Eldest opened his mouth, then closed it.

"Two daughters are a disgrace," said the priest. "You, the Eldest of the Land, are shamed this night. Your shame can only be cleansed with blood."

A shudder ran through my father's body and escaped in a long sigh. "The babe's mother is dead," he said. "Is that not blood enough?"

The look on his face was unfathomable to me. The twisted pain and sorrow mirrored my own. Once again I wondered: Did the Panther Master love my mother?

Did he love me?

But there was death in the High Priest's eyes. "You know the law," he said. "If a man fathers two daughters and no sons, one daughter must be given to the Beast. You are Eldest of your people. You must set the example for all. You must choose, Panther Master, and choose quickly."

I was caught in a snare. When I moved to run, Wolf Tongue stepped in my way. His movements were like those of a wild animal, too fast and too fluid to be followed. I saw how his muscles tensed like those of a panther prepared to leap, and he raised his knife. There would be no escaping this man.

The baby's cries were becoming more desperate. My head spun with the sound, and all my instincts cried out to protect. There, before the Eldest and the priest, trapped in that small slice of eternity where only death waited, I looked down into my sister's face.

She was so tiny, and by no means beautiful. She was red, dirty from birth. But she was alive. Her feet were small and perfect, her hands more perfect still. For a split second, black eyes, bright and hungry, gazed up at me. In their blackness shone a light like the stars, like the moon, like the silver song I had heard such a short time ago on this same hillside.

"The time is now," Wolf Tongue snarled, and he crouched before me, his hands reaching for my sister.

I spat in his eye.

For a moment he did not move. He crouched, spit on his cheek, one eye closed. The other focused on me with such intensity I did not think I had more than a few breaths left to live.

It did not matter. I turned to my father and gave him the baby. I did not look at his face, nor did I wait to hear anything he might say. He could not have stopped me one way or the other. He was broken. Everything about this man, this strong Eldest of elders, bespoke his defeat. No, he could not help either my sister or me. So I did not wait for him.

I turned back to Wolf Tongue, who still crouched in place. His knife hand hung limply between his knees. The other slowly wiped spit from his face.

I knelt before him, my hands folded over my heart, and bowed my head.

"No!" My father's voice was sharp behind me. "No, this is not my choice, Wolf Tongue! You . . . you must give me time!"

But there was no time. Wolf Tongue must have my blood. I had insulted him. I belonged to the Beast now.

Wolf Tongue gave no sign that he heard the Eldest speak. I felt him staring at me, felt the heat of his yellow eyes. He must have seen how my body quivered with terror as I knelt in his shadow. But I would not back down.

His knife hand never moved. The other, however, reached out and touched my cheek. In a low voice, he whispered to me:

"No one dares stand up to me. No one, little beauty."

His touch was loathsome. I struggled to breathe, to make my lungs expand. But I met his gaze eye for eye.

Wolf Tongue ran his tongue over his teeth, which gleamed white even on that clouded night. Then he stood, towering over me.

"Hear my words, Eldest," he said, without breaking my gaze. "For a time, you will keep both daughters, and no shame will rest upon your head. But when the Beast requires blood, then you will give him his due."

The next instant, he was gone, vanishing silently as a dream. I, my mind so full of fear that I could make no sense of what had just happened, remained where I knelt. I felt the Eldest's arm around my shoulders, lifting me to my feet. I heard my sister's whimpers.

"Come inside," the Panther Master said, "my brave Starflower."

The midwife waited for us, sitting beside the still body of my mother. She held in her pudgy hands a stone cup of the foul brew. Her gap-toothed grin made me sick as I entered our house, propelled from behind by my father. I held my sister tight.

The midwife's hands moved quickly. "Come here, child," she signed. "Bring the babe to me. I will feed her this; then you must go to the village and find her a wet nurse since the mother is dead."

I was numb. I considered running. But I knew without even a glance at the Eldest that this would be useless. Heart heavy, I knelt before the midwife and watched the woman dip a finger into the cup, then lift the brown liquid to the baby's desperate, sucking mouth.

My sister gave a cry at the bitter taste. Then the cry shriveled away and vanished as the cursed medicine took effect.

It is the will of the Beast that lowly women should not voice the wicked thoughts of their hearts. They must go forever silent in the world of men, speaking only the language of their hands and faces. Now nothing but the greatest pain would give my sister a voice. Otherwise, she would remain as mute as I am.

2

I BECAME A WALKING CURSE.

Everywhere I went, little Fairbird strapped to my back, people turned their faces from me. Women were cursed from birth as it is, but a woman-child who was supposed to be dead was that much more unlucky. Mothers kept their children from me and made certain that my shadow never crossed theirs. Girls with whom I had played silent games now ran at the sight of me.

I did not care. They were cruel old cats, every one of them! Yet even as I scorned them and their scorn of me, I understood. We are each of us allotted so much time for our lives. Whether the Beast commands this time or not, I cannot say; such things are beyond my knowledge. I do know what the priests taught: When a life is demanded, a life must be given. That is why they sacrifice before the wars, so that the sacrificed lives might substitute for those warriors who otherwise owed their blood in battle.

Fairbird had not died at her time. And no one had paid her blood price.

While the contempt of the women and the rejection of my playmates were painful, the fury of the menfolk aimed at my father was worse. As though it were somehow the Panther Master's fault that a daughter was born and not a son. Had my mother lived, I know the blame would have fallen upon her head, and the Panther Master would have needed all his cunning to save her from the elders' bloodthirsty hands. As it was, they focused their anger on him.

The Crescent People withdrew their sworn allegiance. The North Walkers retreated to their territories and made war against any tribe that dared approach them. Many others rejected the Eldest's leadership. The peace that had maintained a tentative hold on the Land since the early years of my father's rule were replaced with bloodshed. And it was my fault.

But the High Priest had spoken. Fairbird was safe from the Beast. At least until he saw fit to claim his due.

My life remained separate from the wars. When the campaign seasons came, my father went to battle with his loyal men, and I did not see him for months at a time. I kept to myself, walking in my mother's footsteps. I cooked. I planted. I weeded and harvested. I repaired the house when the summer storms tore bits off the roof and knocked in one wall. And I cared for Fairbird. I became a woman well before my time.

So the years passed.

Fairbird grew from babe to lovely child. I don't know if others would think her as beautiful as I did. In my eyes, she was perfection. I could see so much of my mother in her, especially when her tiny hands formed the words I taught her. I brought Fairbird up in the way I believed my mother would have raised her.

And always, I searched for her true name. Mother was not alive to know it as she had known mine. I must discover it for myself. No child should live a life unnamed. Though my father called her Fairbird, I knew there must be something deeper still. A name he had not given but that was as much a part of her being as her own black eyes.

Let me speak now of spring, one year gone. The gnarled fig trees disguised their disfigured limbs in clouds of pink, and ancient mangoes put forth clusters of delicate flowers that filled the air with a mild, sweet scent. Starflower vines, thick and lustrous, encroached upon the orchards and were pruned back, their severed branches used to adorn our doorways and rooftops for good luck. And my father set out with his men to war upon the Crescent People.

My life would always be one of solitude, I knew, save for Fairbird. And in solitude there was shame. It was best, of course, for a girl to be given to a man. Unwed women were often cast out of the village, for women are unlucky at best, and if they do not have a man to serve, they are useless. Not that the wives enjoyed a happy lot. It was rare for a wife to love her man as my mother had loved the Panther Master. Still, at least they had a place in the village.

Since the night my sister was born and I took upon myself the curse of unshed blood, I knew I would never wed. I was the Eldest's daughter, and I would keep his house and tend his crops until such a time as he might choose a new bride. Then he might cast me out, me and Fairbird too.

So far I had been fortunate. Though victorious in his campaigns, the Panther Master never brought home a new bride. I had long since ceased fearing my replacement. I had a place in the community, unwanted though I might be. I did not need a man. Isolated as I was up the hill from the village, I rarely came in contact with the village lads my age. I knew they hated me, as did all of Redclay Village, but their hatred manifested itself in treating me as though I did not exist.

One day, all of that changed.

I always took Fairbird with me when I fetched water. When she was little, I could strap her to my back and carry her as well as the heavy skins. At four years old, she was too big for me. Curious as a pouncing puppy, she would scamper off after the smallest butterfly—impossible to keep a hold on! So I would tie a string to my waist and another to hers, and lead her thus down the hill to the stream.

The stream flowed just past the outskirts of the village to the gorge, where it dropped into the river far below. I dared not take my water from any streambed near Redclay, however. I did not wish Fairbird to see how the other women feared her. Therefore, twice a day we would make the long walk down to where the stream ran to the gorge. There was a bank where I could fill the skins and also look down to the rushing water below us.

It was a grand sight, that river running beneath our feet, cutting the ground so deeply. It must have been about its task of carving the land for hundreds and hundreds of years, since before the Beast became our god. I loved to watch that white water, charging and roaring and powerful. I would hold Fairbird and stand on the edge of the gorge, looking down that long way. The river wound through the rock, then vanished into the wild forest that grew below.

One midsummer evening, when the sky was beginning to cool from the harsh heat, I took Fairbird to our customary watering place. She was tired and petulant that day, flinging herself to the ground and signing "No!" more often than I liked. I often wondered if I had given our mother nearly as much trouble! I was tired and harried by the time we reached the stream at the gorge edge . . . which is why, I believe, I did not see the boys.

They must have known I came this way. I had never thought to vary my route or habits, never felt the need for secrecy. I was the Eldest's daughter. I was ignored and shunned, but I never feared for my safety.

The moment I saw them, five great lads—only just too young to make the rites of passage into manhood and join the warriors—my stomach sank with foreboding. They sprawled on the banks, hot and irritable, some of them dripping from a recent watery brawl. Their dogs lounged nearby, scuffed from fighting one another but docile for the moment. Their ears pricked when they saw me, and their barks alerted their masters.

I drew up short at once, standing there as still as a hunted doe, my waterskins clutched under each arm, my sister tied to my waist.

Five pairs of eyes turned to me.

Just at that moment, Fairbird decided to make one of her dramatic falls, flinging herself to the ground. She tugged me off balance, and I nearly fell myself, dropping one of the skins.

The biggest of the five boys laughed. "Look what we have here," he said. "The blight!"

"A pretty blight," said another with a look that made me shudder. "Prettiest blight I've ever seen."

A third slapped this lad on the shoulder saying, "Don't kiss her, Killdeer! You'll break out in boils, so they say!"

"And is that the little sacrifice?" a fourth boy asked, pointing to my sister. There was cruelty in his face.

I dropped the other waterskin and hastened to pick up Fairbird. She was too far gone in her sulk to realize the danger before us. She wrapped her arms around my neck and wept silent tears into my shoulder for some grievance I still don't know. My attention was fixed on the second boy, who had gotten to his feet. He wasn't the biggest of the bunch, but I knew him by reputation: Killdeer, the son of one of my father's warriors. He was a sullen-faced youth who hated his father with such a grim passion that many wondered how long it would be until one of them killed the other. But I scarcely cared about that. What mattered to me was what he had done to his dog.

All the village boys are given dogs the year before their manhood rites. These dogs will later follow them into battle and are as much a part of a warrior as his right arm. My father, as Eldest, had several great lurchers that accompanied him everywhere. I loved these dogs. In the winter months, it was my duty to care for them. They were such powerful animals, with fiercely loyal hearts. And they loved me. I was, in their eyes, as much their better as the Eldest himself, and they obeyed me, and I learned their ways and handling.

I would have loved to have my own dog. A wild fancy for a woman.

Yet Killdeer, by virtue of his sex, was given a bright and bouncing young pup. I remember watching it from a distance, thinking how smart and lively it was, so eager to please. Within a month, it was not the same animal. In so little time, Killdeer turned that eager pup into a snarling, wolfish, hateful creature, cringing from its own master, ready to tear out the world's throat. It would be a terror in battle, Killdeer boasted. But it would never serve him as it might have. He had beaten the love out of it.

So it was with anger rather than fear that I watched Killdeer approach me. "What do you say, pretty blight?" he said to me, a wicked smile on his mouth. "Want to kiss me and give me boils?"

I bared my teeth at him. He drew back a moment. It must be unsettling, I thought, to have a curse threaten to bite. Then his smile grew. "Or maybe I'll take the little blood sacrifice. You'll give a kiss to get *her* back, won't you?"

He lunged for me, taking hold of my sister. I turned away and drove an elbow into his side. He grunted, then by sheer force of size, wrenched Fairbird from my arms. Still attached to her by the cord, I staggered and fell. Fairbird's face twisted in a silent scream at the pain of the cord digging into her skin.

The sight filled me with such rage, I hardly knew myself. I was on my feet in an instant, flying at Killdeer. I had not the strength to punch that sullen face of his as it deserved, so I grabbed his hair instead, giving it such a vicious tug that he howled and dropped Fairbird. My sister, panicked, flung her arms around my knees, her body shaking. Overbalanced, I let go of Killdeer's hair and landed in the dirt, still tangled up in Fairbird and that fool cord.

A growl filled my ears.

I turned and found myself facing Killdeer's lurcher. The young dog's lips were drawn back, revealing its teeth. Saliva dripped from the end of its muzzle, and its eyes spoke its longing for blood.

I did not move. I knew from experience with my father's dogs that the only way to take mastery is to show no fear. Before this creature, ready at a moment's notice to tear off my face, it was nearly impossible not to cower. I know that is what Killdeer and his cohorts expected, and I heard them laughing in anticipation.

But I was not afraid, not after that first split instant of surprise. Instead, I was filled with a deep, heartrending pity.

This loveless creature had no true name. Unloved, it stood before me, broken even in its strength. Nameless, it would be no more than a brute all its days.

I did not fear that dog. Rather, I searched, gazing into its eyes to plumb the depths beneath.

Then I saw. I knew. A name that I could never speak. But I knew it now, and knew what this dog was meant to be had it known a tender master. And so I looked upon its snarling, frothing face and I loved it.

I do not know how long we were like stone in place. I remained crouched, one hand on the ground to support me, the other clutching Fairbird. The dog stood frozen in that snarl. Then suddenly the lurcher's ears went back and the teeth vanished. It lowered its muzzle and whined gently. Placing its forepaws out before it, it lowered its body to the ground, the picture of submission.

I put out my hand and grabbed it by the back of the neck, gentle but firm as well. It snarled and feinted an attack, but I did not move. If I flinched, I would lose my arm to those dripping jaws. Once more, the dog whined and put its nose between its outstretched paws. Its tail twitched faintly.

Killdeer, who had been too stunned by this display to speak, suddenly roared: *"Frostbite!"* He took a step and clouted his dog across the head, sending it sprawling and yelping.

As though in a dream, I heard a shout. The next moment, an enormous red dog hurled itself into Killdeer. Snarling and screams rent the air. I would have screamed myself if I could, but instead I sat with my arms wrapped around Fairbird, struggling to get to my feet. Somehow I couldn't make my limbs move. I saw the other four boys piling upon the red dog and Killdeer. Then Killdeer's own lurcher flung itself into the fray, dragging the red dog away from its master. The other boys hastened to restrain their own dogs from joining the fight. Killdeer was too shaken from the attack to do anything, and I could see poor Frostbite getting the worst of the battle.

Another shout. I turned to see a young man I did not know emerge from the gorge. He cried out, "Bear!" and plunged into the tangle of fighting dogs without hesitation. He grabbed the red dog and, with strength I would not have thought possible, hauled the animal off of Frostbite. Then he whirled upon the other boys.

"Get away from here! Go!" he shouted, his face like thunder. He was older than they, though not by much. They looked at one another, calculating their numbers and trying to decide whether they ought to attack this stranger. "Do you want to fight me?" the stranger said, his voice menacing. He took a step toward the largest of the lads, one hand still holding his dog, the other forming a fist.

The boys fled, taking their dogs with them. All except Killdeer, sniffling like a child. He had forgotten Frostbite.

The stranger turned to me and Fairbird. "Down, Bear," he said, and his dog immediately dropped to the ground, its eyes alert, watching its master. The young man, however, stepped over to me, and much to my astonishment, offered me a hand.

"This seems a fine beginning to my duty in Redclay," he said. "A good brawl, a good service. A lucky omen, I wonder?"

I stared at his hand. The men of the village never put themselves out to help a woman unless their own woman is threatened in some way. Yet this stranger offered me aid! Embarrassed, I didn't know which way to look.

Fairbird, however, felt no reserve. With a brilliant smile, she pushed away from me and took the stranger's hand. He, with a shrug, helped her to her feet instead. Fairbird clung to him, swinging his arm back and forth, and beamed up at him, her brown, tear-stained face transformed from its terror. He grinned back at her, then turned and watched me as I picked myself up, brushed off my skirts, and quickly untied my sister's lead.

The stranger looked me up and down. "Of course," he said, his grin widening a little, "I should not be surprised. Boys that age are louts. They think tormenting a beautiful girl is the easiest way to catch her eye."

I stared at him. For one thing, it was odd for him to refer to my attackers as "that age" when he could scarcely be much older. That superior tone did not suit my liking, or so I told myself. But his other words touched something inside me I had not known existed.

Beautiful?

I realized I was blushing and quickly looked away. I saw Killdeer's lurcher lying on its side.

With a gasp, I hastened to the dog, my fluster forgotten for the moment. The poor thing was panting, its eyes rolling and its tongue lolling. I realized then that Frostbite was female. And she had flung herself at the great male in defense of a master she hated. My heart surged, and I put my hands on her with as much tenderness as I could, checking her hurts. A wound in her shoulder gaped and would need stitches, and one ear was almost completely torn off. I found myself angry that such harm had been done to this brave animal. As my anger had no other focus, I cast a dark glare up at the stranger.

But he, gently setting Fairbird aside, knelt down beside me. "Poor thing. She should have stayed away from Bear. He wouldn't have hurt her owner, merely scared him as he deserved. Maybe a little more than he deserved. Bear is not one to turn from a fight."

So it was her fault? I wanted to ask, my eyes flashing. It was just as well that I had no voice.

"Can you help her?" the stranger asked me next. "I am trained for battle and have no knowledge of healing. But if you know what to do, I'll carry her to your home and assist you."

The notion of walking back to the village with this stranger following me was somehow frightening. But I knew I would never get Frostbite home by myself. Biting my lip, I nodded. Then I got to my feet and swung Fairbird up onto my hip, keeping her well back while the stranger knelt and gathered the poor dog into his arms. Frostbite snarled and snapped, but he was no more afraid of her than I had been. She must have sensed something in him to trust. . . . That, or her wounds were too great. Either way, she relaxed in his arms. He spoke a sharp word to his dog, which rose to follow but remained a good many paces behind.

Then the stranger turned to me. "Lead on."

Leaving the waterskins behind, I did as I was told. We were an odd procession, I with Fairbird in my arms, he bearing Frostbite, and the huge red dog pacing just behind. I was thankful that the Eldest's House stood on the near side of the village and I would not have to lead the stranger through the center of town. As it was, I could not meet the eyes of those we passed, and they, rather than ducking away to be certain their shadows did not cross mine, stood and stared.

The stranger took no notice of this. His face was fixed, and he looked neither to the left nor the right. He spoke not a word until we began the climb to the Eldest's House.

"Stop a moment," he said then.

I obeyed and turned to look at him. His face had an amused expression, one eyebrow raised curiously. "This place cannot belong to any but the Eldest Panther Master," he said, looking up at the house on the hill. There was no mistaking it. It was bigger by far than any other to be seen, set up high to oversee Redclay. Wherever the stranger came from, I was certain, no elders from his tribe lived in a house so grand . . . though this one housed only me, my sister, and the Eldest.

I nodded, though there was no need. He already knew he was right. "Are you a slave of the Panther Master?" he asked.

My father kept many slaves taken from the wars to work his fields. But they lived in small huts on the fringes of the village. None of them ever came near the Eldest's House. I shook my head, raising my chin. Though a woman and a cursed woman at that, I was no slave.

"Are you then . . ." And here the stranger laughed shortly and shook his head. "You aren't the Eldest's daughter Starflower."

I stared at him a moment, wondering what that laugh of his meant. Then I answered with a cool nod.

Here he tossed back his head and gave a real laugh, startling poor Frostbite so that she struggled in his arms. Adjusting his grip and clucking soothingly to the dog, he cut his laugh short. When he had quieted her again, he looked me up and down. I felt a bit like a fine cow he was considering buying. But his smile was warm.

"I am Sun Eagle," he said, "son of Darkwing, elder of the Crescent People. I come in advance to Redclay to tell your people of Eldest Panther Master's victories. The Crescent People are once more united to the tribes under his rule. In a month's time or less, the warriors of the Crescent People will come to Redclay and pledge their spears to the Panther Master forever."

Here he stopped, and his bold face wore, if only for an instant, faint traces of bashfulness.

"To seal the vows," he said, "I am to wed Maid Starflower."

3

EANRIN

"GOOD CHOICE."

The voice that spoke was near, Eanrin thought. But it was difficult to tell for certain in the blackness. There were other sounds here, many voices crying out in many languages. Those were fainter, yet not necessarily far away. It was, Eanrin thought, as though the voices themselves were so small that they almost could not be heard. But his ears were quick, especially now when his sight was, for the present, smothered.

He tried to think. It was difficult in all this darkness, but he forced himself to stop and put at least a handful of thoughts together. The first was the realization that he was not falling. Or at least he didn't seem to be. He wasn't entirely certain that one could move at all in blackness this deep.

He also realized that his voice was one of those screaming.

This embarrassed him, and he immediately closed his mouth. What a faint, pathetic sound it had been. Certainly not worthy of the Bard of Rudiobus.

"Of course, in the end, there wasn't another choice, was there?"

Oh yes! He'd almost forgotten. Someone else was here. Someone whose voice was much bigger than the tiny voices all around. Eanrin turned about, searching, but remained as blind as ever. What was more, though he could have sworn the voice had spoken right in his ear, he could not feel the sensation of a body near to hand or hear any sound of breathing. All his cat's senses strained for some other indication of a presence. But there was nothing. Only those tiny screams that were too small to understand.

"You must choose your own way. Let no one else direct you! Choose your own way, and it will always lead you here."

Eanrin didn't tremble. He was a man of Rudiobus. He was not afraid. Instead, he asked, "Why are all those people shouting?"

"They are crying out for their rights."

Eanrin took a moment to consider this. "What are their rights?" he asked at last. He could scarcely hear himself speak. But whoever stood beside him in the dark seemed to have no difficulty.

"To choose their own paths," it replied. "To live their lives without obligation. To be the gods of their own worlds."

Once more Eanrin considered. Then he asked, "Why are their voices so small?"

"Because I have given them what they demanded. I have allotted them worlds in which they may reign divine. And those worlds are small."

"How small?"

"Very small."

Eanrin tried to lick his lips. But the darkness was so penetrating, he couldn't be certain he had a body anymore. Still, he wasn't afraid. After all, nothing had happened yet to cause him any real alarm. He had fallen down a chasm, yes, but the fall appeared to be over, and he appeared to be unharmed. The darkness was thick, but it wasn't as though darkness could actually hurt anyone.

Another thought finally formed in his brain. "Am *I* a god?"

The voice, which now seemed to be laughing, said, "Not yet. Your world is rapidly shrinking. Soon, it will have room for no one but you.

Then you will be a god. Then you will not hear these other voices. In your world, there is room for you and no one else. In your world, you will reign uncontested."

The words rang clearly, far above all the little voices. These were shrinking into a dull hum, though the smaller they got, the more violent they sounded in their incoherency.

"Wait," Eanrin whispered. "When I am a god, will I be . . . alone?"

"Yes."

The word pressed down upon him, crushing. Eanrin wasn't certain that he had lungs, but if he did, they could no longer draw breath.

"When you are a god, you can only be alone."

He wasn't certain he had shoulders, but if he did, they were bowed under the weight.

"And yet who would not choose to be a god?"

He wasn't certain that he had a heart, but if he did, it no longer beat.

A sudden light burst through the blackness.

The brilliance was painful to Eanrin's unaccustomed eyes, but it proved that he was not blind, so he turned to it. How far away it was, scarcely more than a pinprick, but swiftly approaching. Against his will, his arms outstretched, but when he opened his mouth to speak, he found he had no words.

A rhythmic pace beat upon his ears. A loping gait, unhurried, unthwarted, deliberate as it advanced.

"He's coming!" spoke the voice in the darkness behind Eanrin's shoulder. "He will be upon you soon!"

"Who is coming?" Eanrin formed the words without sound. Shading his eyes, he strained to peer into that brilliant glare.

"Quick, take my hand!" Eanrin felt something touch him in the dark. He shuddered and stepped away, but the voice spoke with still more urgency.

"If you do not come with me, he will catch you, and you will lose everything! Everything you are. Do you understand me? So voracious is his appetite, he will devour you!"

"Who will?"

"The Hound!" hissed the voice, made small in its terror. "The Hound is coming!"

4

STARFLOWER

SUN EAGLE CARRIED WITH HIM my father's name mark, a large red bead with a black panther painted across it. This he presented to the older men, those who were past the age for battle but who stood guard over the village while the fighting men were gone. Though the bead was certainly genuine, they remained uneasy with the presence of a Crescent lad. Until the Eldest and his warriors returned, Sun Eagle would know only uneasy hospitality in Redclay. Many cast him dark glances and even muttered threats when he passed by.

"Traitor's son," they called him.

To avoid as much unpleasantness as possible, he hid away in the most unfrequented quarter of the village: the Eldest's House, home of the cursed children.

I was no more at ease in his presence than any other in my village, though for different reasons. But as the days passed, Sun Eagle proved himself a quiet, well-spoken young man. He seemed to sense my discomfort, and rather than take advantage of it as other young men might, he kept his distance.

I watched him as I went about my daily tasks, this stranger who, if he spoke the truth, was to be my husband. As an elder's son, he did not assist me in any of the household work but spent much of his time whittling a new spear shaft or chipping away at a sharp rock to make the head. His movements were deft, and I could see that his work was fine. I had often watched my father go about similar tasks during the winter months. I thought Sun Eagle's work perhaps equal to the Eldest's.

Fairbird adored him. She was forever lingering in his shadow, frightened as a shy kitten if he looked her way but quickly warming the moment he showed any sign of friendliness. I, however, was less easily won.

One day, I sat in the yard tending to Frostbite's shoulder. The poor dog was slow to recover and made nervous by the close proximity of Bear. But she had learned to trust me since the encounter by the stream, and I loved her. Not for any grace of temper or outward beauty on her part. She was a mean-spirited creature still, willing to bite my hand even as I fed her. And she was certainly no beauty with her shaggy gray coat and long nose. But I loved her. I loved her because no one else had, and she needed love more than she knew, poor beast. And as I tended her wounds, I poured that love through my fingers and hands, stroking her head and ears, willing her to take it in. It was a slow process, but within twelve days, I began to see a softening in her spirit as her longing for affection grew.

I could see Sun Eagle from where I worked. He sat in the shade cast by the house, concentrating on some project. I could not see what it was, only that it was not a weapon. It was difficult to discern more than that, especially while carefully pretending disinterest. So I smeared a soothing poultice on Frostbite's mending skin and told myself that I did not care.

Suddenly I heard Sun Eagle laugh. I turned and saw my sister standing in front of him, a great smile on her face. He was hanging something around her neck. Even from that distance, I realized what it was: a name bead like my father's, like the one my mother had made for me. Sun Eagle had carved it from wood and colored it with pigments.

Fairbird grabbed hold of the cord in order to draw the bead up to her face. Then she turned and ran to me, so excited I thought she would burst with her need to laugh. Aware of Sun Eagle's gaze upon me, I inspected the trinket. It was fine work, especially for a young warrior in training. The dyes were simple, the background a burnt orange, and the figure of a bird done in rich brown. It looked like a songbird, I thought, though it was too small for any detail.

In Fairbird's eyes, it was the most glorious of treasures. So I smiled at her pleasure, signed for her to tuck it inside her doeskin shirt or it might get scratched. She nodded, then ran off with it still clutched between her small brown hands, unwilling to hide it away just yet.

Frostbite whined and pressed against my side. Sun Eagle's shadow fell across us.

"I saw that she had no name mark," he said. Then he crouched before me and gently stroked Frostbite's head. The lurcher trembled but allowed the caress for a few moments before backing away, growling. It would take her time to become used to gentleness. Sun Eagle withdrew his hand, resting his elbows on his knees where he crouched. "Tell me, Starflower," he said, "is your sister truly cursed as they say?"

I hardly knew how to answer. I could shake my head no, but what good was my word against the word of the village men? So I remained still, looking at him, letting my answer rest in my face. *Does she seem a curse to you?*

He narrowed his eyes, then turned away, gazing down the hill to the village. "They say you're cursed as well."

Who would want a cursed bride?

I picked up my herbs, mortar, and pestle. Let the young man think what he liked. It made no difference to me. If my father bade me marry him, I would. If Sun Eagle refused to take me, I would not.

And if the Beast swept down from the mountains and devoured me, then so be it. I have no say, no voice. I am a woman.

These thoughts rolled through my brain as I rose with my armload to return to the house. Frostbite trotted after, keeping close to my heel. Sun Eagle also followed. He did not enter the house after me but lounged in the doorway, watching as I slid the mortar and pestle into place and began rehanging the herbs I had used for the poultice.

"Do you intend to give the dog back to its owner?" he asked.

This took me by surprise. I paused in my task, staring first at him, then down to Frostbite, who sat by my feet. Sun Eagle must have seen how my expression hardened, for he laughed suddenly.

"Ha! Let the lad come get her if he wants her!" he said. "If he has the courage to face you again, that is. That dog is more yours now than she will ever be his. She would tear out his throat at a word from you."

I blinked and swallowed hard at this forthright statement of my power. I looked down at Frostbite, who raised soulful brown eyes up to me. I could not imagine her in battle now. Not after coming to know her. She could be broken, of course, could lose the truth of her nature and be made into a monster again. But the real dog—the one whose true name I had discovered—was not bloodthirsty.

I knew, though, that Sun Eagle was right. She would die to defend me. And she might kill her former master in the process. I placed a hand on the lurcher's head and offered a prayer (not to the Beast, who would revel in blood) that Killdeer would have the sense to stay away.

When I raised my gaze to Sun Eagle again, he smiled at me. It was a warm, knowing smile. A smile that made me think perhaps he saw me. Not merely my silent woman self, cursed and little better than a slave. But me, who I was, with all my longings, weaknesses, and even strengths. He smiled, and I was uncertain how to respond to that look from this young man I was to wed.

At last I came to a decision. I smiled in return.

That moment, we heard the first shout heralding my father's homecoming.

The elders of all the tribes loyal to my father gathered for the betrothal ceremony marking the Crescent People's return to loyalty. Redclay Village had never before overflowed with so many warriors and revelers alike, and the women of the village were hard-pressed to provide food and drink for the men.

At the center of it all were the Panther Master and Elder Darkwing. I had hardly seen my father since his return, for he and his recent enemy, wary of each other, were in constant company, each unwilling to let the other out of his sight. Slaves were sent up to the Eldest's House, ordering me to prepare myself for the betrothal rites.

I was given no information as to what preparations I should make. I did my best on my own, with Fairbird and Frostbite both getting underfoot in their muddled attempts to help and to ensure they were not forgotten. I unwrapped my mother's gown from where it had been stored since her death. She had worn it for her own betrothal, and it was beautiful, I thought. The doeskin was a warm brown, and many colored beads and stones decorated the neck and sleeves. I put it on and, despite Fairbird's help, arranged my hair.

For five years, I had remained hidden, avoiding the village people. Now I would be displayed before all their unfriendly eyes. I would not allow myself to be shamed.

Three maids and two warriors came to the house at sunset to escort me down to the village. I hated leaving Fairbird behind . . . she had never been alone before. Desperately, I signed to Frostbite to watch over my sister, not knowing how much of the command the dog understood. Then, flanked by the warriors and preceded by the maidens—girls I had once known and played with but who now pretended they did not know me—I was led down into the thick of the revelry.

I caught no sight of Sun Eagle in the throng. Men were laughing and shouting, women were scurrying like silent shadows, girls danced in a ring around a great bonfire, and the young boys who had yet to make their passage into manhood watched them and called raucous remarks. Warriors drank heavily, their stoic faces melting into either jollity or anger. Brawls broke out among some.

If this was the solemn ceremony of betrothal and oath swearing, I wondered what horrors awaited me on my wedding day.

At long last I was brought to the center of it all, amid the noise and clatter and roiling smells. The night was deep and lit red with torches. My father wore a great panther skin across his shoulders, his bare chest painted with red claws. He was noble and terrible, a frightening and foreign figure as he presided over the madness. Darkwing, seated at my father's feet in the place of a conquered enemy, wore black feathers in a collar around his neck. Like his son, he was a handsome man, but with a cruel line to his mouth that Sun Eagle had not acquired.

My father put out a hand to me, and I went to him, took that hand, and bowed over it. He must have felt how I trembled, for his other hand rested briefly on my head, an almost tender gesture. Then he turned me to face Darkwing, who had risen and stood before us, his mouth still more downturned.

"In pledge of our newfound friendship, I offer you my daughter," said the Panther Master.

For a brief, terrifying moment, I thought I was being given to this man, not to Sun Eagle. Darkwing turned, however, and drew Sun Eagle forward from the shadows. The sight of the young man's face, while not dear to me, was such a relief that I smiled at him. He saw my smile and perhaps took it to mean more than I intended. He did not smile in return, but his eyes shone in the torchlight. My stomach dropped and my smile vanished. I wondered if it was dread that I felt. Perhaps it was something else, but I was too frightened and confused in that moment to know. The man who was to be my husband was presented before the Panther Master.

"And I, in token of my loyalty, give you my son," said Elder Darkwing. "May the joining of our children mark the eternal joining of our nations." There was bitterness in the elder's voice but truth as well. He would not turn back on his vows.

Then his eyes fell upon me for an instant. I shuddered under his gaze. I saw in that man's face everything he would not dare to say aloud.

Curse! his eyes screamed. *Blight on your father's house! And you will curse my son as well!*

But he had lost the war to the Panther Master. He must pay the price.

I lowered my gaze and scarcely dared to look up again, even as my hand was joined with Sun Eagle's and the rites of betrothal were performed by a young, skinny priest in a wolfskin robe. He trembled as he spoke the words, and I saw his hand shake as he sacrificed the goat. The terrible bleating of that animal rang in my head, and I thought I would be sick. But at our wedding, many more awful sacrifices would be given to the Beast, and these would be made by Wolf Tongue himself. How I dreaded that night to come!

Before it could take place, however, Sun Eagle needed to make his passage into manhood. This, I learned, would take place in three days' time. A week later, when Sun Eagle was officially made a warrior, we would be wed.

But what of the Beast? I wondered. Had he forgotten the bargain he and my father had made? Or—and I trembled at this thought—would he simply take my sister when the time came to collect the debt? My heart began to race. I could not marry! I must not!

And I wondered suddenly if this was my father's plan all along . . . to spare me from the Beast should he come down from the mountain. For the Beast would never take any but a maiden. If I was married, I would be safe.

Fairbird! My heart cried out desperately inside me so that I could scarcely hear the young priest's babble or my betrothed's voice whispering in my ear. *Fairbird, my darling! I cannot let this happen!*

Yet what choice did I have?

It was deep into the night before the warriors escorted me back to the hill. They left me at my father's door, and I entered the house so exhausted I could scarcely see straight. I fell over Frostbite, who waited just inside the door. She yelped and snarled, then came back nosing my legs and wagging her tail, cringing as though she expected a blow. Poor creature. I patted her soothingly, then cast about for my sister.

I found her cradled in Wolf Tongue's arms.

My heart ceased to beat. For a moment, I believed I had died and fallen into some dark hell. Then, with a gasp, I flung myself across the room to where the High Priest sat cross-legged before a low fire, my sister sound asleep in his lap. He raised cold eyes to me and put up one hand. I stopped at the gesture as though my feet had grown roots. Everything in me urged to take my sister from him, but fear held me in place.

"Do not wake the child," he said. His voice was low. I thought it would shatter every bone in my body. He lowered his hand to rest on Fairbird's head, stroking her hair softly. "She was exhausted from weeping. She was abandoned in the dark." His eyes flashed at me. "I do not abandon my own. I keep them safe. I keep them close."

I shuddered. Frostbite pressed against my legs, whining softly.

Wolf Tongue looked at me long and hard. Something in his gaze reminded me of the expression on Sun Eagle's face only a few hours before at the commencement of our betrothal. I felt as though something dark and feral had fixed its eyes upon my naked spirit. I wanted to turn and run, to flee this house and this man's presence. But he held my sister. I could not go.

"You have grown, Starflower," said Wolf Tongue. "You are beautiful indeed."

My heart leapt in terror. Desperately I swallowed it back. Then, taking a firm step forward, I held out my arms for Fairbird. My eyes said what my tongue could not: *Give her to me!*

Wolf Tongue, I knew, understood. To my surprise, he stood. He had to bend his head and shoulders to fit beneath the too-low roof, and he seemed a tremendous figure full of dreadful power. But he held out the sleeping child.

"Take her," he said.

I sprang forward. But even as I took my sister, Wolf Tongue's hand clamped down on my upper arm. I struggled to pull away, but it was no use. So I stood still, clutching Fairbird to my breast, and felt the High Priest lean down until his breath warmed my ear.

"You have not forgotten your bargain with the Beast," he whispered. "He gave you back your sister only for a time. Soon he will demand blood."

I closed my eyes, cringing away from those words. But he took my face in his other hand and forced me to look at him. His eyes were oddly yellow and they glowed in the darkness of the hut. Inhuman eyes, I thought, though their expression was that of the earthiest man.

"The Panther Master knows his sin," Wolf Tongue said. "If he tries to thwart the will of the Beast, disaster will follow. You will never wed, Maid Starflower. You will not—"

"Wolf Tongue! Unhand my daughter."

Wolf Tongue's lips curled back in a snarl as he and I turned to the door. There stood my father, spear in hand, panther skin thrown back across his shoulder. I could not see his face in the darkness, but his stance was ready to attack.

"Eldest," said Wolf Tongue, and his voice was a growl. "Tell me, what right have you to make demands concerning the Beast's possessions?"

"She is not the Beast's. Nor is she yours, priest," said my father, advancing into the room, his spear at the ready. The glow of the fire struck the stone, turning it red. "Unhand her and leave this house."

"One of them belongs to my master," said the priest. He backed away from me, though his hand lingered upon my arm. "One of them must pay the blood price. And soon."

"Leave this house," the Eldest repeated. The head of his spear now hovered just before Wolf Tongue's heart. Wolf Tongue looked down at it. He smiled.

Faster than my eye could follow, he grabbed the stone head. Though it must have torn his hand, he wrenched it from the Panther Master's grasp. Flinging it into the shadows by the hearth, he turned to my father, his teeth flashing.

"I give you warning now!" he cried. "If you insist on giving away what does not belong to you, you and all your village will suffer. The Beast has spoken. He will not be denied!"

Then his voice softened, becoming sinister in its gentleness. "Do not think I speak without concern. Your people are my people, Eldest. I have shielded them from the Beast's wrath for many years now, longer than you know. But the Beast is a cruel god when crossed. I cannot stand in his way. Neither can you."

My father, empty-handed, stood in the darkness, and still I could not read his face. At last he spoke:

"Get out."

Once more, the priest growled. But when the Eldest took a step toward him, Wolf Tongue slipped around to the door. There he paused and looked back at us one last time. "You have been warned, Panther Master!"

He vanished.

Silence settled upon the Eldest's House. My father turned to me, but I was afraid and lowered my gaze to my sister instead. I found her wide black eyes staring up at me. I wondered how long she had been awake and how much she had understood. Tears falling down my cheeks, I pressed her close to my heart.

The day before his passage, Sun Eagle came to me in private. I was in the mango grove just below the Eldest's House, harvesting an early crop, still green, which I would set to ripen in covered baskets away from pests. Though my hands were busy, I struggled to keep my mind from pursuing any of the dark paths before it: the Beast, Wolf Tongue's threats, my father's silence. Most of all, marriage and what it might mean for my sister.

To keep these thoughts at bay, I concentrated on the blistering heat of the day, on the sweat gathered on my brow, on the leathery green leaves tickling my face and arms, on the hard skins of the fruit as I plucked them from their clusters.

A shadow fell across me. I looked up into Sun Eagle's solemn face.

"Starflower," he said, "I come to beg a boon of you."

My heart leapt, perhaps with fear, and I nearly dropped the basket balanced on my hip. I cast about for Fairbird, but she was some way up the hill, closer to the house. Only Frostbite was nearby, dozing in the shadow of a silver-branch tree.

"You're not afraid of me, are you?"

I startled at Sun Eagle's words and looked up at him quickly. But he wasn't laughing or mocking. He seemed merely curious. Hastily, I shook my head. I set down my basket, then folded my hands, indicating that I was willing to hear what he had come to say.

"As you know," he said, "I make my passage tomorrow. I shall descend into the gorge and journey into the Gray Wood. When I have killed a beast and returned with its hide, I will be deemed worthy of manhood."

I nodded. This was an ancient custom. The only time men entered the forest down in the gorges was at this momentous point in their lives. Some had returned with strange creatures, fabulous beasts with two heads or many horns, and even stranger still! One man, it was said, had come upon a goat with panther's legs and a mouth full of fangs. But it had never happened in my lifetime. Most of the lads returned with a squirrel or a rabbit, though this did not matter. The courage it took to enter the Gray Wood was enough to make them warriors.

"Your father," Sun Eagle continued, "has told me to keep his name mark and to carry it with me for luck. An honor I scarcely deserve from a warrior such as he!" A warrior who had bested his father in battle. The honor must be a bitter one for Sun Eagle. "But it would honor me still more," he continued, "were you to let me bear your name mark as well."

My hand flew to my throat, where I wore the blue bead painted with a white starflower. My mother had made it for me when I was younger than Fairbird. It was a beautiful piece, more beautiful by far than those worn by the other village girls. My mother had been gifted.

Sun Eagle watched me, his dark eyes intent. He must have known or at least guessed what it was he asked of me. He asked for my trust. He asked for my loyalty. To give him this gift meant so much more than a mere wish of luck.

"Please, Starflower," he said. And there was that look again, that look as though he knew my true name.

My hands trembled as I reached up and untied the leather cord from around my neck. I hesitated a moment, thinking of my mother's hands. I had watched them mixing the paint and carefully decorating the little marker. I had watched them string the trinket on this cord and had bounced with excitement when she held it out to me.

I placed it in Sun Eagle's outstretched hand. He tried to catch hold of my fingers, but I withdrew quickly, though I smiled a little. Then I signed, though I knew he would not understand, words from a song my mother had taught me: "Beyond the Final Water falling . . . won't you return to me?"

I signed it as a blessing. But Wolf Tongue's dark threats lurked on the brink of my mind. I shivered as a shadow of foreboding passed over my spirit. When I raised my gaze to Sun Eagle's, I found his eyes alight. But my own, I knew, held only fear.

"I'll slay a beast," said he, clutching the bead in his fist. "And I'll bring it back to place at your feet. You shall wear its fur as a mantle on our wedding day."

The next morning I stood beside my father at the edge of the gorge. It was near the place where I had met Sun Eagle not many weeks ago. I held Fairbird's hand in mine, and she wiggled and squirmed and kept signing to me, "Where is he? Where is he?" She was devoted to Sun Eagle, though shy in his presence.

I told her to be still with a sharp motion of one hand and turned again to watch the scene being played out below. Elder Darkwing and two of his finest warriors escorted Sun Eagle down the narrow gorge path to the river running below. Bear, Sun Eagle's red dog, followed close behind. There was little room to walk on the riverbank. They needed to tread carefully on sharp wet rocks, for to slip would mean to vanish in the white water. So it was a slow company that made its way along the river's edge below us to the place where the Gray Wood began.

Darkwing himself drove a stake into the ground and tied to it a stout-woven rope. The other end of this rope was looped securely about Sun Eagle's waist. A young man who wandered into the Gray Wood without this anchor to secure him would never be heard from again.

The Gray Wood was an unmerciful predator.

Let the rope be sound, I whispered in my heart. *Let the stake be solid.* Let the threats of Wolf Tongue be empty as the wind.

I could not hear the blessings Darkwing spoke to his son. The river's voice was much too loud and we stood too far away. I saw Sun Eagle salute with his stone dagger. Then he turned to the forest and strode into the shadows without a backward glance.

The moment he disappeared, the mist rose.

It crept from the river like an army of ghosts, white and thick. I saw the men below give each other glances, and then they vanished from my sight. The mist continued to roil and thicken, climbing up the sides of the gorge like some living mass. I turned to my father, but he stood like a rock, staring down into that impenetrable gloom. Fairbird tugged at my hand, terrified, and I picked her up and held her close.

Let the rope be sound! I prayed again. *Let the stake be solid!*

I heard my father's warriors murmuring behind us. I heard the shifting of their weapons. Then the mist spilled over and rolled over us all, a wet blanket over our heads. Fairbird clung to me with a death grip.

I thought I glimpsed something in the smothering gray; a black form clad in a wolfskin, standing on the far side of the gorge, oddly visible at that distance when those standing nearest to me were cloaked in mist. I saw that form, and my hope fled.

As suddenly as it came, the mist dissipated. The sun broke through overhead, and blue sky, hot with summer, relieved our eyes with its brightness. Standing once more, I looked about and saw the faces of the warriors looking as bewildered as I felt. But when I turned to my father, I found him standing as I had last seen him, staring down into the gorge.

I looked to see what he saw. Darkwing was on his knees beside the stake, pulling frantically at the rope, which had gone slack. The two warriors held on to a snarling Bear, who strained against them toward the Gray Wood.

I watched as the elder of the Crescent People dragged the frayed end of the rope out of the trees. Bear gave a monstrous howl, broke from the warriors' grasp, and vanished into the forest.

I knew then, without a doubt: Sun Eagle would never return.

5

Eanrin

Someone took hold of his arm in the shadows. Then, with a tug that nearly dislocated his shoulder, Eanrin was spun about and pulled into headlong flight. "Run!" the voice in the dark urged him.

"Who are you?" Eanrin gasped, though he already knew. In his heart, he knew.

"No time for that now," said the voice. "Run for your life!"

There was no room for thought, no room for anything save terror. He must run! Through twisted, labyrinthine ways, through gasping reaches. All this Eanrin sensed in no more than an instant as he fled hand in hand with that darkness he could neither see nor identify. Anything to escape the Hound! The Hound, who would devour him, body and soul!

How could it have come even here, into the depths of the pit? Eanrin's spirit shuddered at the thought. Was there then no escape? He had fled throughout the turning of the ages; since the moment he drew his first breath, he had lived in constant flight. Eluding that One who would make him, if caught, into something other than himself. Who would break him and reform him until he could scarcely be recognized.

Nothing would be left but the Hound. Nothing, if he did not flee!

In that mad dash through the unassailable blackness, Eanrin's fear-crazed mind played evil games. Flashes struck his eyes like lightning, and in those flashes he glimpsed scenes from his own life, moments he never stopped to count and therefore forgot sooner than remembered. None of these moments were in themselves worth remembering: fine games, high festivities, beautiful women and songs. But he saw them now, with the threat of the Hound just at his heels, and recognized them for the desperate battles they were. How he clung to the only life he knew! How he flung himself into it with every ounce of his strength, hoping to ignore the inevitable footsteps beating upon his fears.

The Hound had always pursued him. He knew it as he fled in the darkness. The Hound had pursued him from the moment of Eanrin's first waking, coursing at his heels every day of his long and weary existence.

A final flash burst upon the poet's vision. He screamed and fell to his knees, though the grip on his arm never relaxed. Covering his face with his hands, he strove to push from his eyes the memory seared there.

The moment upon the battlefields of Arpiar when he stood with blood upon his sword and gazed down into the stricken face of a dead goblin man. The face of Death himself.

"The end of us all," he moaned, rocking himself in the darkness. "The end of us all, without exception."

A voice hissed at him from above. "What are you talking about, little creature?"

"Death!" Eanrin gagged. The name tasted foul upon his tongue. "Death, the inevitable victor."

Someone stood beside him. Until that moment, Eanrin had not been able to perceive any presence save the hard grasp on his arm and the voice. Now he could feel the heat of a body standing beside him. But he dared not open his eyes. Not with that vision still heavy upon his memory. So he sat unseeing, and the stranger beside him did not speak.

At long last Eanrin put out one hand to push himself upright. His fingers touched icy water. He drew in a sharp, hissing breath. "Dragon's teeth!"

"You are safe now," said the stranger beside him.

Eanrin sat up on his knees and wiped his hand on his already soiled shirt. "Safe?" he repeated, his voice tremulous.

"Yes."

Eanrin shivered. He could now feel mud seeping through his clothes. He considered taking cat form, but the mud would be still less bearable then. "He . . . he has been hounding me," he said in a low whisper, shuddering. "I am so afraid."

"You should be," said the stranger.

"I know." Eanrin shook himself, wishing he could somehow shake away the dread that clutched his heart.

"You don't know," said the stranger. "You don't know anything. Have you seen what becomes of those the Hound catches? Do you know what fates awaited the Brothers Ashiun, the first to be caught in that One's jaws?"

"I know," said the poet. "I know what happened to Etanun and Akilun."

"You did not see!" the stranger cried. "But I did. I watched the whole sad drama play out from beginning to end. They lost themselves in the Lumil Eliasul."

Shuddering, Eanrin whispered, "Do not speak that name!"

"It is the name you should most dread. Not the name of Death! Death is only a final release, the last barrier between you and the completion of your Self. The final curtain that must be swept aside before you can become everything you have always wished to be. A god.

"But the Lumil Eliasul won't make you a god. He will make you his slave."

"They lost everything," Eanrin moaned. "They lost everything they had!"

"Indeed, they did. Etanun and Akilun gave up all in the service of that One. And when at last Etanun realized he wanted more, do you think he was allowed to leave freely? Was he granted permission to seek my kiss? No! It is a dreadful thing to be loved by the Lumil Eliasul."

"Poor Etanun," Eanrin whispered.

"Yes, poor Etanun! Brave Knight of the Farthest Shore reduced to rags, to dust. And all because his Master would not set him free to pursue his deepest desire. His desire to be complete, to alone be god of himself, beholden to no one! Is this a crime, I ask you?"

"It's a terrible thing, love," Eanrin said. He tried to open his eyes, but all was darkness. He could not guess if he was blind or lost in a world without light. "Love is the most dreadful end."

"It is!" said the stranger. "Once you love, you lose. You can never have your Self back! Once you allow anyone else to mean more to you than you do, how can you be whole? You are broken, weak, vulnerable to all assaults. It was love that broke Akilun when he went to his brother's aid. And it was love that broke Etanun when, with Akilun's murder upon his hands, he forsook the path I had set before his feet and lost forever his chance to receive my kiss. To taste my fire."

A sob caught in the poet's throat, and he bowed his head, covering his face once more.

"To have the Lumil Eliasul is to have nothing else besides," whispered the stranger. "He will fill you with love, and you will lose your soul to him."

"No matter how hard I flee, still he pursues!" Eanrin cried. "No matter how far, even here in the pit."

"He will hound you to destruction," said the stranger in the smooth tones of a father. "But should you embrace Death, it is you who will have the victory, not he."

"I have tried so many ways to hide!" The poet tore at his own face and mouth with trembling fingers. "I have covered myself in veils of vagueness and foppery. I have dazzled the worlds with my disguises. But he sees through every blind. He knows what I am inside. I cannot escape him!"

"Only Death can liberate you."

"I have scorned his servants, those pretty knights. I wrote ballads about their failures, putting on display their forlorn efforts to all who would listen! But despite my best work, what good did it do? Akilun himself betrays me by his devotion to his Master even when all things were stripped from him. How boldly he marched to his own destruction for the love of a brother who betrayed him. Curse him!" Eanrin squeezed his eyes shut, though the darkness around him poured into his mind even so. "That constancy in the face of disaster . . . it wounds me to the heart! His faith in his Master makes a mockery of my mockery. Those knights, they are traitors to their own nature in their trueness to their Lord!"

"But you, immortal bard, will be true to your nature. You will not give in to selfless love. You will not give up mastery."

The Hound approached.

Eanrin screamed to drown the sound of pounding feet, though he knew that when his voice gave out, he would hear it again, only closer. His scream became agonized words.

"How can I give up what I know? I want it all, not just the best but the second best, the moderate, even the squalid. How can I give up everything I have for love?"

"In the end, it's nothing but a pretty story," said the stranger. A warmth like encircling wings enfolded the poet, deepening the darkness. "Love like that means only one thing: sacrifice. Is that a burden you were meant to bear?"

The poet felt the heat, the close pressure of those wings. "How empty it all is," he breathed, his lungs inhaling scalding fumes.

"To love is to empty one's Self," said the Dragon. "To love is to surrender. To love is to lose."

"I can't," Eanrin moaned. "I can't."

The drum of feet, the steady approach, and the Hound drew nearer still. Through the thick shelter of the wings came a glow. But Eanrin could not see it, even as the light increased and revealed the awful contours of those wings, the cruel scales, the hideous leather folds. He could not see, though his eyes were wide open.

"He has driven you to this place of darkness," hissed the stranger. "Your only hope is Death! He will take you otherwise. Is that what you want?"

"I—"

"You are master of your own world! Do not permit him to take this from you."

"But my world . . . my world was so silent." Eanrin thought of the tiny voices shouting out to the darkness but forever alone.

"And yet it was yours! Will you give up your rule for slavery?" The great wing pushed the poet from behind. "Enter the Dark Water," the stranger said. "You are at its banks. Enter the Dark Water and sink. He will not pursue you there. It is the last haven you can know!"

Eanrin rose. He took a step. He felt the water lapping at his feet, and he trembled.

"Only this way can you be free," said the Dragon. "Go! Swiftly! He is even now upon you!"

The light pierced the shade of the Dragon's wings. It pierced into the gloom of Eanrin's spirit and struck like daggers upon his eyes. Scales fell in a steady stream from his face. They hurt as they fell, and he screamed at the pain, his hands catching at the cascade. Sharp edges cut his hands in ribbons of blood.

But his vision cleared.

He looked up. He saw the Dragon. He saw the face of Death-in-Life, a face that had been his close and constant friend through all the lonely generations of his existence. He saw and was astonished by the ghastly visage, the sordid destruction of beauty, of dreams.

And Eanrin saw that he stood on the edge of the Dark Water. A single step, and he would make the plunge.

But the light was all around them, striking through every sense, and with it a Voice, which was also light, more brilliant than the voices of the sun or the moon, for it was the Voice that had taught them to sing. It sang now and drove the Dragon to furious wailing. Eanrin could hear no words, for the cacophony of the Dragon's screams muddled his ears. He shut his eyes, but the light was still there. He fell to his knees on the edge of the water, curling into a ball, but still the torrential battle of sounds and words and voices calling his name battered him on all sides.

Then, as suddenly as it had come, the noise ceased. Eanrin found himself kneeling in a great quiet. He realized there were tears on his face. This was a strange, painful sensation. He had never before wept. Not he, the brightest and blithest of his kind. He put up wondering fingers to touch his damp face. Then he sobbed and covered his eyes with his hands, catching his tears until they overflowed onto the ground, dropping into the pile of scales scattered at his feet on the banks of the Dark Water. When at last his sobbing eased and he could look down, he saw those scales gleaming wetly. And he realized how close he had been to becoming a dragon himself.

Light glowed gently, reflecting off the tears. The scales themselves remained only black. The light was steady, white and pure. For a moment Eanrin glimpsed the face of the Hound. Long and noble, with solemn black eyes surrounded in a golden aura of soft fur. When he blinked, however, the vision was gone.

The Hound was vanished; perhaps he had never been.

But the light remained.

A silver lantern sat before Eanrin, there in the depths of the pit. It was small and delicately wrought, and in its heart glowed a light more potent, more beautiful, more colorful than starlight.

Eanrin recognized it at once: Akilun's lantern, the fabled Asha. A gift from beyond the Final Water, crafted in the realm of the Farthest Shore. Akilun himself had died grasping it in his hands.

"And so I might die," Eanrin whispered. "So I might lose myself."

He put out a hand. It glowed with life in the light pouring from that lantern, but it trembled as well. He took hold of the lantern's handle and stood.

A Path appeared at his feet, leading away from the Dark Water.

6

STARFLOWER

OATHS WERE FORGOTTEN that day. Even as I watched Elder Darkwing from above the gorge, I could see his new loyalties fading from mind. Battle would have broken out in an instant with all the Crescent warriors gathered in Redclay. I felt the tension mounting behind me as I stood on the gorge edge. I felt the blood heat rising in the men, both my father's loyal warriors and the furious men of the Crescent Lands.

But when Darkwing and his two warriors at last climbed from the gorge—Darkwing with tears staining his face—my father stepped forward and said, "We are dismayed at this loss. I will send men into the forest to find your son."

Darkwing's eyes flashed. "Murderer," he snarled. "You are behind this."

"No," said the Panther Master. "This is not the doing of any man in Redclay."

"No. Not any man," said the elder. Then his gaze fixed upon me and my sister, standing in the Eldest's shadow. "This is the work of the curse you brought upon the Land!"

I heard the war cries not yet uttered in the men's straining throats. The face of every warrior, though he stood in stoic silence, shouted his desire for battle.

But the Eldest said simply, "My men outnumber yours."

"Are they yet *your* men in light of this treachery?" cried Darkwing, casting about to all those gathered.

And for a moment, I wondered. I wondered if the time of my death had come, and the deaths of my father and sister. Darkwing's words were like poison among the men. Would they, in light of their master's sin before the Beast and this evidence of the curse's work, turn upon him now? My heart stopped beating. I could scarcely even think of Sun Eagle and his fate. My arms tightened about Fairbird, and she was like stone in my arms.

The Eldest said, "Take your people and go, Darkwing. Mourn for your son as is right. Then we will meet again and see what is to be done."

Darkwing's hand crept to the dagger at his side but did not touch it. His gaze locked with the Panther Master's. I knew that whatever decision he reached would determine our fates. If he believed he could best my father and made the attack, I did not doubt that half my father's warriors would turn upon us as well.

But the Panther Master did not back down. His face was calm and sad, as though he looked into the future . . . a dreadful future, but one that did not include a battle that day.

Darkwing's hand slowly dropped away from the dagger, then passed across his face as though to wipe away traces of his tears. His shoulders bowed like an old man's as he turned and descended into the gorge. One by one, his men followed. They did not stop to take provisions. They left as swiftly and silently as shadows.

They could not escape our cursed land soon enough.

After that began the dark time. War broke out once more with the Crescent Tribes, more bitter and bloody than before. It lasted late into the winter, and only in the worst winter months did the men of Redclay return to our village, my father among them. He had not been wounded in the fighting, but his face was that of a dying man. His skin had a yellow cast, and his eyes were hollow. He scarcely looked at my sister or me when he entered his house. He allowed me to feed him and serve him as always, but he did not speak to us. Rarely did he go down to the Long Hall in the village to sit among his warriors.

My mind was a tumult during those months. More than ever, the people of the village avoided me. The village women would not permit Fairbird and me into the fields, and we more often than not lived on whatever I could harvest from the Eldest's garden. Every day I woke afraid, and when I put down my head to rest at night, I thought I heard someone crying up from the gorge. Sun Eagle, far away and lost, a phantom in the darkness:

"Can anyone hear me?"

I would cover my ears and curl into a tight ball upon my pallet, but still his voice would ring in my mind. My father, true to his word, had sent warriors into the forest to search for Sun Eagle. But they had found nothing, not even the other end of the broken rope. He was lost forever. So why did I keep hearing that ghostly cry?

Then one night, deep in the coldest darkness of winter, it stopped, and I never heard it again. That night I made the signs of passing for my betrothed.

"May he walk safely through the void beyond the mountains," I signed. "And may the Songs sing him to life."

I could not say exactly what my feelings were at Sun Eagle's loss. Horror. Guilt. Sorrow, I believe. I scarcely knew him. But I think had our lives been otherwise—had I not been a living curse—I might have made him a good wife.

Amid all those other feelings, however, there was one even stronger: relief.

I hated to admit it, but it was true. For now Sun Eagle was gone, I should not marry. And this was best. I knew it could not be long now.

It happened in late winter just on the verge of spring. The warriors were already beginning to gather to prepare for the spring sacrifices before marching off to war. It was the night before they set out on this long pilgrimage to make their blood offerings that we heard the sounds.

Just before sunrise, when the world was still dark but edged with the first gleams of light, I was startled from a restless sleep by frenzied animal screams. It was as though some creature was being torn apart. And rising with the screams of that luckless prey were hideous snarls. I had heard hunting dogs make similar noises, but never like this. I had even heard wolves calling in the night, and on one occasion, the haunting cry of a panther.

But this was unnatural. It was as loud as thunder, and it shook the earth! Whatever made that cry was a monster so great that even the ancient giants trembled in their stone sleep.

The screams of the first animal died, but then another took up its place. Something was among the cattle in one of the far fields, I realized. Something was among the cattle, going through them, slaughtering. Something vast, something the likes of which we had never seen before.

Fairbird lay beside me, her hands over her ears, her mouth open in a silent scream. I gathered her to me, and she, in her terror, pressed her face to my shoulder and bit down upon my gown. Her little teeth tore down to my skin, but I did not move her. I held her close and stroked her back but could not shield her from those unnatural sounds. They carried into the center of our spirits, ravishing all sense of safety or hope.

I knew then with absolute certainty: The Beast was come down from the mountains.

It seemed like hours later before I heard word. My father and his most trusted men ventured out to the far fields. There they found the Eldest's great herd slaughtered. Not a cow was left alive. Not even those calves had been spared that had been isolated in preparation for the spring sacrifices.

The Eldest was stern and seemingly unafraid when he marched with his men back into the village and announced to his people what had transpired. Everyone had heard the evil sounds. Everyone knew that this could be no natural work, even those of us who had not witnessed the carnage firsthand. No pack of wolves, no matter how large or how vicious, could have made the sounds that had shattered the morning only a few hours ago.

"It is the work of some devil," declared my father, yet his voice did not shake as he spoke. The sun shone down upon his tired face and made him look once more the strong and noble leader he had always been to his people, a man who would serve the needs of the nation before considering his own.

In all but one point.

I shivered and dared not draw near the crowd but remained out of sight, Fairbird held tightly by the hand. Frostbite had followed us, cringing, her tail tucked. She too was frightened by what she had heard. She was my loyal shadow, however, and would not be left behind.

"It is the work of some devil," I heard my father say again. "But do not fear. We shall hunt it down! We shall stop this monster before the day is through!"

I watched how the people looked at each other; I saw the disbelief in their eyes. They knew this was not the truth. They knew, as did the Panther Master, though for the moment he refused to admit it.

Suddenly a deep laugh rumbled through the crowd. I watched as people parted, backing away nervously, clinging to each other, men and women, young and old. And through the gap they made, I saw Wolf Tongue.

He strode down the middle of the village, his long wolfskin heavy about his shoulders. He laughed as he came, a cruel, derisive laugh, right in the face of his Eldest. The Panther Master stood like a rock, and I saw the spark of fire in his eyes. I knew, however, that he would not dare strike the High Priest. Even the Eldest may not strike a holy man, especially not one so favored by the Beast.

Wolf Tongue stood before his Eldest, still laughing. When at last he spoke, his voice was low, but silence held the village in such a grip that I knew we all heard every word he said.

"Do not think you can thwart the will of the Beast," he said. "I've seen it happen before. So have you. Have you forgotten the days of your grandfather already? Have you forgotten his fate when he too thought to keep from the Beast his due?"

He turned suddenly to the village, his arms outspread. The wolfskin fell back to reveal his naked torso beneath, scarred from many battles. He was a big man, muscular and awful in his history of bloodshed during the many long years he had served his god. I realized then, for the first time, how old Wolf Tongue must be. For he had always been the Beast's High Priest, as long as anyone could remember. Yet his body was that of a warrior in his prime, and his face was both young and old. What an unnatural life he must lead in his close communion with the hideous divine.

"Do not forget!" he cried out to all of us. His voice, like the awful sounds we had heard that morning, seemed to shake the village to its foundations. "Do not forget the horror loosed upon your grandsires when they failed to heed my warning! They called your servant a liar and refused to satisfy the Beast's demands. They refused to give him the woman he required of them. But she belonged, by rights, to your god! Who among you remembers the screams? Who among you remembers the slaughter? I remember as though it were yesterday. I remember mothers wailing, children lying in pools of blood, warriors choking on their own gore. I remember your elder slain, mauled beyond recognition! You remember, do you not, Panther Master?"

He turned once more to my father, and the proud Panther Master shrank under his gaze. Wolf Tongue's words were painting that dark night of long ago across his memory.

"You were there," said Wolf Tongue. "You were a small child, and you saw the death of your grandfather. You remember."

He did. I could see how my father crumpled beneath those memories, melting from the powerful warrior into that small, frightened child witnessing things innocent eyes should never be made to see.

"Give the Beast what he asks!" Wolf Tongue's gaze swept out across the village. "Give the Beast what he asks!"

"Yes," muttered one man. "Give him what he asks." Then another took up the sound. Soon the men were shouting, and even the women raised fists in the air in agreement. "Give the Beast what he asks!" all cried.

My father was as silent as a woman before them.

Wolf Tongue turned suddenly, and his gaze fixed upon me where I hid. I realized he had known where I was all along. I gasped and drew back into the shadows of the outer buildings, but he was striding toward me in an instant. Frostbite yelped and fled before me up the hill. Though I tried to follow, I could not make my feet move. The High Priest's hand came down upon my shoulder.

The next thing I knew, he had taken Fairbird. I fell to my knees as she was pulled from my arms, and watched as Wolf Tongue flung my sister across his shoulder and strode back to the crowd. Her eyes and mouth were wide with terror, and her tiny hands reached back for me. She seemed so far away, miles and miles beyond my help.

Oh, Fairbird!

Holding her in his arms, Wolf Tongue strode to the middle of the crowd. He raised one hand, and instant silence fell. Then he spoke, this time in a voice so soft, so gentle, I would have thought he soothed his own children. It was like pure honey in its sweetness, and for a moment, even my heart calmed.

"My only thought," he said, "is to protect you. Helpless as you are before the wrath of the Beast, I long to stand between you, to give you shelter from the storm of his fury. But how can I?" he persisted. "How can I, if you resist me so? The Beast has made his will known. If you will not give him the blood he requires, he will take it from you in other ways! Today, livestock. Tomorrow, your children!"

Women gasped and clutched their little ones. Men brandished spears and stone knives, shouting battle cries. But those who had seen the carnage in the field knew there could be no fighting this enemy. The cry was taken up again, "Give the Beast what he asks!"

"The Eldest has two daughters!" cried the High Priest. "One belongs to the Beast by law!" He raised my sister, struggling uselessly in his grasp, high above his head. And the Eldest, standing behind Wolf Tongue, hid his face in his hand.

In that moment, I thought I hated my father.

Teeth grinding, my fingers like claws, I tore into the crowd. None, not even the largest men, dared stand in my way. I tore and kicked and even bit as needed until I broke through them all. I leapt at Wolf Tongue with the fury of a wildcat, clawing at his bare chest in my efforts to reach my sister. But he held her out of my reach. Leaning forward, he whispered so that only I could hear:

"Will you spit in my eye again, lovely one?"

If only I had been born a man! If only I'd had a spear in my hand at that moment! How different would be the story I tell you now!

But I had no weapon. I had not even a voice. I had only my decision, made long ago on the dark night my sister was born.

My eyes spoke everything I had to say. Wolf Tongue understood. His own eyes flared with triumph and . . . hunger, I thought.

I took a step back. I held out my arms. Wolf Tongue placed my sobbing sister in my grasp, and I hugged her as she wept into my neck. Then I walked slowly away from the crowd. I spared a single glance for my father, but he did not look up. He knew the choice had been made. He knew, as did all the people of Redclay. They parted, letting me through, and I walked between them as I carried my sister back up the hill to the Eldest's House.

Behind me, I heard Wolf Tongue shouting orders to the village. "Prepare the procession. Make ready the rites. We journey tomorrow to the Place of the Teeth!"

7

EANRIN

EVERY STEP WAS A BATTLE OF WILLS. He may as well have walked on burning coals. But there was no fire here, no heat; only darkness on all sides.

Except, not complete darkness. Eanrin's hand trembled as it clutched the handle of Asha lantern. It was unbelievable yet undeniable. He, the Chief Poet of Iubdan Rudiobus, held the Light of Sir Akilun. The glow that lit the many Houses of Lights in the Near World of long ago, before Hri Sora burned those houses to the ground and banished the lights, leaving shadows in the wake of her flames.

And following that destruction, before rebuilding could begin, Akilun himself had journeyed into Death's realm and never returned.

Eanrin had assumed, along with all the Faerie folk, that Asha had gone out when Akilun died. But here it was. He tried to tell himself he was mistaken; it must be some other lamp. After all, he had never seen Asha with his own eyes. Could this not be a replica?

Might it not, rather than lighting his way out of darkness, direct him only into deeper death?

Even as the thought crossed his mind, Eanrin cursed himself for thinking it. No matter how many blasphemous lies he might try to tell himself, he could not deny what he absolutely knew in the depths of his heart. The lantern was real. And the Path it showed him led to safety.

The face of the Hound flashed before his eyes.

"You fool," he whispered, his mind crying out against his heart. "You fool, Eanrin! You have given in. You've accepted *his* way and *his* help. He will devour your soul at last."

But his heart responded with a shrug. After all, it was follow the light or remain in blindness. It was accept the aid of the Hound or succumb to the will of the Dragon. Was there a choice in the end?

"I should never have rescued Imraldera," he said. "I should have left her by the River and gone my own way. If I had, I would never have been made to look into the face of Death. At least, not for many generations to come."

Again he cursed and closed his eyes, wishing he could block the lantern's light. But it glowed down into the farthest reaches of his mind, separating truth from lies.

"I'm glad I saved her. I'm glad I've been brought to this place."

The light flared brighter still. Eanrin opened his eyes hesitantly, afraid of the sudden brilliance. But it was gentle even in its power, and he found that he could bear to look upon it. He could also now get some sense of where he stood. A tunnel led as far as he could see both before and behind. His feet were turned up an incline, his back to a gaping descent. He knew, without knowing how he knew, that not many paces behind him the Dark Water still waited.

Shuddering, he faced forward and squared his shoulders. As he went, his gaze shifted more and more often to look at Asha, to study the wonder that he held.

It was silver and delicate, made by craftsmen of such skill, Eanrin could not begin to guess who they were. Surely not the goblins, even before they forsook their craft. Nor dwarves, for its beauty was of a different kind than their work. No one he knew in all of Faerie could have done something like this. But still more amazing to his eyes was the light it held.

It was as though one of the moon's own children had come down from the heavens to dwell inside. White as purity, but full of all the colors of all the worlds, it warmed and it cooled, refreshing the spirit. When he breathed, Eanrin took in the scents of spring, of summer, of autumn and winter together, pursuing their ageless, circular dance.

As he looked at it, Eanrin knew that what he had seen on the edge of the Dark Water was no dream.

Guilt weighed upon him. How, in his arrogance, could he have been so foolish? How could he have believed that the work of the Dragon only affected *other* people? Wicked people who deserved their fate if they were willing to listen to those lies. He breathed a long sigh, remembering the scales he had seen at his feet, where they had fallen from his own face. How close had he been to becoming one of the Dragon's brood?

Gazing at the light, Eanrin felt his heart settling into a steady beat. "My life will never be the same," he whispered. "I have forsaken the Dragon. So I must be devoured—"

"Hallo in the dark! Be you living or dead?"

In that moment, Eanrin realized what miracles might occur in these deep places of the world. For, when he heard Glomar's voice ringing in the darkness, he felt a surge of good feeling, of camaraderie, of brotherly affection and even . . . yes, even love. It was a dizzying sensation! He hollered back:

"Lumé's crown and scepter! I never thought I'd see the day when your voice would give me joy!"

There was a long pause. Then, "Dragon-eaten vapors. For a moment, I thought that was real. Ah well . . ."

"No! Glomar!" Eanrin shouted. "Glomar, you blundering oaf of a badger-man, stay where you are!"

"That was more like. Is that you there, cat?"

Eanrin sprang forward, little caring in that moment if he followed the Path of the lantern or not. His longing for a familiar face, a good old Rudioban face, beat all other concerns into nothing. Asha shone upon the startled features of the guard, who had just time to open his eyes wide and exclaim, "What by all the Dragon's brood is—" before Eanrin clasped him in glad embrace.

"You dirt-nosing lug!" he exclaimed, slapping the guard repeatedly upon the shoulders. "Fancy meeting you in these foul parts! To what depths have the mighty plummeted, eh?"

Glomar growled and pushed the poet away. "The darkness has made you mad. Or madder than you were."

"Perhaps," said the poet, stepping back and smiling. Asha swung gently in his hand, spreading its glow up and down the long tunnel. "Or perhaps it is here that I have finally seen the light."

"Little enough light, if any," said the badger. His eyes squinted as though he were peering through heavy murk. "I can hardly see my hand before my face in this tomb. It's a good thing I depend on my nose rather than my eyes, or I'd be lost indeed."

Eanrin blinked, and his smile drooped into a frown. "Are you daft, Glomar?"

Glomar snorted. "I've no time for this. Follow me if you'd like; I'm not opposed to your company in this place, but I am opposed to your wicked tongue. Keep it behind your teeth, and perhaps we'll find our way out of here." He moved heavily past Eanrin, stumping several steps down the long incline.

"Lumé's crown!" Eanrin darted out a hand to catch the captain by his shoulder. "Have you gone blind?"

"Blind? I'm a badger! Blindness makes no difference to me."

Eanrin began to tremble. Asha's light shivered in his grasp. "Can you not see the lantern, then?" he asked.

"What lantern?"

So perhaps Eanrin had gone mad. Visions of dragons and black lakes and hounds! He gazed from Glomar's stern face to the silver light and back again and saw that Glomar, indeed, had no perception of what Eanrin held.

"No," he whispered. "I know what I saw. I know what I *see*, even if he does not! And it's more real than real."

"What are you babbling about, cat?"

Eanrin licked his lips. "I've been down that way," he said. "It's . . . it's a dead end."

Glomar grunted. "I trust my nose."

"In that case, tell it to sniff this." Eanrin lifted the lantern right up to Glomar's face.

"What are you doing, cat?"

"Please, stand a moment and *smell*!"

Glomar had never heard Eanrin's voice so urgent. It was enough to shock him into momentary obedience. He stood where he was, inhaling deeply, though he did not know what he was supposed to smell. The light of Asha fell upon his rough features, washing away the golden man of Rudiobus into the truth of the badger underneath. Eanrin, however, saw no understanding in his face. No sudden revelation of the wonder that gleamed so brightly just before his eyes.

Suddenly the guard snorted. "What is that?" he said.

"What is what?"

"I do smell some . . ." Here he gave a glad, wordless cry. "Come on, cat!" he said, turning, taking Eanrin's arm, and running up the inclined path. "I smell it now! Fresh air, this way!"

It wasn't at all what Eanrin had expected. But as long as the badger-man hastened in the direction Asha was indicating, he supposed they couldn't get into too much trouble, at least, no worse than they were already in. He hastened after his rival, watching how the lantern lit the Path one step ahead of Glomar's scurrying feet. Only a single step, but it was enough.

Eanrin wondered how long he had been so guided without knowing it.

"How did you end up here, cat?" Glomar asked after they had progressed some moments. "Did you fall for the vision too?"

"What vision, Glomar?"

The captain growled. "Nothing. Nothing at all." He was silent several paces. Then, "Seriously, though, how did you end up in this tomb?"

"Tomb?"

"Yes, tomb. Don't tell me you didn't know."

"Didn't know what?"

"Gah! I should never expect a straight answer from you, should I?"

"Lumé's crown, Glomar," Eanrin cried, tempted to kick the captain's heels, "I wish I had some idea what you were going on about! By the

Flowing Gold itself, I know of no tomb, nor visions. I fell into a pit, a nasty, dark, and stinking pit. And what with one thing and another"—there was little use, he decided, in trying to explain the Dark Water or, still less, the Hound—"I ended up here. With you, more's the pity. But I know nothing of any tomb."

"Must be the city playing its tricks again," Glomar said with a shrug and continued along his stumping way. "It's getting stronger, I shouldn't wonder, the longer Hri Sora is awake. They're feeding off each other. I can smell it. Here in the dark places I sense what I couldn't up there under the red sky. Hri Sora is getting stronger."

Eanrin frowned, surprised at the captain's words. He had felt no such sensations himself. But then, his adventure had obviously led him an entirely different route than Glomar's, and his senses had been distracted.

"What tomb are we in?" he asked the badger-man.

"*Hers,*" Glomar said, his voice sinking to a low growl. "Or at least, hers before she became *her*. Before she took the fire. This is the tomb for the last Queen of Etalpalli, and her name has been melted away from above the door."

Eanrin shuddered. "Hri Sora is the last Queen of Etalpalli," he said.

"Hri Sora is its mistress," said Glomar. "But she is not queen."

Were they, then, still in the tomb as Glomar believed? Eanrin wondered. Or were they both now in the Netherworld, still near the Dark Water? If Glomar had died in the tomb, and Eanrin in the fall, then there could be no doubt the Netherworld was their fate. Terrible thoughts for an immortal to consider, and Eanrin found his mind rejecting the notion. He focused once more upon Asha.

"Light," said Glomar.

"What?" Eanrin looked up, wondering if the captain had suddenly perceived the lantern after all. But no. He saw beyond the glow of Asha another, more distant source. A pinprick of daylight.

The tunnel had an end. *But what end?* Eanrin wondered.

It didn't matter. He and Glomar were instantly running, Asha swinging lightly in Eanrin's hand, still guiding, though neither looked to it for guidance. The daylight seemed forever away, but they were immortal and lived without thought of Time, so *forever* mattered less than the need to somehow get there. How long they ran in the dark could not be measured in minutes or hours. But run they did, neither speaking, both hoping beyond hope for an end at last to this blackness.

Suddenly the pinprick was a window, then the window was a door. The two men of Rudiobus burst through from darkness to light, momentarily blinded. They cried out, whether in joy or pain, neither could guess. It was impossible to emerge from that tunnel, like a newborn bursting into the world for the first time, and not make a cry. And they fell upon the ground and lay for some while.

At last Eanrin raised his head and looked about.

Then he gasped and sat up. "Glomar!"

His companion lay beside him, still groaning, feet splayed out behind him. Eanrin grabbed him by the hair atop his head and gave a little shake. "Glomar, look around you, man! A fine mess this is."

Glomar huffed and spluttered what might have been curses had they been coherent and pushed himself up onto his elbows. "Lumé smite me," he growled, shaking his head. "We're in the dragon-eaten Between."

So they were. They lay on the banks of the River, beneath the shadows of the Wood, and both could hear the roar of Cozamaloti's not-too-distant falls.

Eanrin leapt to his feet, then realized his hands were empty. He cast about like a lunatic, searching the banks, even stepping down close to the water. The River snarled at him, and he backed up quickly, his eyes wide and his hair bristling. The River was not one to soon forget an offense. Eanrin scrambled over slippery rocks onto a higher tuft of ground, searching.

It was no use. Asha was gone. Perhaps it had never been. Eanrin ground his teeth. Curse that Hound! Curse that Light! He was back where he'd started from and he'd . . .

"Dragon's teeth," he breathed. "Dragon's teeth and tail. I left her behind."

"Gleamdren!" Glomar cried, rallying himself and getting to his feet. He stood on the River's edge, shaking his fists, his face red with anger. "We left her, cat! The queen's own cousin, lost to the dragon's clutches!"

Out of habit Eanrin fumbled for his comb, gnashing his teeth when he remembered he'd lost it. Running his fingers swiftly through his hair, he stepped down beside his rival. He spoke firmly, his face set. "We've got to go back for her, Glomar."

"Right you are!" cried the captain. "I'm not leaving Etalpalli without her! I'll not rest until Lady Gleamdrené Gormlaith is safe once again!"

"Oh. Yes." Eanrin shook his head, frowning. "How silly of me. Her too, of course."

8

STARFLOWER

THEY SET A GUARD around my father's door that night. As though
it were necessary! Foolish men. By myself, I might have slipped
past them and vanished into the night. I could have crossed the gorge,
on into the Crescent Lands and farther north, finding myself a home
among people who did not know my face.

But I could not escape with Fairbird. And if I left without her, they
would surely give my sister to the Beast.

Thus a guard was unnecessary that night. I sat before my father's
hearth, my sister curled up in my lap, Frostbite's shaggy body pressed
against my thigh. Where the Panther Master was, I could not guess. Perhaps trying to work some persuasion upon Wolf Tongue. That would be
like persuading the giants of old to rise up from their stone sleep! Wolf
Tongue had been too long in the Beast's service to remember what mercy
was. If he had ever known.

Fairbird slept. I wished I could enjoy a few hours of peace, sleeping beside my little sister as I had done since the night of her birth. But there could be no sleep for me that night. I tried to think instead. If I was to be wakeful, I wanted to be mindful, grateful for those final hours with Fairbird and my loyal dog. I wanted to store these memories for the long march I had ahead of me, on the north-facing road to Bald Mountain.

I couldn't do it. I couldn't possibly remember as I should. Even now, it fades. The play of light on Fairbird's cheek . . . I see the glow, but do I remember how vibrant the color, how soft the contours of that little face? I don't know. And Frostbite, growling and showing her teeth even as she slept. She sensed my fear, poor creature. How she would have protected me if she could!

Dawn came.

Had it been enough? I asked myself as light crept through the low doorway and I got to my feet and found a stake, a mallet, and a rope. Had I loved her enough? Had I treasured the moments with my sister, even when she drove me to distraction? Even though she had been the cause of my outcast state? Oh, Fairbird! I know your true name! I cannot remember when I learned it. Perhaps I always knew without realizing what I knew. Your secret is mine, my darling, treasured in my heart! And I would die a thousand deaths for your sake. You are my strength . . . and my downfall.

Frostbite woke at my movements in the house. She gathered her gangly legs under her and got to her feet, shaking away sleep and following me to the door of the Eldest's House. The guards stood before the door, and I saw no pity in their eyes. I hesitated. I could not begin to guess at the consequences if they did not let me complete this final errand.

I took a step. The older of the two planted his spear before my feet. He did not have to speak. I read the warning in his face.

"Let her pass."

My father's voice drew my gaze. To my surprise, I saw that he sat some little way off, his panther skin drawn about his shoulders. He did not look at me or even at the guards. How had he known I stood there?

"Let her pass," he said. "She must secure the dog."

My guards exchanged looks. But the Eldest had spoken, and Wolf Tongue was not there to contradict. Unwillingly, the older man stepped

back, withdrawing his spear. Moving slowly, so as not to seem frightened or harried, I passed between them, around the house, and down
the southern side of the hill. Frostbite padded after me, her head low.

I selected a place where the earth was hard and where shade from the
mango grove cast relief from the heat. It would require some effort to
drive in my stake, but once in place, it would hold. The morning was
swiftly dawning and already promising to scorch. Sweat dripped down
my face, but I focused all the pent-up frustration of the previous night
into my task. I struck with my mallet as though I struck at the head of the
Beast! I could feel the eyes of the guards above watching me at my work.

The patter of hurrying feet gave me brief warning. The next thing
I knew, Fairbird's arms were about my waist, clinging. I dropped the
mallet in my surprise. With some effort, I pried open my sister's grasp,
turned around, and knelt so she could fling her arms around my neck. I
held her, rocking her and stroking her head as I had done so many times
before. How much of the goings-on did she understand, I wondered?
She had been terrified yesterday while held in Wolf Tongue's grasp, but
did she comprehend his demands? Did she know the fate in store for me?

At last I pushed her back. "Fairbird," I signed with shaking hands,
"you must watch over Frostbite for me while I am gone."

"Where are you going?" Her hands were so frenzied, I could scarcely
read the signs, but her face asked the question with perfect clarity.

"Far away," I replied. "Far, far away."

"When will you come home?"

How to answer such a question? I drew her to me once more, my
mind desperately searching for what to say. The guards above were shifting, their spearheads sharp against the brightening sky. I had little time.

Once more, I pushed her from me so I could use my hands. "Fairbird,"
I signed, "I know your true name. I am going to our mother now, and
where she is, I will have a voice as strong as any man's! Listen for my
voice, Fairbird. Listen for me calling your true name. And when you hear
it, we will find each other again. I promise you!"

She did not believe me. How could she believe such wild fancies?
"Don't leave me," she signed.

The guards would call me soon, and if I did not come when summoned, they would fetch me. I did not want Fairbird to see that. So I set her firmly aside, retrieved my mallet, and went back to driving the stake in deep. She pulled at my clothes, tears falling down her cheeks. I dared not look at her.

At last the stake was placed. I took the rope and called Frostbite to me. The poor dog had sat nearby, whining as she watched Fairbird cry. I tied the rope to her neck and secured the other end to the stake. I tested my knots. They would hold. They had to!

I turned to Fairbird again. "Watch over Frostbite. She needs you," I signed. I turned to the dog next. "Watch over my sister. For me, dear one!" I could only hope she understood me. The dog wagged her tail, but her ears were back and her eyes sad. I patted her once. Then I turned to go.

Fairbird lunged for me, grabbing my hand and tugging for all she was worth. She nearly pulled me off my feet in her desperation. I knelt. There was no stopping my tears now. They coursed down my face unhindered. Beasts and devils eat those spying guards for seeing me cry! But I could not stop myself.

"Fairbird," I signed at last. "Fairbird, go sit with Frostbite."

Defiance flashed through her eyes. But then she bowed her head and did as she was told. She sat cross-legged, and Frostbite lay down to put her head in her new mistress's lap.

I marched up the hill to where my guards waited. And I listened to Frostbite's forlorn howls. But more painful to my ears was the awful silence of my sister.

Our journey was long. We crossed many rivers, descending the gorges, canoeing across, and climbing the other side. We passed through many hostile lands. But the warriors of those lands laid down their arms at a word from Wolf Tongue. The Beast would have his prey. And afterward . . . who could say where loyalties would lie?

Warriors headed our procession, cruelly armed but painted for sacrifice, not for battle. Behind them came three priests, all dressed in deerskin dyed red, their faces painted in black streaks, like tears, but with swirling patterns and dots. Behind these walked the elders of all the villages and lands loyal to the Eldest.

My father walked behind them, rich and powerful in his skins, his face painted red and black. He was so stern, so handsome, and silent as death.

I made the long journey with twelve other maidens. They wore black, and their feet were bare. They represented each tribe of the Land, even those not loyal to the Eldest. For even those tribes who warred against each other must pay homage to the Beast. He, their great god and greatest enemy.

When we passed through the Crescent Lands, I glimpsed Elder Darkwing and his warriors some way off, watching our progress. Darkwing wore the same collar of black feathers I had seen him don on the night of my betrothal. At that distance, he looked like some strange, dark spirit. I feared he would order an attack. Even from so far away I could feel his desire for vengeance. I wondered if Darkwing heard, as I had, the voice of Sun Eagle crying on dark nights.

But the sight of Wolf Tongue was enough to stay his bloodlust. No one liked to thwart the Beast's favorite.

Many weeks we journeyed, for our destination was far. People of every tribe gathered in a crowd behind us, camping so near us at night that I could often discern their whispering voices above the crackle of our campfires. The Beast had ravaged many a town when he came down from the mountains to demand his dues. The people of the Land were frightened. They wanted to be certain their god was satisfied.

At long last I saw the great mountain, tallest peak in the whole range, rising on the horizon. Once upon a time, it had been called Lady Whitehair, for its peak was covered in starflower vines that gleamed so bright at night that one could see the glow from great distances. It was said that mountain had once been the queen of all the giants, a great and terrible beauty.

All her beauty was gone since the fire fell from the heavens and smote that mountaintop. The blaze on Lady Whitehair was visible even as far as Redclay Village. And when it at last burnt out, all that remained was Bald Mountain. Cursed ground on which no living thing would flourish again.

It was there my fate awaited me.

At long last we began the mountain climb. I had never traveled so far north before and had certainly never been to the mountains. As we ascended those dizzying heights, I gasped in wonder at the world spread far below me. The mountains extended forever all around the Land. It was said that nothing existed beyond them. To cross over the Circle of Faces was to pass into the Void where the dead wander lost. I thought this must be true. The mountains were so high and so shrouded in clouds and mist, there could be nothing beyond them.

We spent the night before we reached the Place of the Teeth on the lower slopes of Bald Mountain. How evil was the ground beneath me! I smelled poison of bygone years, the poison of hatred beyond all bearing. No wonder it was here that the Beast demanded his gifts be brought. The dead mountain was a fitting site.

Our followers on this pilgrimage had increased so much by this time that the whole slope of Bald Mountain was alight with campfires. It was as though the dragon had fallen to burn the mountain a second time. All were afraid to sleep in darkness here, where the Beast dwelled, never seen but ever present.

But Wolf Tongue was with us as well, and he stood watch throughout the night. I could see him from where I lay among the twelve silent maidens with whom I traveled. I saw how our campfires reflected in his yellow eyes. His face never turned, but those eyes darted here and there, observing the night. How I feared that gaze would fall upon me!

But it never did. Since the moment I took my sister from his arms, Wolf Tongue had not so much as looked at me.

Morning dawned. The maidens in my company cut their feet in careful patterns, cringing at the thin red lines they inflicted on themselves. The Beast demands such cruel worship! I, however, was not cut. A perfect offering must be unblemished. Instead, I was dressed in my mother's white doeskin wedding gown, and my hair was crowned in starflowers, bloodred in the young light of that new day.

The Eldest approached me, as handsome and stern as he had been when we began our journey. He held in his hands a wooden bowl full of lamb's blood. This he handed to me. As I took it from him, I dared to look into his face. Briefly, oh, so briefly, our eyes met.

How difficult I found it to read the face of this man who was my father! Everything I saw contradicted everything I believed. Surely I was mistaken. I was a woman-child. I was a blight. I was of less value to him than his slaves. I was marked for death.

Surely he could not love me.

The way to the Place of the Teeth is secret. Only Wolf Tongue knows the hidden paths, and only those he allows may follow him there. Those shadowing our procession of holy men and virgins could not join on that final ascent. They tried, of course. Curiosity will drive many a soul to dreadful extremes. But as we climbed that lonely trail, I felt the shift. The air went cold for an instant. When I looked behind me, the path I had just traveled was obscured, and the people who followed had vanished from my sight.

The maidens with me trembled but bowed their heads and hastened on. The priests and warriors proceeded without pause.

My hands shook. I watched the blood sloshing in the wooden bowl I held, desperate to keep from spilling a single drop. Such importance rested in that one task! Not to spill. Not to spill. Not to think of Fairbird. Not to think of what waited at the end of my climb. Not to spill.

I did not want to weep but could not stop. But I shed no tears for my own sad fate. I cried for those people who had followed behind. They only wanted safety for their families, just as I wanted safety for Fairbird. They wanted to know that the Beast would be satisfied.

The sun was high above us, filling the valleys below with brilliance. I gazed out across the expanse of the Land. I could not begin to imagine how many villages dwelt below me within the shelter of the Circle of Faces. Tonight, I would save them.

But what about tomorrow? No matter what befell me at my journey's end, I knew the dread under which they lived would not be lifted. It will never lift so long as the Beast is god.

See the truth, Starflower.

The words came to my mind like a memory. But a memory of what?

I did not know the voice that spoke them. It was not the voice of any man in the village.

See the truth and speak.

The sound was clearer than any I have heard before or since. When I heard it, I for a moment saw everything around me as a fragile dream. The dead mountain, the priests, the maidens, even Wolf Tongue himself . . . they were nothing but phantoms. What was real was the voice, and it rang down from the heavens as though sung by the sun himself.

Speak, Starflower!

What was it my mother had said all those years ago, before Fairbird's birth? *"You must learn to search out the names of things,"* she had signed to me. *"And one day, you will speak those names aloud, and in speaking, you will be stronger than death or life-in-death!"*

I remembered what she had said then as I marched to my death. But I shook my head and drove the memories away. The phantoms around me became solid once more. The sun was silent as it burned through the sky.

I would never speak. I had no voice.

Looking ahead, I saw the Teeth: great jagged stones that stood upright like the lower jaw of a wild animal. Among them stood Wolf Tongue, his arms upraised as though to catch our procession in a strangling embrace. Still he did not look at me, but his eyes burned bright.

I realized in that moment that I feared Wolf Tongue far more than I feared the Beast. The Beast was an idea. I had never seen him. I had heard his voice in the night, inhuman sounds that echoed through the village. His shadow had held my people captive for generations, his thirst for blood sated only through subservience and sacrifice. I had witnessed the carnage of the wars in which he reveled, the ongoing enslavement of the women who lost their voices to his demands.

Still, he was distant. Intangible, like fear itself.

Wolf Tongue, however, walked among us. And Wolf Tongue bore me a grudge.

Our party neared the summit of Bald Mountain. I saw the bloodstains on the jagged Teeth, dark against stone. There were five stones, four at the corners of a great slab, the largest jutting from the center. I watched as four torchbearers, their torches as yet unlit, took their places around the central Tooth.

Wolf Tongue, robed as ever in his skins, stood with the scarlet-robed priests on his left and the elders of the villages on his right.

See the truth, Starflower.

The Eldest approached, and the hooded maidens parted to let him pass. He stood before me and wrapped his large hands around mine as they held the bowl of blood. He led me from among the maidens and up to the slab. I could feel the eyes of everyone upon me. Only my father would not look at me, even as my eyes silently pled with him. It was no use. So I stared down at the blood and at the Panther Master's hands.

The slab was smooth and cold, though the day was hot. My bare feet walked on the bloodstains of many generations. Animal's blood. And man's.

"You will be stronger than death. . . ."

Wolf Tongue took the bowl of blood. The Eldest backed away from him. I wanted so much to cry out for mercy, to beg him, if he loved me, to stay! But he was gone already, lost amid the crowd.

". . . or life-in-death."

"The hour is nigh, Starflower," Wolf Tongue whispered. "Kneel."

I knelt. He tied my wrists with biting cords and secured me to the central stone. There was no need for this, however. The moment he placed his hands upon my shoulders, I could not move. Darkness overwhelmed me, filling my heart and mind, so powerful that I almost forgot my fear. I was helpless as I knelt in the shadow cast by the stone. I bowed over so that my hair covered my face and brushed the slab beneath me.

Wolf Tongue danced. It was a strange, animal dance, without music, without beauty. He poured the blood from the wooden bowl onto my neck. The stain flowed through my hair and down my mother's white dress.

"She is marked with blood," declared the High Priest. "She is marked for the Beast." His voice was like echoing thunder. He raised his arms above his head, shouting out to the mountains themselves: "We offer you our purest, our best, Lord of the Mountain!"

We waited.

For hours, we waited. Sweat mingled with the blood on my neck, which matted in my hair. It was too hot, and the presence of Wolf Tongue standing so near too overwhelming for me to put any thoughts together. The Beast would not come while everyone watched. I knew that much. I was safe for the moment. Safe . . .

My mother's dress. With my head bowed to my chest, I could see how the bloodstain had traveled down my torso to the waistband. Such a pity. It was to have been my wedding dress.

The sun began to set. One by one, the four torches were lit and set in grooves upon the corner stones. The clouds went orange and red, then deepened into the purple of twilight. A constant wind twisted through the Teeth and whipped my hair across my face. My hands bound, I could not move to push it back.

Suddenly the wind was gone. With it went the torchbearers. Behind them followed the warriors, the elders, and the twelve limping maidens. Oh, Father! Must you leave me too? I dared not look up, for I knew I would find he was already gone. At last even Wolf Tongue slipped down from the slab. I heard his heavy tread as he moved down the mountain trail, out of sight. Even he fled the night's coming terror.

Speak, Starflower . . .

9

WITH MY FOREHEAD PRESSED against the central stone, I knelt, blood soaked and ringed in red torchlight. Too long had I lived as an outcast, but I had never been so abandoned. I felt the pressure on my shoulders where Wolf Tongue had grabbed me and forced me to my knees as firmly as though he still stood over me, holding me in place. All the half-formed plans I had made during the weeks of our journey fled my mind. All the battles I had thought to fight, all the resolve for courage in the face of my end. There could be no fight, no courage.

And yet, I thought, *it could be Fairbird waiting here.*

But it wasn't. Fairbird was safe. She was far from the Beast's shadow, and the price of her life was paid. With this thought came warmth, peace, even. Like the first breath of spring chasing away the cold months of winter. How it stole into my mind in that deathly place I do not know, but there it was. I could bear my own death, my own pain. How would I have borne knowing she sat in this circle of stones? Such a fate would be far, far worse than death. But that fate would never be. My Fairbird would live. She must!

Can you hear me?

The cry of that sad voice again touched my mind. It was the same voice I had heard as I climbed the mountain. For the first time I realized with some surprise that it was no memory. It spoke to my mind from the outside.

Someone was calling me.

I turned where I sat. The cords on my wrists bit down deep if I moved too much, but I was able to look around me a little. The torchlight acted as a shield preventing me from seeing anything that might be in the darkness beyond. The night was perfectly still, without a breeze, and the torches burned straight and tall. Their crackle was the only sound to break the stillness. It was as though the Place of the Teeth was cut off from the rest of the world.

Can you hear me?

I can! I can! I wanted to shout. Oh, are you close? Can you untie my bonds? But I had no voice. I could hear but could not respond.

My mouth opened in a scream that, though silent, rattled me to my core. They were gone. All my people, my father, everyone! They had abandoned me, and I could not so much as cry for help! I gnashed my teeth, lifting my gaze to the looming crest of Bald Mountain, just visible above the torchlight. But I could scarcely lift my head, so heavy was the darkness weighing upon me. I struggled against it, furious.

The torches went out.

Plunged into sudden blindness, I lay still, afraid even to breathe. But my ears were sharp, and there were no other noises to disguise the approaching footsteps. I turned my head in the direction of the sound, toward the higher slopes of the mountain. Someone was descending. Straining my eyes, I saw a tall black figure. Like a fluid shadow it passed over the ground and climbed up onto the slab of bloodstained stone.

Yellow eyes flashed in the night.

"Starflower," Wolf Tongue whispered. "You are mine at last."

I should have known. I should have guessed from the night of my mother's death when he gazed upon me with so much hunger.

There was no other Beast in the Land. Only Wolf Tongue.

He looked down on me, blocking out the stars with his great broad shoulders. I gazed into his eyes, gleaming with their own light. Wolf's eyes. He was a strange, otherworldly creature. My body quivered like one hunted. I read the story his eyes told, a tale of fire and betrayal and death.

But, I thought—and this was the strangest thing—it was not my death I saw in his gaze.

He smiled. The night was heavy, but it could not hide that smile. My stomach heaved with terror, and I twisted around, my arms pulled painfully to one side, pressing my back against the jutting stone.

"You are so beautiful," said Wolf Tongue. "So beautiful when you stand before me, unafraid, defiant. You make me think of the one I loved and lost. She too was brave and strong. But so much more beautiful when I had her cowering before me, submitted to my will! Just as you, my lovely Starflower, will be more desirable when at last I have broken that spirit of yours. Then, and only then, can you be mine."

I could not breathe. The cords chafed my wrists until they bled.

"Tonight," said Wolf Tongue, "I shall make you what I want."

The moon peered over the rim of the mountains, breaking through the thick clouds.

See the truth, Starflower!

"Tonight," said Wolf Tongue, "I shall do more than kill."

Moonlight reveals the truth of things. So my mother taught me. It streamed down upon the Place of the Teeth, covering me, covering him. It was cold and terrible, scattering shadows, showing the world for what it was.

See and speak!

The change came upon him. The shadows of spells that surrounded and shielded him during the day fell away. The High Priest threw back his head, his face contorted in a scream. His hands reached to the air, claws lashing at the night. His throat stretched and thickened, his face lengthened, and a wild, black fire leapt from his eyes and mouth. At last a howl—like a wolf's but human, like a man's but animal—burst from him and filled the air.

And I knew the secret of the terror that had long held the Land captive. The Beast, half wolf, half man, stood before me.

I screamed. It was agony, like teeth tearing me up from the inside out. I should not have been able to make the sound. But I looked upon that monster's face, and no curse could bar my screams.

A shout rang out, a battle cry such as I had heard many times from my father's warriors. The Beast stopped and turned, and I, my fear slashed into silence once more, struggled to see around his hulking body.

The Eldest leapt upon the slab.

He stood, armed with only a flint dagger, small before that monstrous form. Their eyes locked. What silent words passed between them, I do not know. I could not see from where I was tied. But I heard the Eldest, my father, shout his battle cry again, and he sprang forward. He was a man alive once more, not the living corpse he had been since the night of my mother's death. The Beast swung a huge arm at him, but he ducked and was only touched upon the shoulder. It was enough to knock him flat, and for a terrible moment, I thought he would not rise.

The Beast turned to me. I felt the brush of his teeth against my neck. I felt the heat of his breath upon my skin. But the Eldest was up again, throwing himself against the monster. He wrapped his arms about his hairy body, and the two of them rolled in a mass of snarls and shadows. I saw the spark of the Panther Master's flint knife striking against stone. They fell off the slab into the darkness below the Place of the Teeth, where I could not see. Then I heard the roar of the Beast.

The knife had found its way home.

I startled and struggled when a dark figure jumped back onto the slab. Even when I realized it was the Eldest and not the Beast, I writhed in terror at his approach.

"Easy, Starflower," my father said as he strode quickly to the stone. His knife and hand were soaked in dark blood. "Easy, my child."

He knelt and swiftly cut the cords. Released, I fell to the stone, gasping for breath. My father's hands were on my shoulders, lifting me up and leaning me against him. "Can you stand?" he asked, his voice urgent. "Can you walk?"

With his help, I got to my feet. My limbs were numb from the hours of kneeling, my head light with fear. His arm was around me, however, and he half carried me two steps.

But it was he who collapsed.

Horrified, I fell to my knees beside him. Only then did I see the gaping wound in his side. Father! My hands, hampered by the remaining cords still clinging to my wrists, flew over his body, feeling for his heart, his pulse. He lived! Only just, but there was life. He lay headlong upon the stone, drawing shuddering breaths. I pulled him and tugged, desperate to get my arms around him, and his blood mingled with the blood Wolf Tongue had poured on me.

I heard him speak. His words were slurred, and I bent my head to his mouth. He gasped as though this would be his final breath. As he let it out, he said only:

"Run."

I heard the Beast moving down below the slab. My heart beat in my throat as I sat up, as I stood.

"Fool!" I heard the snarl from the darkness. "Decaying, mortal fool!" He panted with pain, but his voice was full of enraged life. "You cannot kill me! Only my own children have the power to end my life! You are nothing, you insect, you crawling little maggot!"

The Beast would be upon us in a moment. He would finish my father, if he was not dead already. And then, he would finish me.

A flash of gold caught the tail of my eye.

A strange sight in the darkness, pure and shining. I turned to it, my fear momentarily forgotten in wonder. Something bright stood away up the mountain, and at first I could not discern what it was. Then I realized, and my wonder increased.

It was a Hound.

Follow me.

The voice sang in the night. The same voice I had heard calling me as I sat awaiting my death. The same voice I had heard the night my mother died, singing calm, singing comfort.

The Hound turned and sped away into the night, up the mountain and away.

I did not think; I could not anymore. Terror and sorrow had bound my mind so tightly that no thoughts could form. I felt a vague certainty that the Beast would pursue me if I ran, and that perhaps my father would be left to die in peace. I flung myself from the slab and ran, leaving behind the Place of the Teeth and the crumpled body of the Panther Master. My bare feet scraped and bled upon the rock.

Follow me.

My feet were as though winged, and I fled such distances in mere strides! As though the wind itself had caught me and pulled me along like a fluttering leaf. Ahead I saw the shining Hound, and he was beautiful as he loped through the black night, guiding like a star. He led up and up, over the crest of Bald Mountain, where the stench of poison was strongest. But I scarcely smelled it then. Instead, I gazed upon the lower slopes of other mountains, where life yet flourished and starflowers gleamed.

The Hound led that way. *Follow!*

I heard the noise of the Beast's pursuit. His labored breathing, his growls, and the scrape of his claws upon stone filled my ears. But as I pursued that Hound, I knew that the Beast could not catch me, not so long as I ran along this strange, enchanted path.

Roaring filled my ears, the roaring of the River Way.

It was said that only one passage led through the Circle of Faces: here in the north, where all the rivers of the Land form into one and cut passage through the rock. It was said that when it breached the far side of the Circle of Faces, the Great River plummeted forever in a vast waterfall, never reaching the bottom of the Void. I looked upon it now, and the currents of the river were white, like the froth in a rabid dog's jowls. Only a fool would steer his craft into those waters. Only a fool would pass through the mountains and fall into the darkness of the Void.

The Hound, graceful in his every stride, loped down the dead mountain to the banks of that river. There the water flowed into a subterranean cavern, passing under the final smaller mountains that formed the Circle of Faces. Into this cavern, the Hound vanished.

I halted at the riverbank, my arms swinging to catch my balance. I could not run that way! Into that dark, where I would be blind and helpless! I was trapped. The river blocked me, and the mountain rose behind me, so sheer that I wondered how I had even descended.

I looked up the way I had come. I saw the Beast.

Like an unrelenting nightmare, he rolled down the mountainside, his gaze fixed upon me, his quarry. All trace of humanity had vanished. He was all wolf now, enormous, bigger than a horse. My hesitation had cost me. In a moment, he would have me in his massive jaws.

Follow, my child!

The Beast or the darkness. Such was my choice.

I prayed: *Lights Above, look down and light my way!* Then I took to my heels and dashed into the cavern. The river swirled about my feet. I could see nothing save the distant glow of that ethereal Hound far ahead. With the growls of the wolf echoing in my ears, I pursued that light. Would the Beast chase me even in this dark? I did not doubt it. And the deeper I went, the more the darkness oppressed me, the more present was his voice howling behind me.

"You were meant to be mine! *Mine!*"

How long I fled that subterranean way, I cannot guess. My feet were sore and bleeding, my limbs bruised, my bones aching. Sometimes I missed my footing in the dark and fell into the water, which carried me hard and fast until I thought I might drown. But the swiftest currents never held me long. I was always cast out upon the blind shore, and the Hound was there, still leading, still guiding.

At last I saw the end of the long cavern, where the water flowed freely out into . . . into what? The Void? The end of all things? It did not matter. No choice remained to me. I must follow the Hound, whether plunging forever with the waterfall or stepping, without existence, into the Nothingness.

"Wait!" cried the dark voice behind, inhuman and ghastly. "Wait, my Starflower!"

My steps slowed despite myself. I kept moving, but fear of the unknown nearly drove me back into the known fear of the Beast's embrace. Far, far ahead the Hound gleamed. But he was so distant, so eerie. And the end of the tunnel waited, as certain as I still breathed.

"Do not venture beyond the safety of the Land!" cried the Beast, and his voice was desperate. What could he have to fear? That I would escape him? But why should that make him tremble so?

I could hear his panting breath behind me. My feet slipped and stumbled on wet rocks I could not see.

"There is nothing for you out there, my beauty," said the wolf. I could sense the nearness of his massive body. My heart raced. Each moment, I wondered if I would feel his teeth tearing into me.

"Do not leave the shelter I have created," he said. "I have made the Land safe, dependent on nothing but me. I am your great protector."

Every step I made was a battle. The end of the cavern was so near! I could see the faint outline of a dark sky that seemed bright as day compared to the dark in which I walked. Cringing, I forced myself another step, another two steps.

"I have cared for the mortal creatures of this nation. For generations, I have been their guardian! My love is great and terrible, too much for your mind to understand. But you will learn. I will teach you."

The voice changed. It was no longer that of a wolf. It was a man who stood just behind me in the darkness now. I dared not look around.

"Come back with me, Starflower. Do not pass into the emptiness beyond. Come back with me, and I shall make you a goddess."

One more step. I must not give in! One more step, just one more.

Why did he not grab hold and drag me back? I was weak to the point of breaking. I could not have struggled against him.

"Come back with me, my love," he said, his voice a growl filled with the horror of his desire. "Step off that Path you follow, and come back where you belong."

If only I were dead! If only he had slain me upon the stone!

"You were always meant to be mine."

I lifted my foot. The distance was too great. I could not make it, could not force my body a single pace farther. I could not—

Follow me!

The Hound was before me, bright and huge and golden. He should have blinded, so potent was his brilliance in the dark of that cavern. Instead, it was as though my eyes were opened for the first time. I saw clearly the path on which I walked. I saw that the Beast could not follow or catch me.

Energy surged through my heart with hope and courage. My hand caught at the Hound, clutching the long, silky hair of his back. Then he was running, and I was dragged along in his wake. He plunged into the river. Water swept over me, cold and dark, but there was light as well, for my hand still gripped that golden fur. My bones should have been pulverized. I should have breathed in the river water and perished. Instead, I was carried swiftly out of the cavern in a rushing tumult.

I came to myself on a thin strip of land. Night was heavy around me, thick with stars. There was water on both sides of me, lapping at my shaking body. I sat up, shivering, alone. But for all this, the first thing I noticed was my gown.

My mother's wedding dress had been washed white once more. The blood was gone.

I looked around me, searching for the Hound. But he was nowhere to be seen. Far ahead I saw the haze of distant land, though in the night my eyes may have fooled me. Behind me loomed the mountains, the cavern, and the mouth of the tunnel from which the river issued.

So this, then, was the Void. This separation from all that I knew. From my sister, my father, my home. It was worse than the fall I had imagined. It was worse even than Nothingness, for in Nothingness I could not have known pain.

My hands shook as I raised them and made the signs of passing. For my father, the Panther Master, who died because—oh, Great Lights, Great Songs! Because he loved me! Against all reason, all expectation, he loved me, his silent, worthless offspring. He loved me enough to give his life.

And when I had finished, I made the same sign for myself. I too had died that day, died to the person I had been. I can never return to the Land. Therefore, I am like one dead.

"*Starflower!*" The Beast's voice, human in its pain, echoed from the deeps of the earth. "*Starflower, do not leave me!*"

I gagged in my terror, my hands faltering in their signs and clenching into fists. Would he pursue? The river could not have carried me far. Could he pick up my scent and come after me even now? I dared not wait to find out. Though everything in me longed for rest, even the rest of death, I forced my body into motion. I staggered and sobbed in pain as I fled down that narrow isthmus of land.

And even as Wolf Tongue's lament haunted me, so the voice of the Hound, unseen but near, urged me on my way.

PART THREE

1

ETALPALLI

THE GIRL SHOULD BE BROKEN.

Midnight hovered with smothering thickness above Omeztli Tower. Hri Sora sat with her children on either side, her quick eyes following every movement of the mortal girl's hands, reading each variation on that gentle face.

She should be broken! The Dragonwitch licked her lips, burning them with the smoldering coal of her tongue. The girl was mortal and frail. After such an encounter with the wolf, she should be shattered to pieces. The humiliation should in itself have been her undoing! The abandonment, the horror of her weakness put on such prominent display. Dreadful fate, to be so shamed!

Yet the creature's hands faltered only when they spoke of her sister, her father, or that wretched dog she seemed to value. And, though Hri Sora sought it throughout the long telling of that sorry tale, she could find no hate in Maid Starflower's eyes.

"On the far end of that narrow stretch of land, I entered the Wood," the mortal signed. "I thought as I passed into its shadows that it was like the Wood in the gorge where Sun Eagle was lost. If this is so, my heart aches even more at his fate. This is a terrible place, this nightmare into which we have fallen."

One of the brutes lying at Hri Sora's side whined. With a hiss, Hri Sora cuffed it into silence. Let the beasts be mute in her presence. She had, for the first many years of their lives, been mute in theirs! She had listened to their squabbles and snarls, unable to raise her voice to bid them cease, powerless even before her own offspring.

Not anymore.

She turned remorseless eyes upon the silent maiden before her. The girl's hands were still, her gaze fixed upon the cowering Dog. How pitiful she was! Not only bound in the repressions of her people, but bound still more in the repressions of love. Yet Hri Sora felt no pity. Contempt burned like hatred in her breast.

The girl should be broken of such foolishness. She should have learned by now that love was the greatest, the final chain. It had brought her so low, laid her out helpless before the eyes of the worlds.

And yet she dared stand in the Flame at Night's presence, gazing with compassion on the wretched Black Dog.

Hri Sora spoke aloud, glorying in the freedom of her own voice as she never had before: "So you fell in with Eanrin of Rudiobus and, charmed by the guile of his voice, allowed him to lead you and leave you in my demesne."

The girl stood motionless a long moment. Then she signed, "I chose to accompany Eanrin. Just as I chose to accompany your children."

"Chose?" Hri Sora laughed, and the laugh was bitter in her mouth. "You are a woman of the Land. You never have a choice."

Starflower closed her eyes and bowed her head. Hri Sora smiled at this subservience. This was much more what she would expect from one who had gazed into Amarok's eyes and seen her own frailty reflected there. Shattered spirit, ruined heart . . . and this mortal, unlike the Flame of Night, had no fire on which to fall back.

Then Starflower signed, "Did you choose, chieftain, to destroy your city?"

Fire poured from Hri Sora's mouth as she leapt to her feet. It fell from her tongue in a violent stream. The mortal girl should burn! She should suffer the ultimate penalty for her insolence! How dared she speak to the Flame at Night on subjects she could not understand? The Black Dogs scurried into the shadows, their tails tucked, and Lady Gleamdren screamed from within her cage.

When the fire died, the Dragonwitch looked down to find Starflower crouched, her head covered with her hands. The coward! She did not deserve to die so glorious a death as by fire.

Hri Sora spat out ashes and snarled: "Were you worth anything, mortal beast, you would understand the choices of a queen. Act on what wisdom you do possess and ask no questions concerning matters far beyond your comprehension."

Starflower, though weak from hunger, exhaustion, and terror, gathered her shaking limbs and got to her feet. How she feared she would faint in the presence of such horror! But she had not fainted when faced by the wolf. She would not permit herself to do so now. No, she would die first.

Hri Sora saw the expression on the girl's face and read every thought therein. *It is well,* she told herself, though she hated to admit it. *If she were broken, how could she do what you require of her?*

The Dragonwitch settled back into her low seat, assuming a relaxed pose, though her veins throbbed with the heat of her desire. Desire to see her dearest wish come true—the wish she longed for more than she longed for her wings. She had thought it possible to see that desire fulfilled only if she first recovered those wings. But now . . . now it seemed so close, so possible, she could almost taste the sweetness of satisfaction.

And if she could fulfill her desire without requiring the Dark Father's assistance, so much the better. It never paid to live in debt to that one.

"Will you return to the Land, mortal?" Hri Sora asked, hoping her voice did not betray her eagerness.

Starflower shook her head.

"Of course not," said the Dragonwitch. "Weak as you are, you dare not return to seek your vengeance."

The girl's hands moved in a flash. "I desire no vengeance. As long as Fairbird is safe, that is all I need."

"Fires of heaven!" Hri Sora cried. "Are you really as much a simpleton as that?"

She wasn't. Hri Sora read the truth in the girl's face. The dragon smiled a slow smile. The girl was weak. Her very strengths were her weakness! To love was to be exposed, to love was to bare one's neck to the axe. And Hri Sora, the stronger by far, knew how to take that weakness and make of it what she willed.

"You've already thought of it, haven't you?" she whispered. "You've already considered the repercussions of your actions. You fled, little one. You fled the Beast and deprived him of his blood price. Did you think he would let it go unpaid? Or did you somehow think the life of your father would pay for the blood you withheld from your god?"

Starflower struggled to meet the Dragonwitch's gaze. But her heart heaved in her breast. No, she would not faint, although the truth stood before her with such ghastly reality, she thought she might die.

"Your sister is not safe." Hri Sora leaned forward, twisting her long neck so that she could catch Starflower's eye. "She will never be safe so long as the Wolf Lord lives."

A tear slid down the mortal's dirty cheek.

"He might wait," said the dragon. "A season, a year, ten years perhaps. But you know as surely as you breathe, the Wolf Lord will demand his dues. And when he does, who will cut Fairbird's bonds and bid her flee to her exile?"

Now was the moment. The girl shuddered from exhaustion, unable to resist the truth she had known since the moment she first turned her feet in flight, the truth she had struggled to repress. Now was the moment, and what a sweet moment it was! Hri Sora salivated at the taste of victory so near. Her saliva scalded the stones at her feet.

"You must return. You must see that the Beast is slain."

Starflower slid to her knees. She could not weep, though she wished she could. Her fatigue was too great. And how heavy was the load upon her shoulders! *Fairbird . . . sweet Fairbird. Will it all be in vain? Will our mother have died to bring you life, only for you to be taken? Will our father have been torn to pieces by his own god, only for that same god to take his offspring as well?*

"I cannot slay the Beast," she signed.

"I did not say you should," replied the Flame at Night. "I said you must see that he is slain."

Starflower gazed up at Hri Sora. She studied that face, so reptilian and yet so vulnerable. The eyes revealed the fire scarcely suppressed inside; she knew full well how swiftly it might emerge. Was that hatred, so intense, meant for her? Starflower did not think so. She could see the contempt, but she did not think the Dragonwitch hated her. Nevertheless, hatred dominated her, body and soul.

"What did he do to you?" Starflower signed.

"What?" Hri Sora snapped.

"What did Wolf Tongue do to you that you so desire his death?"

Hri Sora's hands hid her face. Did the Dragonwitch weep? Starflower knew little about dragons, but she was certain there were no tears left in this pitiful creature's body. Her only release was her flame, which she now struggled to swallow back.

The dragon shook herself at last, as though having succeeded in a great battle of wills. When she spoke, her voice was brittle. "I wish him dead. That is all you need know," she said. "He is my enemy, this self-styled lord of his mortal demesne. He sets himself up as master, but he is nothing! He stole that land and crafted it into his weak little semblance of true Faerie kings' realms. This is a crime among all the lords and ladies of the Far World and must be punished!"

Starflower knew the dragon lied. However, she discovered that, after all she had been through, she had no wish to die in a blaze of fire. So she did not allow her hands to form the questions they wished to ask. The Dragonwitch might keep her secrets as she willed; they weren't too difficult to guess. Starflower peered into the shadows of the tower and saw the Black Dogs watching. They were the Beast's children, she knew beyond doubt. The dragon's too, she guessed. Unloved, unwanted, made less than they might have been.

Anger flared in Starflower's heart. But she was at the Queen of Etalpalli's mercy. It was as her captor had said: She had no choice.

"What do you propose, chieftain?" she signed.

Hri Sora, her rant for the moment ended, smiled slowly. "What do you mean, mortal child?"

"You wish to see the Beast dead. So do I. But such a wish will never be if we ourselves do not act. You know this, and you know more about the monster than I do, though I have lived all my life under his thrall—"

"All your life?" Hri Sora laughed harshly. "All the long, what—fifteen, sixteen years? You are a breath, a moment! You know nothing of what you speak."

Starflower drew back her shoulders. "If I am nothing, chieftain, then let me go."

"Oh, I will! I will, indeed! I will release you from the bindings of my realm. I have no wish to keep you here, no more than you wish to stay."

And now the bargain, Starflower thought. *Now I find out why she did not already slay me.*

"But everything has a price, my child," Hri Sora continued. Her voice was that of the Dark Father. "Everything has a price."

The cat and the badger ran along the River's edge, the badger barrelling forward without a thought, the cat jumping and dancing aside to avoid letting his paws touch the water. The River had not forgotten. It would dart out a hand and drag him under in a second if he was to let his guard down. He should know better; he should take himself far from here as fast as possible! Only a fool or a sop would return to Cozamaloti under such circumstances.

"Call me a fool, then," Eanrin muttered as he ran, head and tail low. "But, Lumé love me, don't call me a sop!"

Being the faster of the two, he was ahead of the badger. But his pace slowed as he drew near the storming falls. They were bigger than the last time he had been this way. Not only were the falls themselves deeper, but the breadth was so great that he could not see the far end of the bridge, which vanished in heavy mist across the way. Cozamaloti gave such a long, continuous roar that it drowned out even the petulant anger of the River.

Eanrin put his ears back, and his eyes were wide as moons. He thought he might prefer to stand on the brink of the chasm in Etalpalli than look into the face of Cozamaloti again. At least the pit was dry!

"Hurry up, cat," panted Glomar, drawing up beside him and taking man's form again. He choked midpant as he got a good glimpse of the falls. "By the sin-black beard of my king! Tell me we've come to the wrong place."

The cat looked up at the guard. "Afraid, Glomar?"

"Not a bit of it!" Glomar's voice trembled.

With a shake of his whiskers, Eanrin became a man once more, sitting cross-legged at his rival's feet, gazing out at the crashing white water. He was pale, and his voice was so small that it could not be heard above Cozamaloti. "I am."

"It wasn't like this when last I came," Glomar said. "She must have realized I was trying to enter and opened the gate for me. I . . ." He licked his lips. "This will be much harder." Then he scowled down at the cat. "What I don't understand is how you, *you* of all people, managed to pass through this way! Did Hri Sora unbar the gate for you as well?"

Eanrin shook his head. He thought of Imraldera, snatched by the River's strong arm, dragged under, hauled toward those falls. The ignorant little mortal maid, lost and far from everything she knew. And yet . . . what a wonder! How brave she had been in the face of what must be utmost terror to her. He couldn't begin to guess at her story, where she had come from or why. But he remembered how she had bravely squared her shoulders, her eyes blazing, and started off through the Wood with the commanding stride of a queen! Certainly, she had almost walked— several times, in fact—straight to her own doom. But she was no coward.

And despite all the sorrows and curses of her own life, she had followed him to Etalpalli and worked so hard to help him.

"Brave girl," he whispered so that he could not hear his own voice. There was movement in the mist. His quick cat eyes focused, pupils dilating. Something just beyond his range of vision approached.

Eanrin got to his feet, taking a tentative step or two, ears still listening to the vengeful River, but eyes fixed upon the bridge.

"Ah well," said Glomar, coming alongside him. He did not like to see the cat show more courage than he. Cats were notorious cowards, while badgers were renowned for their valor. By all the Faerie queens, Glomar wasn't about to let that slip today! "She is a woman worth jumping for, isn't she, Eanrin?"

The mist shifted. Eanrin peered intently, telling himself his eyes lied but wanting to believe them. Then, a glimpse of light in the darkness. A gleam of golden-white fur; dark eyes more compelling than suns and moons.

"Lumil Eliasul," Eanrin whispered.

The mist swirled. The vision was gone.

"Eh?" said Glomar. He gave the poet a sidelong glance. What a strange expression had come over that sardonic face! In that moment, Glomar wondered if he indeed stood beside the Eanrin he knew. Had some phantom imposter taken his place? "Come again?"

"I said . . ." Eanrin cleared his throat. "I said yes. Yes, she is." And he strode down to the bridge.

It swayed and groaned terribly when his feet touched it, and he wondered if Hri Sora had put some new protection on her realm and the bridge would break before he could even make the leap. It did not matter. In that moment, Eanrin began to understand something he had never felt the need to consider before the events of the last few days. Before he found the dragon woman sleeping beneath the caorann tree. Before he had seen the Hound.

"Make the leap, make the leap," he muttered as his feet stumbled and staggered on the swaying bridge and his hands clasped at the ropes suspending it. "Make the leap, not for yourself. Not for yourself, Eanrin! Life is too long to live that way." He glanced down the forever drop, and his stomach surged to his throat. "Oh, great merciful beards of monkeys!"

His heart beat a drummer's quick march, and his limbs were like water. But he would have climbed over those flimsy ropes and hurled himself into rushing torrents in another moment, shouting for Etalpalli and hoping, hoping . . .

Footsteps reverberated along the flimsy boards. Eanrin turned. A figure appeared through the mist.

"Imraldera!" the poet cried.

She could not have heard him, not above Cozamaloti. But within a few more paces, she caught sight of him and paused. Then—miracle of miracles!—she smiled.

Perhaps it was a trick of the mist. Perhaps it was his own fool of an imagination inventing nonsense in the wake of his near death and harrowing journey. Eanrin did not care. With a whoop, he bounded across the bridge, little caring how it swayed under his weight. Her eyes widened, and she clutched at the ropes on either side, bracing her feet. He covered the distance in moments and they stood face-to-face, gripping the bridge and staring at each other. Her smile was faded to almost nothing, and her face was pale. Droplets from the heavy mist beaded her black hair.

"Brave girl!" Eanrin cried, though she could not hear him. "Brave, brave girl!"

Then he took her hand and led her back. For now, he wouldn't think about returning to Etalpalli or of rescuing Lady Gleamdren. He wouldn't consider how Imraldera might have escaped the Black Dogs or Hri Sora. She was safe, and she needed to stay that way. He must get her off the bridge as soon as possible and away from the River.

They met Glomar a few paces out. The bridge was too narrow. Eanrin motioned for him to turn around so they might all reach the land. But Glomar's face lit with a brilliant smile, and he pointed and gestured wildly, paying no attention to Eanrin. He was speaking, but Eanrin could not hear him, nor did he bother to try understanding. "Yes!" he shouted back, equally inaudible. "Yes, she's here and she's safe!" He raised Imraldera's hand to show that he held her. "Now back up, you lump of a badger, back up!"

Glomar wouldn't turn. He continued gesturing and tried to push past Eanrin, making the bridge sway still more wildly. It gave a jerk and a drop, and everyone's heart stopped. Only then did Eanrin look around to see what had excited Glomar so.

Lady Gleamdren, wet and ragged with a face fiercer than any dragon, stood but a few paces behind Imraldera, her face red with screaming things that no one wanted to hear. There was murder in her eyes as she looked from Eanrin's face to his hand holding Imraldera's.

Eanrin let go his hold. Swallowing hard, he turned back to Glomar, gave him a push, and the four of them hastened off the bridge and back to the Wood. As they scrambled up the bank, their ears cleared of Cozamaloti's dissonance enough to be filled with Lady Gleamdren's.

"Well, I like this! Look at the pair of you! Do you have anything to say for yourselves? You *left* me behind in that dragon-blasted, smoke-stinking city without a thought, you pigs, pigs, *pigs!*"

She continued on in this vein until they reached the shelter of the forest, still within sight of the bridge but far enough away that Eanrin could breathe easy again. He tried to focus on Gleamdren—who was difficult to ignore, standing just under his chin, her angry face upturned to his, gifting him with the full force of her wrath—but his gaze kept straying to Imraldera, who stood quietly a few steps back.

"And allowing a *maiden* to do a *man's* work!" Eventually, Eanrin hoped, Gleamdren's voice might give out. Not for a few hundred years, perhaps, but eventually. "And *such* a maiden too! A mortal? Have you no feeling, Eanrin? Have you no *feeling* at all? *Are you listening to a single word I am saying to you?*"

"Yes, delight of my eyes," Eanrin said. "I am indeed. So is Glomar, if you care about that, which I'm sure you don't, but you really should because he's been a good sport through all this nonsense—"

Glomar growled, disliking the sound of his praises spoken by his rival. It did not matter, for Gleamdren burst out again.

"Good sport? You call my peril *good sport*? Was this nothing but a *game* to you, Eanrin?"

"No more than it was to you," Eanrin said darkly.

Gleamdren's jaw dropped. She went from red to purple as she struggled to draw a complete breath. One rancorous gasp and her fury would have been unbearable indeed. But just then, Midnight descended.

The Black Dogs stepped from Etalpalli into the Wood Between.

2

"G ET DOWN!"

Eanrin and Gleamdren dropped at Glomar's whispered command, pressing their bodies flat to the woodland floor. Eanrin, his nose quivering at the too-familiar scents assailing it, carefully lifted his head to peer down to Cozamaloti. His cat's eyes struggled in the impending Midnight, but he could see the two enormous forms stepping off the bridge. Their eyes gleamed.

"It's all right," Gleamdren whispered much too loudly for anyone's comfort. "They weren't sent for us."

"How do you know that?" Eanrin hissed.

She stuck out her tongue at him. "I've been in the Dragonwitch's company for some time now. It's difficult *not* to overhear a plot or two!"

"What are you talking about?"

"What do you think I'm talking about?"

Another movement caught Eanrin's eye. He turned his scowling face from Gleamdren to dart a quick look up. He choked on his own breath. Imraldera was striding swiftly down to the River.

"Ah! I told you she was a witch, Eanrin!" Glomar growled. "She's brought the Dogs upon us, you see." The captain reached out and grabbed the poet's arm. "Quick, man, let us find a safe Path to Rudiobus, or we're all lost."

"No," Eanrin muttered. "It isn't true." He sat for the space of three heartbeats, cursing his own cowardice. Then he was on his feet and sprinting after the girl, praying the Dogs would not catch his scent and knowing they must have it already. "You fool!" he heard Glomar call after him, but he ignored the badger-man and caught up with Imraldera.

"What are you doing?" he demanded in a low voice, turning her to face him. She shook her head and pushed him away, pointing back up the incline to where the others hid. "No, no!" Eanrin snapped. "I'm not leaving. Not until you tell me what is going on."

She rolled her eyes helplessly and shrugged. Eanrin could feel the Black Dogs watching them from below, but the girl did not seem afraid, merely tired and frustrated. She raised her hands and began to sign, but Eanrin caught them both. "That's no good, my dear. We're going to have to play at guessing, but never fear, I'm a quick guesser. Tell me, did you make a bargain with Hri Sora? To rescue Gleamdren?"

To his dismay, after an instant's hesitation, the girl nodded.

"Great dragon's teeth and flame!" His hands tightened on hers. "You offered yourself in exchange for Gleamdren!"

But here she shook her head hastily. Pulling her hands free, she tried again to sign. She pressed a hand to her heart, then pointed to the Dogs. Her eyes pleaded with him to understand. And Eanrin did try for all he was worth, his eyes round and worried as he struggled to guess at any possible explanation. He knew so little about her! He knew she was mortal and cursed. He guessed, from the cords he had cut from her chafed wrists, that she had been a prisoner of some sort.

But nothing about her made sense. Not in the context of the dreadful Black Dogs, those merciless hunters who dragged their victims to Death's realm. For in Imraldera's eyes he saw only love.

He had not recognized it before. Their time together had been so short, and he had been unable to read or understand her for most of it. Following his encounter on the edge of the Dark Water, however, he found himself looking at her with new eyes. He could see the love in her every move and expression. Not love for him, no. How could she love someone like him? He was foolish even to consider it. But love for . . . for someone. Or something. Love that could not be quenched even when standing in the presence of Death's own brood!

The Black Dogs snarled. Midnight surrounded Eanrin and Imraldera as the monsters drew near.

"Please, Imraldera," Eanrin said, wishing she would let him take her hands again. But she took a step back from him. How ghostly she looked, her white dress shining faintly in that darkness. "Please tell me you haven't given yourself to Hri Sora."

She shook her head.

"Is that no, you have, or no, you haven't? Dragon's teeth!" Eanrin ran his hand down his face. The Dogs were closer now. He could hear their rhythmic breathing. If he did not move soon, it would be too late. Those great jowls could swallow him in a second. Against his will, his feet carried him back, first one step, then two.

Imraldera made a sign he did not know, perhaps a blessing, perhaps a farewell. She turned and strode down to the Black Dogs until she stood between them, her tiny form framed by their hideous bulk. She cast a final look up at Eanrin.

Then she was gone. She passed into the forest, and the Midnight trailed behind her as the Black Dogs followed.

"Dragon's teeth, dragon's teeth, dragon's teeth!" Eanrin tore at his hair, took a few running steps after, backed up, darted forward again, and stopped. "Don't get involved. She means nothing to you! The affairs of mortals are none of your business. What does she matter? Her life is only a moment. She doesn't concern you! She doesn't . . ."

He whirled and darted up the incline. He found Glomar and Gleamdren waiting for him there, sheltered by friendly trees. Glomar was speaking to Gleamdren, but her attention was not on the guardsman and his faltering attempts at pretty words.

"There you are!" she cried when Eanrin appeared. "Is this how you intend to demonstrate your devotion? Running off after mortal wenches at the drop of a hat? I thought you a man of high feeling, Eanrin, a man of taste! I thought—"

"What do you know about Imraldera's arrangement with Hri Sora?" Eanrin demanded.

"Imral-who?"

"The maid, the mortal maid. What bargain did she make with the dragon? You said you overheard a plot or two. Tell me what you know about this."

"Oh, so you weren't behind it?" Gleamdren threw up her hands. "I thought at the very *least* you had concocted this fool arrangement for my release! Am I really to believe that you were so hapless you had to let this mortal do your thinking for you?"

Eanrin was within breaths of taking Gleamdren by the shoulders and giving her a sound shake. His voice became a growl, so low, so full of menace, that even the queen's cousin must take notice. She gasped and stepped away from him as he spoke:

"Gleamdren, by the golden staff of my order, if you don't tell me what you know, I'll retract every poem I ever wrote in your honor."

"Oh!" Her hands pressed to her heart. "Oh, you don't mean it, Eanrin!"

"Every rhyming couplet."

Her mouth opened and closed several times. Then, in a tiny chirp, she said, "Hri Sora wants her old enemy, Amarok, destroyed. The mortal agreed to help. The Black Dogs are escorting her back to her homeland, and there she is to do the Dragonwitch's work. All on the condition that I was to go free and you two were to be released from the city."

Eanrin stared at Gleamdren. None of it made sense! His mind sifted through the information, struggling to find pieces that might fit together. Who was Amarok? Why would Hri Sora send Imraldera back to the Near World, and why with the Black Dogs as escort? How could the gentle maid possibly be an instrument for the Flame at Night's vengeance?

And why, in the midst of all these horrors, would Imraldera concern herself with his, Glomar's, and Gleamdren's safety?

It was too much. Too much! For a mind as old as memory and a life lived longer than the mountains and rivers of a hundred worlds . . . it was more than Eanrin could bear.

"Curse that Hound! Curse that lantern!" Eanrin snarled, grinding his teeth. "I shall never be the same."

"What?" Gleamdren demanded. "What are you muttering, Eanrin? The girl is gone, thank Hymlumé's grace, and we are free of that wretched, wretched city. You certainly have done nothing of which to write epics, but at least you can escort me home. And here I thought I would return in company with a score of suitors, not two sorry little— Eanrin! Where are you going?"

The poet, running back down the incline, did not pause but called over his shoulder, "I'm going after her! I'm going to help!"

"Eanrin! Lumé love me, cat, if you take one more step after that creature, I will *never speak to you again*! Eanrin, do you hear me?"

But it was too late. Whether the poet had heard or not, he was gone, vanished into the Wood and pursuing the trail of Midnight. Gleamdren stood aghast, her hands on her hips.

Glomar crept to her side. "If I may be so bold, my lady, I should like to offer you my—"

"Be still!" Gleamdren turned eyes full of sparks on the captain. "I don't know who you are, nor do I care. Take me home at once, do you hear? I've had enough of this adventuring to last me a lifetime!"

So it was that Lady Gleamdrené Gormlaith, on the arm of a single escort, was returned to the welcoming bosom of Rudiobus. And wherever she went for generations after, she could hear the women giggling behind her back, "A *hundred* suitors, Lady Gleamdren? Have you bothered to count them recently?"

Omeztli stood empty. The black corridors echoed nothing but silence; the bustling life of Etalpalli was forever stilled. The queen's tower looked out upon a ghost city. It was barren and forlorn save for its last inhabitant.

She sat on the tower's roof. And she was as empty as Omeztli.

Her hand pressed to her chest, feeling that place where her heart had once pulsed. Usually it was warm with the blaze of her inner furnace. But now even that was dulled to almost nothing. She felt as hollow as a dead tree.

"You'll never get your wings now."

The Dark Father stood behind her. She sensed his presence with distaste but did not move. Her gaze was fixed on the far, blank horizon of her demesne. Even her hated offspring had left the city. Her prisoners were swiftly putting distance between themselves and Etalpalli. The vastness of her solitude was impressive, to say the least.

"You let Bebo's cousin go." The Dark Father placed a long-fingered hand on Hri Sora's shoulder. She wanted to flinch but wouldn't. "She was a good chance. She is weak, at the mercy of her own vanity. You could have wrung the secret from her had you made the effort."

In the cold clarity of her mind without fire, Hri Sora acknowledged the truth of her Father's words. But it did not matter. Learning Gleamdren's secret would not have guaranteed her the Flowing Gold. And even had she succeeded and laid the fabled treasure at the Dark Father's feet, who could say if he would have honored his side of the bargain? He was a liar. He was the inventor of lies.

But this way—if it worked, if the girl was smart and did as she was told—this way, Hri Sora's deepest desire could be fulfilled. And the Death-of-Dreams himself could not stop it!

"I'm no fool, my daughter," said her Father. "I can piece together this little puzzle."

He needed no motivation, and she did not care to give him any. She sat as though stone. He laughed to himself, and embers fell from his mouth and singed her tatty hair.

"You came back from your second death stronger and more beautiful than tongue can tell," he said. "The Flame at Night rekindled! And you dared laugh in my face and tell me your fire was the greatest to burn in all of Time. To prove your words, to make your defiance complete, you declared before all your brethren in the Netherworld that you should do what I dared not try. You would rise to the vaults of heaven and devour Lady Hymlumé, the moon herself, destroying the harmonies of the Sphere Songs forever.

"You flew far and you flew fast. You rose to the highest reaches. You looked Hymlumé in the eye, and the worlds felt it when she, frightened, stumbled in her dance and lost the beat of her Song. How powerful you were, my daughter! How glorious beyond all created beings!

"But I am your Father. I will not be undone. You will not defy me to my face and go unpunished.

"I stripped away your wings. I stripped away your dragon form and left you in the frail, wingless body of a woman. And there you stood before the moon. And she looked upon your pathetic state and said: *'Poor little thing.'*

"It was too much for you, wasn't it, my darling? In despair and disgrace, you flung yourself from the heavens, willing to die your third and final death rather than be pitied. The flame of your fall was like the destruction of worlds, fire spilling from your mouth, lashing from your hair, your fingertips. Your screams shattered the sky. And you streaked to your destruction, striking that mountain in the Near World with such force that the fire could be seen far and wide. It burned for days, for months, possibly for years as counted in that mortal world. When at last it died away, the nations assumed you had met your final end.

"But that wasn't how it went, was it, my child? You didn't die. You lay exposed upon that bald mountain peak for a year or more. But you did not die.

"At last you woke. Your fire was gone, and your shell of a body was empty. You wandered down the burned slopes of that mountain, helpless as a new babe, no memory of yourself or your past glories. The mortals of the Near World found you. They took you in as one of their own, and you became no better than they. A Faerie queen turned dragon turned beast of the dust. And so you lived for years. . . .

"What made your fire return, Hri Sora? What finally kindled that memory of flame? You blazed back into Etalpalli ten years after your death was declared, destroying them all. And you brought those monstrous children with you.

"I am no fool! I can guess at your story as easily as though you told me!

"You met Amarok the Wolf in the Near World. He took you for his bride. He, a self-styled lord, a lowly shifter, a devil in animal form. When you were Queen of Etalpalli, he would not have dared look you in the eye. When you were a dragon, he would have fled before your fire!

"But he saw you then, reduced to this helpless state, wingless, witless. What a prize you were! More valuable in his eyes than you could ever have been to Sir Etanun."

Here the Flame at Night's body convulsed. Smoke streamed black from her nostrils. But she stopped and drew it back, breathing it deep and swallowing it down. She could not lose her mind so soon! She could not let the flames overtake her again! She must wait. She must wait for her children's return. She must hear whatever news they might bring.

Oh, let it be word of death! Let it be word of vengeance!

"How you must have longed for his death," breathed the Dark Father. "It need be only one death for him, for he is no true Faerie king, this thief of mortal lands. But when you came to yourself, when you recalled your fire and blazed once more, you did not kill him. Why not, Hri Sora? Why did you not destroy Amarok?"

The Dragonwitch bowed her head. She could not bear to admit it, though she knew the Dragon must have guessed already. His laugh told her that she was right.

"He knows your name. He knows your lost name just as you know his. The name that should be forgotten. He knows who you really are!"

The Dark Father leaned down, his hands upon her shoulders, and whispered in his daughter's ear: "*Ytotia*. My Lady Who Dances."

With a moan, Hri Sora pulled away, burying her face in her hands. If only she had tears with which to cry out her shame! How could she have let him discover her name? In what moment of madness or passion had she let it slip? Now, as long as he hid within his own self-made demesne she could not kill him. Amarok, her lover, her enslaver, her dear and hated one! He had made her think she loved him. He had made her believe she was weak and mortal, that it was her honor to be his bride. How she had rejoiced when she carried his children, how she had wept with joy when she bore him twins! Those monsters.

He had made her a silent woman.

Foolish! Hateful! She had loved because she knew no better, and she had made herself vulnerable before him. The fiend. The Beast, unfit to lick the soles of her feet! And he must die. He must die, for she had loved him, and love was not to be borne!

But her flames could not hurt him in his own demesne, stolen though it was. If she'd been in full power, with her wings and her mighty dragon form, the tale would have been different. No one in the mortal world could withstand the Flame at Night!

Her wings were gone, however. Her power reduced. She could not kill Amarok.

No matter! He could not stop her flight from the Land, her escape through the mountains and out into the world beyond. He could not keep her children from her, so the three of them fled and stood beyond the Circle of Faces, beyond his power. Then she had called him. She knew his Faerie name. She had heard of Amarok the Wolf, if only in passing, generations before she took her Father's kiss. She stood on the isthmus separating the Land from the Continent, and she called to him.

"Amarok! Wolf Lord! Come to me and meet your doom!"

He could not resist the call of his true name. And the moment he stepped beyond the Circle of Faces, her fires would consume him.

But then, the worst truth was revealed. His voice called back to her from the caverns: "Ytotia! My ladylove! Your voice has no power over me!"

The sickening. She felt it even now like a knife in the gut, the strength of her name spoken on his lips. Or rather, the name of a Faerie queen who was gone but whose memory, however faint, yet lived within the Flame at Night. For though Ytotia was long destroyed, her name spoken in Amarok's mouth still held power. Enough to prevent Hri Sora from commanding him.

With a roar that blasted the mountains and boiled the ocean on either side of the isthmus, she cried: "Stay in your prison, Wolf Lord! Stay in your stolen world! But know this, my husband, and know it well: The moment you set foot beyond the Circle of Faces will be your last. For I shall send the Black Dogs, your own two children. And they will rend you to pieces and drag your spirit to the Netherworld where you belong. So I have vowed in fire!"

Hri Sora, sitting on Omeztli's rooftop, whispered again, "So I have vowed in fire."

"It will never work, you know," said the Dark Father. "You've sent the mortal girl to her doom. She cannot lure Amarok from his demesne. She is but a pretty toy! He will catch her and do what he wants with her. She cannot hope to trick him. Is Amarok a fool? He made a dragon and queen into his willing bride! He is not about to fall prey to the manipulations of a mortal wretch."

"I gave her his name," said Hri Sora. "She has his Faerie name."

The Dragon laughed mockingly. "It matters little. The girl is a mute! The name is useless to her as long as she cannot speak it."

"That," said the Dragonwitch with something almost like a smile, "shows how much you know."

3

IDNIGHT RESTED HEAVILY upon the Wood, but the Black Dogs remained out of sight. So Imraldera sat alone in that dreadful place, knowing that her escorts were near, yet not knowing how near, scarcely able to see her hand before her face.

At least they had permitted her to stop awhile. And it was well that they did, or their cursed errand would have met an untimely end. She could not bear the thought of one more step without rest! Not without a sleep untroubled by dreams . . .

When was the last time she'd slept? she wondered as she lay down upon the hard forest floor, adjusting her body around roots and rocks and fallen branches. Lying on the burned stones of Etalpalli, her head pressed to the chest of the cat-man poet, listening to the fading strains of his lullaby; she had slept then. It had not been a restful sleep, but she had, at least for those brief moments, felt safe.

Safety was far from her now, with the Black Dogs so close and the weight of her task crushing her heart.

She must go back. The old life beckoned with the insistence of death. Imraldera had not thought it possible that she could so swiftly be convinced to return to the Land. Though her life had been one of few joys or pleasures, it was the only life she knew. By returning, she tossed that life, so hardly won, into the jaws of Death. The Beast would be waiting for her. He might even now crouch at the cavern entrance where the river burst free. How long had it been since she fled? A few days, perhaps? A few hours? Would the Beast have already returned to the lowlands?

Would he have returned for Fairbird?

"Starflower."

The girl startled at the voice speaking from the darkness. She sat up, twigs and leaves sticking to her matted hair, staring into the impenetrable Midnight. She waited, hoping the speaker would reveal himself. Nothing followed, however. Perhaps she had dreamed it in her loneliness.

She lay back down, shivering though it was not cold, and pillowed her head on her arm. Her eyes would not close but continued straining against the dark. And in her mind, she kept seeing a flash of teeth in the moonlight, and she heard a dark voice saying:

"You were always meant to be mine!"

This must be her fate. Even though her father had given his life to fight it, even though she had fled into the Void and discovered the terrible worlds beyond, still she was driven back. Even if Hri Sora had not made this dreadful bargain, she knew she would have returned eventually.

Because it was true: Fairbird was not safe. She never could be safe as long as the Beast lived. Therefore, as long as the Beast lived, Imraldera must continue fighting him. But how could she, silent and small, hope to combat a vicious and cunning monster many hundreds of years old?

"Starflower."

Once more she sat up. Her heart jumped to her throat. Was it the cat-man? But he did not know her name, nor did his rival. No one out here in the world beyond the Circle of Faces knew who she was.

She waited. Again, nothing followed: no second cry, no sound in the underbrush, not even a warning growl from the lurking Black Dogs. It was either sit like a statue forever or lie down and try to rest. So she lay down again, this time firmly shutting her eyes.

Death. She was sent to lure Wolf Tongue to his death. To trap him, to deceive him, just as he had once trapped and deceived her.

Oh, Mother! she cried out in the echoing silence of her mind. *What sort of monster have I become?*

"Starflower."

She was on her feet in an instant, spinning in place, her eyes peering desperately into the darkness. Her heart thudded in her throat, but for a moment her exhaustion was forgotten in tense preparation for yet another flight. The Black Dogs would pursue her, yes. But better that than to sit here and listen to ghostly voices!

"Starflower."

Someone stood just behind her.

She drew a long breath. She felt the close proximity of the stranger, someone tall, someone strong, but she dared not turn to face him. Nor did she dare to flee. Raising trembling hands, she signed, "Who are you?"

"You know me, my child."

Her heart surged at the words. She did! She did know! She knew that voice better than her own father's. She had never heard it speak words like these, the words of a man. Always before it had rung from the heavens, whispered in the moonlight, sung in the silence of her mind. And she knew his name, a name she had long wondered at, a name she had seen her mother sign in prayer or praise.

"He Who Names Them!" she signed. "You are the one my mother knew, the one who gave the names to all living things!"

"You go into great peril, Starflower," he said.

She longed to turn around, to see his face, but she did not dare. She bowed her head instead and signed: "I have lived my life in peril."

"Live it now in triumph, my child." How fluid was the sound of his voice. It wasn't like a man's voice, she realized, though at first she had mistaken it for such. Nor was it that of an animal. It was altogether unique. Speaking into her spirit, it reverberated there, and she knew she would never forget that sound. "You have followed my paths many times in fear. Follow me now in trust. Trust me, Starflower, and do as I tell you."

"But I am going on a dragon's errand! My way has become dark as this Midnight."

"Yes," said he. "Your errand is one of wickedness and will leave you broken." How gentle were his tones, and yet his was a voice that could destroy nations. "But trust me, my child, and I will make yours a mission of freedom, not of vengeance. I will make you the liberator, not the murderer."

"How can I be anything other than a murderer?" Imraldera signed. "I would give my life for Fairbird, but must I give his death instead? He is loathsome and he is dreadful, but . . . but what makes me any different if I go through with this pact?"

"It is a dark path, Starflower," spoke the Lumil Eliasul. "But I will see you come to no harm. And when you emerge victorious, the worlds will know you are mine. And they will wonder at the works you perform in my name.

"But you must see the truth. You must see who this Beast is. Look at him with your heart, Starflower. You must see his true name, the name which no one has ever known. And when you know his name, you must speak it."

"The Dragonwitch told me his name."

"See the truth, Starflower."

"I do not know how to see!"

"When you see, you must speak."

"I have no voice!"

"Imraldera. Wake up, my dear."

The girl startled upright, blinking hard in her efforts to drive off the darkness. It would not lift, and she remembered with a sickening rush the Midnight and the Dogs. But there had been more, hadn't there? A voice she knew, a promise given . . .

"I don't know how you can sleep in this murk. You mortals are a strange lot, I tell you."

Shaking herself, she forced her eyes to focus. To her surprise, she found Eanrin sat beside her, cross-legged. He grinned wanly and held out his hand. "Hungry?"

He offered her fruit she did not recognize. She snatched it up and, little caring if it be enchanted or poisoned, devoured it so fast she scarcely tasted it. The cat-man chuckled as he watched her, then produced more. The second piece went down more quickly than the first. By the third piece, she began to notice the flavor, sweet but with a sour hint. It was larger than a fig, more crisp than a mango, with a thin outer peel and an inner pulp of odd texture but full of juice that eased her thirst as well as hunger. Her stomach growled in gratitude and, embarrassed, she placed a hand over it.

Eanrin shook his head and produced a fourth fruit. "One would think you had never seen an apple before. Or have you?" he added as an afterthought and raised his eyebrows musingly as he considered this point. Imraldera ignored him and ate, thinking even then that she would never be satisfied.

"Strange company you have chosen to keep," Eanrin said, glancing about. The Black Dogs remained hidden, but he knew they were aware of his presence. They had been given no command concerning him, however, not since they had chased him through Etalpalli. He hoped they would leave him be. "Gleamdren told me of your bargain with Hri Sora. Brave girl. Foolish too, absolutely! But brave. So we're returning to your homeland, are we?"

Imraldera, her hunger ebbed somewhat, stopped chewing a moment. She frowned at the poet. He shouldn't be here, she realized. He should be on his way back home, his lady in hand, triumphant and carefree. But here he was, sitting under the gaze of Hri Sora's deadly children, slicking back his hair with his hand. His shirt was more muddy and tattered than ever. He was stained and disheveled, yet he sat like a dandy and smiled as though the worlds must be blessed by his very existence.

Behind that smile lay a tremulous hesitance she almost overlooked. Was he afraid she would turn him away?

"I can see you thinking," Eanrin said, shifting a little uncomfortably. "You're probably wondering what the blazes I am doing shadowing after you like some love-struck kitten."

She blinked, and her hand holding the apple core dropped to her lap.

"I assure you," the poet hastened on, "that I mean to accompany you purely out of a sense of obligation. You freed my lady Gleamdren. You danced right into Etalpalli the Unassailable, stood before the dreaded

Flame at Night to make your demands, and danced right back out again. The conquering heroine, freer of prisoners and warrior maiden of great renown. I should like to write an epic in your honor . . . but alas! Such is not the work my audience has come to expect of me. No. I shall have to pay my obligation through practical rather than artistic means. That is, if it's all the same to you?"

Who would have thought a cat's face, even in human form, could look so pleading?

Imraldera reached out and took one of his hands. She squeezed gently, filling her eyes with gratitude. If there was one thing she needed out here in the Between, it was a friend.

Eanrin gazed back at her, his expression shifting between an uncertain smile and an uncertain frown. Then he took her hand in both of his and raised it to his lips. "So it is decided! I am your servant."

Imraldera blushed and hastily rose, brushing away the dark seeds left from her meal. With a motion of her hand, she pursued her way. She did not know this Wood. She did not understand the Paths she walked. She knew the Black Dogs flanked her. She knew as well that she hated walking the Path they chose for her.

But something had changed. The Path was no longer so dark at her feet, though the Midnight itself had not lifted. And when she raised her eyes to peer ahead, she thought she glimpsed golden light, distant but steadily shining. She thought of her dream and wondered if perhaps it was no dream after all.

And Eanrin, falling into step behind her, sang softly to himself:

> "Oh, woe is me, I am undone,
> In sweet affliction lying!
> For my labor's scarce begun,
> And leaves me sorely sighing
> After the maiden I adore,
> Bravely marching to Death's door. . . ."

The Wood gave way at last, and Eanrin, for the first time he could remember (though perhaps there was a forgotten time or two in the generations of his life) stood on the brink of the Near World.

The ocean lapped the shores at his feet. A narrow stretch of land extended out over those placid waters, leading toward the hazy horizon of tall mountains in the distance. Eanrin shook his head, surprised at a sight of such majesty here in the mortal realm. Odd, for though he smelled mortality all around him, it offended his nose much less than it once had.

Imraldera stepped from his side down to the water's edge. The ocean wind caught at her long hair and the tatters of her white gown, billowing them behind her like contrasting flags. She looked smaller even than before, offset by the vast expanse of water and those looming peaks. But there was strength in the set of her shoulders.

Midnight fell as the Black Dogs stepped from the Wood. Eanrin shuddered, glancing from right to left as they drew alongside him. But their eyes were fixed upon the girl; Eanrin might as well not have existed. One of them sniffed loudly, raising its ugly nose. Then it howled, a low, mournful sound.

Imraldera turned. With swift motion of her hand, she ordered the monster silent. It crouched to the ground, its body quivering, a black, voiceless shadow.

The strange party made their way along the isthmus, Eanrin avoiding the water lapping on either side as much as he avoided the Dogs. These faded into little more than phantom wraiths, invisible against the night. The mortal world was no place for beings such as they.

The journey must have been long, but they followed a Faerie Path, which carried them swiftly across the distances. At length they stood at the far end of the isthmus, and towering above, sheer and impassable, were the mountains. Eanrin sensed what these were in the Far World of Faerie. Giants! Stone giants! Nothing more than rock and silt in this mortal realm of dust and decay; yet their nature remained at their core.

"The Circle of Faces," the poet whispered. He knew now where they were. Turning to Imraldera, he exclaimed, "You are from the Land Behind the Mountains! I thought no living creature dwelled therein, not anymore.

What a marvel you are, my girl, to have found your way out! Even I know that nothing enters and nothing leaves the Hidden Land." He scratched his head then, making a face. "Which will make things a bit difficult for us, yes? If we are to venture in, I do hope you know the way."

She nodded. With firm steps that belied her quailing heart, she led the poet and the Dogs to that place where the rivers escaped from their subterranean way. The rushing water nearly overwhelmed the isthmus. But Eanrin spotted what the receding tide slowly revealed: a small stretch of dry land leading into that dark cavern. It was narrow indeed, but it looked solid enough. He touched Imraldera's arm and pointed. She nodded, unsurprised.

Then she turned to the Dogs. They had hidden themselves from Eanrin's eyes, deeming him useless. But Imraldera saw them clearly. She signed a command she had used for Frostbite and her father's lurchers: "Stay."

The Black Dogs sat. One growled. One faintly whined. Otherwise, they were like stone.

"Are they not coming with us?" Eanrin asked, uncertain if he was relieved or dismayed. After all, as dreadful as the monsters were, they were a known dread. Whomever the Flame at Night had sent them to face—whomever she could not face herself—was unknown and therefore more to be feared.

Imraldera beckoned to the poet and, moving carefully, crossed the land bridge into the cavern. Eanrin followed, leaving behind the Midnight to step into darkness deeper still. But this, at least, was a natural dark. He smelled earth and dirt, and thought for a moment that Glomar would have been much better suited to this mission.

Suddenly the hair on his neck stood on end. A sensation of utter cold wafted over his spirit. Freezing and smothering, it was familiar, too familiar. Rather than a flowing, living river, he smelled the stagnant stench of the Dark Water.

"Bravely marching to Death's door," he whispered, then cursed violently, his voice echoing and reechoing in the dark. "What have we done?"

His fey eyes struggled to see in the dark, but he could just discern Imraldera's form a few steps ahead as she felt her way along the cavern wall. "Wait!" Eanrin cried, leaping forward and grabbing her arm. He felt her whole body convulse with terror, and she whirled about and gripped his arms as though holding on to life itself. He peered into her face and realized that her mortal eyes could see nothing in this place. She was walking blind.

"We must go back," he told her.

She shook her head.

"We can't go on this way. I know this Path!" he insisted. "I've walked it before, though not in this place. This is the Path of Death!"

Her grip tightened for a moment, then relaxed, as though she forced her muscles to obey. She stepped out of Eanrin's grasp and turned back to feeling her way, her steps slow but firm.

"Imraldera!" Eanrin cried, hastening to keep up with her. "Don't you understand? You go to your own destruction! That's what it means to walk this Path. You will die!" A piece of his mind whispered, *I will die too.*

But in that moment, he did not care.

This is what you have always feared, he realized. *This is the final weakness.*

He shook off the thought and reached for Imraldera again. She was beyond his grasp and moving swiftly. Two steps more, and Eanrin gasped in surprise. For they no longer walked Death's Path. Only a few paces before, without twists or turns, they had been on that inevitable road to the Dark Water. Now the darkness of oppression gave way to the natural darkness of underground, and the stench of demise was replaced with the smells of deep places, cold and dank but not fetid.

They were once more under the mountain. And they followed the Path of the Lumil Eliasul.

It was strange to walk Faerie Paths in the mortal world. In the Between or the Far World, it was as natural as breathing to be carried over those far stretches of land in a stride. In the mortal world, it was a nauseating sensation, and Eanrin often had to stop and let his head clear of dizziness.

In those times, Imraldera waited for him. She, for all her mortality, seemed less affected. Perhaps because it was her land. Perhaps mortals were bound to their demesnes, much like Faerie lords and ladies. Imraldera was, Eanrin still insisted, a princess, and she would feel that bond as only those of royal blood would.

At last they left the caverns below the mountains and emerged, blinking and gasping, into daylight. They were both streaked with dirt and damp, but after their many adventures, this scarcely made a difference. Imraldera, who had been blind as they traveled underground, was obliged to stand for some moments, letting her eyes adjust. This gave Eanrin time to take in the world around him.

He was surprised by the freshness in the air, having expected yet again to be overwhelmed by mortal stinks. But it was as clear and heady to him as the breezes of Rudiobus itself, if warmer. He liked the smell of the forests growing here, the low shrubs and rich mosses. This was a good land.

But as they began to climb the mountains, still following the Path of the Lumil Eliasul, Eanrin grew uneasy. Something was wrong; something was false. Bald Mountain loomed above them, and Eanrin wrinkled his nose as the faint remnants of poison reached him. The Flame at Night had fallen here, he realized. This was the Near World mountain she smote after her plunge from the heavens. He saw the barren slopes where no living thing would thrive again; he saw the scorch marks upon the earth. Something much worse was amiss here, if he could but sniff it out.

Imraldera led him along the Path, up the dead mountain. They climbed into the freezing reaches near its summit, but the cold could not touch them on the Faerie Path. From that height, Eanrin beheld the Hidden Land for the first time: the green fields, the deep gorges wherein the rivers flowed, stretching to the far horizon and beyond sight.

"Your kingdom," he said to Imraldera. But she gave him a puzzled look and shook her head. It did not matter. She was a princess, say what she would.

They picked their way down the far slopes of Bald Mountain. Imraldera's steps became more hesitant, and she stumbled dangerously once or twice. This was not a terrain on which to lose one's footing. Eanrin doubted she could fall so long as they pursued this Path, but he did not like to take the chance. He took hold of her arm, and she allowed him to assist her in the more difficult descents.

Her body shuddered in his grasp, and her dark face went ashen.

Eanrin stopped as though he had hit a wall. The scents of lies and deceits overwhelmed him, and he swayed where he stood.

"Lumé's crown!" he swore. "What is this horror?"

They stood on the slope just above the Place of the Teeth. In the cold light of the sun, the red bloodstains upon the stones showed darkly. The Teeth tore at the sky, and from them Eanrin felt the force of the darkness holding the Hidden Land in its grip.

Indeed, Imraldera could be no princess. No one could rule a land like this. No one, that is, save a Faerie imposter.

Eanrin understood, suddenly, the power behind the curse that kept Imraldera silent. A Faerie beast had crept from the Far World and stolen this land to make a false demesne. He had set up these stones, fed them with the blood of sacrifices, and turned this realm of mortals into his hunting grounds. He had made himself a god among the weaker beings. Wrenching the land from their power, he had bound it to his spirit in ways it was never meant to be bound.

It was a breaking of the Old Laws, a crime against Faerie lords and ladies. A crime against all worlds!

Eanrin turned to Imraldera. Her arms were wrapped about herself, and she stared down at the dreadful stones. The poet looked at her scarred wrists, from which he had cut those cords; then he looked at the central stone. He knew, or guessed at least, what had happened. The Beast had demanded this girl as the next sacrifice. He would have taken her blood or . . . or possibly more.

Fury rose like fire in Eanrin's breast. He strode down to the dreadful stones and struck them with his fists. "Evil, evil curse at your birth!" he shouted.

Imraldera cringed and backed away. Did Eanrin, now that he knew of this place, also believe in the curse? He was not of this world, after all. Perhaps he understood the Beast. Perhaps he sided with the god of the Land and also pronounced women a plague of nature.

Perhaps she had no friend.

Kneeling, she took up a stone. She had come this far. If he, her only companion, turned on her, so be it. She would fight! Fairbird must be saved, and the Beast must meet his end. Eanrin could not stand in her way.

The poet turned, and his face was that of a fierce animal ready to tear into its prey. Imraldera's heart plunged to her stomach, and she braced herself, ready to hurl her stone as the cat-man strode back toward her.

Then he spoke: "The Faerie Beast will know we have breached his territory. It is the way of it, even in a false demesne. They set up protections on their borders, and they sense when those protections are broken."

Imraldera's grip on the stone relaxed. She drew a shuddering breath and nodded.

"We must be prepared," Eanrin continued. "I wish you could tell me everything. Curse the monster for taking your voice! But I can guess at most of it, I think. And some, perhaps, I do not want to know."

He drew a deep breath and turned from Imraldera to gaze down into the Hidden Land. She could strike his head with her weapon. She knew where to hit so that he would fall senseless to the ground, never to move again.

She closed her eyes, whispered a prayer, and let the stone she held drop to her feet. She must trust someone. If she was wrong and Eanrin proved false, so be it. She would not live her life in constant fear of men.

Eanrin turned slightly at the crack of the falling stone. Again, he guessed at many things but chose not to look around. He had made his decision. He would see this adventure through, no matter what became of him in the end.

4

THE LAND WAS BLOODIED with war. Men fought brutal battles, brother slaying brother in a hopeless quest for supremacy. No man could reign supreme over this land that belonged to the Beast. The blood spilled by each warrior poured into the ground and fed the power of the dark god.

And the curse of silence held the women mute. Even if they dared think, "Surely there must be another way!" they could not speak it. They were slaves, shadows passing through the years of their short existences, unable to change what might be.

The season for campaigns was high, and the men were away at their wars. The cat bypassed the fields of blood as best he could, trotting through the villages instead. Every village was the same. Hollow-eyed women tended to the old men and the boys too young for battle as though they were minor gods. The cat would cozy up to one or another, occasionally receiving a pat for his purrs, once or twice a bite of meat. Usually he was repaid with kicks, however. These women to whom no kindness had been shown had little kindness to spare.

Eanrin searched each village with great care. Imraldera, once more scratching signs in the dirt, had been able to give him only a vague idea of what he sought. Through all the disjointed scribbling and a long guessing game, he had learned that he must find the king's village (though Imraldera had insisted there was no king, merely her father). To reach this village, he would have to cross four gorges and four rivers. He must look for the soil that was red and the house upon a hill. In that house lived a child and a . . . something. A cow? No. A lizard? No, no. A walrus? No!

"Not a . . . Iubdan's beard, not a dog!"

Yes, a child and a dog. Another dog. As though there weren't already dogs enough bound up in this adventure! The cat sighed as he padded his sleek way across the landscape. But Imraldera had been firm in this. He must find the house on a hill where a child and her dog lived. After a little guessing, Eanrin discovered that this was her sister and that Imraldera, above all, wanted to know that the girl was all right.

"But what about the Faerie Beast?" Eanrin had asked. "Are we not here for him? Gleamdren said Hri Sora sent you to find him. He will be aware that someone has breached his borders and may even now be looking for us. We must be wary!"

But Imraldera shook her head. The child and the dog . . . they were of first importance. The child must be safe. The Beast would come second.

Nevertheless, Eanrin insisted she remain behind and allow him to venture into the Hidden Land alone. "I won't be long," he told her. "There are Faerie Paths throughout this kingdom, and not all of them are controlled by the Beast. I'll use those and be back before you know it.

"But," he added with an earnest clasp of her hand, "if you see any sign of the Beast, promise me you will run. Don't wait for me. Just run. As fast as you can. Get out of this place and never return."

Imraldera gave him a long look. Her face held an expression he could not read. If only he knew her language of hands and faces!

Then she nodded and patted his head as though he were in his cat form. When he started on his way, she stood at the Place of the Teeth and watched him, looking small and vulnerable but as brave as he had ever seen her.

What a creature this mortal maid was. What a spirit, bigger than life itself!

There had been no sign of the Beast as Eanrin made his way into the low country. He wondered if perhaps the Path of the Lumil Eliasul that Imraldera followed was imperceptible to the master of this demesne. That would be a bit of luck! If such were the case, Eanrin could take all the time he needed to search for that child and that dragon-bitten dog.

Crossing the rivers was the worst part. When he came to those, he was obliged to take his man's shape and, under cover of night, climb down into the gorge. There were forests in these gorges through which the rivers ran. To his surprise, when he inspected them, he discovered they were part of the Wood Between. How strange that the mortal realm would be so close to the Between and yet remain so hidden and separate from all other worlds.

But then he sniffed the rivers and realized: They were barriers. They were enchanted waters set in place long ago to serve as protection. While those within the Land could pass into the Wood and become lost, creatures of the Wood could not come out. Not so long as these rivers were in place.

He wondered how the Beast had gotten in. The rivers should have prevented his crossing into the world. But from the smell of the earth, the Beast had been here for centuries. Perhaps he had come before these waters flowed. Who could say?

Eanrin found canoes tethered to the shores of these rivers and, though he was no waterman, managed to cross through calmer waters and climb the gorges to the tablelands above. In this way he crossed all four rivers and came to the place where the soil was red.

So it was that an orange cat with a plumy tail strolled into Redclay at noon one day, head high like a reigning monarch surveying new territory. Other mangy toms gave him dirty looks, and one or two offered to fight. But he was much larger than any of these and soon sent them running. Queen cats hissed and hid from him. He didn't smell quite right. They were no fools; they knew a true cat when they smelled one. This one was certainly a cat, but he was so much more, and this they did not like.

But the people of the village ignored him. To them, he was just another cat. So he passed as though unseen through their midst, searching for a child with a dog.

The difficulty was, there were many ragged little urchins living in Redclay, and more than a few of them had great watchdogs standing guard while their mothers worked. How could one particular girl be picked out of all of these? The cat sat awhile in the village center, pondering this question.

Then he realized: None of the girl children, mute as frightened rabbits, had dogs. Only the boys.

That should narrow his search, he decided. Imraldera had been quite clear on the subject. The girl he sought had a dog. Also, that girl lived up a hill.

Eanrin turned to gaze up at the house on the hill overlooking the village. It was impossible to think of it as the house of a king or princess. It was little more than a glorified hut as far as he was concerned, larger than the rest of the huts making up the village to be sure, but a hut no less. He trotted up the hill to investigate more closely.

He halted halfway. He smelled the Beast.

The smell was intense, that contrast of immortality against all the mortal surroundings. Not the immortality of Rudiobus, of Bebo and Iubdan; no, this was a different scent altogether. It was full of the blood of this stolen demesne.

The cat's ears flattened and his tail bushed to twice its size. Growling in his throat, he backed down the hill, staring at the house as though any moment he expected the Beast to emerge. He was just another Faerie. Not a queen or a king. But this Faerie had been drinking in the fear of enslaved subjects for generations, and this had made him powerful. Eanrin crawled back down the hill and took shelter in the shadows cast by the nearest hut. He disliked the notion of meeting this self-styled god face-to-face.

"How did you get caught up in this wretched affair?" he muttered to himself. "And for what purpose? None of this is your business. The girl is nothing—"

But that wasn't true. Eanrin closed his eyes, and across his memory flashed the light of a silver lantern in a dark place, and the deep eyes of the Hound. He cursed and tried to shake the images away, to smother them back.

How long he crouched there debating his next course of action he could not guess. But suddenly his nose twitched as he caught a familiar scent. "Imraldera?" he whispered, sitting upright, his fear of the Beast momentarily forgotten. Was it her scent? No, it couldn't be! She had remained in the mountains, far from here. It was dangerous for her to come so near to the Beast. Paths of the Lumil Eliasul aside, he was sure to sense her!

Footsteps drew near, bare feet treading softly on the dirt. She was coming this way! Did she think to climb the hill? Did she think to face the Beast here, in the center of his realm? No!

The cat leapt out of hiding, springing into the middle of the road, his back arched and his ears back. A gray dog, its face whitened with age, snarled at him, but he hissed and darted at it with his claws. It drew back, surprised.

A girl stood just behind the dog. She looked down on the cat, one eyebrow raised, then put a gentle hand on the dog's back. "Shhh," she murmured, though in her muteness she could scarcely make the sound.

Eanrin stared. This girl was not Imraldera. But she was the same age and the same height, and she looked enough like Imraldera to be her . . .

"Lights Above us!" the cat swore, though to the girl and the dog, it sounded like a growl. The dog showed its teeth, its ears back.

"Shhh," said the girl one more time, gently patting the dog's shoulder. Then she proceeded on her way, carrying a heavy skin of water up the path to the house on the hill. The dog gave Eanrin a last snarl, then fell into place behind the girl, moving arthritically, for it was old.

"A girl and her dog," Eanrin said, watching them go. "How strangely Time moves here in the mortal world."

Keeping his body low and straining every sense for any warning sign of the Beast, he followed the girl up the hill. He found her around the side of the house, emptying her waterskin into a large trough. It was uncanny how closely she resembled Imraldera! The same cheekbones, the same nose. The mouth was different, though. It had a distinctly downward turn, as though she had never smiled and perhaps did not know how. And her brows were drawn together in a line that looked as though it would never soften.

Imraldera, though run-down and worn to the bone with fear and sorrows, was free in her heart and spirit. This girl was a slave through and through.

She drew a sharp breath and looked up, her frown deepening. A shadowed form appeared in the doorway. The smell of immortality was stronger than ever, and Eanrin saw the Beast for the first time.

He wore a man's shape, but his wolf nature was impossible to disguise. It was in his face, in the way he moved, in every breath he took. Rapacious and wild, but cunning as well. His eyes were sharp as ice but yellow as fire. They were familiar eyes. Eanrin shuddered as he recognized the Black Dogs in that face. The resemblance was remarkable. But while the Black Dogs were mindless save to obedience, this man—this wolf—was a master of many fates.

He stepped from the house and approached the girl as she finished emptying her skin. "Fairbird," he said, and Eanrin saw the girl tremble. "I enjoy watching you as you work. Does this bother you, child?"

What could she answer? This man was her god. But, Eanrin wondered, did she know? Did she realize that this person was the Beast holding the land captive? Or had the Faerie kept his true self secret? After all, mortal eyes do not penetrate so far. She might not be able to recognize the wolf in that face.

She could not answer in words. She bowed her head, finished her task, and set the skin aside. Then, as though wishing to pretend the man did not exist, she turned to go about her next task. But the Beast stepped forward and blocked her way.

"I look forward to this time," he said, his voice low. The dog near the girl's feet growled, but he ignored it. "I look forward to your visits at my house. Do you know, I asked that you be sent to fetch my water and prepare my meals. I could have had any girl in the village. I asked for you."

She would not look at him but stared at her feet. Her dog pressed against her thigh, still growling. What a pitiful creature it looked, so old and decrepit standing in the presence of ageless power. But it growled in the face of that power and did not back down. The Beast bared his teeth at the dog. "Brute animal," he snarled and raised his hand to strike.

The girl, however, threw herself on her knees and wrapped her arms around the dog's neck. Eanrin was surprised. He hadn't thought the little maid capable of demonstrating such passion. But she clung to the dog, burying her face in its gray fur, waiting as though she expected the Beast's blow to fall on her instead.

But the Faerie stepped back, a smooth mask hiding the anger on his face. "Fairbird, Fairbird," he crooned. "Sometimes I fear that you are little more than a mouse. But you have some spark in you after all! Not as *she* did, though. Not as she did . . ."

He said no more. The girl got to her feet and, still without looking at him, motioned her dog to follow and fairly fled down the hill. Whatever tasks she had meant to complete were forgotten now in her desire to get away. And the Beast did not stop her. He watched her instead, and the look on his face was hungry indeed, but also frustrated.

As lovely as Fairbird was, she was not her sister.

Eanrin, his body flattened to the ground just out of sight, watched the scene and trembled at what he saw. Imraldera had made him promise to do as she asked. First, he was to find the child with the dog. He had done that.

Then he was to tell the Beast that she waited for him at the Place of the Teeth.

But how could he do that? He saw the look on that monster's face, and he knew what it meant. He knew what fate awaited Imraldera should the Beast set on her trail again. He would run her down for sure! His was the nature from which the Black Dogs inherited their hunting instincts. And if those mindless beasts were lethal, surely their father was worse by far!

"She travels the Paths of the Lumil Eliasul," Eanrin whispered to himself. But would it be enough? Perhaps if he gave the Beast his message and then fled with all speed across the Land. If he reached Imraldera first and gave her fair warning. Her plan was suicidal. But what other choice did they have?

He didn't have to tell her.

His tail lashed at the thought. He could return to her up in the mountains and tell her the child was dead. He could tell her there was no point in continuing this madness because it was too late. Then they could run away together, back into the Wood! She need never revisit this dreadful land, never face that monster again.

Eanrin felt sick inside. He hated himself in that moment, he who had never before thought of himself without love and self-satisfaction.

"It would be useless anyway," he muttered. "The Black Dogs would get her. Hri Sora wants to see this creature destroyed even more than Imraldera does. She will have given them orders to kill the girl should she fail her task."

As soon as he said it, he knew it was true. There was no going back. Forward was the only option, forward into an uncertain future. They had trod the Path of Death already. They would tread it again together.

The Beast had vanished inside the hut. Eanrin, still a cat, crept to the doorway and crouched there, listening to the breathing of the wolf shaped like a man. Suddenly that breathing caught short.

"I smell you," said Wolf Tongue. "I smell you, Faerie man."

Eanrin swallowed hard. Then he spoke in his brightest, merriest voice. "What-ho, my wolfish friend! Well met, I say, in these odd mortal lands! How came a chap like you to be among this riffraff?"

The answering growl was thunderous. "This is my demesne," said the Beast. "How dare you come here? This is my land and has been these many centuries now! How did you pass the rivers?"

"Oh, you know, I have my ways," said Eanrin. His cat's eyes could just discern the creature's shadowy form moving toward him in the darkness. He backed away, ready to bolt, feeling safer in the open sunshine. "Secret ways to and fro. I'm known for my guile, even as you, my lord, are known for your thievery."

"Cat." The Beast spat the word like a curse. He appeared in the doorway, still a man, and stared down at Eanrin where he crouched. "You are not welcome here."

"No more are you, I imagine," Eanrin replied with a careless flick of his ears, though his heart raced madly. "Unless you want to try and tell me that these mortals *asked* you to come and steal their land."

"What business is it of yours?" Wolf Tongue cried. He would have liked to snap up the cat in a single bite and be rid of him. But he dared not. Not if there was a breach in his land allowing Faerie folk through. He must learn the source of that breach, and soon, if he was to close it and secure his territory once more. "Why should you care what I do with these maggots?"

"I find myself caught up in all sorts of business not my own these days," said the cat, smiling. "But curiosity always was my downfall, you know."

"It will be in the end, I have no doubt," said Wolf Tongue. He took a menacing step out of the house. Eanrin crawled back a few paces. "How did you break those protections and infiltrate my realm?"

The cat said nothing.

"The rivers keep all Faerie kind out," said the Beast, "save those brought in by a man of this land. Thus was I given admittance. A young man making his rite of passage came upon me in the Wood. I convinced him that if he took me back into his world, I would make him a king among his people. He agreed and led me back, and so I crossed the river gates that would otherwise have held me at bay. And I did indeed make him master of his people . . . and I became his god! So have I worked to make this realm my own, to make myself a power as great as any Faerie king or queen.

"But I will not permit others of our kind to enter here and contest my rule! So I ask you again, and I will not ask a third time: How did you pass the rivers?"

"I come," said Eanrin quietly, "on behalf of Maid Imraldera."

Wolf Tongue stared at him. "Imraldera," he breathed, the name rolling slowly off his tongue. "Imral . . . the star . . ." A slow, terrible smile spread across his face, and he was more wolfish now than when he ran upon four feet. "You come on behalf of the Starflower." His look was ravenous and he gnashed his teeth. "How I loved her!"

"Loved her?" Eanrin stood upright as a man. He cut a small figure beside the towering Wolf Tongue, and his bright shock of hair contrasted against the darkness of that other. "You say you *loved* her?" He shook his head, grimacing. "You have never loved anyone but yourself all your life!"

Wolf Tongue's smile grew. "And you have?"

Eanrin stared into that terrible face, and he saw his own reflected there. A beast. An immortal beast. His voice shook, but he spoke his next words loudly, flinging them in Wolf Tongue's face as a challenge.

"The Starflower has returned to her land!" he cried. "She has returned to finish her business with the god of her people. She waits for you even now at the Place of the Teeth!"

With those words, Eanrin spun about and ran. Taking his cat's form, he hurled himself down the hill, streaking like lightning. And only just fast enough! No sooner had those words crossed his tongue than the Beast lunged for him. He felt the brush of teeth against his skin. He felt the heat of breath upon his fur. Had he hesitated even an instant, those jaws would have closed upon his spine and snapped him in two.

He hurtled through the village, a bright orange streak, darting for the nearest Faerie Path he could find and praying it did not belong to the Beast. Howls filled the air behind him, and he knew that Wolf Tongue had taken his true form.

The race was on.

5

IMRALDERA STOOD ON THE EDGE of the Place of the Teeth, watching the landscape far below. She understood many things that she could not have begun to imagine the last time she came to this place. She knew what lay beyond the Circle of Faces. She knew that the Void was no Void but in fact held worlds far greater than the world she had always known and found sufficient.

She gazed upon the Land of her people, the Land that belonged to the Beast. The naming of things had always come easy to her. The night her mother died and Fairbird drew her first crying breath, Imraldera had studied her sister until she discovered her true name, and wondered then if perhaps she had known it all along. Later, she had gazed into Frostbite's snarling face and known what the dog had been intended to be, not what it was. Even the Black Dogs, waiting now just beyond the ring of mountains . . . even they had names, though their souls were suppressed to the point of extinction.

The name of this land was Sorrow. But what, she wondered, was the true name of its master?

"When you hold the name of a Faerie Lord, you hold power indeed."

So had the Dragonwitch said. And she had given Imraldera, as though bestowing a gift, the name by which the Beast was known in the worlds beyond.

Amarok. Imraldera rolled the word around in her mind. Though the language was foreign to her, the meaning translated itself: Ravenous. Cunning. Cruel. How could Wolf Tongue have any other name? It was too accurate to be doubted. She had gazed into his eyes. She had seen the desire. She had watched through all the years of her life how he feasted upon the fat of her land and grew strong, and she knew he had been at this feast since long before she was born.

Amarok. Her hands tried to form the word, to make the signs. There was no word quite like it in her vocabulary. She signed *hungry.* That wasn't true. She signed *brutal.* That too was incorrect. She frowned. The shadow cast by the central stone fell across her face. But her hands could not form the name.

"Say his name," Hri Sora had said, *"and he will do your bidding."*

Imraldera clenched her fists and drew a long breath. She stood in the middle of a bloodstain, whether human or animal she could not know. In her mind's eye, she gazed upon her future, the path she must follow. She saw only death. Her death, perhaps. Perhaps the death of her enemy. But death, one way or the other. Could such an end be right? Could such an end be pure? Or was holiness always bloody?

The mountain growled.

Imraldera felt rather than heard the reverberations beneath her feet. The stone Teeth quivered to their roots, and Imraldera herself stumbled and nearly fell from the stone. She caught hold of the nearest rock, clutching its sharp contours to support herself. And she gazed down into the valleys below.

He was coming. She could not see him. But she knew beyond doubt. The Beast was returning to Bald Mountain.

The god of the Land ran across the long expanse of his demesne. His head was low, his claws tearing the turf in painful gouges, scarring the countryside in his wake. He covered miles in a stride, his eyes fixed on the point beyond the horizon where his prey awaited his coming.

The Land shuddered at his passing. The people, his worshippers, hid their faces, weeping at what they thought was their imminent doom. But he passed them by without a glance. He had but one purpose in his heart.

Her! The escaped one! The one who fled through the watery pass she could not have known, following some guide whom she trusted more than she trusted him!

But she had returned to him. She waited for him now. She had passed into the worlds beyond and found them more dreadful than the love he offered. He would have her at last! He would have her and keep her as he had been unable to keep Ytotia. Ytotia's flame could not be suppressed forever. This girl was mere mortal dust—but not for long. He would transform her into one such as he, and if her mortal frame could withstand the change, she would be a worthy consort to his godhood.

So he ran, and Bald Mountain watched his coming, and watched also the girl standing upon its slopes, small among those jagged teeth on the sacrificial stone. It did not watch the orange cat streaking just ahead of the hunting wolf, for in the grand poetry of the story playing out below, that creature played no role. Only the girl and the wolf, a tale as old as Time itself. Girl and wolf; maid and monster. The dead mountain knew the symmetry of the worlds, the fixed laws of stories being lived. It had watched them all since it was Lady Whitehair, tall and glorious.

So the mountain paid no attention to the Bard of Rudiobus making that last mad, exhausted scramble up the secret Paths to the Place of the Teeth. And Imraldera, as she stood waiting—every muscle tensed to run, forcing herself to stand—did not see him until he sprang suddenly onto the stone and collapsed at her feet.

"Run now!" he gasped, his form flickering between cat and man. "The wolf is upon you!"

The sun sank, staining the sky red, hurling shadows across the mountain. Imraldera stared down at the cat. Her eyes, memory dazed, saw her father lying in a pool of blood.

"Run!" he had said, his last word. And she had obeyed, leaving him

behind, leaving Fairbird, leaving her people. She had deprived the Beast of his due, and what price had her people paid in her absence?

"Run!" Eanrin cried. "It's our only chance!"

And what of Fairbird?

Her mouth twisting in a silent scream, she whirled about and leapt from the stone. Even as her bare feet scrabbled in the soil, the wolf appeared below and in a single, powerful leap, landed among the Teeth. Imraldera heard his sharp intake of breath, and her limbs froze. She turned and stared at the monstrous form—large as a horse, black as sin, her oppressor, her god.

"Starflower!"

The Eldest's daughter gazed into the face of the wolf and, just as she had that night under the cold moonlight, she saw death there. Tears filled her eyes, even as her heart refused to beat and her legs refused to obey her and run.

"Starflower!" the Beast cried. "You have returned to me!"

Maid and monster. Girl and wolf.

He was a man now, standing on the edge of the stone. His eyes were as yellow and intent as a wolf's, and his gray wolfskin fell back from broad shoulders. His arms reached out to her, ready to embrace, ready to kill. "You have returned," he said. "You know the truth, deep in your heart. You have known it since the night you dared spit in my eye. You are as vicious as you are beautiful! Not the demure, silent maiden, not you, Starflower. You were always meant to be mine."

Her mouth was dry. Her body shook. Her mind screamed, *Run!* But if she did . . . if she ran that Path leading over the mountains and down into the water deeps of the river cavern . . . if she led her enemy through that dark way and emerged at last into the Midnight where his children waited . . .

Imraldera stared at the Beast, her fear overwhelming. All thought, all reason, all puzzling through the dangerous questions was reduced to silence.

"Come to me now, my pretty one." The wolf in man's form gnashed his teeth, and blood fell from his lips. "At last," he whispered. "Let me take you and make you what I want."

Suddenly Wolf Tongue screamed. A barrage of fur and teeth and claws had leapt into his face, snarling for all he was worth. The cat tore viciously at his eyes and ears, slipping through his furious fingers, scrambling around behind his shoulders to cling just out of reach. The Beast roared and became animal once more, lashing and writhing in his efforts to get the tiny monster off his back. In the midst of their ugly howls, Imraldera heard Eanrin shouting, "Run, fool girl!"

She came to her senses in a rush, gasping at the pain of it. Then she was running, fleeing up the mountain Path once again as the sun sank and night overcame the world. She knew who she was, she knew where she had been, and she knew what lay before her.

A shriek cut the darkness behind her. A death cry? Sickness tore at her heart. Had immortal Eanrin met his doom? But she could not think of that. She must run, and faster! Up the highest slopes of Bald Mountain, where the air should be so cold her blood would freeze, so thin her lungs would collapse.

The wolf was behind her. She felt the pound of his pursuing feet. *Oh, cat! You should have left me by the River! You should have abandoned me to the Black Dogs and let me walk this Path alone!*

She stumbled as she ran, cutting her hands upon sharp stones, and her feet bled just as they had the last time, leaving red footprints in her wake. The Path turned downward, and she slipped and skidded, nearly collapsing altogether. But the Hound was ahead and the wolf behind, and she could not stop, not yet.

"When you hold the name of a Faerie Lord, you hold power indeed."

Fear! Was that his name? That spear of terror he plunged into the hearts of his worshippers? Amarok the Wolf. The Father of Fear.

See the truth, Starflower.

The song sang into her heart. She clutched it like a lifeline pulling her along when everything in her begged for release, for collapse, for an end. This Path was all she had to cling to now; no more reasoning and no more hope, just run, run, run!

See the truth and speak.

The river flowed ahead, cutting through the mountains and deep underground. Imraldera followed the Path, feeling as light and tossed about as an autumn leaf, prey to the whim of greater forces. But Fairbird must be safe. And if that meant death, so be it! Imraldera plunged once more into the darkness of the cavern, where she was blind and the roar of rushing water filled her ears. No gleam of gold to relieve her here. Nothing but darkness all around and the wolf just behind.

See and speak.

She was blind and she was mute. But she would not give in, not yet!

Her hand traced the cavern wall, and her feet sometimes nearly slipped as the river flowed past, ready to tug her under. The Path she walked was magic, however, and led her safely through those underground miles. She should have died down there the last time. By rights, she should die there now. But instead she saw the gleam of light far ahead. Sunlight! Night had come in the world above, come and gone, and daylight reigned once more. But where was the Midnight? Where were the Black Dogs?

"My love."

The wolf's voice, so near behind, was enough to shatter the spirit. She staggered and collapsed against the wall. He was close. His voice was a monster's, but a man's hand reached toward her in darkness.

"You fled me down this Path before," he said, "and where did it lead you? Back to me, Starflower. Back to me, where you belong. Why fly from me again?" His voice was a snarl, but it pleaded with her. "My own, my love. You will only be brought back to me a second time. Such is your doom; you cannot escape it. I am your god, and I have decreed it so."

He could not touch her, not while she stood upon this Path. But his words sank into her heart, and she feared the truth of them. Girl and wolf . . . inexplicably joined. Only death would sever his hold upon her, upon Fairbird, upon the Land.

See the truth.

She pushed herself upright, forcing her eyes to look ahead, to look to the daylight where the river emerged from the deep places of the world and roared out into the sea beyond the Circle of Faces. One step, then two. She felt the wolf reaching for her; all his will strained against her, begging her to stay.

"Starflower—"

The river caught her.

Just as it had the last time she fled, it swelled about her legs and snatched her up, carrying her through the darkness. She should have drowned; her bones should have been crushed. But the Path was true and swift. It did not lie. It carried her beyond the darkness, out into the blazing light of day and cast her upon the shore of the narrow isthmus, beyond the reach of the mountains, beyond the reach of her god.

Imraldera lay gasping for some time, uncertain of herself and her fate. At last, her arms shaking and her legs protesting in agony, she forced herself to her feet and turned to face the long cavern.

The wolf stood at its mouth. His eyes were full of black fire, and his fists raised in furious protest. "No!" he shouted, his voice carrying above the roar of the river. "Come back to me, love! Do not leave me again!"

The silent girl stood trembling, water dripping from her hair, her nose, the hem of her dress. She stared at the Beast and he raged at her. But he did not step beyond the safety of the mountains.

The Black Dogs were nowhere in sight. Perhaps they were near, but Imraldera could not say for sure. There was no trace of Midnight. She was alone upon that stretch, ocean on either side, mountains before, haze of a distant horizon behind. She and her enemy were the only two beings left in the worlds.

But he would not approach her.

He beckoned, his voice desperate as he spoke. "I will give you a voice. That is what you want most, isn't it, my lovely? I took it from you, but I can give it back. Return to me, and I shall give you everything you want!"

She stared at him, her brow set in a line, her lips gently parted.

"Say his name," said the Dragonwitch, *"and he will do your bidding."*

Imraldera raised her hands to sign, but they did not move.

See the truth and speak! sang the voice in her heart.

What truth was she meant to see?

"I will make her suffer," said the wolf. He paced back and forth along the edge of the water, just within the shelter of the cavern. "I will make that sister of yours suffer. I will tear into her just as I tore into your father when you left me the last time! You love her, I know. You would die for her. But will you live for her, Starflower? Will you return to me and live out your life as you were meant to for the sake of that girl?"

Hatred. That must be his name. She stared at his hideous face, distorted by his own unsatisfied lusts, and she hated him.

See the truth.

"I can't!" she screamed in the silence of her mind. "I can't see what you want me to see!"

But you have already seen it.

"I don't know what you're talking about!"

Let me show you.

Imraldera gasped.

She stood in a memory upon the bank of a stream. She saw herself crouched on the ground at the feet of several angry lads, Fairbird clutched protectively in her arms. A gray lurcher snarled at her, saliva dripping from her jaws, hatred in her eyes.

Imraldera watched the girl who was herself gazing into that distorted face. And she remembered. She remembered what Starflower had seen.

Every living creature must hear its true name spoken before its soul may wake and live. Otherwise, be it man or beast, it is no more than a husk living a brutal, animal existence. The soul is a seed that must be watered, or it will lie forever dormant.

Frostbite, bruised and kicked and ill-treated, was a soulless creature when she snarled in the face of Starflower. But her spirit longed for an awakening. She longed to hear her true name.

Starflower, lying on the riverbank surrounded by enemies, had looked at that animal, and she had loved.

Imraldera shook herself, blinking as she returned to that place between oceans, standing before the Beast. She saw him, saw what he had been meant to be. What loss or neglect had stunted the growth of his spirit so that it might as well never have existed? She could not guess. Or perhaps he had chosen this living death. Perhaps he had rejected all hope of true life for the sake of the godhood he so desired.

It did not change what he had been created to be. It did not change his true name, the name that lay hidden behind all others.

The girl looked upon the wolf, and her eyes were opened at last.

"I know your name," she signed.

"What?" snarled the wolf. It was against the laws of the Land for menfolk to speak the silent language of women, but he had ruled this Land too long not to know all the workings of his slaves. "What did you say?"

"I know your name," she signed. "The name you wish no one to know."

"My, my!" He smiled. "Who told you that? Your wanderings must have taken you far, little Starflower, if you came to the lands where people knew Amarok of old. Amarok the shifter. Amarok the loner. No lord was he! No master of men, no director of fates. I was scorned by kings and queens who thought themselves my betters. But Amarok is made of more than dust, and the creatures of dust are subject to his whim!"

He stepped to the edge of his demesne, his feet just within the shadow of the cavern. "Go on, Starflower. Speak my name. It means nothing, for I know yours as well. Or did the people among whom you walked not tell you that side of the story? You can only control the power of a name so long as yours remains secret. And you have no secrets from me, my love. I am your god."

"I know your true name," she signed, and her hands shook as they formed the words.

Speak!

A taste like fire but purer, like scalding water, filled Imraldera's mouth. From her lips, bursting like a liberated fountain and filling the air so that all might hear, she sang out in a loud voice:

> *"Let me praise the One Who Names Them.*
> *He named this child from the Beginning,*
> *Before the worlds were made!"*

The wolf swore. His voice jolted from the inside out, as though his heart were breaking in two, and fire leapt from his eyes. But Imraldera, gazing upon him, declared the truth to the monster's face. In a whisper, she spoke his true name:

"Beloved."

A howl of rage shook the Circle of Faces. The wolf sprang from hiding, murder in his eyes. How dare she? How dare she speak that vile word, that word that contained slavery to his ears! He would devour her. He would crush her between his jaws and remove all memory of her from the face of the world. And when he returned to the Land, he would put her sister to the same death, and the silent women would be silent forever!

He forgot, for an instant, the Dragonwitch's vow.

"Know this, my husband, and know it well: The moment you set foot beyond the Circle of Faces will be your last. For I shall send the Black Dogs!"

Midnight smothered the world. Darkness full of tormented dissonance. Whether the Dogs themselves saw the creature upon which they fell, who could say? But they set upon him in a hurricane's rush, their eyes flashing, their jaws slavering, their teeth stained with the blood of their father.

Imraldera covered her face and cowered from the dreadful sight, unwilling to look. But she could not stop her ears to the screams.

"My own! My own!" cried the Beast.

And the Black Dogs dragged him to the realm of Death.

6

A HUSH FELL upon the world. Not a hush of silence. Gentle noises
rang so much clearer following the horror of the Black Dogs' coming and going. Waves lapped at the isthmus, murmuring. The river, its
roar dulled by distance, poured from the mountains into the sea. Clouds
gathered, drawing misty rain with them, which fell upon the girl kneeling
on that lonely shore, her head cradled in her hands.

It was done. The wolf was slain. Her people saved.

But Imraldera wept for Amarok.

She understood now as she had been unable to before. With each tear
that fell, she understood better, and her heart ached with the knowledge
it now bore. For she had looked into the face of her enemy and she had
loved. And then, she had stood by at his death.

"There is but one thing that separates the living spirit from the brute."

She looked up into a face she could not recognize in the heavy mist.
But the voice she knew.

"Only love sets you apart. Only love makes you more than an animal.
Without love, you are no better than the Beast himself."

The stranger before her knelt down and took her hands in his. She still could not see his face clearly in this gloom. But she saw his eyes. Dark, flecked with gold, full of kindness. His was a gaze in which she might rest.

"Amarok was intended to be more," said the stranger. "The seed of goodness remained inside where it was planted. Had he submitted to love, that seed would have grown and flourished. As it was, his soul was a dry desert. But you saw, Starflower, if only for that moment, what he was meant for. Love for your sister was not enough. Love for her is as natural to you as breathing! The love you needed, my child, is unnatural and can be learned only with pain. Yet there is power in that love beyond all created understanding!"

Imraldera drew a shuddering breath and let it out with a sob. That final vision filled her mind, that vision of blood and roaring darkness, the pain in the Wolf Lord's dying voice. What might he be now had he lived a life of submitted humility rather than stolen divinity?

But the One who named the Beast *Beloved* drew her to him, and she wept upon his shoulder. The task was done. Her people were safe. And though her heart ached, it still beat. She had not become what she loathed. How dreadfully close had she walked to that edge? She could not guess.

"Starflower," said the stranger, stroking her hair with the tenderness of a father, "will you now speak love throughout your days?"

Imraldera drew back to look into his face once more. She saw in his eyes what he asked of her: A life of service, of burden. These things, however, did not frighten her. All she feared was returning to the life of slavery she had always known.

She saw in the eyes of the Lumil Eliasul that he offered a life more whole and free than any she had ever dreamed. Imraldera took a deep breath. Then she nodded.

"I have loosened your tongue," said the Lumil Eliasul. "You may speak!"

She opened her mouth. Her tongue tingled as though she had bitten fire. Licking her lips, she struggled to form the words that were always waiting to be spoken.

"My Lord," she said, and her voice cracked and trembled. "My Master."

There in the veil of mist, the One Who Names Them knighted the Silent Lady who now sang. And she knelt before him, words pouring from her heart and falling, stumbling, from her tongue, uncertain but full of joy even as she mourned the death of her enemy. For now she knew better what it meant to love and to be loved. And in loving, she found her spirit opening ever more to the greatness for which it was intended.

"Are you ready, Dame Imraldera, to do my bidding?" asked her Master.

"I am," she replied.

"I am sending you back into the Wood," said he. "To the Haven where once the Brothers Ashiun dwelt, offering succor to those in need and protection to both the Far World and the Near. You will take up the work that they began, guarding the gates I have set between the worlds and teaching the people of both worlds to walk my Paths. And I will give the keeping of records to you so that this story and others like it may not be lost to the memories of mortal and immortal alike."

Imraldera nodded. But more tears caught in her throat, and she could not for a moment speak. *Fairbird . . .*

But there was no returning to the Land. She was no longer Maid Starflower, the silent daughter of the Panther Master. She was Dame Imraldera, Knight of the Farthest Shore, Lady of the Haven.

Oh, little sister!

The Lumil Eliasul placed a hand upon her shoulder. "First, gentle dame, go and speak to your sister. Tell her that the curse is lifted, and she need be silent no more."

———

Was it a dream?

Imraldera stood once more alone on the isthmus, and the mist was receding. So much of her life these days seemed either a dream or a nightmare. Had she invented, out of the sickness of her sorrowing mind, the comfort she felt even now surrounding her heart?

She shook her head and slowly put her fingers to her mouth. "No," she whispered. "It was no dream."

A growl drew her gaze swiftly to one side. Approaching out of the mist, she saw the form of a great Dog. But it dwindled. Still growling, it became a gangly child, its sex indeterminate, its eyes those of a wolf. There was blood on its face, blood not its own.

It saw Imraldera and stopped growling. Its peaked features grimaced with confusion and it whined softly.

Imraldera put out a hand. The words came with difficulty from her unpracticed tongue, and her voice was low and rasping. Yet there was gentleness when she spoke.

"Come to me, little beast. Let me wash your face and hands. I will love you, and I will help to make you whole."

It took a few hesitant steps toward her. A bony hand reached out as though to catch hold of her and the possibilities it saw in her eyes. It was a creature divided, two entities in one. Child and beast, neither dominant, each driving the other mad. But the seed was there, only waiting to be watered.

"Come," Imraldera said, extending both arms. She ached to embrace that lost little soul, to find the life inside that gaunt frame. "Come here to me. Be safe."

It took another step.

Then its littermate appeared, as like to the first as a mirror image, only its eyes were given way to madness. It too was stained with the blood of its own father, and there was no child in that face, only monster. It snatched its sibling by the hand, snarling, froth dripping from its mouth. Two Dogs turned tail and fled Imraldera's presence, dragging their Midnight behind them as they returned to bear word to their mother.

Imraldera wiped tears from her face. "I hope we will meet again," she signed with tear-stained hands. Then she pursued the Path into the cavern, back once more to the Land of her birth.

The cat lay in a crumpled heap upon the sacrificial stone. But he was alive. Or at least he thought he was. He could feel every single aching muscle in his body and no fewer than three distinct bites out of his flesh and fur. So he must be alive, for what that was worth.

Before coming to full consciousness, he took on his man's form, hoping that might help. It didn't.

Opening his eyes, Eanrin saw his own hand lying before him on the gray stone. There was blood on it, perhaps his own. With a groan, he pushed himself up, glad to find all his limbs attached. One arm was numb, however, and he suspected a break. Dragon's teeth! At least his kind healed quickly. There were teeth marks on one leg and across his shoulder, but nothing deep, thank Hymlumé's grace.

"Imraldera," he whispered.

Gasping, he struggled to his feet and turned about, searching for any sign of the girl. Had she taken advantage of what little time he could give her and fled this place? Or had the wolf overtaken her in the end?

He tottered to the edge of the stone and leaned a shoulder up against one of the Teeth for support. His lungs heaved, dragging air slowly in and out. What a place of horror this was! A Faerie Circle of dreadful purpose. The wolf must have built it himself ages before, when he took this mortal realm and made it his demesne.

But . . .

Eanrin gasped and pulled back, only just in time. For the great stone against which he leaned suddenly melted away, vanishing into nothing. "Light of Lumé!" Eanrin cried as the other stones and the great slab itself vanished, leaving the poet to fall through the air and land hard on the mountain slope beneath.

The Place of the Teeth was gone. So then was the wolf.

Eanrin picked himself up and, limping, started up the mountain Path, uncertain where he went but vaguely thinking that Imraldera had gone this way. If the wolf was dead, perhaps she lived. Perhaps she had succeeded in extracting Hri Sora's revenge. He would not let himself consider that she might be dead.

The Hound stood before him.

At first, Eanrin was too exhausted to realize. Then he drew back with a cry, the fear of centuries compiling into that one moment. He saw again the Dark Water; he saw the lantern. He saw the choice that lay before him, the choice of godhood or life as a servant. What a terrible choice it was!

"No," he whimpered, clutching at his wounded arm and limping several steps back down the mountain. "No, please. I've done enough. I've helped the girl just as you wanted me to."

The Hound did not move. His gaze never wavered.

"I'll never be what I was before. Everything has changed now that I've met her! I know I will be a different man. But please, let me just go home to my own world."

"Your world is marred and shattered."

Eanrin felt himself shaken to the core at that voice. He felt the ugly truth of his soul striving to flee. But there was no escape from the gaze of the Lumil Eliasul. The cat was hounded down at last.

"Strange, piteous, futile man," said the Hound. His voice held all sorrow and compassion. "How desperately you have fought all that would make you whole."

Eanrin shrugged, wincing but still trying to make light. "I've been a good man. I've never harmed a soul. I've minded my own business. If I've pursued a life of laughs, who's to blame me? I've only ever been myself."

"You have the worlds at your feet," said the Hound. "But you have not love."

"I do!" The poet shook his head. Why were tears coursing so hot upon his face? He dashed them away furiously. "I have loved my life! I have loved Lady Gleamdren and my verses. I . . . I don't deserve slavery."

"What do you deserve, Eanrin?"

"I deserve to choose for myself. I deserve my freedom . . . and yet you chase me down, driving me before you!"

"You know where the road you walk will lead you. You have seen the Dark Water."

"I was minding my own business," the cat-man whispered, "but you had to set upon me. You're worse than the Black Dogs, and they hound a fellow to Death!"

"I hound you to life."

"And what kind of life?" Eanrin's voice became a growl. "I've seen what happens to your servants . . . beatings and imprisonments. Homelessness and hunger while they strive to achieve the impossible! Don't think I don't know what awaits me if I place myself in your service. I remember Akilun and Etanun when they first stepped into the Near World and made such names for themselves among the mortals! And I remember when all that changed. When Akilun was turned from every door. When Etanun's name became a byword for traitor! I know what becomes of your servants. Their reputations are soiled among all who once loved them!"

"And yet, they are glorified."

"They are brought low by dragon fire!"

"Yet not destroyed."

"They are weighed down with sorrow."

"And uplifted with rejoicing."

"They have nothing!"

"They possess everything." The Hound stepped forward, and he was bigger, brighter, more beautiful than anything found in the Far World or the Near. "All things are given to them," he said, "for I have bestowed power upon them in my name. They are my servants, and though all the weapons of darkness are hurled against them, they will endure. I have placed my love in their hearts, and it overflows from them in love for others. And so they become great even as, in your eyes, they shrink into nothing. Even as you curse them, so shall I bless them."

"Even Etanun?"

"Yes, even Etanun."

"After what he did?"

"Even Etanun."

"He betrayed you! Has he simply to apologize, and all is forgiven?"

"No. This is a mystery both more simple and more complicated than you may yet understand. But my love covers his wrong."

"I don't believe you."

"That is because you do not know my love," said the Hound. "Your heart has not yet learned that truth. That truth which is pain, which is sorrow, but which is beauty beyond any a loveless life may understand."

"I am afraid." Eanrin shuddered as he saw now the deepest secret of his soul. The secret he had kept hidden even from himself all the long ages of his existence. "I don't want to love. I will be hurt if I do."

"You were born in fear, Eanrin. But my love casts out fear."

"How?"

And suddenly the Hound transformed. He was a figure of still greater glory, clothed, but only just, in a man's shape. Tall and shining with a face bolder than the sun, the Lumil Eliasul, the One Who Names Them, the Giver of Songs.

"Will you take up your burden, Eanrin of Rudiobus?" he said. "Will you become a knight in my service? Will you, the masterless, call me Master this day and forever?"

In the end, Eanrin decided, there was only life or death. He saw now how small he was, another beast among beasts. No better than Hri Sora or Amarok or any creature who made themselves their only standard and their only source of truth. After all he had been through, Eanrin knew he could no longer live that way.

"I will, my Lord," he whispered.

The Lumil Eliasul smiled. "Rise!" he cried. "Clasp my hand and come, Knight of the Farthest Shore!"

Eanrin put out a trembling hand and found it firmly grasped.

He stood alone upon the slopes of Bald Mountain. His wounds were healed, his body whole. Eanrin looked down on his shredded, dirty shirt, at the muscles and limbs beneath. Nothing broken, nothing bleeding. Then he pressed both hands to his heart, and here he discovered a marvel.

He had spoken to the Lumil Eliasul. He had given away his life forever.

For the first time in all the immortal generations of his existence, he realized that he lived.

With a joyful cry, he leapt forward, running on the Faerie Path, up the mountain and down the other side. He found the rushing river, and he rushed as fast or faster still, feeling the surging power of life and love in his limbs. To be bound was to be free! To be free was to be bound! He understood now. Later, doubts would return. Later, he would struggle with his bondage to duty, just as any cat must. But for the moment—and what a moment it was, the brightest and truest in all his long immortal life—for the moment, he understood.

He must find Imraldera! That thought gave his feet wings. He must find her and tell her what had happened, what he had seen and—Lumé love him—what he'd agreed to become! He must tell her everything!

If she lived.

All the joy crashed down in that one moment of pain. What if, after all this, she was gone? What if he had failed her in the end, and the wolf had caught up with her?

"No," he growled. "No, that cannot be."

New urgency drove him now along the Path, and he did not smile. He followed the river to where it plunged beneath the earth. Only a few more paces and he would vanish once more into the darkness, searching and searching.

But there was no need.

"Imraldera!" he cried, surging once more to the very heights of joy. For she appeared at the mouth of the tunnel, blinking and dazed, her face streaked with tears. When she saw the poet careening down the slope of the riverbank, however, she smiled. She opened her mouth but had no opportunity to speak, for he reached her in an instant and scooped her up in his arms. Pressing her close and swinging her about, he shouted: "You've won! You've won! You bested the Wolf Lord, you marvelous creature! I will never doubt you mortals again . . . well, not *never*. But I will think twice before doubting; I swear on my hand! Oh, you amazing girl!"

Without thinking, he pressed a kiss to her cheek. A hot flush rushed to his face, and he dropped her unceremoniously and quickly put his hands behind his back. "That is . . . I'm glad to see you whole."

Imraldera placed a hand to her cheek, her smile a little lopsided but still present on her face. Then she reached up and gently touched the poet's scarlet face.

"Eanrin," she said, her voice rough and low, "I know your true name."

"Well, of course you know my name, my girl. Everyone knows Bard Eanrin. I've told you, I'm the most famous . . . Hold on! Did you just . . . Imraldera, my dear, did you just *speak*?"

7

WATERSKINS DRAPED OVER HER SHOULDER, Fairbird made her slow way down to the stream. She avoided the other women and did not take her water from the same streambeds as they. There was no reason for this. No one was unkind to Fairbird, especially since she was a favorite of the High Priest.

But when she was a little girl, her sister had taken Fairbird to a private place and always gathered water there, just the two of them. Now Fairbird did the same.

She preferred solitude, with only Frostbite for company. They had begun life as outcasts. And when that dreadful day had come and her sister was taken from her, when the women of the village came up to the house on the hill and brought Fairbird down to their homes, it made no difference. Fairbird shut herself up inside, hiding under a shell much thicker than silence.

As a child, she had been glad when the Eldest did not return, though it meant years of war for the tribes of Redclay. The Eldest had taken

Starflower from her. If he would not give her back, well, he might as well not return himself.

The silent girl, her face pinched, her mouth always frowning, made her way down to the water and knelt to fill her skins. Frostbite lowered her grizzled muzzle to lap at the stream. Fairbird stroked the dog's head and down her back, feeling the protruding bones. Her faithful companion was growing old. How lonely her life would be when the lurcher died.

Suddenly Frostbite growled and lifted her dripping muzzle. Fairbird sat upright and turned to look where the dog's gaze was fixed. A woman she did not know stood downstream near the edge of the gorge. Had she just climbed up? Was she a woman of the Crescent Tribes? A victim of the wars, fleeing for safety? Her dress had once been white and might have been fine indeed. Now it was brown and torn. Her face was dirty and streaked, as though she had wept many tears. A refugee for certain, she looked no more than Fairbird's own age.

Frostbite growled again, backing up a step or two. Fairbird placed a soothing hand on the dog's head, then turned to the girl. "You have come to Red Clay territory, near Redclay Village," she signed. "Where have you come from?"

The girl raised her hands and signed in return: "From beyond the Circle of Faces."

Fairbird frowned. At first she thought she must have read the strange girl's signs wrong, and she asked her to repeat herself. The girl obliged, signing the same odd phrase. "Beyond the Faces?" Fairbird asked. "That is . . . not possible."

The stranger's eyes filled with tears. Fairbird watched them fall down her cheeks as she drew nearer. Then Fairbird drew a sharp breath, and Frostbite whimpered. The girl's drawn face was so familiar.

"Who are you?" Fairbird signed.

The stranger came nearer still until she stood no more than a few paces away. Her black hair blew across her face, but she pulled it back impatiently, her mouth opening and closing. Then she spoke out loud.

"My sister," she said, "I have found you."

Fairbird staggered back, tripping over her waterskins and almost falling into the stream. Her heart raced with terror. Blasphemy! A woman with a voice! The Beast would descend upon them, and who would stop him? Not Wolf Tongue! No, though the Beast slay half the women of the village, the High Priest would not move to protect them.

"Sinful woman!" Fairbird signed, her eyes wide with terror. "Sinful, blasphemous, blight among your people! Is this why the Crescent Tribes sent you here? So you could hex us with your wicked tongue?"

The girl's face was very still. What longing was in her eyes as she gazed upon the other girl throwing curses in her face! But at last Fairbird's hands stilled and she stood panting in the stream. Then the stranger spoke again.

"Forgive me. I . . . I did not know how long I left you. My poor Fairbird! So alone."

Fairbird stared. Her face went deathly pale. For the space of three breaths she did not move. Then she gnashed her teeth, and her hands tore the air as she signed: "Who sent you? Was it Wolf Tongue? Because I will not accept his advances! Who sent you to torment me with the memory of my sister?"

"Fairbird," the stranger said, "I am your sister."

"Liar!" Fairbird's hand lashed the word like a curse. "My sister died ten years ago. Offered in blood debt to the Beast. She died in my place. She died and left me with the curse of guilt. She died and she left me!"

The stranger took a step forward, her hands outstretched. They were very alike, those two women. Neither tall, both slender, their dark hair falling away from faces full of sorrow. But in the one face there was hope, while in the other there was only despair.

Imraldera, still struggling with the newness of the words upon her tongue, said, "Fairbird, my darling—"

"Away from me!" Fairbird signed. She turned to flee, nearly falling over Frostbite as she went. She grabbed the dog by the ear and tugged, urging her to follow her back to the village, away from this woman with an unholy voice. Let the skin lie in the water and rot! She must get away, and she must not remember.

But Frostbite would not be moved.

The old dog, her mind as slowed by age as her body, stood with her lips drawn back. Her cloudy eyes could see little, and her ears did not know the voice of the stranger. But her nose . . . her nose was as good as it had ever been.

Suddenly the dog yelped. She tore from Fairbird's grasp and flung herself upon the stranger. Fairbird gasped, thinking her lurcher would tear the girl's throat out in her efforts to protect her, and she flung herself after, desperately trying to catch hold.

But the dog, still barking and yelping, stood with her paws on the stranger's shoulders, licking her face and whimpering, her tail wagging as though it would break. The stranger wrapped her arms around the dog's hulking body, burying her face in the gray, musty fur.

Fairbird stared. She had been betrayed so many times in life. First, her mother died before she could know her; then her sister was cruelly wrenched from her by a father who appeared as cold and heartless as stone. Only Frostbite had been true. Only Frostbite had remained by her side as the darkness of her god threatened to swallow the last shreds of hope she clutched for herself.

Now even Frostbite betrayed her. It was the final blow.

With a sob, she turned to flee.

"Wait!"

Fairbird stopped. Something in that voice compelled her to stay, to hear words that might be as arrows.

"I told you once," said the stranger, "that when you heard me speak your true name, I would return to you. Will you hear me now? Will you let me speak the name that is truly yours? If I speak it, will you know me at last?"

Fairbird stood as silent as she had lived.

"Gift," the stranger whispered, putting Frostbite gently from her and approaching Fairbird's rigid form from behind. "Love Gift. Gracious Gift. Gift of my mother to me, to my father, to the worlds. That is your true name, Fairbird. You are my Gift."

Fairbird's hands trembled. She signed, "I killed my mother. I killed you."

"You gave us reason to die, my darling. You gave us reason to die, and in that, you gave us reason to live."

Her eyes stricken with tears, the silent girl turned to the one who spoke.

"My Fairbird," whispered Starflower. "My sister."

Then suddenly Fairbird was in her arms. She was a young woman now, but she felt no more than five years old as she buried her face in the shoulder of that stranger who was no stranger but who was in fact the dearest of her heart. She wept and felt the tears of her sister falling in her hair and down her neck. Frostbite, in her joy, pressed up against their legs until they fell over in a pile.

They lay together, the three of them, nobody speaking and nobody signing, trying to explain. Frostbite knew best. Let joy be joy without words! And they followed the old dog's example.

But at last the time for stories came. The girls' hands flew as they talked in the silent language. But at last Imraldera came to the end of hers, and she put her hands in her lap.

"The curse is broken," she said out loud.

Fairbird shook her head. "I cannot believe it," she signed. "How can a god die?"

"He was no god," said her sister. "He was Faerie kind, a creature of the Gray Wood."

"He has been our god for generations."

"Sister, listen to me!" Imraldera took Fairbird's face in her hands. She could still see the child whom she had snatched from Wolf Tongue's grasp and whom she had told to sit by Frostbite and stay behind. Fairbird was grown up now, and so beautiful. What a terrible thing was the Faerie world, filled with immortals caring nothing for time! Eanrin had explained much to her on their journey to Redclay, things Imraldera had not wanted to understand.

It did not matter. The child Fairbird was gone, but Fairbird herself was present. And they had so little time.

"The curse is broken," Imraldera said again. "You are free. You may speak as boldly as any man, and you can make them listen. You must tell them, Fairbird! You must tell the other women. It was the Giver of Names who freed you. It was he who gave you your name and now gives you a voice. Do you understand?"

Fairbird's brow drew together. "But I cannot speak. I am not brave like you."

"You can," Imraldera said. "Open your mouth, sister. The time of slavery is ended."

She placed her hands on Fairbird's lips and parted them. And suddenly the other girl gasped as though drawing her very first breath. In her throat, like a rushing torrent, words sprang up and poured out. She found herself speaking, singing even, and though each word was halting on her tongue, they were loud and strong. In voices unlovely but full of joy, the two sisters sang songs their mother had once sung only in the silence of her heart.

When they were finished, Imraldera rose. "Frostbite," she said, and the old dog came to her. Not the spry young pup she had rescued from Killdeer, but a tottering old dam. Yet her cloudy eyes were full of love and loyalty. Her soul had been awakened and it would not sleep again. "Guard Fairbird," Imraldera said, stroking the dog's head. "Keep her safe, as you have always done. The Beast is dead, and the people are free, but freedom can be so terrible when new! Keep her safe as long as you live."

Then she turned to her sister and embraced her. "We may never meet again in this life," she whispered.

"I mourned you these many years," Fairbird replied, and her new voice trembled. "I will mourn no more. But please, Starflower, come back to me one day. I know you must go. I know you must follow the Giver of Names as you promised. But come back to me, at least once more."

Imraldera kissed her sister's cheek. And then they drew apart. Fairbird stood with Frostbite by her side and watched the young woman follow the stream to the gorge and then descend.

"The Beast is dead," Fairbird whispered. How strange the words tasted. "We are free."

"So your name is Starflower?"

The two lonely travelers walked slowly along the Faerie Path winding through the Land. Imraldera, used to silence, did not speak and rarely looked at her companion. But Eanrin was not one for long silences. And the girl looked so down after her parting with her sister. A distraction was well in order. "Starflower," he repeated. "Hmph. It's very . . . ethnic, I suppose. I like Imraldera better. Mind if I keep it up, or are you going to insist on Starflower?"

Imraldera shook her head. There was little use in arguing the point, and she knew it. So she smiled and shrugged and continued on her way.

The poet grinned back. "Your sister is quite nice," he said, seeking to lighten her heart. "She'll do well, I believe. She's gotten by for ten years without you, and I think the knowledge that you are alive and well will get her through many more. I know how you women are too! As soon as she gets used to having a voice, it'll be all anyone can do to stop her! Take my lady Gleamdren, for instance. That lass can chatter a man's ear off and still find more to say!"

Imraldera gave the poet a sideways glance. He was hiding something, she thought. Hiding behind his lively prattle and flippant ways. But she was a reader of hands and faces, and she saw something more behind his eyes.

"You . . ." She paused, struggling still to form the foreign words. "You have met the One Who Names Them."

Eanrin's face went white as a sheet. He swallowed and stared down at the Path for many strides. Imraldera watched his jaw clench and unclench as he considered what to say next. She reached out and lightly touched his arm. He came immediately to a halt, shifting his gaze from the ground to her hand but still not looking her in the eye.

"You faced the Beast for me," she said. "You fought for me. I thought you were dead." She smiled at him, though he did not see it. "You met the Giver of Names instead."

Eanrin nodded.

"What did he say to you?"

And now it was the poet who was struck dumb. He found he could not yet speak of his encounter, of the words that had passed between him and the Lumil Eliasul, of the promise he had made.

"He showed you who you are, didn't he?" Imraldera said. "And he showed you who you could be."

"That . . . yes, that about covers it," the poet said, his voice hoarse. He drew a long breath and spoke through grinding teeth. "Imraldera, I—"

"Do not be afraid, Eanrin," Imraldera said, reaching up and placing her fingers on his mouth to quiet him. "He knows your true name. Even as I do. You have nothing to fear."

Then she was moving on her way, progressing down the Faerie Path through the land of her birth. Eanrin fell in step behind.

"He is dead."

Hri Sora stood on the brink of Omeztli's rooftop. She felt the presence of her children behind her, and she did not need a look or word to know their story. She smelled Amarok's blood.

"My love," she hissed, spitting embers that fell into the darkness below. "My love is dead. I am safe."

He had seen her vulnerable. He had made her his. And now he was gone.

"What need have I for wings?"

The Dragonwitch threw back her head and laughed out loud. Her children, standing in the shadows of the stairway, cringed back and hid themselves. The fountain of her fire rose to the sky, celebratory flames falling over the dead city in red and orange.

"I am the firstborn!" she cried. "Even wingless, I am powerful! Even wingless, my will cannot be thwarted! I am more dreadful than all my brothers and sisters. Those who trifle with me will know my wrath!"

So she laughed and danced and made merry. Until suddenly she stopped with a terrible sob and fell upon her knees. Oh, for the sweet relief of tears! She screamed, clutching her gut where the fire roiled.

It wasn't enough!

She had been humiliated before the worlds. She had been made weak and pitiful. And though she was firstborn of all dragons, she had needed— it was poison even to think it!—she had needed a *mortal* woman to do her work for her.

Cursing, she spat out the venomous fumes of her inner furnace. Her children took flight, their tails tucked, hiding in the darkest recesses of the city. And they watched as Omeztli, the queen's ancient tower, melted under Hri Sora's flame and collapsed into a pile of molten rubble.

The Dragonwitch lay buried beneath the wreckage. The fire was consuming her mind, and she knew she would soon be lost to it once more. But before she went, she vowed:

"I will have vengeance on the mortal girl. On her and on all who have wronged me. When next I rise, they will burn!"

8

Q UEEN BEBO STOOD before her long mirror, Lady Gleamdren at her elbow. "Take this, my dear," said the queen and, removing the crown from her head, passed it to her cousin. Gleamdren obeyed and stepped back, her eyes round with surprise at what Bebo did next.

For the queen picked all the pins out of her knot of golden hair. With a shake of her head, she set it free, and gold cascaded in glorious bounty down her shoulders, down her back, flowing to the floor and behind her in a stream of light.

"There," said the queen with a smile. "Let the secret of the Flowing Gold be secret no more."

"Your Majesty!" cried Gleamdren, horrified. "What will Iubdan say? When the worlds know the secret of his great treasure, will you be safe?"

Bebo laughed, for she knew the true source of her cousin's concern. Lady Gleamdren enjoyed the prestige of being one of three to know Iubdan's secret. For long generations she had tended Bebo's hair, tying it up in ribbons, securing it with pins, and hiding it beneath crown and veil so that none might guess at its radiance. With the secret out, full half of Gleamdren's allure would fade. Bebo saw the pout forming on her cousin's mouth, and though she well knew Gleamdren's faults, she loved her dearly even so.

"I will be safe," she said, patting the pretty maid's cheek. "When the Faerie lords and ladies realize that the Flowing Gold is attached to the very head of Bebo, they will think twice before sending thieves with barber's shears! And perhaps we shall have no more of dragons and witches endangering my people for the sake of a secret."

So it was that Bebo swept down from her chambers to meet her husband beside Fionnghuala Lynn, and all the Merry People of Rudiobus gathered there beheld the shining river of her hair. Many sighs of wonder and, soon after, of understanding filled the air as they realized what Bebo revealed.

Iubdan's thick brow shot up at the sight. "Well, I suppose I couldn't keep it to myself forever," he said, taking his wife's hand and drawing it through the loop of his arm. "It was a grand game while it lasted! And if the Faerie folk set upon us and steal the Flowing Gold one strand at a time, you, my queen, even bald, will always be my greatest treasure."

Bebo smiled and patted his hand. Then they turned to gaze across Gorm-Uisce, for they had felt the approach of one of their kind on the borders of their realm. All the court of Rudiobus lined up behind them, straining their eyes to see who sat upon Órfhlaith's back as she skimmed the surface of the lake.

But Bebo's gaze was downcast, and a smile played upon her mouth, for she knew already who came. So did Gleamdren, standing at the queen's right hand. Her face was demure, but those near enough could hear her teeth grinding.

"What!" Iubdan exclaimed when the green-gold mare drew near. "Is that who I think it is?" He leapt forward into the shallow waters, little caring how he soaked his bejeweled sandals. "Eanrin, fool cat! Is that you? And do you—oh, Hymlumé have mercy!—do you bring yet *another* mortal maid to Rudiobus?"

Eanrin, his scarlet cloak and cap long gone, his white shirt browned and torn with travel, yet wore the brightest smile ever seen among the

Merry People. With one arm, he waved to those gathered by the gate, while the other wrapped protectively around Imraldera's waist. He lost his balance when Órfhlaith gave a sudden burst of speed; he would have landed in the lake had not Imraldera caught him in time. So it was with this undignified ending, one leg wrapped over the horse's back, the rest of him scrambling for purchase, that Eanrin made his return to Rudiobus.

"My lord and king!" he cried, sliding from the mare's back with a thump but righting himself and sweeping immediately into a deep bow. One would have thought he still wore his gold braid and velvet. "I return to you from far-off lands and bring good tidings!"

"Do you indeed?" Iubdan's bushy eyebrow lowered as he inspected his bard. "Well, you're a bit late when it comes to Gleamdren. Glomar brought her back safe and sound near a fortnight past. We feasted him proper, but you'll have to write a ballad or some such in his honor as soon as you get the chance. Otherwise it's not an official rescue. He said you were ensorcelled by a witch and unlikely to be heard from again." His dark gaze shifted to Imraldera, still perched on Órfhlaith's back. "Is this our witch, then?"

Imraldera blushed, but Eanrin shook his head and cried, "No indeed, good king, she is a heroine. Who among you—" He swept his arm as he addressed the gathered throng. For a moment, his gaze caught Gleamdren's and he faltered. Her eyes were hooded like a snake's. Licking his lips, he hurried on. "Who among you recalls the name of the shifter, Amarok?"

The response wasn't as immediate as he would have liked. There was some muttering, someone whispering to his neighbor, "Was he the wolf? The one who disappeared into the Near World a while back?" The neighbor shrugged.

"Yes!" Eanrin cried, resolved to make an epic of the event despite his audience. "The dreadful Wolf Lord, bane of the Wood, scourge of the Near World!"

"I don't know if I'd go so far as to call him a bane—"

"He is vanquished!" the poet persisted. "Yes, and vanquished by none other than the lovely maiden you see before you. Princess Imraldera, daughter of the mortal king in the Land Behind the Mountains."

He turned to Imraldera then and helped her down from Órfhlaith. She glared at him. How many times had she told him she was no princess? But he only smiled back and presented her to Iubdan and Bebo. She bowed to them after the manner of her people and signed "chieftain" to each.

"Hmph," said Iubdan. "Did you run her beneath the caorann tree, just to be sure?"

"I assure you, my king," said Eanrin, "she is as mortal as they come."

"You've said that before."

"It's true this time!"

"Is it?" When Queen Bebo spoke, all others silenced. She stepped forward and placed her childlike hands upon Imraldera's face, tilting her chin up so that she might look in her eyes. Imraldera had thought that she gazed into the faces of ancients when she met Eanrin and the Flame at Night and Wolf Tongue. But as she and the little Queen of Rudiobus studied each other, Imraldera began to tremble. This face, she realized, was as old as the sun and the moon.

"Brave Starflower," whispered Bebo. "You looked upon the Beast and saw worth. I said that only true love would rescue Lady Gleamdren. Rescue Gleamdren, yes, and so much more!"

And to the surprise of every watching eye, Bebo leaned forward and kissed Imraldera upon the forehead. "Welcome to Rudiobus, sister," she said.

The people of the mountain cheered. Eanrin beamed, as proud as though he'd done something grand himself, and once more caught Gleamdren's stare. He ducked his head and stepped around to the other side of his monarchs. Iubdan threw up his hands and said, "Well, that does it, then! The girl is welcome, and so are you. I do hope you have a song up your sleeve, cat, or I'll demote you and make Glomar Chief Poet. Just see if I won't!"

The Hall of Red and Green had never before seen such dancing or such music. The torchlight shining on Bebo's golden hair reflected in the eyes of all the revelers, driving them near mad with joy and merriment. Oh, to be subjects to such a queen as she! And to be ruled by such a king! So they danced their wild dances and sang their wild songs, sometimes in animal shape, sometimes clothed as men and women.

Imraldera stood to one side, away from the throng, and watched with eyes darting like a frightened doe. These dances were nothing like the dances of her people. They were manic yet full of laughter. And Eanrin, she thought, was the wildest of them all.

He took the center of the hall at one point and, at Iubdan's behest, burst into a song he claimed to have composed on the spur of the moment.

> *"Oh, Gleamdren fair, I love thee true,*
> *Be the moon waxed full or new!*
> *In all my world-enscoping view*
> *There shineth none so bright as you."*

Imraldera heard murmurs of approval all around her. Eanrin was, after all, the Prince of Poetry, so his work must be genius. Though she considered herself no expert, Imraldera could not help wondering if the song was as brilliant as all that. Gleamdren's reaction certainly wouldn't lead one to think so. Imraldera watched as, after the poet ended with another of his elaborate bows, he swept up to the dais, where Gleamdren stood behind Queen Bebo's throne. He pressed his hand to his heart and, from what Imraldera could make of his face from across the room, spouted professions of undying devotion.

Imraldera frowned. Eanrin's masks were remarkably good. It was difficult for her, especially on so short an acquaintance, to read his face and hands. But she thought whatever words he said were full of color but no substance. He was playing a part and playing it well, but the truth of the matter she could not guess.

Gleamdren's reactions were as plain as the sky. She gave the poet one withering look, then turned up her nose and marched away without a single word.

Eanrin cringed and hunched his shoulders, the picture of shame. The next moment he was back on the dance floor, laughing and singing with his brothers. What a strange creature he was. So cat and yet so human.

All these people were strange to Imraldera. Every one of them was both man and animal, just as Wolf Tongue had been. But unlike Wolf Tongue, there was no malice in these merry faces. They were as bright and frothy as bubbles on a stream.

This is no place for me.

Imraldera sighed as the thought came to her. But it was true. When Eanrin had offered to bring her to his homeland so that she might recover from her journey before setting off again, she had willingly agreed. But she knew now that this was not right. Her thoughts drifted longingly to home and hearth . . . to Fairbird and Frostbite . . . to her mother, long dead, and yes, to her father. All those dear ones who had loved her and whom she had loved. They were her home. But they were far from her now.

She was Starflower no longer. She was Dame Imraldera, Knight of the Farthest Shore. From this day on, her journey would be her home.

She slipped from Ruaine Hall, down the long paths of Rudiobus Mountain. It was cold here compared to her homeland. The people of the mountain had given her clothes like theirs and taken away her mother's ruined wedding dress. The sleeves of her new gown were long and draping, edged in gold. Rich and beautiful, this gown, but restricting, she thought. And it did not cut the chill of the caverns. Nevertheless, these corridors were brightly lit and decorated with greenery. So different from the tunnel beneath the Circle of Faces!

No one stopped her as she made her way back to Fionnghuala Lynn. Guards saluted her as she went. She smiled shyly to them and hurried on.

Órfhlaith waited for her at the gate.

"I thought you would come," said the mare.

Imraldera, growing used to men's speech in the mouths of animals, startled when she realized that Órfhlaith had spoken in the language of horses. Yet the words had translated in her mind, and she understood perfectly. She bowed politely. "I . . . I wish to return to the Wood," she said.

"Of course," said Órfhlaith. "You have a duty to your Master now."

Imraldera nodded. She climbed onto the mare's back and clung to her scarlet mane. Órfhlaith turned, and her dainty hooves made little ripples as she started out across Gorm-Uisce.

"Wait!"

Órfhlaith drew to a halt, and Imraldera turned to look back. She saw the poet in cat form standing there on the lake's edge, his tail straight up and his eyes round. "Imraldera!" he cried and suddenly he was a man again. With a curse, he plunged into the lake and waded after them. The water was up to his knees by the time he reached Órfhlaith, and the mare laughed at him.

"*Wet!*" Eanrin snarled. "Every time I'm with you, I end up wet! Give me a hand up, why don't you?"

"Why?" Imraldera asked. "What are you doing?"

"I'm coming with you."

"No," she said quickly. "You can't. I must return to the Wood. I must find the Haven of my Master and restore it—"

"And you think you're going to do that alone?" The poet rolled his eyes. "You'll end up lost in a devil's pit before you've gone two paces. Or you'll stop and drink enchanted waters, or you'll take directions from the old man at the Crossings, or any number of the fool things you mortals are inclined to."

"Eanrin—"

"I won't hear of it! You need a guide. Someone who knows the workings of this world." His face was as woebegone as any kitten's in a bath. "Please, my dear, give me your hand, and let's have no more of this debate."

Imraldera pursed her lips. Then, shaking her head and telling herself she would regret this, she gave the poet her arm and, with a great deal more splashing, helped him onto the mare's back. They crossed the lake and dismounted on the edge of the Wood.

It was so vast. Imraldera stood on its edge, peering into the shadows through which she could see so little. She felt as though she struggled to see her future, a future she had never imagined, more frightening than death. And yet she felt that now, for the first time, she lived. She was the Silent Maid no longer. She had a voice, and with it she would speak the truth, even in the very depths of the Gray Wood.

"What do you think, my girl?" Eanrin said, folding his arms. "Are you ready for another adventure?"

"I don't know," she replied.

"Me either." Eanrin grinned. "But the glorious unknown waits for no one! Shall we off?"

Imraldera's stern mouth relaxed, if only for a breath, into a smile. Then she strode forward, disappearing into the foliage. The poet meowled and darted after, and the two of them vanished into the shadows. Órfhlaith, standing a while on the edge of Rudiobus, thought she caught the faintest whisper of the poet's song:

> *"Oh, woe is me, I am undone,*
> *In sweet affliction lying!*
> *For though my labor's scarce begun,*
> *It leaves me sorely sighing*
> *After the maiden I adore,*
> *Who marches bravely to Death's door.*
> *Be bold, my heart! Now is the hour!*
> *You've dared to love the Maid Starflower."*

AUTHOR'S NOTE

MANY OF THE THEMES found in *Starflower* were inspired by a beautiful poem written by Francis Thompson. The poem is called "The Hound of Heaven," and Thompson succinctly (after the manner of poets) expresses so much of what I want to say rather less succinctly (after the manner of novelists) in the story I just shared with you. I encourage you to read the poem in full but thought I'd include the first stanza for you here:

> I fled Him, down the nights and down the days;
>   I fled Him, down the arches of the years;
> I fled Him, down the labyrinthine ways
>   Of my own mind; and in the mist of tears
> I hid from Him, and under running laughter.
>   Up vistaed hopes I sped;
>   And shot, precipitated,
> Adown Titantic glooms of chasmèd fears,
> From those strong Feet that followed, followed after.
>   But with unhurrying chase,
>   And unperturbed pace,
> Deliberate speed, majestic instancy,
>   They beat—and a Voice beat
>   More instant than the Feet—
> "All things betray thee, who betrayest Me."

ABOUT THE AUTHOR

Anne Elisabeth Stengl makes her home in Raleigh, North Carolina, where she lives with her husband, Rohan, a passel of cats, and one long-suffering dog. When she's not writing, she enjoys Shakespeare, opera, and tea, and studies piano, painting, and pastry baking. She studied illustration at Grace College and English literature at Campbell University. She is the author of *Heartless*, *Veiled Rose*, *Moonblood*, and *Starflower*. *Heartless* and *Veiled Rose* have each been honored with a Christy Award.

COMING SUMMER 2013

THE NEWEST
TALE OF GOLDSTONE WOOD

Dragonwitch

Timeless fantasy that will keep you spellbound.

Don't Miss the Rest of the
TALES OF GOLDSTONE WOOD!

To learn more about Anne Elisabeth Stengl and her books, visit anneelisabethstengl.blogspot.com.

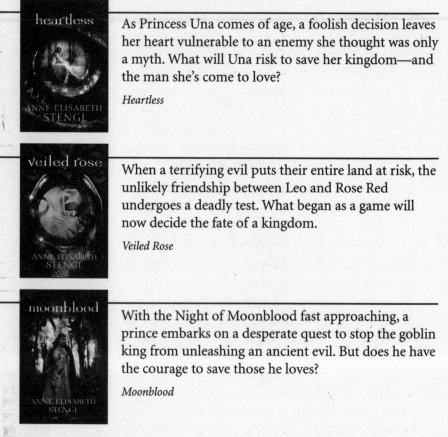

As Princess Una comes of age, a foolish decision leaves her heart vulnerable to an enemy she thought was only a myth. What will Una risk to save her kingdom—and the man she's come to love?

Heartless

When a terrifying evil puts their entire land at risk, the unlikely friendship between Leo and Rose Red undergoes a deadly test. What began as a game will now decide the fate of a kingdom.

Veiled Rose

With the Night of Moonblood fast approaching, a prince embarks on a desperate quest to stop the goblin king from unleashing an ancient evil. But does he have the courage to save those he loves?

Moonblood